"What is it you want of me?" Shannon asked, coming directly to the point.

"To strike a bargain," Miles Cort said. "I know what you want, and who you are. If we can both get what we want, we'll have a deal."

"You can't know much about me from that newspaper ad," she said tartly.

Cort grinned. "I know that you are a twenty-nine-year-old single mother with a seriously ill eleven-year-old daughter. That you are working on some damn fool book, and that because of your daughter's illness, your back is to the wall financially."

Shannon was stunned, then angry. "What gives you the right to pry into my private life?"

"Money and power. I had to be sure you were the right person for the job."

"But I'm not looking for a job. I'm looking for a patron of the arts."

"And have you found one?"

Shannon stared back at him, not answering.

"Face it, your ad was the act of a desperate woman."

She glared at him. "Then what do you want?"

"I want to be your patron."

"What?"

Cort smiled. "I'll be your patron—after you do a job for me. That's the deal. Take it or leave it, my dear. The choice is yours."

The Patron

TREVOR MELDAL-JOHNSEN

PINNACLE BOOKS
WINDSOR PUBLISHING CORP.

PINNACLE BOOKS

are published by

Windsor Publishing Corp.
475 Park Avenue South
New York, NY 10016

First Printing: August 1989

Printed in the United States of America

PROLOGUE

The knock came softly at the door. He groped for a button with his right hand and listened to the light hum of machinery as the back of his bed slowly rose to bring him into a semiupright sitting position.

"Come in," he said.

The door opened and she hesitantly entered. His hungry stare bolstered her confidence and she stopped about five yards from the bed and smiled. "Hi."

"Good evening, Dana." Clouds of thick red hair fell to her shoulders, framing the pale skin of her face. She wore a tight backless dress of a glistening green satin to match the color of her eyes. He knew the skin of her back was sprinkled with light pink freckles. He had seen the lush young woman of about twenty-four before.

"Shall I pour us a drink?" she asked.

"Yes." This was her third visit. Usually he had his people bring a different woman each time, but Dana's combination of innocence and enthusiasm had captured his interest. He watched the movement of her buttocks as she walked across the room to the bar. When she reached the counter she placed her handbag on it and turned her head to smile over her shoulder.

"Scotch on the rocks, right?"

"Yes," he said.

She turned and he listened to the clink of ice in the glass and watched her reach over for the bottle of Glenfiddich. He wasn't supposed to drink hard liquor, but on these nights he allowed himself one drink, convinced it aided his performance.

He allowed his attention to wander to the other side of the room. The closet door was slightly ajar and he could see her from another angle, reflected in the full-length mirror. He admired the curve of her profiled breast, the translucent skin of her bare arm, the concentration with which she poured whiskey first into one glass and then the other. He felt his blood thicken.

And then, as he continued to watch her in the mirror, she took something from her bag and dropped it into one of the glasses. She jiggled the glass slightly in her right hand and then picked up the other one and turned, the smile fixed on her face as she approached the bed.

"I've been looking forward to visiting you again," she said, allowing a note of flustered embarrassment to enter her voice.

He stared back at her, reminding himself that she was, after all, an actress.

He pressed the panic button on the side of his bed. It would ring in the security room in the basement, and it would also activate the buzzer his head of security carried with him wherever he went.

"Here," she said, handing him the drink in her right hand.

"I'll take the other one," he said, reaching out.

She was good, he had to admit. With barely a flicker in her eyes she handed him the glass he had requested.

He took a sip and let out a grateful, "Ah. Wonderful." Then he said to her, "Drink yours."

"In a while," she said, moving to place it on the night-stand. "First I want to take care of you."

He reached out and grabbed her wrist with his left hand

6

before she could put the glass down. Their eyes met and held.

The door burst open and two men entered the room at a run. Both carried revolvers and leveled them at the girl.

"It's all right," he said. "I wanted you to watch Dana. She was just about to have her drink, weren't you, Dana?"

Her pale skin seemed to grow a shade paler as she realized her predicament, but she looked back at him levelly and said, "It was just to knock you out. It's harmless. I was promised. I wouldn't do anything to hurt you."

"Drink it!" he ordered savagely, and released her hand.

"Sir," his head of security interceded, "don't you think we'd better—"

"Shut up!" he said, not taking his eyes off the girl. "Now drink it or I'll have these men shoot you!"

He watched her hand tremble as she lifted the glass to her lips. She closed her eyes and took a gulp.

Slowly she brought the glass back down, a smile of relief forming on her lips as she opened her eyes.

But it was a short-lived reprieve. Three seconds later she began to gag and fear rushed into those once-seductive eyes and she dropped the glass, her hands clutching at her throat as if to douse hungry flames.

She groaned once, a horribly claustrophobic sound, and fell to the floor.

The man who had spoken got to his knees beside her and felt for her pulse. "It must have been poison. She's dead," he said, looking up at the man in the bed.

"Any damn fool can see that," the man retorted. "You shouldn't have made her drink it. I wanted to find out who sent her."

"Someone who wanted me dead, that's who. Now get rid of her and find out if she can be traced here."

"Yes, sir," the head of security said, rising. "Obviously someone knew she was coming here. She wouldn't have done this on her own."

The man sipped the whiskey he still held in his right

hand. "No, she had no reason to want me dead that I know of. But check her background, her contacts. Find out everything you can about her. God knows I have plenty of enemies in this town. But I don't know that any of them hate me enough to murder me. See if she's connected to anyone. A relative, a lover. Look into it with all your resources, understand?"

"Yes, sir." He nodded at the other guard, who picked up the dead girl and slung her over his shoulder. "Is there anything else, sir?"

"Get her the fuck out of here. And don't screw up."

"Yes, sir." The two men left.

Alone again, the man drained his whiskey. This shouldn't have happened. The girls were picked at random. He'd decreed that they shouldn't be professionals. They were chosen by his people from the virtual ocean of out-of-work actresses, dancers, models, and others who filled the city, drawn from every nation in the world in their search for fame. The girls were offered an extremely large sum of money to fulfill his desires and maintain their discretion.

No, it was unlikely that his people had randomly picked someone who was connected to any enemy. There was a more likely explanation. She had come twice before.

Goddamnit! He had violated his own rule and look what happened, he thought, his face flushing with anger. He took a deep, calming breath and resumed his inspection of the problem.

Someone must have got to her. Or someone had told the enemy who wanted him dead about her. "Yeah, he had the same woman twice. Maybe there'll be a third time." Something like that must have happened.

That narrowed the field down, he thought, pleased at his deductions.

He sat in the same position for an hour, examining the possibilities. He thought of the battles he had fought and the wars he had won, the millions of dollars he had made

8

and lost and made again, the casualties he left in his wake when he had to—the business partners, the employees, the women he loved, the mutual betrayals, the children who now hovered around him like vultures.

Ah, yes. He had more than his share of enemies. He had always done what he had to do to get the job done his way, regardless of consequences and without regrets. It was an overriding philosophy that simplified all he did. It enabled him to win more often than he lost.

I was a lion, he thought proudly. King of this jungle.

He thought that what they didn't know was that he was still a lion. All the instincts were there. An old lion perhaps, but an experienced one.

There was a rat somewhere. All he had to do to find it was set a trap. It wouldn't be difficult. A rat was no match for a lion.

Satisfied now that he knew what to do, he pushed a button and the bed fell slowly back, taking him with it.

CHAPTER ONE

The party attracted the usual crowd of writers, editors, literary agents, advertising and public relations people, most of whom Shannon knew. A few were friends, but most were only acquaintances and she wondered why she had come. There was too much noise to allow meaningful conversation and it was preordained that the already substantial din of conversation would rise commensurately with the amount of liquor consumed.

The relationships in the room were intricate, perhaps even Machiavellian at the core, Shannon suspected. There were camps and cliques, rivals for attention, and competitors for money, all operating under the thin guise of sociability. They stood in clumps, like walled-in city-states of older times. Admittance depended upon credentials and prior allegiances.

Shannon listened halfheartedly as the advertising man beside her concluded the story of how his company had just won a large account.

"So we hired fifty clowns to picket their corporate headquarters, demanding that they give the account to us. Can you imagine that? Fifty people in full clown regalia—an entire circus!" He rolled his eyes comically. "The media attention was worth a million bucks. TV stations, the *Post*.

10

The company had no choice but to pick us, based on our initiative alone."

A small, sharp-featured man with shrewd eyes, Billy had a high opinion of his charm and ability. She kept running into him at these parties and he kept regaling her with stories of his brilliance—as if to make up for his height, which was six inches less than hers, she thought uncharitably.

God, am I feeling bitchy tonight or what? she asked herself.

The party was being held by Oliver Wasserman in his Upper East Side apartment. Oliver was a friend and her editor at a magazine she worked for as a freelancer. She had stopped in more out of courtesy than anything else, and only intended to stay a short time.

"Billy!" The loud, jocular voice rose above the din, emanating from a man who approached them swaying. "Introduce me to the gorgeous lady!"

Shannon allowed herself a mental groan. Twenty-nine years old, long-legged, and slim, with the wide, curved mouth, intelligent green eyes, and gamine features of an eighties Audrey Hepburn, Shannon was normally used to this kind of attention. But tonight her patience was limited. A tall (five nine) brunette, she found her looks to be both a hindrance and an asset. They got her into doors she might have been denied entrance to and also drew admiration, which was usually nice. But she was an intelligent woman and resented it when men couldn't see past the pretty face and lissome body.

"David Morton, Shannon Ross," Billy said without warmth.

"And what do you do?" David asked, bleary eyes scanning her body.

"I'm a free-lance magazine writer," she said.

"Well, if your writing is as good as you look—" he said with a leer.

"Excuse me," she said politely, and moved away.

11

"What'd I say?" the man's voice rose behind her.

She felt a hand on her arm. It was Oliver. "Having a good time?" he asked.

"Not particularly. I'll be leaving in a few minutes, I think."

Oliver smiled at her quizzically. "Anything in particular, or just life in general?"

A tall man with thinning gray hair, the perennially amused expression he wore was as much a part of his face as the thin, aquiline nose. They had known each other for five years, had a brief four-month affair three years earlier which they both agreed had been a mistake, and miraculously had remained friends. He was one of the few people she could communicate with honestly, without fear of embarrassment or recrimination.

"Life, I guess," she said, forcing a smile.

"I thought it would do you good to get a break from Melissa for a little while," Oliver said half apologetically. "You've been a hermit lately."

"I thought so, too, but . . ." She waved a hand at the room. "It's the same old crowd. I mean, they're fine, but probably what I really need is time by myself."

They stood talking on one side of the room. Greg and Margaret Chapman, who had a daughter the same age as Shannon's child, came toward them, expressions of concern on both their faces.

"I was so sorry to hear about Melissa," Margaret said, placing her hand solicitously on Shannon's arm.

"It's a real bummer," Greg agreed. Greg, clean-cut and given to wearing pin-striped, three-piece suits, had been a long-haired campus radical in the late sixties, chanting "Down with the Establishment" and similar slogans. Now he successfully ran the family's ultra-respectable and lucrative stockbrokerage, adding loot to the already overflowing Chapman coffers.

Margaret wore a black silk Christian Lacroix original, Shannon noted. A sharp-faced, slim, immaculately

12

groomed woman, she had once been a magazine editor. That was before she met Greg. She no longer worked. Shannon had known them for about five years, during which time her daughter Melissa and their daughter Yolanda had become friends.

"Is she getting dialysis?" Margaret asked.

Shannon nodded. She had hoped for just an hour on this one evening not to have to think about Melissa's plight.

"That's mucho bucks!" Greg said.

"For a free-lance writer with no medical insurance?" Oliver asked ironically.

Margaret's mouth formed an O. "You don't have insurance?"

"No," Shannon said, feeling stupid. Hell, everyone had insurance. Why of everyone she knew was she too dumb and too poor to think of it? On the other hand, how could she have predicted that her daughter would suffer kidney failure?

"What are you going to do? Are there some kind of public assistance programs you qualify for?" Margaret asked.

Shannon hesitated. "Well—"

"Yes, there are, but there are other costs," Oliver interceded.

"I'm afraid so," Shannon said with a shrug. As a free-lance magazine writer, even a fairly successful one, she made a passable living—most of the time. She was a brilliant investigative writer and had once even been nominated for a Pulitzer Prize for a magazine series she had written, but that was then and this was now. Past triumphs never guaranteed current work. Still, even though her income was sometimes unpredictable, under normal circumstances she made enough to support herself and her daughter in a modest manner. These were not normal circumstances, however.

"What you need is a patron," Oliver said with a smile.

"A patron of the arts!" Greg said, delighted at the idea.

"I think they went out with Queen Victoria," Shannon said.

"Artists should be supported by the wealthy," Oliver argued. "Here you are, a talented young writer who can barely make ends meet. That Valentino book you've been working on for years should qualify you for patronage."

The biography of Rudolph Valentino, one of the first male sex symbols of film, was her pet project. But it was a project she couldn't afford to do. It required voluminous research and so far she hadn't been able to cajole a publisher into financing her labors.

"I don't think the wealthy give a damn about writing," Shannon said glumly. "The only reason they invest in art is because paintings can bring a profit."

"Hey, you never know," Greg said, the topic of money causing his face to flush. "I have some pretty far-out clients with more money than they know what to do with. They have to give some of it away. All you need to do is con them into thinking your project is worthy, that it has social relevance or something."

"Thank you very much, Greg," Shannon said heavily. All she needed was another worthless suggestion.

Oliver laughed, but her irony escaped Greg. He was on a roll. "Put advertisements in all the papers for a patron," he said. "I know! Advertise in the West Coast papers. They're strange enough out there to go for anything."

"Yes, but is there any real money out there?" asked Margaret, who had become something of a snob since marrying into money.

"Are you kidding?" Greg asked incredulously. "The money's moving there, from Asia, from here, from Europe. They're awash in the stuff."

"Well, thanks for the suggestion," Shannon said. "I think I'll have to come up with something else though."

"Well, if there's anything we can do to help, just ask," Margaret said, her eyes sincerely seeking Shannon's.

"Anything at all," Greg added.

"What are you going to do?" Oliver asked after the couple wandered off to amuse themselves elsewhere.

"I really don't know," Shannon said. "Melissa's dialysis treatments are covered by Medicare and Medicaid, and when a donor kidney turns up, the transplant will be covered. As for everything else Melissa needs, she'll get it, even if I have to go into debt for the rest of my life."

"Well, patronage isn't the answer," Oliver said. "Those people are your friends, and they're loaded. Notice how they jumped to help. Believe me, Shannon, if I had the money to help Melissa I'd give it to you in a minute."

"It's too much to ask of anyone," Shannon said, touching his hand gratefully. "Don't worry, I'll think of something. Anyway, I'm going to take off now. Thanks for inviting me."

"Want me to call you a cab?"

"I'll walk a little and then get one," she said.

"You'll be okay?"

She kissed him on the cheek. "I'll be fine. I'll call you soon," she said. "Now let me say goodbye to a couple of people and then I'm out of here."

It was a pleasant spring night with only a slight chill in the air. Shannon walked slowly with her hands in her jacket pockets, hardly noticing the passing joggers or the people walking their dogs. Turbulent thoughts of eleven-year-old Melissa filled her mind.

It had all happened so quickly, so unexpectedly, she still found it hard to deal with. First had come a thunderous blow of shock, then waves of grief, then disbelief, and now a kind of angry acceptance of the situation. All in all, it had been and still was a roller-coaster ride of emotions.

She vividly remembered the visit to their family doctor. Melissa had been mysteriously ill for too long, with infections and an apalling loss of energy. At first the doctor

15

had laid it down to some virulent virus, but then he decided to do some tests. When the results came he had called her into his office and spoken to her in an almost embarrassed tone.

"The results of the tests that we've got back so far suggest that there's a problem with her kidneys. I'm sufficiently concerned to want to get some help in pinning down the diagnosis. Ah, by help, I mean I'd like to call in a kidney specialist to help us evaluate the situation."

Then came the kidney specialist, Dr. Ivan Feinstein, and another round of painful and laborious tests, all of which Melissa endured with her typical dignity and bravery.

It was curious, but she had never before realized how deep her love was for her daughter. Oh, of course, she knew she loved her, but under the stress of the tests, during which time Melissa was hospitalized, it was almost as if she became Melissa. She felt it every time a needle was injected into her child. She felt Melissa's bursts of fear. She felt the confusion and uncertainty, the sense of being a pawn in some game over which she had no control. All she could do was be there for Melissa and hope she didn't show her own fear. A calming, safe, stable influence, she told herself in a daily chant. That's what she had to be. It was all she could be.

If the memory of her visit to their doctor was vivid, the day Feinstein came up with his diagnosis was etched in her mind forever.

On the day of judgment, Feinstein met her in Melissa's hospital room and inclined his head to indicate that he wanted to talk privately to her. They went into a small office he had borrowed for the occasion. As soon as they sat, he placed his elbows on the desk as if for support, and said, "I'm afraid Melissa is very ill. She has chronic kidney failure. A large percentage of her kidney function has been lost."

She remembered thinking incongruously that he didn't

look afraid. He stared at her without expression, as if it was something he had told a thousand mothers before. She looked back at him through a haze, her heart thumping wildly in her chest, gripping her hands together until the knuckles whitened, while he went into the details.

The bottom line, when all the talk was done, was that both Melissa's kidneys were almost useless. Cysts had replaced virtually all of the normal tissue and the organs were functioning at less than five percent of their capacity. To survive, she would need dialysis treatments three times a week until a donor kidney could be found and transplanted—an event which could happen in a few months or a few years.

"The problem is the donor's kidney tissue has to match as closely as possible to Melissa's," Feinstein explained. "If they don't match to a certain level of compatibility, then the chances increase that the donor kidney will be rejected.

"Then there's also the matter of who is ahead of her in line, waiting for a kidney. There are a lot of variables to contend with."

And there was more—a lot more than she could assimilate in one sitting. He talked of dialysis and shunts and potassium and diet and medication and anemia and artificial kidneys and nephrectomy and more. She understood perhaps half of it. All she really understood was the increasing feeling of dread that clutched her heart.

"Look," she said finally, getting to what she saw as the crucial point. "A person can survive very well on one kidney from what I understand. Can I give Melissa one of mine?"

"A living related kidney donor provides the greatest chance of success," Feinstein said with a nod of his head. "The best chance is an identical twin, then there's a full brother or sister, and then a parent. We'll have to do tests to see if your kidney is (a) healthy and (b) compatible."

"What's the first step for me?"

"Tissue-typing. A series of blood tests."

"Well, let's get started," Shannon had said.

In the meantime, a small operation was performed on Melissa as a prerequisite to dialysis. A fistula, an internal device connecting an artery directly to a vein, was inserted in her arm under local anesthesia.

Melissa came through it bravely, but Shannon was her mother and she could see the stress on her daughter's face. It felt as if it was imprinted on her own features.

"Good evening!" a handsome male jogger said as he passed her. She looked up, shocked. She had totally lost any sense of where she was.

Oh, God! Shannon thought miserably as she walked down the street. She had traveled about seven blocks since leaving Oliver's party. She looked around for a cab, but of course there was nothing to be seen. She sat on a bench to give her feet a rest, her thoughts returning to her or deal.

Her next harrowing experience had been a meeting with the hospital social worker. She found out that Medicare and Medicaid would cover the costs of dialysis—but only after her own financial resources were exhausted.

She sat in a small office before a thin, young black woman named Elsa Roche and listed her assets on a government form. These included a three thousand-dollar savings account, which she had religiously refused to touch for a couple of years.

"There's no problem with the main eighty percent of the costs," Ms. Roche explained. "But before the remaining twenty percent is covered by the government, you are going to have to use that three thousand toward it—and any other money you have."

"You mean that the government is going to make me destitute before it helps me?" Shannon was outraged. Because she had actually earned some money and frugally saved a portion of it, she was going to be penalized.

18

"Well, that's not the way they look at it," Ms. Roche said benignly.

"I was saving that money for an emergency!"

Ms. Roche looked at her blandly through thick tortoise-shell glasses and said, "Well, what would you call this?"

Shannon had never asked for any kind of public assistance in her life, even when times were hard. By the time the interview was over she felt thoroughly degraded.

She stopped in the corridor before a soft-drink machine. Her throat was parched, whether from thirst or nervousness she didn't know. She put two quarters in the machine and waited. Nothing happened.

Savagely, violently, she had hit the machine with the palm of her hand, her face cruel and harsh. The machine seemed to cough and a can spilled out.

When she reached the apartment after finally finding a cab, Shannon paid the baby-sitter and went into Melissa's room to check on her. She was sleeping soundly, her face relaxed. Shannon leaned over and pulled the cover up to her shoulders.

You could look at that face and never think anything was wrong, she thought, turning and walking away.

"Mom?"

"Hi, sweetie," Shannon said, returning to the bed.

Melissa gazed up at her with befuddled eyes. "How was the party?"

"Oh, it was fine," Shannon said.

"I'm glad you went." Melissa yawned and said, "Did you have fun?"

Melissa had encouraged her to go against her own inclinations, saying that she needed to get out more often.

"Sure," Shannon said, "it was fun."

Melissa smiled.

"You'd better get back to sleep," Shannon said.

Melissa pulled the blankets up to her chin and snuggled deeper into the bed. "Good night, Mom."

Shannon bent forward and kissed her cheek. "Good night, sweetheart."

She went back to the small living room and poured herself a glass of wine. Taking off her shoes, she put her feet on an end table and leaned back on the couch, her mind retreating to the final blow that had come just two days earlier in the form of a telephone call from Dr. Feinstein.

Shannon had been sitting at her desk, staring blankly at a piece of paper in her typewriter. Although exhausted after dialysis the day before, Melissa had regained an enormous amount of energy by morning and had gone cheerfully to school.

"I'm sorry," Feinstein said weightedly. "We've finished the tissue-typing, and although the match is okay, it won't be suitable. Melissa's blood reacts to your kidney."

"What?" she said, not quite understanding him, perhaps refusing to.

"Your kidney isn't suitable for Melissa. We have to find another donor."

"But why not? I'm her mother," Shannon protested. "Perhaps there's been a mistake. Couldn't we re-do the tests or re-check them or something?"

"I'm sorry," he said again. "This isn't that unusual. What about the father? Can you locate him?"

"I haven't heard a thing about him since Melissa was born," Shannon said. "He dropped out of college and disappeared. He could be dead for all I know."

"Can you try and find him? There's a possibility that he could be a match."

"I'll try," she said. "But I hardly knew him. I was just a kid then. I can't even remember where he was from!"

"Any other living relatives?"

"No. We're all alone."

"Well, do your best. In the meantime, Melissa's on the list for a kidney."

Shannon was engulfed with disappointment. "On the list" was small consolation. Melissa would have to continue indefinitely with her ordeal—facing the needles three times a week. In between she would suffer the physical and emotional swings that went with dialysis. Whichever way you looked at it—as a curse or as a life-saving treatment—there were no two ways about it: Melissa would continue to suffer.

As a mother, particularly a single mother, she had learned to feel and share her daughter's pain from the moment her baby had burst from her womb. Every little cold, every fever, every illness from influenza to chicken pox, every moment of danger from when Melissa had first learned to cross the street by herself to her first overnight visit with friends, had filled Shannon's mind—sometimes with concern, at other times with pain. She had suffered with Melissa when a friend first betrayed her, and fought for her when a sadistic teacher victimized her. Melissa's survival was as important to her as her own, and inextricably tied to it.

She had done all she could to keep Melissa safe and happy in an unsafe world, but in spite of all her efforts, she had failed. Her daughter now faced dangers that made those earlier setbacks seem like nothing in comparison.

It was too much for both of them to bear. Why did this happen to us? Shannon thought miserably. Perhaps she had done something to deserve this—she hadn't lived the life of a saint—but Melissa was an innocent. If a God existed, he surely wasn't a just God. If it wasn't for the fact that she still hoped faintly for a miracle and felt a superstitious urge not to jinx it, she would curse him for it. After finishing the conversation with Feinstein, she had put her arms on the desk and lowered her head to them, the sobs bursting from her throat.

It was three in the morning now and she sat alone in the living room, a glass of wine in her hand, her restless mind refusing to let sleep enter.

21

The comment at Oliver's party about finding a patron had been made as a glib social joke. A laughable solution to her problems, but one Shannon couldn't get out of her mind.

Why should patronage be such an absurd idea? she thought.

There was an abundance of historical precedents. The word had its roots in the Latin *pater*, father, and then *patronus*, support. Someone who supported as a father does. Michelangelo had patrons, so did da Vinci. It had always been simply a matter of connecting up with the right person, the one who liked your work, or who wanted to contribute to the culture, or who was motivated by reasons of prestige, or even guilt. The artists had never cared about the motivations, only about their work. They took whatever help was offered.

There was even a precedent of sorts today. In our modern age, foundations acted as patrons by giving grants to worthy people or groups they deemed worthy in the arts. The problem was, as she had discovered earlier, grant money wasn't very much and the competition for it was horrendous. It also took forever to get.

She had applied a couple of times some years earlier and been turned down, mainly for a lack of credentials. It was almost impossible to get a grant for a book if you'd never written one, unless you had a string of impressive degrees—which was a ridiculous situation, when you thought about it.

Maybe patronage wasn't such a stupid idea. Perhaps there were still patrons out there somewhere, wealthy people who thought art was of benefit to society and wanted to give something back for all they had received.

It wasn't like begging, Shannon assured herself uncertainly. She had something to offer in return. Many people had told her she was a talented writer and she had the track record to back it up to some degree. Furthermore, her book was important. Rudolph Valentino had been a major cultural phenomenon, one that had inspired and influenced later filmmakers' audiences. Why wouldn't someone support a project like that?

"Because they don't give a shit," Shannon said aloud, shaking her head.

She was dreaming. It was ludicrous. Totally impossible. Ridiculous even to consider it. She'd have to come up with a better solution than that, and fast.

But there was no better solution. Not one that she could think of. God knows she'd tried. And what greater justification for lunatic actions than desperation?

Why not? she thought finally. She had absolutely nothing to lose. Why the hell not?

She did about fifteen versions of the advertisement before finally going to bed at five in the morning. She labored over the wording as thoroughly as she did for any of her articles. The version she finally settled on read:

Diligent, excellent, credentialed young non-fiction writer in financial straits seeks a Patron to invest in her future while she completes important biography. Contact Box

It was a joke, she told herself. It was stupid. It was not only desperate, but insane.

She listened to these thoughts and others, and then pushed them all aside. Perhaps it was all of those things, but if there was even the slightest chance that it would work . . .

The next day she placed the advertisement in *The New York Times*, the *Los Angeles Times*, and the *San Francisco Chronicle*. It was an investment she could ill afford, costing her $137.42, plus long distance telephone charges, but she did it anyway. And then she waited.

CHAPTER TWO

Melissa turned her serious green eyes on Shannon and said, "You're starting to look like a model again, Mom. It's gross. All your bones are showing. You've got to eat more protein."

"My diet's fine." Shannon was walking Melissa to school and they stood at a traffic light, waiting for it to turn green.

Melissa wrinkled her upturned nose in disgust. "Yogurt, salad, and vegetables! Ugh! You need some meat. More chicken. Fish even. We learned about it at school. You have to use all the food groups."

"Meat's expensive," Shannon argued.

"Isn't chicken cheap?"

Nothing was cheap when you had only a little money, but Shannon's firm policy was not to whine to her child about money problems. Growing up was difficult enough in today's world, without taking on the adult's responsibilities.

"We'll eat more chicken, if you like," she said.

"Do you think some people are born vegetarians?" Melissa asked obliquely.

"I'm not a vegetarian," Shannon said defensively, knowing this was a discussion she couldn't win. "I don't buy a lot of beef or pork because it's expensive."

"I was born a carnivore," Melissa said definitely.

The subject was dropped. Melissa had made her point.

They crossed the street and stopped in front of the school entrance. "Bye, honey," Shannon said, leaning down to kiss her.

"Bye, Mom," Melissa said, and ran to join a group of friends.

Shannon watched her for a moment and then turned to retrace her steps home.

She passed the window of a furrier's shop. Mink and blue fox draped the shoulders of the two mannequins. Sometimes she wished she had money. Not only for the luxuries that occasionally caught her fancy, but for Melissa. The poor kid was always wearing secondhand clothes and she didn't exactly have an abundance of toys. Not that she ever complained. They had never starved, somehow always managed to make ends meet, and Melissa accepted her lot with the dignity of a truly noble soul— something Shannon suspected children possessed in its pure form at birth, but which tarnished with so-called maturity under the guidance of their elders.

She'd had Melissa when she was seventeen and almost been talked into giving her up for adoption by her parents when the young father disappeared into the abyss of America, never to be heard from again. But she had refused against all logic and advice, driven by a mysterious love for the seed growing in her womb. She had never regretted it. Melissa was the most precious thing in her life.

Her own parents had died by the time Melissa turned three and, as an only child herself, Melissa was all the family she had. In many ways, she was more like a sister than a daughter. Funny and bright, Melissa possessed a wisdom and maturity beyond her years. As one friend said, "Melissa was born thirty years old."

She smiled to herself at Melissa's dissertation on diet. Her strong maternal streak tended to manifest itself in a

25

protective attitude toward her mother. And even to her relationships with men. Would-be suitors had to pass the gauntlet of Melissa's approval. If she didn't like a man Shannon dated, she made her attitude unmistakably clear—to both Shannon and her date.

Not that there had been all that many dates in recent times. Currently there was a man she had been out with for two weeks in a row—Tim Matasky, a successful advertising copywriter, thirty-two, straight, and never married. Melissa thought he was "pretty neat." Shannon hadn't made up her mind how much she liked him. Although he was fun to be with, she suspected his intelligence was only skin deep. She was getting fussier with age, she admitted a trifle regretfully. Consequently she hadn't had much luck with men lately. That heady romantic feeling she'd had as a girl had eluded her for years.

Finally! Home was in sight. Breathing heavily from the long walk, she resolved to start exercising more.

The apartment was on the second floor of a three-story building, consisting of a living room, which doubled as her office, and a bedroom, which she shared with Melissa. Although small, it was functional enough for the two of them. Thank God for rent control! The apartment wasn't much, but in today's open market it would fetch three times what she paid in rent.

She went directly to the answering machine on her desk. No calls. As a free-lance writer, the telephone was her lifeline. She'd done stories for magazines around the country and the subjects of her profiles were often out-of-town celebrities. Her phone bill each month was often more than her rent.

She drank water from the kitchen faucet, then returned to her desk to sit and stare blankly at the half-completed page in her typewriter. The subject of her story was a well-known artist, or rather his art collection. In twenty years this colorful character had cleverly collected the work of his fellow up-and-coming artists—and amassed a collection worth a fortune.

She was having difficulty finishing the story. To begin with, the subject had been fascinating, but it had only taken a few interviews for her to realize that he was simply avaricious and vain. Character assassination wasn't her forte, but she felt obliged to report what she had discovered and it was giving her trouble. Somehow, though, the conflict seemed overshadowed by the problems she faced with Melissa.

A massive file of papers loomed on the other side of the desk. She looked over at it longingly. That was what she really wanted to spend her time doing. Valentino's biography, which she had been working on for almost three years, was a labor of love and, she decided during despondent moments of low self-esteem, a luxury.

She had tried to sell the idea to book publishers a few years before, but no publisher wished to provide an advance to fund her research, particularly to a writer who had never published anything longer than a magazine article. One house had expressed great interest, but only wanted to see the project when half the manuscript was done. Then they would perhaps discuss a contract and an advance. Catch-22.

In the meantime, it was an expense she couldn't afford. She had done a lot of research in local libraries and interviewed a number of the few remaining actors who had known Valentino, but most of the work had to be done in Los Angeles—months and months of it to do the job properly.

Sighing, she looked away. More important problems faced her. She couldn't afford self-indulgence. Not now. She had to finish this damned article so she could get paid for it and get assigned another. She needed the money.

* * *

Her first letter came on Wednesday. She picked it up at the *Times* office and read it in the lobby.

It was handwritten, the black ink thin and spidery.

Dear Young Writer:

Your ad filled me with disgust. Why don't you do what everyone else does and get a job? If people worked harder instead of expecting a free ride, this country would be grate again. I think that you and your type of people should be rounded up and sent to government work camps until you learn how to do it instead of leaching off other hardworking people. I hope you starve. That will teach you a lessun.

Yours,

An American.

Jesus, Shannon thought, crumpling it up to throw it away. People who wrote letters like these never signed their names. In spite of the three misspellings, the hateful message was clear. Then, like the good writer she was, she straightened out the letter and put it in her purse. She'd keep a file. One never knew when it would come in handy. There might even be, a story in it one day.

By the end of the week she had received five letters, two of which she paid to have sent overnight from the *L.A. Times*.

One was from a literary agent, asking to see the work in progress on the chance that she could sell it. Another was much like the first, a diatribe against freeloaders. A third was from a lady on the Upper East Side offering her a job as a housekeeper at four dollars an hour plus room and board. "You will be able to work on your job after dinner each evening," she wrote. "Of course, the dishes would have to be done first."

The fourth was from a young man who was looking for a sex slave. He would provide room and board in return for services rendered. "You would have to obey my every wish and command at any time," he wrote, "but you will discover a sexual fulfillment you have only dreamed about!"

The final letter came from a sympathetic librarian in Pasadena, California, who recommended a book called, *How to Get a Grant for Your Project.* She wrote, "Grant money is not substantial, of course, but perhaps it could help. I've met many writers who are unaware of this approach and I thought it might help you to at least suggest it."

Bless her, Shannon thought gratefully. But it wasn't really a viable alternative. She'd already discovered that.

In the days that followed there were no other answers to her advertisement.

Her investment had been a miserable failure.

Attempts to find Melissa's father were also proving fruitless. She had only known Mark Keller for one youthful summer when she was still in high school. He was three years older, a student at the University of Oregon visiting New York for the holidays.

They had met at a coffee shop in the Village one evening. It didn't take long for a handsome, long-haired, worldly student who could quote poetry and other great works of literature to seduce an awestruck and willing young girl with bohemian leanings.

The next night they went to his room. It was just half a block from the coffee shop, down a dirty alley, and up some rickety stairs. There were posters of Jimi Hendrix, the Doors, and Bob Dylan peeling from the walls, and a mattress on the floor.

They met four times in the next two weeks and then Mark ended it, saying she was too young. About a month later, she found herself pregnant. She went back to his room, but was told that Mark had left a week earlier. His neighbor, a bearded artist, had no idea where he had gone.

"Maybe Europe. He said something about Europe." The landlord had no forwarding address for him.

Their conversations had been about art and writing and music and politics, not families and other mundane historical facts. She knew literally nothing about him, not even where his real home was. She wrote to Mark Keller, c/o the University of Oregon, without result until, after school started, she finally called and found out that he had dropped out. They had no address for him either.

At that point, she gave up. She had already faced the major ordeal, which was to announce the pregnancy and her desire to have the baby to her parents. After recrimination and tears and other dramatics they realized she had made up her mind and they had no choice but to help her. She had no need of Mark Keller. Besides, she told herself, he had dumped her. She had to face the fact that it was even more unlikely once he knew about the baby that he would have a change of heart.

Now, almost twelve years later, she wished she had not given up so easily. As far as she could discover, Mark Keller no longer existed.

Utilizing her journalistic skills, she spent a day on the telephone to various officials at the University of Oregon and this time did get an old home address, an apartment on the East Side in Manhattan. There was no further information available other than that he had been majoring in English lit. when he dropped out. His name was on no alumni lists.

She went to the apartment, a decaying old three-story brown building, and spoke to the landlord. He had bought the building three years earlier, after the death of the owner, and had no Kellers living there and no records of previous tenants. She spoke to the tenants, but none of them remembered a family by that name.

She then called every Keller in the telephone book, running the gamut of reactions from interest to outrage. Only one of them had a son named Mark. He died in Vietnam and would have been forty years old this year, his mother told her with some bitterness.

She didn't know what else to do. For all she knew, he might also be dead. Or Mark Keller might not have been his real name. Or he wouldn't be interested in giving up a kidney for a daughter he'd never seen. Or it wouldn't match anyway. In any event, for now she was stymied. She decided to put it aside until inspiration struck.

The letter came on a Friday. It was delivered to Shannon's apartment by Federal Express.

She signed for it and closed the door, staring at the package. Beverly Hills. A magazine assignment for an L.A. magazine? She wasn't working for one at the moment.

She looked at the return address: Douglas, Collins & Henderson. Fine Anglo-Saxon names. She had no idea who they were, but they sounded like accountants.

Tearing the strip off the package, she opened it. It contained a letter and a sealed envelope.

The elegantly gold-embossed letterhead—Douglas, Collins & Henderson, Attorneys-at-Law—and below the heading a string of names of two dozen associate lawyers.

"Dear Ms. Ross," the letter read, "regarding your advertisement which recently appeared in the *Los Angeles Times*, we have been authorized to approach you on behalf of our client.

"Our client, who wishes to remain anonymous at this time, has instructed us to send you the enclosed round-trip airplane ticket to Los Angeles and for your return to New York. Said client is interested in your proposition and wishes to meet with you to discuss it further. All your expenses for the trip will be reimbursed by our client.

"Please telephone the undersigned collect at your earliest convenience and inform us if you can make the trip on the prearranged dates, as inscribed on the tickets.

31

"We look forward to hearing from you.

"Yours sincerely,

"Joseph Collins."

Scarcely thinking about it, Shannon opened the other enclosed envelope. First-class American Airlines tickets to Los Angeles for the following Wednesday, and returning on Thursday.

She called Oliver at the magazine.

"How's it going?" he asked, pleased to hear from her.

"I'd like you to check something out in your morgue files for me," she said brusquely.

"What?"

"An L.A. law firm. Douglas, Collins & Henderson. In particular, one Joseph Collins." She gave him the address. Wilshire Boulevard in Beverly Hills.

"Sure," he said. "What's this all about?"

"I'll tell you later. Can you check it and call me back?"

"You mean now?"

"ASAP."

"I'll call you back as soon as I find something," he said.

Only then did it strike her that the letter had been sent to her home address! How on earth had the lawyer or his client found out who she was and where she was? Her ad had given a coded box number at the newspaper for replies. The person placing the ad was guaranteed privacy. That was the whole point of having a coded number. It was theoretically impossible to find out who had placed the ad.

She puzzled over it for fifteen minutes and then the telephone rang.

"Yes," she said.

"Douglas, Collins & Henderson," Oliver said. "Old L.A. law firm. Very respectable, very reputable, and very, very powerful. Big clients, both old money and the relatively new. They include old L.A. families, major corporations, and wheeler-dealers in the movie business. Joseph Collins is one of the founders. Born Joseph Kalinsky.

32

Changed his name and apparently made it work. Very wealthy. A scion of L.A. society. That's all I know."

"Hmm."

"Come on, what's going on?"

"You know the ad I put in the *Times* for a patron?"

"Yeah, big surprise, kid. You told me it didn't pan out."

"It just might have," she said.

She thought about it for a day and then called Mr. Joseph Collins in Beverly Hills. The secretary put her through to him immediately.

"Thank you for calling," he said. "Are the arrangements suitable?" He enunciated his words carefully, but there was a slight tremor of age in his thin voice.

"I need to know more," she said. "I need to know who this client of yours is before I travel across the continent."

"I'm afraid my client has demanded confidentiality," he said, sounding truly regretful. "I can give you no information except that which was in the letter."

"Well, how do I know that this is not something criminal or dangerous or unsafe for me?"

"I can personally vouch that such is not the case. I have known my client for a long time and know my client to be honorable and respectable. I'm sure you have found out something about the reputation of our firm. You have my word that your safety is not in question."

"How did your client get my name and address?" she asked. "It was a confidential newspaper box number."

"I do not have that information. However, my client is not without his resources," he said drily.

"And willing to use them," she said unnecessarily.

"Ms. Ross, my client wants to meet with you and discuss your advertisement. If interested, my client will make a proposition. You will then be free to return to New York on Thursday."

"I don't know."

"Perhaps you should then consider it further and telephone me when you do know," he said mildly.

"No," she said, suddenly making up her mind. "I'll come. Wednesday on the American flight. What do I do when I arrive? Where do I go?"

"You will be met upon landing at LAX," Collins said.

"By whom?"

"I do not have that information. But I'm sure whoever it is will find you. Now, if there is nothing else . . ."

"I do have one problem," she said hesitantly. "My daughter is ill and is going to need nursing care while I'm away. It's going to be expensive, and—"

"We will, of course, reimburse those costs," he interrupted smoothly.

"I see. Thank you," she said.

She hung up the telephone. It was crazy. She was going to fly three thousand miles to meet a stranger. The lawyer hadn't even divulged the gender of his client—man, woman, or hermaphrodite. And yet, what the hell, she told herself. This was exactly what she had wanted. It was why she had put the ad in the paper in the first place.

The funny thing was, she realized for the first time, she had never really expected a response. She had known all along that it was fruitless gesture born of desperation. Now, suddenly, long after she had completely given up her illusions, there was a response that actually seemed to be genuine. She was thoroughly shocked and more than a little nervous. She felt as trepidatious as a child whose bluff had been called by an authoritative adult.

CHAPTER THREE

Shannon handed the flight attendant her empty cup and stared blankly at the pages of a magazine on her lap, trying to avoid further conversation with the New York businessman sitting beside her. He was self-centered and boring and she knew that if she encouraged him even slightly he'd suggest they meet sometime in Los Angeles for "dinner and a drink."

She couldn't help it, she was excited, and had been for days. She told herself realistically that she shouldn't allow hope to rise—the disappointment would be that much tougher to bear. But it was hard not to at least consider that she might have found a solution to some of her immediate problems.

Besides, without hope, life would be insufferable.

The dialysis procedures had been following each other with monotonous regularity. Three times a week she took Melissa in and sat there for four or five hours while her daughter's blood went through the cleansing process. Melissa usually didn't feel much like talking during these periods and spent the time dozing, watching television, or reading. Shannon knew that after a while she would be able to drop Melissa off and pick her up afterward, but for now she felt her presence offered something.

In the meantime, in addition to her other problems she

was worrying about Melissa's schooling. No matter how they tried to arrange it, she was missing significant periods of school and falling behind in her studies. "Perhaps if you hired a private tutor," one of the teachers suggested, not unkindly. "That way she could make up the work at home or while she was having her treatments."

A tutor was out of the question. There was no way she could handle the expense. She tried as often as possible to help Melissa herself, but her own work was suffering and they were desperately low on money. She was getting a few magazine assignments, but in the face of dwindling available time she found herself working late into the nights to complete them. The effort was showing. She was exhausted most of the time and had even noticeably lost weight. She felt trapped on a merry-go-round that wouldn't stop.

Out of everyone she knew, Oliver had remained a true friend, a fact that filled her with gratitude. He wanted nothing and was willing to give everything. He listened, gave advice, offered to loan her what he could afford, got her work, and, when he became aware how wan and pale she was growing one day after she dropped a story off at his office, he showed up at her house with three bags of groceries that night and offered to cook dinner.

"This is too much like charity," she said, too tired to put any conviction in her voice.

"And you're going to refuse it?" he asked, raising an eyebrow.

She shook her head dumbly and then burst into tears.

"Come on," he said, encompassing her in his arms. "I know how tough this is for you, but I also know how tough you are. You're both gonna come out of this okay."

"God!" she mumbled against his shirt, which she had thoroughly wet. "It's just so . . . so . . . endless! It just goes on and on and on, getting harder and harder. I thought that if you persisted things got easier, but this

36

doesn't." She tried to stop crying, not wanting Melissa to see her like this.

"Listen, one day they are going to find a kidney for Melissa, babe. When that happens an end will be in sight."

"If she doesn't reject it," she said morosely. "One of the kids in that unit has rejected three kidneys so far. There aren't any guarantees."

"Of course not. There aren't guarantees for anything. You should know better than that! But at least there is hope. You can't ask for more than that."

"Oh, God," she said, pulling away from him. "I know you're right. It's just . . ."

And so her life had been.

The seat belt and no-smoking signs came on and soon the aircraft began its descent into the murky, smog-laden Los Angeles basin. Thousands of houses stretched forever below them. Glistening blue swimming pools sat like jewels among a patchwork of monotonous gray rooftops, dull greenery, and busy streets.

"I hate this city," the man sitting beside Shannon muttered. "I don't know how they can even call it a city. Can't walk anywhere."

Shannon felt only excitement. She'd heard the same cliché uttered by New Yorkers a thousand times, but walking wasn't high on her list of priorities. She had been to L.A. twice before to do interviews, and each time the city had fascinated her. It was a strange place indeed, with no real center to it, but the vast urban sprawl linked by hundreds of miles of freeways contained a vitality totally different from New York's.

The trip over the country had been splendid. She had never flown first class before. There was ample space in which to stretch out, better food, free drinks, and the flight attendants treated you with deference. For once she didn't feel exhausted after a long flight. She could see why those who could afford it refused to travel any other way.

She thought of the meeting ahead for the hundredth time in the past two days. Who was this potential benefactor? What did he really want of her? Was what she was doing safe? What if he was some kind of criminal? Why the secrecy and the middle man? She shrugged the questions aside irritably, just as she did each time. She couldn't "think" the answers; she'd have to find them out. She'd made her decision and now she'd have to play the hand. There was no turning back.

The Boeing 747 landed without a bump. A nervous couple near the back of the first-class cabin applauded.

Shannon disembarked and walked down the narrow tunnel to the gate. Someone would be waiting, the lawyer had said.

And so there was, just behind the barrier. A burly man in black chauffeur's uniform held a card on which was neatly printed in black ink, "Ms. Shannon Ross."

"I'm Shannon Ross," she said, approaching him.

Face expressionless, he took only an instant to inspect the lithe young woman. She wore a short pale-blue skirt, a blue-and-white striped cotton jacket over a silk shirt, and flat, open-toed shoes.

"Do you have luggage, ma'am?" he asked, touching his cap.

"Just this." She swung the small carry-on bag.

"Allow me," he said, taking it from her.

"Thank you," she said.

They walked down the stairs and boarded the escalator.

The chauffeur stood in front of her. After a quick glance back to make sure she wasn't blocking any fast-moving passengers, Shannon moved forward and stood beside him. He was about an inch taller than she, stocky, with broad shoulders, black hair, dark eyes of indiscernible color, and craggy features. His nose looked as if it had once been broken. Shannon wasn't used to chauffeurs and didn't quite know what to say to the stern man beside her. She began with the obvious. "What's your name?"

"Andy Paxton, ma'am."

She stuck out her hand and said, "Pleased to meet you."

Was that a smile lurking at the corner of his mouth? He took her hand. "Likewise, ma'am."

"Where are we going, Andy Paxton?" she asked lightly.

"Beverly Hills, ma'am."

"To see whom?"

He turned his head and met her eyes and said without inflection, "I was told not to answer any questions, ma'am."

Shannon nodded and stared back at him. "Are you taking me somewhere safe, Mr. Paxton?" She watched his reaction intently.

"Absolutely, ma'am," he said, an offended stiffness entering his voice. "You have nothing to worry about on that score."

"Thank you," she said, and stepped behind him.

The limousine, white and long, with a television antenna sticking up from the back like a flag of prosperity, waited at a loading zone, unticketed and ignored by two policemen standing nearby. The air outside was warm and heavy with a slightly noxious odor. She was glad she had chosen cool clothes.

Paxton opened the door for her, watched her slide in, then closed it. He got into the front and said over his shoulder, "There's a bar in front of you, ma'am. A television set and a radio. If you need anything else, please let me know." And then the glass window between them glided to a close and she was alone.

The seats were made of soft, dark leather. She slid the bar door open and saw wine, gin, vodka, brandy, champagne, and ice. She closed it again and looked through the shaded windows. Little could be seen of the terrain beside the freeway except for the slender palm trees that rose like sentinels on both sides. In the distance ahead she could see the rows of high-rise buildings along Wilshire

Boulevard and beyond those the indistinct outline of the Hollywood Hills.

After fifteen minutes they took the Sunset Boulevard exit and drove east toward Beverly Hills. The road wound past the UCLA campus and then the limousine smoothly turned left and entered the gates of Bel Air.

It was a sudden change of scale: the houses were larger, the trees older and taller, the foliage thick and lush. Long driveways behind closed iron gates gave tantalizing views of rolling lawns and mansions. There were other limousines on the road too, along with Rolls-Royces, Jaguars and Mercedes Benzes. An impatient red Lamborghini screamed past them and took the curve ahead at about eighty miles per hour.

This was one of the things she liked about Los Angeles, Shannon thought. She'd noticed it during her last visit as well. In New York wealth was more discreet; here they flaunted it openly. This candid approach to life carried over into other activities as well. Individualistic eccentricities seemed to be more tolerated here. Social doors opened more easily. Or so it had seemed, based upon her limited experience.

They turned into a driveway and stopped before huge gates. By now she was thoroughly lost in the maze of roads. Last seen somewhere in Bel Air, she thought with black humor. Silently the gates swung open, and the limousine crawled forward.

Fruit trees. Beyond them a lawn, neatly planted rows of roses in bloom. It seemed like acres. And there—a house. Too small a word to describe it. Without doubt a mansion. Two stories of Spanish architecture, of adobe and white plaster and green ivy. A building that sat there like a colussus with enormous windows behind a verandah that ran the whole width of it. Beside it were other smaller houses and a garage large enough to hold half-a-dozen cars. God knew what was behind the mansion, she thought. Perhaps it went on and on, a mile or two of house.

The limousine crunched to a halt on the tarmac directly in front. Paxton got out and opened the door for her.

"Here you are, ma'am. I hope you had a comfortable ride."

"Yes, thank you," she said uncertainly. The house, the grounds, the mere size of it all awed her. She had the incongruous thought that she was a pretender, that her whole life was a sham. While she had been sitting at various typewriters writing trivial stories that had seemed important to her at the time, someone else had been creating this, and all the wealth it implied.

Paxton led the way up the steps, across the porch to the front door. He opened it and stood aside for her to enter.

The hall was the size of a tennis court. A dark hardwood floor glinted under the shattered light of a crystal chandelier hanging from the second-floor ceiling. Obviously expensive paintings and tapestries hung on the walls and a white marble staircase wound its way upstairs. The center of the room was covered with a thirty-by-twenty foot Persian carpet, an Isfahan, she guessed, remembering the research on carpets she had needed to do while writing a story.

Oak doors led to rooms on either side of the hall. At the far end of the hall a woman stepped from one of these doors, moved toward them, but then turned and entered another room.

Her attention went back to the paintings. Was that a Monet on the wall to her left? It had to be. A country landscape of brilliant color and light. Beside it was a Pissaro, she was sure.

She stood there astounded until Paxton interrupted her. "This way, ma'am," he said, opening a door to her left.

They entered what appeared to be a combined study and living room. Paxton pointed at a cluster of stuffed armchairs around a couch. "Please sit down. Someone will

41

be with you shortly." And then he disappeared, closing the door through which they had entered, leaving her alone in the center of the room.

Books filled the far wall of built-in shelves. A desk sat at the other end of the room, its surface unmarred by paper. Behind the desk, framed photographs coated the wall, hundreds of them. She took two steps toward them and peered forward. They were all movie stars. Marilyn Monroe, Bogart, Hepburn and Tracy, Ginger Rogers, Fred Astaire, and on and on, the Hollywood greats of the past. All the photographs were signed, too, she saw, although she couldn't read the writing from this distance.

She stepped closer, then changed her mind. Turning, she went to the couch and sat, crossing her legs and clasping a knee with her hands. Someone in the film business, she thought. The photographs made it very likely that her potential benefactor was involved in the motion picture industry.

The door opened and a slim, blond-haired woman of about thirty entered.

"How do you do? I'm Lynn Reid," she said, walking over to Shannon and holding out her hand.

Shannon stood and gripped the firm, dry hand. Ms. Reid wore glasses shielding her blue eyes and her hair was tied back, giving her a severe appearance. She wore a knee-length gray skirt and white blouse and seemed very businesslike.

"He'll just be a few moments longer," she said. "Is there anything I can get you? A drink? Some coffee?"

"A cup of coffee would be nice," Shannon said.

"Very well," the lady said. "In the meantime, please make yourself comfortable."

She turned and left the room. Shannon sat again. A secretary. She had to be "his" secretary.

A minute later, a middle-aged woman entered. The woman she had seen in the hall? She carried a silver tray, with a silver coffeepot, sugar bowl and milk container, and a cup and saucer made of china slightly thicker than an eggshell. She placed the tray on the table before Shannon, saying, "Your coffee, ma'am. Will you be needing anything else?"

"No. This is fine. Thank you," Shannon answered.

Once again alone, she poured the coffee, added a spoon of sugar and some milk, and stirred the liquid with a silver teaspoon.

The coffee was strong and flavorful, unlike anything she had tasted before. She took a few sips then put the cup down and stretched her legs. She was a little tired, she realized. It was late afternoon in New York, early afternoon here. A three-hour time difference. At nine o'clock it would be midnight according to her internal clock and she would no doubt be truly exhausted.

The door again. And something—with Lynn Reid standing behind it—rolled into the room.

It took Shannon a full two seconds to realize that she was watching a motorized wheelchair move toward her.

In it was a man.

Burning black eyes stared at her from above a hooked nose, wide thin-lipped mouth, and square chin. It was the face of a determined man, a man she guessed to be in his late sixties, a man she recognized immediately.

Miles Cort, a bona fide Hollywood legend.

Her memory spilled out facts faster than she could assimilate them. Like Howard Hughes, he had made his money first as an industrialist. Whereas Hughes had made his money in aircraft and machinery, Cort's wealth came when he took over his father's food packaging and distribution company, a giant in the field, along with Hunts and Del Monte, S&W and others. Like Hughes, he had entered Hollywood as an independent producer. Then, in 1950, at the age of thirty, he bought Charisma Films, an ailing studio, and made it into a major studio. Unlike Hughes, Cort loved film above all else. Food packaging did not interest him and, in 1955, he sold the now greatly expanded family food business for a fortune.

In the fifties, Cort used great stars to make great films, many of which were now considered classics. In the sixties, his company entered television production, but toward the end of that decade it began to run into financial problems due to some monumentally expensive feature film flops. In the mid-seventies Cort sold his companies and went back to where he had started—independent production. He made a couple of lackluster movies, but the times seemed to have passed him by. A number of important critics called his films "old-fashioned." As far as Shannon remembered he had retired from public view a year or two ago after suffering an illness, some kind of stroke, she thought.

All this and more flooded her mind. Cort was generally considered to have been the last great studio head in the old mold, a peer in spirit if not age of the Zanucks and Warners and Harry Cohn and Louis B. Mayer—those autocratic and despotic studio bosses who got films made by the hundreds. Like those men, he knew film and loved it. It was an age gone by, lost to the accountants and lawyers of present-day Hollywood.

"Sorry to keep you waiting," Cort stated. "Damn fool telephone call kept me upstairs."

He was a large man in spite of the wheelchair, with his big shoulders, broad hands, and thick, stubby fingers. His oversized head seemed to wobble on his neck. The most curious thing about him was the voice—high-pitched, almost feminine in tone, although the inflections were decidedly male: aggressive, impatient, powerful.

"That's all right," she said. "I was just enjoying a cup of coffee."

"So, you're Shannon Ross." He wheeled his chair to within two feet of her. Those black eyes examined her relentlessly before he continued. "I've read your magazine work. Like it. You're a good writer."

44

"Thank you."

"And I'm Miles Cort. Heard of me?"

"I recognized you immediately, Mr. Cort."

"Hmm," he grunted, apparently pleased. "Know anything about Hollywood?"

"I've interviewed directors and actors. I watch movies, I've been working on a book about Valentino, I—"

"But you have no close connections?" he interrupted. "No desire to write screenplays? No network of contacts to fulfill your aspirations here?"

"No," she said.

"Good," he nodded. "That's what I want."

"What is it that you need me for?" she asked.

Cort looked up at his secretary who stood silently behind him. "She looks tired," he said to her. "Long journey. Probably like a nap. Show her to the guesthouse." He turned back to Shannon. "We'll talk over dinner. Have a rest. Get freshened up."

Not waiting for her agreement, he pushed a button on the arm of his chair, wheeled backward, did a smart ninety-degree turn, and headed out of the room.

Shannon felt like a child who had just been offered food, only to have it snatched away. She looked blankly over at Lynn.

"Mr. Cort is a very busy man. He doesn't mean to be short with you, it's just his way of doing things," Lynn said, a slightly amused slant to her lips.

Shannon was disappointed. Her curiosity was killing her, but she hid it and said, "Well, I guess I could use some freshening up."

"I'll show you to your room," Lynn said.

Shannon picked up her suitcase and followed her. They went back into the main hall, through a door into a hallway, and out the side of the house.

"Have you worked long for Mr. Cort?" Shannon asked, picking her way along a shaded flagstone path.

"About four years." Lynn turned her head. "Here's your guesthouse."

It was a small stucco bungalow draped in glowing crimson bougainvillea. Lynn opened the door and ushered Shannon in.

"There're two bedrooms, living room, study, a full kitchen. Of course, if you need anything else to eat or drink, just call Maude, the head housekeeper. She'll take care of all your needs."

Shannon put her suitcase down and stood in the middle of the room.

"Oh, one other thing," Lynn said. "There's a telephone here for your use, but I must ask that you not call anyone until you've talked to Mr. Cort at dinner tonight. All right?"

"I have to call my daughter," Shannon said. "She's expecting to hear from me. It'll be too late after dinner."

Lynn hesitated, thinking about it, then said, "I suppose that'll be fine. However, please don't tell her where you are or who you are seeing. Mr. Cort demands confidentiality."

"Agreed," Shannon said.

"Very well. Dinner will be at seven. I'll come and get you." Lynn gave a short nod and left.

Shannon looked around the room. Some guesthouse. Not only luxuriously furnished, it was four times the size of her New York apartment.

More intriguing at the moment was what Cort wanted. Obviously he wanted something and he wasn't about to become her generous patron out of the goodness of his heart. Something that demanded no close Hollywood connections. Perhaps he wanted to hire her, but for what? Writing? She hadn't been looking for a job. That wasn't what she had sought in a patron. She already had her Valentino project to work on.

She sighed then. Now was no time to jump to conclusions. She had no choice but to wait and see exactly what was involved. Someone in a desperate situation such as she was in no position to act the prima donna.

She went to the bathroom. Most of the space in the room was taken up by an oversized floor-level Roman tiled tub with a built-in Jacuzzi. The shelf was laden with bath oils and salts.

"I think I could learn to like this," she muttered to herself. She'd soak in the sybaritic splendor of the tub, then call Melissa, and then take a nap, she thought.

"Oh, God," she said aloud. She'd just noticed a telephone in the bathroom. Hell, she could call Melissa while bathing! For some reason, the idea, perhaps because it was so far removed from her normal living circumstances, made her chuckle.

Her immediate future decided, she set about making it a reality by removing her clothes.

Promptly at seven, Lynn Reid knocked politely on her door. Shannon had managed to pack two changes of clothing into the small carry-on bag and now wore a long beige skirt and a floppy satin shirt. Lynn Reid, she noticed, still wore the same gray skirt and blouse.

As they walked through the garden, now magically glowing from strategically hidden outdoor lights she hadn't noticed during the day, Lynn asked if she found her quarters comfortable.

Rather than say how she really felt about them and appear like a country hick, Shannon murmured a simple "Very nice, thank you."

In truth, she was overwhelmed. From the down pillows on the bed, to the oversized television, stereo VCR, and vast selection of movies to watch, to the fully stocked bar and refrigerator filled with caviar, delicatessen meats and cheeses, the sheer sumptuousness of it was almost beyond belief.

Lynn, as if having read her thoughts, said drily, "It

may not be an original thought of his, but Mr. Cort is a firm believer that living well is the best revenge."

"What's that wonderful aroma?" Shannon asked, enchanted by the sweet, heavy smell that saturated the night air. For all she knew, Cort had machines that spewed it out like perfume.

Lynn shrugged disinterestedly. "Probably daphne. There are bushes of it around. It seems to exude the scent only at night."

They entered the house and went through the main hall to the wing opposite the office where she had first waited. Lynn flung open two double doors and stood aside. "Enjoy your dinner," she said.

Cort was already at the table, a thirty-foot-long slab of red mahogany. Above it were three chandeliers, miniature versions of the gigantic one in the main hall. More expensive oil paintings hung on the walls.

"Forgive me for not rising," Cort said, still in his wheelchair at the head of the table. "Perhaps you would care to sit beside me?"

Apparently they were the only two eating dinner. A place was set for her to his immediate right and she sat there obediently.

"A white wine?" he asked.

"Thank you."

He took a bottle from a silver ice bucket to his left and skillfully poured it into her glass.

"To our future efforts," he said, raising his glass.

The wine was like nectar, dry but bursting with flavor.

"It's wonderful wine," Shannon said, putting her glass back on the table.

"The best Chardonnay California has to offer," he said with satisfaction. "I'm not supposed to drink. Damn fool doctor. I gave up almost everything, but damned if I'll give it all up."

He wore a dinner suit and tie, she saw. Able to observe him more closely now without being disturbed by surprise,

48

she saw that although his hair was gray, he still possessed most of it. Deep lines creased his face, but instead of emphasizing his age they gave him an attractive dynamism. A face of experience. He must have been an extremely handsome man in his forties, she guessed. His most striking feature, however, were the obsidian eyes. Alert, watchful, they seemed to reflect light in their depths.

"What is it you want of me?" she asked, coming directly to the point.

"To strike a bargain," he said. "I know what you want, and who you are. If we can both get what we want, we'll have a deal."

Shannon felt a flash of irritation at his presumptuousness. She'd always prided herself on a certain complexity of character and had shot more than one man down for claiming to "know" her intimately after one or two dates.

"You can't know much about me from that newspaper ad," she said tartly.

Cort grinned. His white teeth were capped and perfect. "I know that you are twenty-nine years old and having a hard time of it as a free-lance writer, even though you have a good reputation as a professional who delivers what she promises.

"I know that you are a single mother and have an eleven-year-old daughter named Melissa who is seriously ill. That you're seeing an advertising copywriter, but that it probably isn't serious. That you are working on a damn fool book about Valentino, and that, financially, because of your daughter's illness, you have your back to the wall and are finally ready to face the realities of life. I don't need to know more than that to present my deal."

Shannon was stunned for only a second, and then her surprise was replaced by anger. "Quite apart from your opinions about my career, how in the hell do you know all— What gives you the right to pry into my private life?"

Cort allowed himself a tight smile, not at all taken aback by her vehemence. "Money and power, my dear," he said placidly. "When you have those, it's a simple matter to find out about people. You don't think I would invite you here without first finding out if you're the right person for the job. It was simply prudent of me to do so."

Shannon shook her head. "I wasn't looking for a job. I was looking for someone to support a project I'm working on. A patron of the arts."

"And have you found one? Did you get any offers?"

She stared back at him stubbornly, not answering. The bastard already knew the answer, she thought.

Cort's grimace was not without sympathy. "Patrons disappeared in the nineteenth century. Nobody gives a damn about art or artists anymore, not unless they can make a buck from it. Face it, your advertisement was the act of a desperate woman clutching at straws."

Shannon's anger suddenly deflated. What was the point? He was right, of course. It had been a foolish thing to do, even more foolish to expect results. As for his prying? It was a perfectly reasonable action on his part.

She took another sip of the seductive wine and said, her voice flat, "Then what do you want?"

Cort had been leaning forward, watching her reactions as he spoke. Apparently he saw what he needed to see because now he settled back into his chair and his voice became more relaxed. "I want to be your patron."

"What?"

Cort smiled. "You can't get anything worth a damn for nothing in this world, my dear. I'll be your patron, in a manner of speaking, after you do a job for me. That's the deal."

"What job?" she asked, interested now in spite of herself.

"Forget Valentino, he's dead. Long gone and barely remembered. Besides, he was just an actor. I have something better for you. I want you to write the biography of the greatest man still alive in Hollywood today."

"Who?"

Cort lifted his wineglass toward her in a silent toast. "Why, me of course, my dear. Who else? Me. Miles Cort."

Shannon sat alone on the porch of the guesthouse, rocking slightly on the cushioned patio chair. The smog had evaporated with the night and now stars were visible through the velvet foliage. Nearby, a mockingbird kept up a song of calls. The smell of daphne still clung to the air.

She had told Cort that she would let him know her answer in the morning before she left to catch her flight. After dinner she had excused herself, refusing a cognac, and returned to the cottage. She had found her own supply of cognac in the bar, poured herself a glass, and gone outside to think.

Her thoughts wandered away from Miles Cort's proposal and returned to her daughter. For some reason at that moment, memories of her conversations with Dr. Feinstein vividly intruded. There was, for instance, that time just before Melissa's first dialysis treatment. "There's one thing you should know," he said soberly. "An eleven-year-old is developmentally at the absolutely worst age for fear of needles, and we use needles to start each dialysis treatment."

"Is this true of all kids?" she asked.

"I don't know of any exceptions."

"How do they get over it?"

"With great difficulty, and some children never do. I've never seen nurses physically restrain anyone, but there's a moment when treatment is starting where they always wonder if they'll have to."

Another thing he said that clung to her mind like a parasite: "On an average, kids on dialysis need blood transfusions about every six weeks."

"Are they safe?" she asked, the headlines leaping into her mind.

"There are serious risks," he admitted soberly. When he saw the expression on her face, he said, "Let me explain . . .

"In all people with kidney disease, the hormone in the bone marrow stops helping to produce red blood cells. With adults, we have drugs to help produce these red blood cells. However, if we gave kids the drug it would cause them to stop growing."

He shook his head. "They need blood though. They lose blood during the treatment, they lose it because of waste products in the blood, and the red blood cells have a decreased life. Transfusions are crucial."

"But the blood is tested, screened, isn't it?" she asked.

"Of course, but there are risks. I'd be derelict if I didn't tell you about them. Blood always poses a big problem. The testing isn't a hundred percent foolproof. At a certain stage of incubation, nothing shows in the blood. There's always the danger of infections with hepatitis and, of course, to a much lesser degree, with AIDS."

"But the blood is tested for AIDS," she protested.

"Blood is tested for the AIDS antibodies, not for the virus," he said. "If someone contracted the disease last week and gave blood today, the antibodies wouldn't show up."

"But can't they store the blood until it does?" she asked incredulously.

"Not long enough."

"God," she said. "That's terrifying." Not only that but barbaric. Medicine the science was suddenly vulnerable to the whims of the gods.

Feinstein nodded. "It's a risk, a real one, but it is minimal when the percentages are taken into account. At least for the time being. When the disease really spreads . . ." He left his sentence unsaid.

There was no need for him to say more. The ramifications were obvious. Nor did the percentages interest her. Not when her daughter's life was at stake. But what could she do but acquiesce? The hideous thing about this whole experience was the lack of options. Years ago—during her childhood, in fact—people died of kidney failure. Now they could be kept alive. But there was apparently no progress without risks. The scales were always balanced somehow.

"Can she use my blood?" she asked.

"Not enough," he said.

They had also been required to choose between two types of dialysis—hemodialysis and peritoneal dialysis. Both had their advantages and drawbacks.

Hemodialysis, she was told, used an artificial kidney machine to cleanse the blood about three times a week. Peritoneal dialysis involved a catheter placed into the abdomen and had to be done every night. In their case, if they chose peritoneal dialysis, Shannon would have to be trained for a couple of weeks and then she would do the procedure.

It came down to a matter of lifestyle. Because of her work, there was always the possibility of travel and she was in no position to afford home nursing care for Melissa when she was away. She allowed Melissa to make the decision, however. After hearing all the pros and cons, Melissa decided on hemodialysis.

And then there were the first dialysis patients they had seen— four children. Three were black and one was Oriental.

"They handle their ordeal in different ways," Feinstein had muttered to Shannon. "Some of them do homework during the treatment, some of them sleep, and some watch television."

The Oriental, a girl of about fifteen, though small for her age, was, as he said, dozing. One of the boys was reading, the other two watched television.

53

"They all look so wiped out," Shannon said sympathetically.

Feinstein nodded. "By the time they come in here, they usually are. The toxins have built up in their bodies in the previous two days. They're exhausted after the treatment. By the next day they start to feel better."

"And then almost immediately, by the next day, bad again?"

"Yes," he said, his mouth tight. "But at least they're alive."

"Jesus," Shannon said, unable to keep the disgust from her voice. It was a hell of a way to live, a cyclical ride between feeling good and feeling bad.

And it had proved to be exactly that for Melissa.

The eager howl of a baying dog brought Shannon back to the present. This was Bel Air, a bastion of wealth and privilege. All she had to do was say yes to Miles Cort's offer and she and Melissa would be able to enjoy all the benefits it brought.

Shannon smiled grimly to herself in the dark. She already knew what her answer would be, and so did Cort. She was going through a charade dictated by pride.

As their dinner progressed, he had offered her a sweetheart deal, an unbelievable deal, in fact.

"Why me?" had been her one of her most pressing questions. "With your money, you could hire anyone with marvelous credentials to do your bio."

"I read that series you did on labor racketeering. A damn fine piece of work. And it was obvious that it took courage to do it. Besides, what did you get for that? The Pulitzer?"

"No. I was nominated."

"Well, you should have goddamn won it."

"Thank you," she said. "But there are other good writers. Ones who did win the Pulitzer. So why me?"

"I want someone who's not stupid about the subject of Hollywood, but someone who's fresh, able to approach it from an unjaundiced viewpoint. Also someone who doesn't owe any favors around town. This town's full of hack writers. I need another one like I need a heart attack," he had said. "Besides, I've always hired people who are hungry. They're not fat, contented cats. They work harder, do a better job."

He outlined the terms of his deal:

She would start work immediately, stopping all her other projects.

She would move onto the estate and live in the guesthouse.

Her daughter could stay with her. A dialysis machine would be set up and a private nursing staff would be provided to give the treatments. A tutor would also be provided so Melissa wouldn't have to miss school.

She would end any relationships with current boyfriends and commit herself to six to twelve months of work.

In return, she would be handsomely paid. And she would be paid regardless of whether the book found a publisher or not.

All her expenses would be covered.

All her daughter's medical expenses would be covered. Lifetime medical expenses, and he would try to locate Melissa's father.

After completing the biography she would get a substantial fee, enough to keep her living well for at least three years, during which time she could work on whatever she wanted to.

She had sat there wordlessly after Cort outlined the bargain. He had then added another carrot. "I have many contacts, powerful people," he said. "I will also utilize them with all my power to see that a kidney is found for your daughter."

"I don't think it's possible to buy a kidney," Shannon said.

"When you have enough money, everything is possible," Cort said.

"I'll need to think about it," she stammered finally.

"What's to think about?" Cort had asked, spreading his hands. "This is everything you need and want!"

"I can write the truth?" she asked hesitantly.

"As you see it. You'll have full access to my papers and everyone I know. An unlimited expense account. Secretarial and research help if you need it."

"Why are you willing to spend so much money on this book? You're talking about a fortune."

"I'm worth somewhere around two hundred million dollars, my dear. What else am I going to spend it on? This book will tell my story, set the record straight. It's important to me."

"I'll give you my answer in the morning," she said.

He paused, then said, "Good. Call me on the telephone. My extension is number one."

Why had she hesitated? she now asked herself. It was everything she wanted, or, at least, needed. Why did she even go through the silly pretense of indecision?

She knew that answer, too. Cort was offering her too much. He was buying her. This was a powerful and determined man, and he wanted something done. She'd had enough experience working with egotistical people to know that no matter how much "truth" they wanted, they didn't want it to conflict with their version of it. Right now, Cort thought he'd let her write what she saw fit; later, it would change and there would be problems. But those were future hurdles, and to be expected. They went with the territory if you were a writer and, above all, she was a writer.

"And someone is offering you what seems like all the money in the world to write," she said incredulously to herself.

More important, however, was his offer to help get a kidney. God, if he could do that! If, instead of waiting one, two, or three years, Melissa could get a kidney sooner and end this horrible dialysis treatment, that was worth everything else put together. Could he do it? Would it be legal? Did she care if it wasn't? This was her daughter's life. Any shortcut was justified.

She swirled the cognac in her glass and took a sip. As smooth as silk, it probably cost eighty dollars a bottle.

"Idiot," she said.

She put the glass down and went inside. She picked up the telephone in the living room and dialed "one."

"Yes?" Cort said.

"We have a deal," she said. "I'll do it."

"Good. In that case, we don't need to meet in the morning. Go back to New York, take care of your affairs, and be back, ready to start in two weeks. Lynn will take care of all the financial details and logistics. Good night."

She stared at the silent receiver in her hands and smiled wryly to herself. She was now a hired hand. She had her orders.

CHAPTER FOUR

Orson Cort, the oldest son of Miles Cort, looked up from the trade magazine he was reading as his secretary entered the doorway of his small office.

"Wife's on the line," Wanda said. She was a thin black girl with long legs and what he considered to be a splendid ass, which was essentially why he had hired her.

"Yeah," he said. Picking up the telephone, he watched Wanda turn and saunter out of vision, her buttocks gliding against each other in tight designer jeans. She'd only been with him two weeks and wasn't much of a secretary, but one day he was going to dip into that pot of black honey. He was sure it would more than make up for her lack of typing and spelling skills.

"I don't think much of your new secretary," Barbara said cuttingly, startling him with the coincidence of their thoughts. "Her telephone manners could do with improvement. She always sounds like she has gum in her mouth."

"Is that what you called about?" Orson asked. Barbara had been his secretary for six months until he married her in 1988. Since then she had never approved of his choices to fill her position. They were either too pretty or too stupid, or a combination of both.

"Are you sleeping with her yet?" Barbara asked.

"Just because I fucked you, doesn't mean I fuck all my

secretaries," Orson said, not for the first time. "Keep in mind that I wasn't married when I met you. Besides," he added with an ambiguous chuckle, "You're a big enough cunt to keep me satisfied. What is it, anyway?"

"I want to know if I can call a wallpaper company for the dining room?"

"What for? The wallpaper's fine in the dining room."

"I told you last week," she said sharply. "It doesn't go with the furniture. We need to change it, get a lighter color."

"Shit!" he said. "Didn't we just talk about money two days ago? Didn't I just explain that things are tight right now and that a few things would have to wait?"

"It won't cost that much," she said.

"You'll just have to put up with what's there a little longer," he said. "As soon as I get this deal off the ground you can paper the whole house inside and out. When the old man croaks you can go buy a new house here and another one in Santa Barbara."

"He'll outlive us all," she said bitterly. "I'm not going to wait around for that to happen."

"Well, just wait on the wallpapering."

"When will you be home?"

"Late. I have a dinner meeting with Fowler."

"The money man?"

"One of the money men," he said. "Listen, I got to run. See you later. Love you, baby."

He hung up and glowered down at the phone. Bitch! She was fifteen years younger than he was and behaved like it most of the time. His fifth wife, she was turning out to be a mistake, just like all the others. She thought that because his name was Cort he was made of money. In reality, he was struggling. If he didn't get this movie project off the ground, she wouldn't have a house left to live in, let alone wallpaper.

He looked down at his ostrich leather boots and then brushed some paper shavings from his blue jeans. Then he took his tweed jacket off the back of the chair, slung it over his shoulder and left his office. Stopping at Wanda's cubicle he said, "I'm taking off. If anyone calls, say I'm taking meetings and can't be disturbed."

"Sure. Will you be back?"

"No, you can split early," he said.

He hurried through the corridor, nodding politely to a passing man and shouting out a "hi!" to another. Slim, and of medium height, Orson had brooding dark features dominated by bulges below his eyes which some people said looked like poached eggs. All in all, in spite of the fact he was only forty-two, there was something somber and older about his appearance, as if each year had left its cumulative mark.

He walked out to the parking lot and climbed into the silver Mercedes Benz he leased for $310 a month. The small office he rented on the Burbank Studio lot and the Mercedes were necessities for someone who called himself an independent producer. A secretary was another image-raising asset. In truth he didn't have enough work to keep Wanda busy, but she was an actress, willing to be paid a pittance in order to be on the lot and be seen, hopefully to "make contacts." It was all part of the Hollywood game. You had to look good, even if you weren't. Half of being successful was getting other people to believe you were already there.

He drove past the guard at the gate and made his way to the freeway. The traffic was already thickening as early birds tried to get out of the city. Heading west, he took the Laurel Canyon exit toward the Hollywood Hills. Just before the slope upward where the more expensive homes began to appear, he turned right and parked in front of an apartment building.

He was not, as he had told his wife, having dinner with money man Fowler. With all his talk of access to vast financing, Fowler was turning out to be just another flake jerking off at having access to glamour.

60

He walked to the building, stopped at the door, and pushed the buzzer for number 22.

"Yes," the voice came over the intercom.

"Delivery," he announced, and pushed the door open as the buzzer sounded.

He took the stairs to the next floor, rang the doorbell, and waited. There was a movement behind the peephole and then the door opened.

The woman wore a red satin dressing gown, belted tightly at the waist to show the curve of her hips. The V of the neck allowed a tantalizing but minuscule glimpse of something black and lacy. Curly blond hair fell in waves to her shoulders. She stared at him, her blue eyes wide with surprise, saying nothing.

He grinned wolfishly at her.

"Where's the delivery? What do you want?" she asked finally, a girlish tremble to her voice.

He pushed the door open further, stepped in and then closed it behind him. "You," he said, leaning back against it.

"Get out or I'll call the police." Her eyes were wary now. "Open that door and get out."

"How are you going to call the police?" His eyes slid over to the telephone beside the couch. It was a good twenty feet away from her.

She stepped back, fear entering her face for the first time now. Then another step, half turning her head to look longingly at the telephone.

"I'll scream," she said, her hands raised to her chest as if to protect her breasts.

Orson took a step forward. "Nobody will hear you."

"What do you want from me?"

He took another step and then reached out a hand to move her arm aside and touch her right breast. He could feel the hard nipple through the satin. Using thumb and forefinger, he squeezed it.

"What do you think?"

61

"No," she whispered, then turned and ran for the telephone.

He was on her before she had gone six feet, his outstretched hand grabbing the back of her hair and pulling her short. She screamed once, a short, sharp yelp and then stood there with her back to him.

He released her hair and put his hands on her shoulders. Stepping forward he pushed his crotch into her ass so she could feel his growing hardness.

"No," she said again. He swung her around so that she faced him and then pulled her closer so that her body pressed against his. Heavy and humid breath brushed his face. He leaned back at the waist and dropped his hands to cup her breasts. He was also breathing hard now, his cock visibly straining against his pants.

"Please don't hurt me," she said in that girlish voice. "I'll give you anything you want. Money. Jewelry."

"That's not what I want." He pulled at the bow of her belt and the gown spread open about six inches. With the back of his left hand, he pushed one side away to reveal her full left breast and her lacy bra.

Black, transparent in parts, it was open in the center— a circular hole from which protruded a hard brown nipple.

"No!" she screamed, pushed against his chest, and ran for the telephone again.

He caught up with her just as she reached for it, grabbing the collar of her gown and throwing her down on the couch.

She lay there on her back and looked up at him, the gown concealing nothing now. He looked at her crimson-painted toenails, up the pale creamlike skin of her spread-eagled legs and settled his gaze on the tiny panties, slit open to reveal the swell of her shaved crotch.

Bending slightly, he reached down and ran the palm of his hand down until his fingers found the opening. He explored it skillfully, watching her lips part and her eyes half close, listening to the sharp intake of her breath.

"You're dripping wet," he said thickly.

Her eyes opened and she looked up at him with a different expression, languorous, satisfied, her hips thrusting up ever so slightly against his hand.

"I'm ready," she said.

As if reacting to a command, he drew his hand quickly away, straightened up, and tore at his belt with clumsy fingers. He kicked his pants off his feet and stood there, his cock jutting up at a forty-five-degree angle.

"You want it now?"

Her own hand crept down to her cunt now. With two fingers she spread it open. "Now!" she said urgently. "Now!"

He fell down on her, not bothering to take off his shoes or his shirt, entering her rising hips almost immediately.

They lay naked on the king-size waterbed, tangled covers below them.

Orson looked over at the now satiated body of his fourth wife and ran a hand lazily across her hip. "You're the best fuck I ever had."

Pat grunted, not bothering to open her eyes at the compliment.

Pat was an actress who, like many others claiming the same occupation in Hollywood, seldom worked. He had met her while producing *Tilt*, a low budget movie that had made him enough money to keep going for six months but had added little credibility to his reputation. Ostensibly dealing with the world of pinball players, the film was little more than a titillating exposure of tits and ass—soft-core porn for the teen market. After appearing briefly at a few small theaters and drive-ins, it languished in video stores and on late-night cable.

Pat had a small part in the movie but attacked it with such vigor she attracted his attention. The fact that she had a thirty-seven-inch bust, long legs, and full lips set in

63

a permanent pout had much to do with his interest, particularly because she made a point of making sure he noticed. After all, he was the producer of the film and a member of the illustrious Cort family. As soon as she felt him nibble at the bait, she dropped her play for the handsome leading man and concentrated on Orson.

He didn't have much chance of escaping, he thought in retrospect. He'd always had a soft spot for well-endowed actresses (some would call it a fatal attraction) and had already married and divorced three of them. Within months after first sleeping with her, he married Pat in 1984, making her his fourth wife. However, as soon as she found out that like most people she knew he was struggling from one month to the next to make payments on his possessions, her ardor began to cool. Within a year, they were divorced. She took what he had in alimony ("Getting blood from a stone," he called it) and they parted ways. Kind of.

The thing of it was, they had great sex together. Had from the first time they had grappled with each other in a trailer on location. She loved these role-playing games, and he found he had a penchant for them himself. And, he discovered after the divorce, without the stresses of marriage, the sex was even better. Not only that, but he didn't have to marry her to fuck her! It was a perfect antidote to what his father despisingly called, "This disease of yours—marrying every broad you fuck."

He frowned at the thought of his father. The old bastard had literally cut him off. Oh, he still got money from the trust fund Miles had set up years before, but it was a piddling amount, a couple of grand a month. He had approached Miles to bankroll the project he was currently trying to pull together, but the old man had waved him away with a snarl. "You've lost too much of my money already. Go lose other people's money." End of subject.

It was true investors had recouped nothing on his previous two films, but that was just bad luck. It could happen to anyone, and had happened to many. But Miles was his father, for chrissakes. Where was his sense of paternal support? Down the toilet with all his other finer emotions. Miles had always been a lousy father and an asshole. Why expect him to change now? But the unfairness of it still rankled. Hell, a lousy million bucks was all he had wanted. Hell, Miles had a hundred, two hundred times that amount.

"How's the new movie coming along?" Pat asked, interrupting his thoughts.

"Great, just great!" he said. It was his standard answer. In Hollywood, you never let anyone know you had your back up against the wall. Like vultures, they'd tear the skin off your back if they knew.

"Do you have the financing together?" she asked, raising herself on her elbow and resting her head on her palm. Her breasts were finally beginning to sag, in spite of a ferocious exercise program, he noticed. In another five or ten years they'd be hanging down to her stomach. For some reason the thought satisfied him. Nobody had a right to stay beautiful, successful, or happy forever.

"I have three companies interested in financing it," he lied. "It's just a matter of choosing the best terms among them."

"Hmm," she said, not making it clear whether she believed him or not. "Is there a part in it for me?"

"Shit! You know I can't give you a part. Barbara would be down on me like a ton of bricks!"

"I don't know why you married that cunt," Pat said, falling on her back and looking up at the the ceiling.

Orson remained silent. He didn't, either. Barbara was a good fuck and seemed to like him at the time. It was generally the reason he got married.

"Is Miles putting money in your movie?" she asked, her words drifting upward.

"Miles won't give me another dime," Orson said bitterly. "The asshole thinks I'm a bum, as you well know."

"He liked me."

Orson grimaced. "He didn't like you, baby. Miles doesn't like anyone. He just liked your ass and wished he could get into your pants. He acts that way with every pretty woman."

"Like father, like son," she said without rancor.

Orson smiled, almost proudly. "Yeah, well, we both have a certain talent in the area."

"Yeah," she said, "if only you had his money as well, you'd be perfect."

"I will," Orson said. "One day I will. Even Miles won't live forever."

"Mmm. What's he worth these days? Two hundred million?"

"Give or take a few bucks."

The thought of money stirred her. She sat up suddenly, her breasts swaying and her eyes bright. "Resuscitation time," she said, her head diving for his groin.

Elizabeth Cort sipped the twenty-two-year-old Beaujolais and looked down the table toward her father, not really hearing what he was saying to her sister Anne. How she hated these weekly family gatherings! She always had. They were simply an excuse for Miles to berate his children collectively.

It was a poor turnout tonight, however. He must be feeling frustrated with only two to criticize, she thought ungenerously.

Miles had five children by two of his four wives. Orson at forty-two was the oldest; and then came Anne who was forty but persisted in calling herself thirty-five and was already on her third husband. Miles's third wife, Rosemary, had borne Stephen, Elizabeth, and Richard. Stephen was thirty-one, Elizabeth twenty-nine. Richard was the baby of the family at twenty-seven. Tonight only the women, Elizabeth and Anne, were attending.

"Where's everyone else?" Elizabeth asked when there was a pause in the conversation.

Miles glowered at her. "Orson has a business dinner, Stephen, who as you know, seldom graces us with his presence, said he was working, and who the hell knows where Richard is. Probably getting into some trouble and expecting me to bail him out."

"I'm sure he's fine," Anne consoled in her usual ineffective way.

"It'll be the first time," Miles said, starting his comment with a grunt.

"He's not so bad, Daddy," Anne cooed. "He's young still. Trying to find himself. He's an innocent in a vicious world."

Other than to emit a humorless snort, Miles let the comment pass. At their last dinner together, after Anne had made a similarly perceptive comment, Miles had pointed out that her insights were obviously derived from a profound source, probably a combination of *Cosmopolitan* magazine and *The National Enquirer*. He was apparently in no mood to try to top that tonight.

Elizabeth looked curiously at her half-sister. Anne was still pretty in a sad, dissipated way, a blond-haired Barbie doll with fine feathers that were losing their distinction and a tall yet full body that men found attractive. Sometimes, however, Elizabeth was convinced there was a vacuum between Anne's ears. She was given to meaningless philosophical comments like the one she had just made. In her twenties she had been an actress of some repute, but now she had little to show for it. She was past her prime in a town that worshipped youth.

The two sisters were opposites in every way. Elizabeth was dark-haired, of medium height, and just missed being plain. Her eyes were her most striking features. Lying in the band of color between hazel and green, they had smoldering depths to them. A passion lurked there, in strange contrast to the rest of her. And yet, if one looked past the carelessly placed makeup, there was a sensuality to her mouth, and her features were perfectly balanced. Her body, too, was trim and athletic. To an observant stranger, it might seem that she had deliberately set out to look plain and unnoticeable. Tonight, while Anne wore a low-cut dress of bright tropical colors, Elizabeth wore severely cut tan slacks and a white blouse.

"How are you feeling?" Elizabeth asked her father.

"Fine. Don't I look fine?" he asked belligerently.

"Yes, you look fine," she agreed docilely. She never fought him. It would be like one woman taking on the Russian Army—a losing proposition, a waste of energy.

Miles poked disgruntledly at his food and said, "I was hoping everyone would be here tonight. I was going to make an announcement."

"Ooh! What?" Anne asked.

Miles placed a piece of filet mignon in his mouth and chewed it vigorously without bothering to answer.

"Hey! The happy family!" Richard sauntered into the dining room and stopped a foot from the table. Tall, with fair hair, blue eyes, and a profile that could stop a shipload of women, he looked down at them, sarcasm curling the corners of his mouth.

Miles washed the residue of his meat down with a hearty sip of red wine, then said, "We're honored you could make it."

Richard sat beside Anne and leaned his elbows on the table. "Sorry, I was tied up on the other side of town." His voice was quite unapologetic.

"Daddy was just going to make an announcement," Anne said with a bright smile at her father.

"A public hanging?" Richard asked hopefully.

"When are you going to get serious about life?" Miles snarled. "Jesus! You haven't changed in twenty-seven years. You think you can go through life acting like a kid. One day I'm not going to be there for you and you're going to find a bottomless pit right under your next step."

Carefully Richard poured himself a glass of wine. There was a wildness in his eyes. It was perfectly obvious to Elizabeth that he was stoned out of his skull. She wondered, as she always did when she saw Miles and Richard together, why her father indulged him so. He'd been in and out of jobs and trouble forever. He made no secret of his liking for drugs and his indiscriminate sexual tastes. Anyone else in the family would have been disinherited long before. Miles not only tolerated it, but supported Richard to a large extent, providing him a generous allowance and allowing him to live in one of the guesthouses on the estate.

She looked from one to the other and realized with a sudden flash of insight that it was because they were so alike. Miles saw himself in the young man. They were both completely amoral, the only difference being that Miles's amorality always had a purpose. So far, Richard had not shown the talent or the discipline his father had developed so early. Perhaps Miles still had hope that one day it would emerge, although the way Richard was conducting his life it would be like the phoenix rising from the ashes.

Richard sipped his wine and then looked at his glowering father, his voice serious for the first time. "Wish on, Miles," he said ironically. "There's no point. I'm already in a bottomless pit."

Miles stared back at him. God, Elizabeth thought for a wild, unbelievable moment, was that sadness in his eyes? But the moment passed before she could be sure and Miles said, "I despise self-pity. It's the weakest of emotions."

Richard shrugged in ironic apology and raised his glass. "To the strength you worship that I lack."

"What is it you wanted to tell us, Daddy?" Anne interjected quickly, consternation showing plainly on her face. Anne hated scenes and would do anything to avoid them—unless she created them.

Miles hesitated, and for a few seconds it seemed as if he would deprive them of his announcement, but then he leaned forward in his wheelchair and said reluctantly, "I wanted to let you all know that I will be having a semipermanent guest soon. I'm about to embark on a new project."

They all looked back at him, Elizabeth with boredom, Richard with ironic attention, and Anne with feigned interest.

"Yes?" Anne asked.

"The young lady is a writer. She will be working with me," Miles said.

"You're working on a new script?" Anne asked disbelievingly.

"No, we will be working on my biography," Miles stated. He leaned back again, and watched them, as if waiting for applause.

"Your biography?" Richard asked, surprised.

"You're working on a book?" Anne asked.

"You've hired her to write it for you," Elizabeth stated.

"Yes," Miles said.

"Who is this person?" Anne asked, a shrill tone entering her voice. "Is she qualified to do a job like this?"

"Is she qualified?" Miles asked, shaking his head in mock sadness. His voice began to rise. "Is she qualified? You're asking me?"

Elizabeth sank in her chair. She could recognize the imminence of an oncoming tirade.

Miles seemed to rise in his wheelchair, but it was impossible. It was an illusion. His legs no longer functioned. The muscles were isolated from the messages of his brain. The stroke had taken care of that.

"I have worked with the greatest writers in this town," Miles thundered. "I have manipulated them and controlled them and made them produce their best work in spite of their various insanities and imperfections and doubts." He slammed his fist on the table. "When Arthur

70

Bennett was too drunk to write, I'm the one who grabbed him and took him up to a cabin at Lake Arrowhead and locked him in it and made him sober up cold turkey and kept him there for three weeks with an armed guard outside his door while he produced his best work. For chrissakes! His only good work.

"So don't ask me about writers. I know writers better than anyone left alive in this town today. If I have a writer, you do not need to question his or her ability."

"Yes, of course, I'm sorry," Anne said, wilting beneath his glare.

"What makes you want to do a biography now?" Elizabeth asked calmly.

Miles spread his palms. "I'm getting old. I'm the last real producer in Hollywood. It's time to set the record straight."

"The gospel according to Miles Cort," Richard murmured.

."You better believe it. Read it and weep," Miles snapped. Then he grinned cruelly, his glance taking them all in. "You will all read it and weep. That much I promise."

The house was silent. His daughters had left and Richard had gone to wherever he went to seek his thrills. Maude, the housekeeper, had taken him upstairs and helped him prepare for bed, as she did every night before retiring. Now Miles lay there, his back propped up, his reading glasses perched low on his nose, studying papers his lawyers had delivered earlier in the day.

It seemed to be progressing well, he thought. In a week or so he would need Joe Collins to come to the house for a face-to-face meeting. Matters were going to get even more complex.

He took one last look at the papers and then tossed

71

them into an open briefcase beside the bed. Leaning down, he closed it and pushed it under the bed.

Damn kids, he thought as he leaned back. None of them would ever grow up. Richard was dissipating into nothing, Anne had wasted the little talent she possessed, Elizabeth was a nonentity, Orson was an idiot, and Stephen was a fool with no ambition. A musician, for chrissakes! He didn't know why he bothered with these weekly dinners. They always made him angry. And yet, the dinners and his money were the only way he had of controlling them. Without his willingness to do that they would probably be even worse off, every one of them.

If only he had the energy he'd once had, he'd straighten them all out. Ever since the stroke had left his legs paralyzed, he'd felt his children slip further away from his influence. They had thought he'd die when that happened. A couple of them had probably prayed for it, he thought with perverse satisfaction. Hell, they could have had a gigantic prayer meeting. There were at least a hundred people in this town who would have joined them. But fuck 'em, he'd fooled them all. Through sheer will and hard work he had progressed from the state of a near total vegetable to a man able to speak and move and express himself again.

He lifted the snifter of cognac from the Louis XIV night table beside him and smelled it appreciatively. Money had its perks, he thought. The bottle was over fifty years old, and he had about two cases left. When he finished those he would buy more, no matter how much prices had risen, and no matter what objections his doctor had.

He heard the sound of the limousine approach the house. Ah, that would be Paxton with his visitor. His head of security, Peter Corydon, or one of his men would be viewing it all through the monitors in the basement security room. Every inch of the estate was covered by cameras, lights, alarms, and dogs. Only invited visitors could enter. It cost him between twenty and thirty grand a month, but it was worth it.

The solid thump of the limo door. In a few moments he would see what Andy had brought. He sipped the cognac, allowing the fumes to rise into his nostrils. Sumptuous. And waited.

There was a soft knock at the door.

"Come in," he said.

The door opened with trepidation and a young woman entered. She was Eurasian, half Chinese, he guessed, with a pitch-black hair that hung almost to her waist. There was a slight slant to the eyes, but her features were more Occidental than Asian. Her body, too, was European, with a firm swell behind the pink silk blouse and long, muscled legs that had obviously seen some exercise.

"Hi!" she said, closing the door behind her and standing there.

"Your name?" he asked, his eyes devouring her. She was delightful.

"Sandy Gee," she said, her accent decidedly Californian. He would have preferred something exotic like Mae Lin, but Sandy Gee would do.

She would be an out-of-work actress and not a professional, he knew. His instructions to Paxton were specific. A different woman every time, unless he requested an encore. This one was young, no more than twenty-three, he guessed. She would have had a blood test for AIDS in the last week, and she would have been paid enough and threatened with heavy enough consequences for any indiscretions to remain silent forever.

He waved his hand to indicate a point across the room. "There's a bar," he said. "Pour yourself a drink."

She moved across the room with the fluid grace of a dancer, bouncing slightly on the balls of her feet. A moment later she approached him, a glass in her hand.

She did exactly as she had been instructed. She sat on

73

the side of the bed and smiled. "What do you want to-night?"

God, he thought with an almost manic glee as he stared into her dark, flat eyes. The power of it! What do you want? He could have anything. He could ask or demand anything. The vistas were limitless. She was his to use as he wished. It was just like the old days in the studio. Nothing had changed. Nothing.

He put his glass carefully on the night table and turned back to her and told her what he wanted.

CHAPTER FIVE

For two weeks following her trip to Los Angeles Shannon moved at such a hectic pace she lost sight of herself at times. There was so much to be done, so many arrangements to be made.

She divided her activities into three categories: work, apartment, and Melissa. Each involved dozens of phone calls and assorted chores.

The easiest problem to solve was what to do with the apartment. She was loath to give it up completely. Bargains were hard to find in New York city, and presumably she would be returning after completing her assignment for Miles Cort. But, as it turned out, she needn't have worried. Two days after informing Oliver she couldn't accept her next assignment and mentioning her plan to leave the city, he told her of someone who needed an apartment—a writer who had just moved into town after selling a novel. The man was flushed with success and optimism. She sublet the apartment to him for double what she was paying, which was still a bargain by any standard. Luckily, he had also arrived with no furniture, so she was able to leave most of hers for his use, rather than having the expense and trouble of placing it in storage.

Apart from the sheer tedium of taking care of bills and

other practical matters, the most difficult problem was handling Melissa's medical needs.

On these matters and more, such as immediate funds for expenses, airline tickets, and other details, she liaised with Lynn Reid. Cort's secretary proved to be a model of efficiency, handling all her tasks with a calm, competent certainty.

They had their final conversation the day before she was due to leave.

"The dialysis equipment and nurse will be here before you are. It will all be set up this afternoon," Lynn promised. "I thought I'd get it in a day early so everything is smooth and running ahead of time."

"Wonderful," Shannon said. Melissa was having dialysis today and wouldn't need another treatment until the day after they arrived.

"The tutor won't start until the following week. I thought it better that your daughter get settled in before having to face schoolwork."

"She'll be grateful," Shannon said wryly. "It isn't her favorite activity."

"As for you," Lynn continued, "the guesthouse has been provided with an IBM computer with a forty megabyte hard disc, a modem, a database program for your research data, and the word-processing program you requested, the latest Wordstar version."

"No excuse not to get right to work," Shannon said.

"Mr. Cort will expect it," Lynn warned.

"Well, thank you for all your help. You've been wonderful."

"It's my job to be wonderful," Lynn replied drily.

Later that evening Oliver came to say goodbye. He sat on the couch with mother on one side, daughter on the other.

"Next time I see you, you're going to be blonde and tanned with a surfer for a boyfriend," he told Melissa.

She hid a smile and said seriously, "I'm going to miss my friends."

"You'll make new friends," he said.

"Yeah, yeah, that's what Mom says all the time. We're going to be living on this estate. There aren't any other kids there."

"You'll meet some," Shannon said cheerfully. "There'll be visitors with kids and we'll go out often."

"Aren't you excited?" Oliver asked Melissa. "What an adventure!"

Melissa finally smiled openly. "I've never been on an airplane before and Mom says the sun shines all the time in California. She calls it 'everlasting sunshine,' " she said with a giggle. But trepidation entered her voice again and she said more quietly, "I guess I'm excited, but I'm also scared. It's all going to be so different."

"That's what adventures are—different experiences," Oliver said.

When he kissed Shannon lightly on the mouth at the door he shook his head. "This is the weirdest thing I've ever heard of. I guess I don't have to caution you about the difficulties these kinds of writing assignments carry."

"No, you don't. I know how egos can soar."

"Well, you also know that above all I hope it works out well for you."

"I'll make it work out," Shannon said positively. "But thanks for being my friend."

Oliver hugged her. "I'm going to miss you."

"I'll call," she promised.

She closed the door behind him and leaned against it. In truth, she was more nervous than any of them, although for Melissa's sake she hid her fears. They were uprooting themselves, sailing into the unknown, literally changing their lives because of the promises of an eccentric old man.

Looked at in that light it was crazy. But examined in

the light of reality, she felt that she truly had little choice. This was the best solution available for her problems.

She sighed and pushed herself away from the door. There was still last-minute packing to be done before she could get some sleep. She had better get busy. It was too late for doubts now.

Melissa finally grew excited at thirty-thousand feet. "Oh, my God, Mom," she said, grabbing Shannon's arm and pulling her toward the window. "See, that's a river! It's so small it looks like a piece of string!"

They sat in the first-class cabin, courtesy of Shannon's generous patron. The flight attendants thought Melissa cute and pampered her throughout the flight. Shortly before landing they took her to the cockpit and allowed her to look over the captain's shoulder. By the time they landed, she had decided upon a career in aviation, not as a flight attendant, but as a pilot.

Andy Paxton was waiting for them at the gate. "Welcome back to Los Angeles, ma'am," he said to Shannon. In his black uniform and peaked cap, his hands clasped behind his back, he was an imposing figure.

"Hi, Andy!" Shannon said with genuine pleasure. "This is my daughter Melissa. Melissa, this is Mr. Paxton."

Melissa held out her hand and Paxton gravely shook it. "I'm very pleased to meet you, miss. I hope you enjoy your stay with us."

"Are you really a chauffeur, Mr. Paxton? You drive a real limousine, like rock stars use?"

"Better, miss," he said, a twinkle lightening the stern, dark eyes. "They rent their limos. Mr. Cort owns his. It's got a television, a stereo system, a telephone, and a refrigerator in it."

"Wow!" she said. "That's rad!"

"It certainly is," he said.

"I've got a ton of luggage this time, Andy," Shannon warned him.

"We'll have a skycap give us a hand," he said.

While they stood on the moving walkway, Melissa strode ahead. "Wow! Look how fast I'm going," she said over her shoulder.

"A lovely girl," Paxton said. "It will be nice to have a child on the estate again."

"Thank you. Do you have any children?" Shannon asked disarmingly.

He was startled by the intimacy for a moment. "No, I don't. I was married once and divorced, but there were no children."

"They're a blessing and a burden," Shannon said softly.

It took half an hour to wait for the luggage and load it into the limousine. Then Andy held the door open and Melissa stood before it in awe.

"Wow!" she exclaimed, clambering in and running her hands over the soft leather seats. "It's as big as my bedroom!"

When they entered the gates of Cort's mansion, Melissa's eyes widened further. No comment this time, however. She took her mother's hand and held it silently. The roses—red, white, and pink—were magnificent. A brilliant plume of crimson bougainvillaea tumbled down the side of the house. A flock of sparrows rose from a lemon tree as they approached and wheeled away in unison. A cream-colored Rolls Royce stood in the driveway. And the house itself was as impressive as ever, gleaming whitely in the sunlight.

"Not a bad little homestead, is it?" Shannon remarked.

"It's rad," Melissa replied. "It's like a movie star's place."

"Better," Shannon said, drily echoing Paxton's earlier remark about the limo. "Mr. Cort made movie stars."

"I'll take you directly to your guesthouse," Paxton said

as the car halted. "Miss Reid will be over to see you in a few minutes, I believe."

With my orders no doubt, Shannon thought, suddenly realizing that to all intents and purposes she was now employed. Not only that, but this almost obscenely luxurious estate was now their home.

After Paxton unloaded their luggage, Melissa eagerly explored their quarters. Three things impressed her most: the size of the bathtub, the fact that she had her own bedroom, and the enormous color television set which she announced after fiddling with it could "get every channel in the world!"

Shannon was impressed by the bouquet of fresh flowers and the obviously expensive bottle of wine in the ice bucket beside them.

"So you like it?" she asked, relieved by her daughter's reaction.

"It's great! Where's the pool?"

"Uh, I'll show you in a little while," Shannon said. She'd have to find out what the rules were for Melissa. Would she have free reign of the grounds? "Let's just wait for Miss Reid."

They both inspected the dialysis machine in Melissa's room. It was computerized, digital, state of the art. "I almost forgot about it," Melissa said wistfully.

"Well, you don't have to do it until tomorrow," Shannon reminded her.

Lynn Reid arrived looking much as she had the last time they met. She wore a dark skirt and pastel blouse and her hair was still tied back. She shook hands with both of them and said, "I hope everything is to your satisfaction."

"It's perfect, thank you," Shannon said, wondering what it would take to break through the reserve the secretary had constructed around herself. Did she have lovers? A private life? Or was her entire being dedicated to serving Miles Cort? Beneath the primly presented exterior was a pretty woman. Did she ever reveal that side of her?

"Mr Cort would like to see both of you in an hour," Lynn said. "That should give you time to freshen up and get settled in."

"Fine," Shannon said.

"I'll come and get you. Just buzz the housekeeper if you need anything."

After she left Melissa said, "She's strange."

"What do you mean?" Shannon asked.

Melissa frowned. "I don't know. She's just kinda, well, stiff. Like she's cold, or shy, or something."

Shannon shrugged. "You're right. I think she is shy. I don't know. I guess we'll get to know her better as time passes. For now, I need to shower and change before we see Mr. Cort. How about you?"

"Can I have a bath?"

"After I have a quick shower, okay?"

An hour later, Lynn ushered them into the study in the main house. Cort was already waiting for them, sitting in his wheelchair, a photograph album open on his lap. He snapped it closed and put it on the table beside him.

Time had distorted Shannon's memories: she had forgotten how black yet filled with flame his eyes were and how his head seemed to dwarf the remainder of his large body. He stared at them both without speaking, no hint of welcome or anything else in those eyes.

"Hello, Mr. Cort," she said. Beside her, she felt Melissa take her hand.

"So that's the child," he said, his eyes taking in the entirety of Melissa.

"This is my daughter, Melissa."

"I hope you enjoy yourself here," he said to Melissa.

"Thank you," she replied politely.

He turned his attention fully on Shannon, the cursory social graces now disposed of. "I suppose you need a day to recover from your trip, but tomorrow I want you to start interviewing me."

Shannon shook her head. "I'll need to do a fair amount of work before I can start the interview process. The first thing will be to look through the press clippings and already existing studio and other biographies of you to give me a feel for you, the times, events. Interviewing you before that would be a waste of time. I wouldn't know where to begin."

Cort gestured dismissively with his hand. "I remember it all. Just follow my lead."

Shannon recognized a challenge when she heard one. She narrowed her eyes slightly and said firmly, "Mr. Cort, just as you know how to produce films, I know how to interview subjects. That's what I do for a living. Research is always my first step. That's the way I work."

Cort stared back at her for a long two or three seconds. She met his gaze without flinching. Then he briskly nodded his head. "All right, we'll do it your way. How long do you need for the research?"

"I'll look at the existing material tomorrow and see what's there. If most of what I need is there, it'll take another two or three days to go through it, take notes, et cetera."

"Good," he said. "I'll be at your disposal. If you need anything, ask Lynn. When you need to see me, tell her."

"I appreciate it," she said.

"Good," he repeated. The meeting was over.

Walking back through the garden, Melissa looked up at her mother. "He's really weird, Mom."

"It's just his manner," Shannon said kindly. "He's been used to ordering people around all his life. But he's been very generous to us, so let's give him a chance."

Melissa wasn't ready to be converted. "I'm not sure that I like him," she said with a set expression on her face.

Ten minutes after returning to the guesthouse there was

a knock at the door. A young man stood there, his eyes noticeably widening when he saw Shannon. He smiled at her. "Hey, I didn't know the writer was going to be such a fox."

He was tall and thin with the same large head as Miles and looked about twenty-six or twenty-seven. A handsome young man, but there was a weakness to his mouth and a nervous skittishness in his eyes, in spite of his bravado.

"Oh," he continued, "I'm Richard Cort, the good-for-nothing son. I live on the estate. Thought I'd come over and meet you."

"Shannon Ross." She held out her hand.

He held it a moment longer than necessary, then looked past her into the house where Melissa was. "You have a daughter!" he said, surprised. "I didn't know you were married."

"I'm not," she said.

He flashed his smile at her again. "Hey, well, if you ever need anything, or ever get lonely, I live in the guest-house behind the main building. Come on over."

It wasn't so much his words or his tone, but the way his eyes scanned her body, lingering at her hips and breasts, that told Shannon what he had on his mind.

"I'm going to be too busy to be lonely," she said pleasantly. "I'm sure your father will see to that."

"Hey, kid, how you doing?" he said to Melissa who had come up to stand slightly behind Shannon.

"Hi," she said.

Shannon didn't invite him in.

"Well," he said uncertainly, "I'll see you both around."

"Goodbye," Shannon said, stepping back and closing the door.

They walked back to the kitchen where they had been preparing a snack. "Now him I don't like," Shannon said to her daughter.

"Me neither," Melissa agreed, adding, "Wow, Mom, these people are pretty strange here."

Shannon smiled at her daughter. "Well, maybe the rich are different."

"What do you mean?" Melissa asked.

"Don't worry about it, okay? Just remember, we're a team. We'll keep each other sane, okay?"

"Sure, Mom. We're a team. Us against the world."

Orson Cort seldom went out of his way to see his sister Anne or their mother Agnes, but this evening, on one of his infrequent visits to the small Santa Monica house where his mother lived, Anne happened to be there. Although they were only two years apart in age, they had never been close. They met during their father's weekly dinners at times, but rarely spoke directly to each other on more than a social level.

He bent to kiss his mother's leathery cheek and nodded at Anne.

"You didn't bring your wife. What's the latest one's name?" Agnes asked.

"Barbara, Mother, as you well know," he said tartly.

"Five wives! How can you expect me to remember them all at my age?"

"You don't have to remember them all. Just the current one." He turned to his sister. "How are you, Anne?"

"Fine." She wore a low-cut blue dress and sandals. It seemed to him that she had put on a couple of pounds in the last few months. A slight sag below the chin made her look more petulant than usual.

"Been working lately?" he asked slyly, knowing she hadn't.

"No, not recently. I turned down a couple of parts," she said, and changed the subject. "So what do you think of Daddy's latest?"

"Latest what?"

"Oh, I forgot. You weren't at the dinner. I was just telling Mother about it. He's going to write a book."

She told him about Miles's announcement that he was hiring someone to write his biography.

"And she's going to be living on the estate?" Orson asked.

"That's right. Working directly with him on the book. Interviewing us all as well."

Orson sat in a thoughtful silence. "He's up to something," he said finally.

Both women looked at him. Orson frowned impatiently at them. "Why would he be writing a bio? That's not like him. There must be something else going on."

"He's getting old," Agnes said. "He wants to immortalize himself in the memories of others before he passes away."

Orson snorted. "He never gave a damn what anyone thought."

"He said he wants to set the record straight," Anne said.

"Maybe," Orson said dubiously. "Do you know anything about the writer. Who she is? Her background?"

Anne shrugged.

"Well, that's the first thing to find out," Orson said. "I don't like it. It's uncharacteristic. I want to find out what's really going on."

"You're making a mountain out of a molehill as usual," Anne protested. "It's quite understandable that after the stroke he'd want to do something like this."

"Is she pretty?" Orson asked.

"The writer? I haven't met her. Come to think of it, I've never met a pretty writer. They're all plain with thick glasses," Anne said, preening with a slight toss of the head.

"Maybe that's what it's all about," Orson guessed.

"A lover?" Agnes said derisively. "In his condition? At his age?"

Orson smiled. "You'd be surprised. I happen to know

he has female visitors on a regular basis. Young and pretty ones, too."

Both women looked at him with rising interest. "How do you know that?" Anne said first.

"I have my sources on the estate," Orson said with a self-satisfied smirk. "Someone has to keep tabs on the old bastard."

"You shouldn't speak of your father that way," Agnes said without conviction. Then she smiled thinly and added, "It's too kind a description."

"Mother!" Anne said, but she smiled, too.

Once Agnes was beautiful. Orson remembered how she had been when she was young: vivacious, talkative, a stunning presence in any room with glossy black hair and a calendar girl's figure. Now she was thin and gray with a bowed back and a lined face. She was still talkative, but gossip was her metier and bitterness her legacy. She had never forgiven Miles for divorcing her after five years of marriage, particularly after bearing him two children. She had, in her oft-repeated resentful words, "sacrificed the best years of my life for him."

She had remarried twice since their divorce, but neither marriage had succeeded, although they had left her financially comfortable. She was by no means wealthy, but she owned the house she lived in and had an acceptable income. The house, bought for thirty thousand dollars years earlier, had, like all Westside property, increased in value in the seventies and eighties and was now worth a little over three hundred thousand.

How she filled her days, Orson had no idea. Gossiping with old friends probably. His mind wandered as the two women chattered on about his father. The bastard was up to something, that much was sure. No way he'd suddenly decide to write an autobiography. What for? He had all the fucking money in the world as it was. Plus he never had and never would give a shit about what people thought of him. He'd always said his films were his legacy, and it was one of the few statements he'd made that Orson believed.

He resolved to make a few phone calls and see what he could find out. It always paid to be prepared where Miles was concerned.

"Yes, I turned down a part last week," Anne was saying to their mother. "There just seems to be no taste in the movies today. They're all designed for kids with short attention spans. It's as if the adult audience has disappeared. I don't know what the industry is coming to."

Sure, Orson thought cynically. Sure she did. If she was offered a part where she had to ride naked on a donkey throughout the movie she'd take it.

"I know," Agnes agreed. She sniffed at Orson. "The screen is filled with the type of films people like Orson make. Vulgar and simple-minded. The golden age of Hollywood has long gone."

It was time to leave, Orson decided. He had better things to do than listen to lectures from the dried-up old bitch.

"Well, gotta go," he said, looking at his watch.

"So soon?" his mother asked, her voice losing its edge and turning mournful.

"Important meeting. Some money men," he said.

Anne smiled knowingly at his lie and he had to suppress the urge to say something cutting. Instead, he kissed them each dutifully on the cheek and left.

The Bijou Club in Century City was an In Place. When the In People weren't there for special events and parties, the Out People who wanted to be In People filled the stark black-and-white rooms, dancing to the million-dollar sound system run by a Jamaican disc-and-video jock and drinking the outrageously priced and exotic, watered-down drinks.

Orson thought he would find his brother Richard there,

and wasn't disappointed. He was sitting at a table with two girls, both of whom appeared under age. Damned if he could tell these days, though. Everything between eighteen and twenty-five looked the same to him. Richard was slumped in a bored position. He was watching the dancers and ignoring his companions.

"Pull up a chair," Richard said when he saw him. "This is Stacy and this is Kim. This is Orson, a famous producer."

"A producer?" Stacy echoed, a thin blonde. Her T-shirt left one tanned shoulder bare, exposing a butterfly tattoo.

"Got any other interesting tattoos?" Orson asked.

She giggled and said to Richard, "He's cool."

"No he ain't," Richard said. "He's my brother."

Stacy giggled again, but Kim, equally thin and a redhead with a sharp, angular face, looked at Orson with interest. "You're a Cort, too?"

While he nodded, Stacy said, "I need another drink." She was slurring her words, but her eyes were glowing. She was stoned out of her mind, he realized.

"I got it," Orson said, flagging a waitress down. "Go ahead and order."

While the girls ordered he took a vial from his jacket pocket and handed it to Richard under the table. "High-grade blow," he said with a wink. "I thought it might come in handy for you."

His brother took the cocaine and put it in his pocket. "What do you want?"

"Why don't you girls go powder your noses," Orson said to the two women.

They stood obediently and walked to the ladies' room.

"Cute," Orson said, looking after them.

"They like to fuck in threesomes. Actually, I think they like to go down on each other more than fucking."

"I want to know about this writer the old man hired," Orson said. He looked at his brother's elegant and handsome face and saw from the glittering eyes that he, too, was wasted.

"She's a looker, but cold," Richard said, staring out at the dance floor and drumming his fingers on the table in time to the music.

"You hit on her already?"

"Reconnaissance. She has a daughter with her. A kid of about eleven. She looks close to thirty."

"Married?"

"No."

"Is she fucking Miles?"

"Beats me."

"I'd like you to keep an eye on her and let me know," Orson said. He leaned his elbows on the table. "The old man's up to something. Do you believe this story about a book?"

Richard looked surprised. He'd obviously never considered it wasn't true. "What? You don't think she's there to write his biography?"

Orson spread his palms. "Why would he do that? He's never been interested in a project like that before. Write a book? Come on. He despises writers."

"Well, why would he say it then?" Richard asked in exasperation. The subject was too nebulous for him to grasp.

"Maybe he's boffing the girl. Maybe he's going to marry her. How the hell do I know?" Orson snapped. "But I'm going to find out. What's her name?"

"Shannon something. Shannon Ross."

"Do you know where she's from?"

Richard shook his head. "I don't know anything about her."

"Well, find out what you can and call me, okay," Orson said. "And keep your eye on what's going on around there as well."

Richard slumped back in his chair. "What's the big deal, anyway?"

Orson shook his head sadly. "What if he was marrying her? What do you think would happen to all his money? How much do you think we'd see when he kicked? Think about that."

"He wouldn't be getting married," Richard said emphatically. "Come on, why would he do that? He gets enough pussy as it is."

"Shit! I don't know. Why does anyone get married?" Orson said, wondering even while he spoke why he ever got married and kept on getting married. He looked gloomily at his brother. "Maybe that's not it, but something's going on and I'm going to find out what."

He got to his feet and said, "Don't call me from the house."

The two women approached, swaying through the crowd. Richard cocked his head in their direction. "You wanna stay and party? That Kim is a wild fuck. Screams to bring the roof down."

"Too skinny," Orson said.

"Models, but they both want to be in movies. They'd do anything for a real producer," Richard said with a cynical smile.

"Are you leaving?" Kim asked regretfully when she arrived at the table. She stood close to Orson and looked boldly into his eyes, a slow smile appearing on her mouth.

There was a moment of temptation, but it passed. "Yeah. See you all later," Orson said.

That fucking brother of mine, he thought as he walked out, he's going to burn himself out before he turns thirty. No, he corrected himself, that was three years away. He wouldn't last that long. Before he turns twenty-nine, he thought. Dead or in jail or dying of AIDS.

CHAPTER SIX

She was studying the life of a complicated man, a life brimming with events, with conflict, disaster, and achievement. It was also a divided life: a public one and a private one, and both were equally convoluted.

Shannon yawned. The soft yellow light of the desk lamp fell on her face, accentuating the dark shadows below her eyes. It was late, almost one in the morning. Melissa had been asleep for hours, but after putting her to bed, Shannon had resisted the lure of the seventy-seven available television channels and continued to labor. She had spent three long days going through the morass of material Cort had provided her with, yet she still felt no closer to his essence than when she had started.

There were scattered facts available, to be sure, but they were like punctuation points in his life. She was much more curious about the missing sentences between the periods and commas and question marks.

His first wife, Isabella, had died in 1942 during childbirth at the tender age of twenty-one. The child, a boy, didn't survive, either. Cort was only twenty-two then. How had this affected him? Did he have three more wives and five children to try to make up for this devastating loss? Or did he simply stop caring after that? His infidelities were legendary and some were well documented in the press. How did he justify them?

Then there was his business life. What really caused his move from the conservatism of established business to the glamorous and risky world of filmmaking?

His infatuation with film had apparently started shortly after the war when he was in his mid-twenties and married to Agnes. When his father died, he ran the family conglomerate with a skill that belied his age, doubling the company's value in a short three years. "It was too easy," he said in an early interview. "I needed a bigger challenge and making movies provided it." Was it really that simple, that cut and dried, or were there more complex reasons?

And his family! My God, she thought, there was a real complexity. She looked at the chart she had prepared earlier in the day to try to make sense yet again of this tangled web of relationships:

Miles Cort (1920-)

m. Isabella, aged 19
   (1940) (deceased)
   died 1942 in child-
   birth

m. Agnes, aged 30 (1945)   Orson (b.1947)
   divorced 1950   Anne (b.1948)

m. Rosemary, aged 22   Stephen (b.1958)
   (1957)   Elizabeth (b.1960)
   divorced 1975   Richard (b.1963)

m. Portia, aged 25 (1976)
   divorced 1980

The Children

Orson Cort (aged 42)
   m. Faith (1967) divorced 1970 (one child)
   m. Clare (1971) divorced 1973 (one child)
   m. Susan (1976) divorced 1980 (two children)
   m. Pat (1984) divorced 1985
   m. Barbara (1988)

Anne Cort (aged 40)
   m. Alex Fine (1970) divorced 1975
   m. Douglas Johnson (1978) divorced 1983
   m. Martin Lawson (1987)

Stephen Cort (aged 31)
   single

Elizabeth Cort (aged 29)
   m. Ellis Brown (1985) divorced 1988

Richard Cort (aged 27)
   single

He was a grandfather four times. If you added up all the marriages, he and three of his children had been married thirteen times. Orson had been married five times, Anne three times, Elizabeth divorced after three years of marriage, and the two sons Stephen and Richard were still single. What were the relationships between Miles Cort and his offspring? He did not strike her as a loving father by any stretch. How had this affected his children? Were they all like Richard seemed when she met him: vain, frivolous, and shallow?

Much of the material she had been given came from the public relations department of Charisma Films, the studio Miles had run. It consisted of press releases, biographies of dubious validity which often contradicted each other, depending upon the era, the writer, and what angle they were pitching, and newspaper clippings of Cort, his studio, his films, and his family. Most of these were laudatory in nature, but of greater interest were the snippets to be found in the gossip columns and the more sensational newspapers.

She learned from these that Richard had been arrested at the age of eighteen for drunk driving, held on suspicion of carrying an illegal substance at twenty-two, and been seen in nearly every nightspot in town with starlets, Brat Pack members, and other chichi L.A. society members. What he did for a living was never explained. Presumably nothing. The overall picture was of a wild rich kid.

Anne Cort, her various marriages and divorces and cyclical career as an actress, was well documented.

Orson Cort was usually called "the producer son" of Miles Cort when mentioned, although one gossip columnist always referred to him as "the B-movie producer son who has achieved the dubious distinction of taking more trips to the altar than his father."

Elizabeth Cort was never mentioned and Stephen Cort was mentioned only once as "the musician son of Miles Cort."

As for Miles, the gossip columns were filled with the antics of him and his wives. These ranged from what sounded suspiciously like a failed suicide attempt by Agnes who drove a car off a cliff, to a public brawl at a party with Rosemary, to sly mention of him in the fifties as "The Reigning King of the Casting Couch." Innuendo was rampant, mainly on the order of "What does Miles Cort's wife think of the fact that he was seen at the Brown Derby with lushly attractive starlet Gloria Morton hanging on his arm and on his every word?" During his divorced periods, columnists speculated on whom he would marry next. Apparently he dated everyone who was anyone and eligible for the part.

On the business side, the main topic was his "toughness," although more than one person was quoted as calling him "ruthless." People did things his way, or they didn't do them—not on his studio lot, anyway. His fights with some of the more notable directors and screenwriters of his era were at times well chronicled, at others merely intimated. One thing was certain; throughout his career he had been a dangerous person to cross. One director, Frank Hamlet, had struck Miles once during an argument on the set. Hamlet, a talented director with the potential to become great if nurtured, had never worked again for Charisma—or for anyone else in Hollywood. He'd ended up directing commercials in New York.

Shannon closed the folder she was studying and leaned back in her chair. Enough! She had to get some sleep. The morass of data was like a jigsaw puzzle. She knew from experience that when she started to talk to the people involved and pull a piece out here and a piece out there, the patterns would slowly emerge.

She would start tomorrow with Miles. The toughest nut first. Right now she had to go to bed. She would probably need all the energy she could muster to deal with him.

She pushed the papers aside, stood up and stretched, lifting her arms above her head, bending back at the waist.

Perhaps just a small glass of very expensive English sherry from the well-stocked bar would be nice before sleeping, she thought. She had to admit it: life on the Cort estate certainly had its little compensations.

"Mr. Cort won't be able to see you until three o'clock this afternoon," Lynn said. "I'm afraid he has other appointments before then."

"That will be fine," Shannon said. "I wonder if I could

get some phone numbers from you. I think because of his schedule I should start interviewing other family members as well. Maximize my time."

Lynn gave her the telephone numbers of all Cort's children, the living wives and a couple of business associates. "You might want to wait, however. I think most of them will be here for dinner tonight—the children, anyway. You're invited, of course, I'll let you know a little later exactly who is coming. You'll have a chance to meet them first."

"What about Melissa?"

"It would probably be better if you didn't bring her. Maude Bagley, the head housekeeper, can look in on her, if you're concerned about her being alone out there. Or I could. She'll be quite safe, I assure you."

"Oh, I know. It's just at her age, being alone is something of a trial. Anyway, I'll work something out," Shannon said.

"Oh, and here's the number of Mrs. Dalquist, the tutor we hired for Melissa. She's very good. You might give her a call and set up a schedule."

Shannon thanked her and hung up. Melissa's safety wasn't a major matter of concern. The security on the estate was awesome. There were alarms, cameras, floodlights, and guards all over the grounds, day and night. Lynn had pointed out some of the precautions soon after their arrival. They both had free rein of the grounds, except at night. If either Melissa or Shannon wanted to walk around after dark it was required that they first call the security station—wherever that was. It was just a number on her telephone, as far as she was concerned—and let them know.

"They're trained to react to movement on the grounds at night," Lynn said obliquely. Shannon's imagination ran wild, picturing sirens, lights, machine guns, and missiles zooming around the estate in some crazed parody of the Fourth of July.

Apparently there was a security chief, Peter Corydon, whom she had not yet met, and a team of between six and ten guards who provided twenty-four-hour protection, generally with two or three men on each eight-hour shift. Security alone probably cost Cort almost five hundred thousand dollars a year. The rationale behind this display of impregnability bothered her.

Lynn's explanation when Shannon asked was that the immensely valuable art collection had been well advertised through various newspaper articles. "The art and antiques on the estate are probably worth fifty million these days," she said, and added, "Mr. Cort believes that prevention is the best cure."

It didn't quite wash with Shannon. She couldn't say exactly why she felt that way. It was more an intuitive conclusion than intellectual. Logically, it made sense to provide security for such wealth, but somehow it seemed excessive to her. On the other hand, she told herself, her experience with vast wealth was somewhat limited. What she knew about the idiosyncrasies and fears of the very rich wouldn't fill a blank page. She assumed that her state of ignorance would rapidly change.

Shannon went outside to the patio and looked past hedges and a dozen species of trees to the rolling green lawn. It was a warm, cloudless day with a slight haze on the horizon. Melissa had discovered the swimming pool on their second day here, and now spent most of her time either swimming or exploring the grounds. She talked a lot to the head gardener, Jesus Perez, a middle-aged Mexican whom she addressed politely as *Senor* Perez. Apparently they had struck up quite a friendship, from what Shannon could make out.

She felt the sun warm her arms and thought lazily of the pool, but concurrent with that was the thought of all the telephone calls she needed to make. She had to earn her keep. She turned and went back into the cottage.

* * *

Miles Cort sat at his desk and sorted through the daily stacks of mail Lynn had placed there for him. As usual, he wore wool slacks and an open-necked white shirt. Invitations, a dozen of them. He seldom went out, preferring that people he needed to see come to the house. He glanced through the invitations quickly, Screenings, parties, charity events, political fundraisers, awards ceremonies. He pushed them aside. Lynn could give them out to his kids as she usually did.

The next stack was personal correspondence. Letters from a few old friends, some pleas for money, an actor wanting a screen test. Pitiful, he thought, without a trace of pity in his heart. The guy still thought he ran the studio.

Junk mail formed the largest pile. He looked through each piece, as was his wont. It always amazed him what people tried to sell: financial newsletters, high-scale catalogues, gimmick items, memberships in various societies, seminars to improve your business, your health, your outlook on life, and more. Sometimes, just for the hell of it, he ordered catalogue items, not because he needed them, but because it gave him something to do. Today, after carefully reading the skillfully written ad copy, he ordered an air ionizer from DAK. The air could never be too clean, particularly in L.A.

The next largest stack consisted of bills which drew his full scrutiny. The estate was virtually a large business. Staff, grounds, equipment, and all the other upkeep cost him a fortune each year. Although his accountant and a small army of assistants took care of the payments, Cort insisted that all bills come to him first, then were sent to the accountant's office. People still tried to slip things past him and he wasn't about to let that happen. "Anyone who lets other people take complete charge of his finances deserves to get shafted," he often told his kids.

Lot of good that did, he thought bitterly. They were all financially irresponsible.

The last stack consisted of daily updates of all his investments: stock, bond, and precious metal accounts; foreign exchange deposits; futures investments; a few businesses he either owned outright or partially; and progress reports on the new ventures he was setting up. These reports were seen by nobody, not even Lynn. She had been instructed to add all mail from his lawyer to the pile unopened in its envelopes.

His practiced eyes scanned the sheets quickly. He'd done it often enough to know that any discrepancies would leap out at him. There were no surprises.

He pressed the buzzer on the desk and thirty seconds later Lynn entered the study.

"Yes, sir?" she asked, walking toward him.

"Will they all be here tonight?"

She stopped in front of the desk. "We have confirmations from everyone but Richard."

"Where is he?"

"I don't know, sir." She hesitated.

"Yes?" he demanded.

"He didn't come back last night," she said.

"So what else is new. Call around and find him. I want everyone here for dinner. All of them, understand?"

"Yes, sir."

"Is the writer settled in?"

"Yes, sir. You have an appointment with her at three."

"Cancel it. Call Joe Collins and tell him I want to see him over here then for a progress report."

"Yes, sir."

"That's all."

She turned and left the room. He looked at the pile of junk mail again. He wanted to reexamine one of the catalogues. A watch that also counted the wearer's pulse had caught his eye. It was worth another look. It would help him when he swam, he thought.

"Come on, Barbara, he wants the whole family there," Orson pleaded.

She slammed the hairbrush on the table and looked at him in the mirror. "He wants his children there. Not the family. I'm not going to go and sit through a dinner listening to him decapitate you one by one. Besides, the old bastard doesn't even know my goddamn name."

"He does too," Orson protested weakly, thinking that she was probably right. A pretty redhead with pale skin, Barbara was ten years his junior at thirty-two. She had a nice compact body, he thought as he looked at her, but the thrill had gone out of their relationship as soon as they had married the year before. Before the legality of matrimony they fucked like rabbits; now they hardly touched each other.

Barbara layered lipstick on her lips, contorting her mouth as she leaned forward. "I'm going out anyway," she said, smacking her lips together.

"Where?"

"A screening at the Academy with Janet and Monty."

"Oh, great," he said sarcastically. "You're going to sit through some dumb movie with the unwashed masses."

"Beats sitting with your unwashed father," she said, rising and walking to the closet. She wore a satin slip that rose slightly around her hips.

Orson's eyes flickered as he stepped toward her. "Hey, we have time," he said, placing his hands on her shoulders from behind.

She shrugged them away. "I've put my makeup on, Orson."

"So put it on again."

"No," she said, slipping away from him and reaching for a dress. "It's too much work." She took it off the rack and walked away, leaving him standing there.

Bitch, he thought, watching her, his forehead thumping

with anger. She had to be getting it on the side. He'd suspected it for a while, but it had suited him not to make an issue of it. Now, as he watched her slip the dress over her head and turn back to face the mirror, he reconsidered. Perhaps he should at least find out who was boffing her. It could give him some kind of advantage.

"Who are you going to the screening with?" he asked.

"I told you, The Adamses. Janet and Monty," she said.

Monty Adams was a small-time producer he had partnered with on one movie and Janet, an actress, was one of Barbara's best friends. He'd call Monty tomorrow, he resolved, even though the little fuck would probably lie to him. They were probably all in on it, he thought angrily. All of them.

"Well, I'm taking off," he said. "I've got to make a stop on the way."

"Have a wonderful time," Barbara said sarcastically. She didn't bother turning around to see him leave.

The man Melissa was talking to beside the pool was tall and slender. From the back as she approached, all Shannon could see was that he had long dark hair and wore blue jeans, sneakers, and a red cotton shirt.

"Hey, Mom!" Melissa yelled out when she saw her.

The man turned, and as she looked into his shockingly blue eyes, Shannon felt for a wild second as if she had just walked into a vacuum lock, a bubble from which all the air had been removed.

"Hi, there! You must be Shannon." A warm smile crinkled the skin around those eyes. The mouth was wide and strong, the nose large. His cheekbones jutted high and angular. An improved version of Miles, she thought, wondering which son he was. Probably a dosage of his mother's genes was responsible for the striking good looks and the mellifluous voice.

"Hi," she said.

"This is Stephen," Melissa said. "He's one of Mr. Cort's sons."

"The musician," Shannon said, holding out her hand.

He took it in a firm grip and shook it. "Been doing your research, I see."

"Just scratching the surface."

He released her hand and looked at her frankly. "You are very beautiful."

"And you are very handsome," she replied.

They grinned at each other and then simultaneously looked down at Melissa. She was watching them both, a thoughtful look on her face.

"Melissa has been telling me all about herself," Stephen said. "She's a very special young lady. Now I can see why." He tousled Melissa's hair, a gesture she normally hated, but now she smiled. "Looks like you have a pretty special mother."

"I told you she was pretty," Melissa said.

"And you didn't lie. From now on I'll believe everything you say."

"Are you here for dinner?" Shannon asked.

"Yes, the command performance." He looked at his watch. "I was in the neighborhood and thought I'd drop in early. Now, if you invited me back to your cottage and offered me a drink, that would help me kill some time."

"Would you like to come back to our cottage and have a drink?" Shannon asked obediently.

He grinned, a smile that warmed his whole face. "I thought you'd never ask."

"So you went to Juilliard to study music?" Shannon asked, impressed.

They sat on the patio, each drinking a beer. Melissa was watching television.

Shannon felt relaxed for the first time since arriving.

Perhaps the fact that she was talking to a "normal" person for a change helped.

She felt totally at ease with him, as if they had known each other forever and were just picking up where they had last left off the conversation. So far, she had told him an abbreviated history of most of her life. He was an attentive listener and obviously interested, peppering her conversation with questions. Now he was telling her something about his.

"I started in high school playing in the band during school hours and in a rock and roll band in my spare time. When I left high school, I thought I'd study classical music to get a thorough grounding."

He grimaced at himself. "Actually, I don't think it was really my idea. My music teacher talked me into it and Miles said that if I was going to be stupid enough to go into music I'd better start off at the best school in the world," he said with a small shrug. "I graduated, but it wasn't what I really wanted to play or compose for the rest of my life. I went from there into jazz, then played in a New Age group."

"And now?"

"I mainly compose. Did a piece recently for the Alvin Ailey Dance Company. Kind of a jazz flavor."

"And your father? What does he think of this?"

Stephen smiled. "He thinks what he's always thought. That I'm full of shit and wasting my life."

"Yes, I kind of thought he would," Shannon said. "But you're doing what you love and making a living, right?"

"I eke out a living," he said. "But I am doing what I want to do. What about you?"

"Well, it's relative," Shannon said. "I'm working as a writer, which is good. I'm working for your father, which is not ideal, but it doesn't take me too far off the track. And it certainly doesn't look as if it'll be boring."

Stephen took a swig from his beer bottle, then asked, "Do you know what you're getting into here?"

She was surprised at the question and hesitated before saying, "No, not really."

Stephen's relaxed composure evaporated. He stared unblinkingly at her, his face suddenly hard and angular. "I like you," he said seriously.

"I like you, too," she said, a little uncomfortable at the intensity in his face.

"So, because I like you, I feel compelled to stick my nose into business in which it doesn't belong and warn you to be careful."

"Of what?"

"My father is a dangerous man," he said. "I don't want to sound melodramatic, but evil seems to follow him. It affects the people around him. Just be careful. I wouldn't want to see you get hurt."

"Oh," she replied, suddenly not knowing what else to say.

"I'm not trying to scare you, either," he said. "I just want you to be aware of the situation. Miles charms or cajoles people into doing what he wants done. He doesn't care what happens to them in the process. He's quite ruthless."

"Well, thank you for the warning," she said weakly.

He looked at his watch and the tension lifted. "Hey, we'd better hustle or we'll be late for dinner."

"I've still got to change," she said.

"I'll see you at the house. Thanks for the beer." He rose, smiled a goodbye, and walked away.

How strange, she thought, watching the lean figure move gracefully down the path. What a weird thing to say about your own father.

She shook her head. That did it. None of them were normal, not one single person she had met here.

"Jesus," she said, and turned and went back into the cottage.

* * *

The dinner was a debacle in Shannon's view. Everyone else, however, seemed to think it was a perfectly normal affair—which only served to support her earlier conclusion about the members of this family.

By the time she arrived, Miles was holding court at the head of the table. She grimaced at her mental pun, but there was no other way to describe it. His "subjects" sat on either side of him, a captive audience, while he propounded his theories on life, particularly his theories on their lives.

He broke off in midsentence when she entered the room. "I'm sorry I'm late," she said. "I had to give my daughter dinner."

"Shoulda brought her," Miles said. "Do you know everyone here?"

She looked around the table while he called the roll, starting at his right.

"Orson." A hostile stare back at her.

"Anne." A vacantly social smile.

"Elizabeth." A cool, speculative look.

"Richard." A bold, admiring glance.

"Stephen." A cheerful wink.

"Sit," Cort said, indicating the empty chair beside Stephen.

She sat, feeling their eyes still examining her.

"She's the writer of my biography. A good writer," Cort said, somehow implying in his tone that compared to her they were all inadequate. "She'll want to talk to all of you. Tell her the truth."

"Like being back in school, isn't it?" Stephen murmured to her, amusement in his voice.

"This is my family. My legacy I leave the world," Cort said heavily to her down the table. "What do you think?" He answered his own question. "If I'da been celibate I would have left the world a better place."

Richard laughed. "If you'd have been celibate it would have heralded the Second Coming."

"Miles is being kind," Stephen said to Shannon. "You should hear him when he really wants to injure us."

She smiled nervously, not replying.

Cort glowered down the table at Stephen. "Injure you?" he repeated, his tone injured. "All I ever wanted to do for all of you was make you into men."

Elizabeth murmured something and Cort turned on her. "What?"

"I said, 'Thanks, Dad,' " she replied demurely.

Shannon couldn't stop a small smile from appearing.

Cort looked at Elizabeth for a blank second, then comprehension dawned. "By men, I mean people able to look after themselves in this world," he explained, as if to a child. "It takes tough people to survive. Show a weakness and the ruthless and powerful are like dogs with a wounded prey. They drag you down and eat you."

"My father has a generous view of human nature," Stephen said to Shannon.

"Experience. Something I've got and you haven't," Miles snapped. "That and intelligence. Together they got me where I am today. And it's because of a realistic view of human nature. You live in some kind of dream world if you think people are any different."

"Right," Stephen said.

"I saw Mother the other day," Anne interceded, attempting to elevate the conversation.

Cort wasn't having it. "How is the bitter old bitch?" he asked.

"She still loves you, Miles," Orson said with a smirk.

"I'll bet," Cort said. "The last time she said a kind word about me it rained for forty days and forty nights." He turned his weapons on his oldest son. "Got the financing for your picture yet?"

"It looks promising," Orson answered.

Cort snorted. "That means you got nothing."

"A number of people are interested, including Columbia, which is talking about distribution," Orson said stiffly.

"Talking about," Miles said derisively. "These days it takes a committee of ten to decide to make a decision, then another ten people to make it. Back in my day . . ."

Shannon watched them, hardly hearing the conversation, if it could be called that. She was more interested in her impressions. Orson and Richard were easy, both nasty pieces of work. Richard tried to hide behind a flippant charm; Orson was more weighty. He had an indulgent droop to his mouth and evasive eyes.

Anne, she decided, was probably exactly how she appeared: weak, undisciplined, and generally fearful of just about everything.

Elizabeth was the difficult one to figure out. Shannon was willing to bet money that there was more to her than met the eye. She looked plain and demure, but Shannon was willing to bet it was a self-created image—almost as if she was hiding her real self from the prying eyes of the world. She was probably capable of a few surprises, Shannon decided.

Stephen was as she had thought earlier, handsome, charming, apparently easygoing and forgiving, but very possibly the toughest one of all beneath the affable exterior.

What a crew! she thought to herself. There didn't seem to be an ounce of familial love among them. And Miles seemed to have no favorites, treating them with equal disdain.

The mood continued throughout dinner with the same sarcastic, desultory conversation. Anne, who alone seemed to crave some illusion of normalcy, kept the conversation going, asking well-meaning questions of them all, but seldom able to continue talking once the answers were given.

The only one who looked genuinely comfortable was Stephen. He treated them all with a slightly amused tolerance, as if he understood all their weaknesses yet refused

107

to judge them harshly. The fact that his feelings weren't reciprocated by the others didn't seem to bother him at all.

After eating, they moved to a large living room where liqueur and coffee were served. Cort sat in his wheelchair, the couches on either side of him forming a semicircle with him at its head. It was much like the dining-room arrangement.

Richard lasted about thirty seconds, then gulped his liqueur down and stood. "I have to go."

Cort looked displeased at the breaking of the ranks. "Where are you going?"

"I have to get ready for a date," Richard said. "A delectable young actress who is infatuated by the Cort name." He half bowed to his father. "I thank you for the use of it."

"Maybe one day you'll grow up and put it to some good use," Cort said.

"That remains to be seen," Richard replied. "Good night all."

After he left the room, Miles turned his attention to Shannon. "You've completed your preliminary research, I understand."

"Yes."

"Good. I'm sorry I had to cancel our appointment today, but I had to meet with my lawyer. Lynn will arrange that we meet tomorrow. I assume you learned a lot."

"From press releases and newspaper clippings? Just the signposts," she said.

Cort's eyes gleamed. "Good." He nodded and looked at the others. "I chose the right woman. No doubt about it."

"I'd like to call each of you tomorrow and make appointments to talk to you," Shannon said.

"I'd be delighted," Anne said.

Orson ignored her, while Elizabeth simply looked at her.

"I want you all to give Miss Ross your full cooperation," Cort said, repeating his earlier edict. "If they don't, I want you to let me know," he said to Shannon.

Shannon noticed his tone of voice when he spoke to her was totally different than when he addressed his children. He treated her as an equal, and with a certain amount of rough charm. He treated them as unwanted children. She wondered how they really felt about him. It was something she would probably discover soon.

After a few more minutes of conversation, Shannon said, "I'd better get back and put my daughter to bed."

"I'll walk you," Stephen said.

It was warm and still outside as they walked slowly along the path to the cottage. That heavy, sweet smell was in the air again. What had Lynn called it? Daphne? It was seductive and demanding. Shannon had an urge to find the plant and bury her face in it.

"Not a pretty sight, was it?" Stephen asked.

"What?"

"Our family. The patriarch and his docile subjects."

"No," she said, after hesitating a second. "It wasn't, It's hard for me to understand. Such bitterness. I have only Melissa. If it ever became like that between us . . . I don't know what I would do."

"It never would," he said, and a kind of longing entered his voice. "There's love between the two of you. It's perfectly obvious. You're not sowing the seeds for anything else."

They reached the steps of her patio and she felt his hand touch her elbow. She stopped and looked at him. "You're a good person, Shannon Ross. I'm glad to meet you," he said.

"I think you are too," she said. "How did you grow up to be relatively normal in the middle of all this?"

"I have my own interests, my own strengths and agenda. I don't depend upon Miles's largesse," he said. "I try not to come here very often, however. It's contagious."

She saw a butter-colored moon low in the sky over his shoulder. It was close to full. The light deepened the shadows in his face and accentuated the glowing blue of his eyes.

"What you said earlier, about your father being dangerous," she said. "He seems like a bitter, lonely old man whose life is coming to an end. I don't see anything else."

The blue eyes grew stony. "You're seeing exactly what he chooses to show you. You don't know him yet. Believe me, I meant what I said. Miles can be thoroughly evil. What you see as only bitterness is pure destruction."

She stared back at him and then shook her head. "Well . . ." She paused, troubled by his words but unwilling to explore them further now. "Thank you for walking me back. I'd better see how Melissa is doing."

"May I call you?" he asked. "I'd like to see you again."

Shannon smiled. "I'll be calling you. The interview, remember?"

"Oh, right. The life of Miles Cort. Well, I look forward to hearing from you."

"Good night," she said.

"Good night."

She turned and entered the cottage, feeling his eyes on her back. What a complex yet attractive man, she thought, closing the door behind her. As she walked through the hall toward Melissa's bedroom, she found herself wondering what his music was like.

Richard pumped up the stereo in his living room. Jim Morrison and The Doors. Now there was a guy who knew all about desperation and hunger. Jesus, he'd crammed more into his short life than a dozen other people who lived the full span.

He'd lied about going out. He couldn't stand listening to his father's dissections. Orson, sitting there like a vulture; Anne, without a brain in her head, trying to deny and ignore the undercurrents; Elizabeth, an inhuman punching bag, just accepting whatever punishment was dished out to her; Stephen, so smugly superior, untouched by it all. Ugh! One more family dinner would drive him to suicide.

There was a knock at the door. He hadn't lied about a date, only about going out.

He opened the door and the woman quickly slipped in. As soon as he closed the door she moved into his arms and lifted her mouth hungrily to his. He felt the mouth mash his lips, the voracious tongue, the grinding of her hips against his.

"I missed you," she said, finally drawing back in his arms.

"Yeah," he said, his breathing ragged. Her passion always frightened him. He liked that. It gave everything an edge. And he needed an edge in everything he did.

She reached her hand down to his groin and gripped it tightly. "Come on," Lynn Reid said, tugging at him. "Fuck me. I need you to fuck me."

CHAPTER SEVEN

They met in a cafe on Sunset Plaza. Orson sat at a marble-topped table inside, near the back of the room rather than at his normal position on the patio from where he could watch the passing women. Richard had sounded excited when he called, saying only that he had something "important" to tell him. Orson had decided to forgo the pleasures of girl-watching in the interests of discretion. The less they were seen together, the better.

He looked at the menu while he waited. Nine bucks for noodles, just because it was called pasta and had an Italian name added. Jesus, you could get away with anything in L.A.

Two women sat a couple of tables away. Both seemed to be in their early thirties and were attractive, with tanned skin and expensive clothes. Both of them were chuckling at something one had said. Neither of them looked at him.

Richard peered around the doorway first and then came in. He wore loafers, pale slacks, and an orange T-shirt. Orson waved his hand.

"Hey," Richard said, sliding into the chair opposite him. No apology for the fact he was ten minutes late, but that would have been too much to expect, Orson thought.

Richard called the waiter over and ordered capuccino.

"Same for me again," Orson said, pointing at his cup.

"Espresso, right?" the waiter asked.

Orson nodded and, as soon as the man left, said, "So what is this important news?"

"The old man's up to something," Richard said. His face looked pale and his eyes were swollen.

"So what else is new?"

"Yeah, but I know what he's up to. It's going to blow your little mind," Richard said with a sly smirk.

"What?" Orson asked, leaning forward.

Richard suddenly decided to get coy. "Why am I doing this shit for you?" he asked, narrowing his bloodshot eyes. "What's in it for me? What are you going to do for me?"

Orson spread his hands. "Hey, all for one, one for all. If I can figure out what the old man's doing and how to take advantage of it, we'll both win. Trust me. Whatever he's doing, I can guarantee it won't be for our benefit."

Richard grinned. "You're not shitting about that."

"So what is it?" Orson said, restraining the impulse to lean across the table and grab his brother's throat.

"He's setting up foundations and putting a fortune into them."

"What?" Orson said. "What kind? Who told you this?"

"I don't have all the details, just the general picture, but it's enough. He's setting up a number of different foundations, each with a different purpose, and transferring a lot of money into each one in the form of securities."

"Charitable foundations?" Orson asked, aghast at the thought.

Richard nodded.

"How did you find this out? Who told you?"

Richard shook his head and stared back at him without answering.

Orson met his gaze and then his eyes widened. "Jesus, you're fucking the Iceberg! You're fucking Lynn Reid, aren't you? She's the only one who could tell you about this."

Richard grinned boyishly. "She's no iceberg, believe me. The woman is hotter than hell."

"Jesus," Orson said, thinking the implications through. After a moment he said, "What else do you know about it?"

"Nothing. That's all she knows. He's doing it all through Joe Collins, the lawyer. She hasn't even seen the papers, just a couple of letters."

"We've got to find out more. How much? How much of his money is he giving away here? Our money. What are the foundations for? Christ, why is he doing this?"

"Probably just to piss us off," Richard said philosophically.

"Can she find out more?"

"Her job's at stake," Richard said.

"Her job's already at stake just for fucking you," Orson said with a sneer. "Tell her we'll take care of her if anything happens."

"Yeah, I already did, but she had a good question," Richard said, putting a sober expression on his face. "She said, 'With what?'"

"Oh, Jesus," Orson groaned.

Shannon's interview with Miles took place in the study where they had first met. While waiting for his arrival, she looked more closely at the photographs covering the wall. They did include, as she had thought, virtually all the past greats of Hollywood. Monty Clift, Gable, Brando, Vivien Leigh, Elizabeth Taylor, and a hundred other recognizable names. Most of the pictures showed a younger Miles Cort sitting or standing beside the star.

The salutations ranged from respectful to friendly to fawning. "To Miles, A Visionary Man of His Time." "To Miles, A Giant Among Mortals." "To Miles, The Most Generous Man in Hollywood." Most of them passed the boundaries of simple admiration.

She leaned closer to the picture of Miles with James Dean. The neat script said, "To the biggest asshole in Hollywood."

"A good thing he died," Miles said from behind her. "I would have killed him otherwise."

She turned to see him smiling at her from his wheelchair. "He was a cocky little bastard," he continued admiringly. "Wasn't afraid of anyone."

"It's a very impressive collection," she said.

"It means very little anymore. Most of them are dead. Where do you want to sit? The couch?"

"Sure," she said.

He followed her across the room and watched her sit. She lifted her briefcase from the floor and took out a tape recorder. Miles looked at it warily. "There are times when I'll want you to turn that off," he said.

"How will I—"

"Take notes," he interrupted.

"Very well," she said.

"So you've met my family. What did you think of them?"

"Uh, they seem very interesting," she said lamely.

Cort smiled at her discomfort. "They're no good. I know it, you know it, and they know it."

"I wouldn't make that judgment. I don't know any of them well enough," she said.

"You will. I want you to get to know them all—very well," he said.

She looked at him curiously. He seemed even more energetic and vital than he had on the other occasions when they had met. The skin on his face was a healthy pink and his dark eyes were bright with vigor. He wore his usual open-necked white shirt.

She examined her notes. "I'd like to start with your childhood," she began.

"All you need to know about my childhood is that if you think I'm the biggest son of a bitch in the world, you

115

didn't know my father." He chuckled. "He beat the shit out of me when I was a kid every chance he got. The bastard taught me that it takes discipline and patience to survive."

"How did you feel about him?" she asked.

"I hated him. The last time he beat me I was seventeen. I hit him back, right in the mouth. He stared at me like I was some awful disease, but he never hit me again. He was still an asshole in every other way, but he never hit me.

"If he hadn't died I probably would have killed him. Just like Jimmy Dean up there. He died when I was twenty-three. Keeled over from a heart attack. Bastard smoked like a chimney. Died in his office while he was boffing his secretary, found out later. Too good a death." He chuckled again.

"Were your parents happily married?"

"He treated my mother the same way," he said, his voice growing quieter.

"What do you mean?"

"He beat the shit out of her every chance he got. She was a gentle woman. Never fought back, just stood there and took it. A stupid woman. It taught me one thing: If someone hits you, you just hit 'em back twice as hard, before they have time to blink. They leave you alone after that."

It was good stuff—for a magazine article. Too general for a book, Shannon realized. Now would come the work, the details.

Cort didn't know it, these guys who wanted their biographies written seldom did, but he'd have to work, too. Generally people thought they could just sit there and chat as the memories flitted through their minds, leaving all the real work to the writer. It didn't work that way. Miles Cort was going to need all the discipline and patience he had.

* * *

116

"All right," she said, "I want you to describe your mother to me with every detail you can remember."

Cort surprised her. For two hours he sat in his wheelchair and answered her every question as fully as he could without, as far as she could tell, evasion. That fact—his frankness—excited her. He seemed to be willing to let it all hang out, warts and all. If the trend continued, she'd have a solid book by the time she finished.

As always, the facts between the lines interested her more than the obvious, stated facts. He had hated his father yet admired him, loved his mother yet despised her weakness. His father had apparently been a man without a conscience, a single-minded barbarian. His mother had been the conscience for them both, tortured by his father's sins. "She used to get down on her knees and pray for him, for chrissakes," he said disgustedly. "After he beat me, she'd make me kneel with her and pray that God would forgive him. To make her happy, I'd pretend, but I really prayed that God would strike him dead. Until I was about eleven, and then I stopped praying."

"Why?" she asked.

"Because I knew by then that there was no God with a fully equipped secretarial staff to answer every pitiful human plea."

After the two hours they had set aside, she felt exhausted. Cort looked as fresh as when they had begun.

"Well, thank you very much," she said as she put the tape recorder back in her briefcase.

"Lynn gave you the name of the service to transcribe the tapes?"

"Yes, she's very efficient."

"Best damn secretary I ever had," Cort admitted. "So, tomorrow the same time?"

"Yes. I'm seeing one of your wives for lunch."

"Which one?" he asked.

She glanced at her pad. "Rosemary."

117

Cort grunted. "Only damn lady I ever married. You'll probably like her. Everyone does."

"So I'll see you tomorrow morning?"

"Yes. Stop in and see Lynn in her office. Make an appointment."

As she walked toward the door Cort said, "You do good work. I knew you were the right one."

"Thank you," she answered.

"Oh, and by the way," Miles said, stopping her again. "I have someone working on finding Melissa's father. What's the guy's name? Mark Keller?"

"Yes."

"I've hired a private detective firm to track him down. I'll let you know when they find out something."

"That's very kind of you," she said.

Miles looked back down at his desk. "The child needs a kidney. I told you when we agreed to our deal that if there's a chance he can provide it, it's worth trying to find him."

"Well, thanks, I do appreciate it," she said.

"If he can be found, they can do it," he said.

Hopefully, she thought as she walked out into the corridor, they would have better luck than she had. Detectives had contacts and resources that she didn't even know existed. Miles was right: If there was any chance, it was worth taking.

She stopped at Lynn's office down the hall. It was, as she expected, extremely orderly. Lynn's desk looked as if it had never been touched, except for the single file she was studying. She looked up when Shannon entered, her eyes clouded by concentration.

"I'm supposed to see him tomorrow," Shannon said.

"How did it go?"

"Very well."

"He likes you," Lynn said.

"How can you tell?" Shannon asked, smiling.

"He hasn't fired you yet," Lynn said seriously.

"I have a contract," Shannon said. "It would cost him a fortune to fire me."

Lynn allowed herself a smile. "He has a fortune. Besides, Miles Cort has never in his life let a contract stand in the way of his desires. I'm sure you'll find out all about that as you interview him."

"Well, that certainly adds to my already fragile sense of security," Shannon remarked, more flippantly than she felt.

"There's no need for concern. As I said, he likes you," Lynn said hastily. She appeared to regret having spoken so bluntly. "To prove it, he wants me to take you out this afternoon to Rodeo Drive to buy some clothes."

Shannon didn't understand. "Clothes?"

Lynn looked almost embarrassed. "Well, he asked me about your wardrobe and I couldn't help noticing that it was, well, limited. So he told me to take you out and buy you anything you needed for the party tomorrow night."

"I'm sorry, I don't understand."

"Oh, I guess nobody told you, but there's a big party here tomorrow night. It's Mr. Cort's birthday. He has a party every year."

"I do have some clothes," Shannon said, with a niggling resentment.

Lynn shrugged. "It's something he wants to do. He says that in order for you to do your interviews with some of the people in the business you'll need an extensive wardrobe as well. He doesn't mean anything insulting by it. It's just his way." She arched an eyebrow. "He gave me a virtually blank check for you."

"That's very generous," Shannon said stiffly.

It was pride bothering her, Shannon realized. It was almost painful for her to consider accepting such largesse. She had made her own way for so long, with very little help from anyone. On the other hand, she told herself practically, the truth was that, for the most part, her clothes were cheap, unfashionable, and old.

"Rodeo Drive?" she asked.

Lynn smiled.

"I have a lunch appointment," Shannon said.

"So we'll go later. How about three or four? Just buzz me when you're ready." She looked back down at the file she had been studying.

"Well," Shannon said, still undecided.

Lynn glanced up coolly. "Think of it as part of the job," she said. "If your new boss wants you to buy clothes, then . . ."

She didn't have time to argue, even if she wanted to. "All right. I'll call you when I get back," Shannon conceded. Hers not to reason why. How did the next line go. Hers but to do or die?

"Good," Lynn said. "I'll see you later then. And I'll let you know then when your appointment to see him tomorrow is."

Rosemary Cort lived in a large two-bedroom Spanish stucco house in the Beverly Hills flats. A tall, silver-haired woman with a gracious beauty that age had done nothing but enhance, she greeted Shannon warmly at the front door.

"You must be Shannon Ross," she said. Her handshake was firm. "Do come in."

The house was expensively but tastefully furnished with thick carpets, dark antique woods, and large modern paintings on the walls. The brightly colored art alleviated any sense of severity associated with the dark, heavy wood. The oak coffee table in front of the couch where Shannon sat was carefully littered with magazines: *Art & Antiques*, *Architectural Digest*, *Lear's*.

"I've just made a cup of tea," Rosemary said. "Would you like some?"

"Yes, please."

"Back in a jiffy."

She returned a moment later with a silver tray, on which sat a teapot, cups and saucers, sugar and milk. She placed it on the table, asked Shannon if she wanted sugar and milk, then poured and prepared it for her, before sitting on one end of the couch.

"So," she said, making herself comfortable, "Miles finally wants to legitimize himself." A mischievous look appeared on her face.

"I'm writing his biography," Shannon conceded.

"And it's about time," Rosemary said surprisingly. "Say what you like about Miles, when it comes to the business of film, he was a major player. He deserves whatever accolades he can get."

Apparently Shannon hadn't hidden her surprise because Rosemary smiled and said, "Miles has many short-comings. He's a dreadful man, any way you look at it, but in Hollywood he has contributed more to the form than any half dozen young and overly lauded filmmakers of today. I wouldn't take that away from him."

"Even though you dislike him so much?"

"I dislike him intensely. But I also love him," Rosemary said.

Shannon put her cup and saucer down on the table. "I'm not sure I understand."

"Have you been married?"

"No," Shannon said, realizing where Stephen had gained his looks. He had the same mouth and eyes as his mother.

"Well," Rosemary began with a sigh, "I was married when I was twenty-two. I had three children with Miles—Stephen, Elizabeth, and Richard. We were married for about eighteen years and most of it took place on a battlefield. When Miles's infidelities finally grew too frequent for even me to overlook, I left him. He found himself a younger wife. The point being that you cannot be that long with a person and go through that much and rationally hate him. When it was all over I had the choice of being hurt and bitter, a victim of the past, or living my life. I chose to live my life."

"That is quite exceptional," Shannon said.

Rosemary shrugged. "It doesn't feel exceptional. Like Miles, I'm a survivor. Victims are not survivors. You, for instance. I'm told you have a child. Yet you've never been married. You chose to keep your child, not to be a victim."

"Of course," Shannon said. To her it had seemed a natural decision then and still did.

"Well, then," Rosemary chided. "Don't be so surprised when other people have the same qualities."

Shannon smiled and removed the tape recorder from her bag. "Do you mind if I record our conversation?"

Rosemary waved her hand languidly.

She turned it on and placed it on the couch between them. "What was Miles like when you first met him?" she asked.

"A lot younger. We both were."

Shannon laughed. "No, I mean, what were your impressions?"

"I know what you mean," Rosemary said. She hesitated and stared thoughtfully out the window before speaking. "He was exciting. He was like a hurricane. Nothing in his path was left standing in exactly the same way it had been."

"Do you mean like roofless homes and uprooted trees?"

Rosemary sighed. "There was that destructive element of course, a lot of it, but there was so much more. You have to understand Miles, what was important to him. It wasn't the money and I don't think it was the power— even though he enjoyed using both. It was the project. The movie. The end goal was to see that film up on a thousand neighborhood movie screens around the world. To achieve that he'd do anything, sacrifice anything or anyone."

"And you admired that ruthlessness?"

Rosemary gave her a sharp look. "I admired the single-mindedness, the sheer sticktoitiveness of his vision. Ruthlessness comes into how the goal is achieved, the methods. The fact was that once Miles had a dream, and each movie he produced was such a dream, he made it into a reality, no matter how difficult the task. He did things that a million other men would consider impossible. One can't help but admire such commitment."

"Yes, I suppose that's true," Shannon said.

Rosemary picked up her cup, sipped once, then placed it back on the table. "Hindsight is interesting," she said reflectively. "I've since come to think that men who have such a persistence of vision are either extraordinarily sane or quite insane. In some cases I suppose there are elements of both. I mean, people can be rational on some subjects and totally nuts on others, can't they? In either case, there is a similarity: They don't agree with what other people consider to be reality. They believe that reality can be changed according to their desire."

"And in his case?"

"Sane or insane? I don't know. I never really understood Miles and still don't. Probably he had elements of both. In the final analysis you have to judge a man by his products. He has produced some great films which will live long after he has gone, and he has done some good works. On the other hand, he has ruined lives and left a shattered family, including children who will never recover from his influence. How would you judge him?"

Shannon didn't answer the question. As a writer/researcher it wasn't her job to judge—not yet, anyway. She wanted to explore further one of Rosemary's comments.

"What do you mean by what you said about the children?" she asked.

Rosemary's mouth grew hard, and for a moment Shannon was afraid she would refuse to comment, but after a moment she spoke.

"I won't comment on the others—on Orson and Anne.

You're perfectly capable of seeing them as they are, but my children I have a right to judge." She stopped and looked at Shannon with a plaintive look. "I love my children, you understand, but I'm not a fool. I'm a realist and I can't ignore what they have become. Richard is a wastrel. He should have been thrown out of the house to fend for himself long ago. Necessity might have forced him to use his abilities. God knows why Miles hasn't done it. Elizabeth is too quiet and secretive and has no ambition whatsoever, from what I can see. She hides herself from the world, is afraid of it. No, I love my children, but I am not proud of them."

"What about Stephen?"

Rosemary suddenly smiled at herself. "Isn't it funny how we focus on our failures? I don't count Stephen among them. He's a fine man, his own man, and whatever he does with his life I'll be proud of."

"I like him," Shannon said unprofessionally.

"Most people do. He has that rare capacity to attract loyalty. I think it's because he likes people and doesn't judge them."

"Yes," Shannon said, remembering the blunt, interested way he had looked at her.

"Have you heard his music?" Rosemary asked.

"No."

"It's quite exceptional. Of course I'm biased, but some of it is unusually beautiful. I think of all the children he is the only true artist."

"And he gets that from you?"

Rosemary shrugged self-deprecatingly. "I'm afraid not. If I taught him anything it was taste, but I don't have an artistic bone in my body—at least, not when it comes to doing. I appreciate art, but that's the extent of my skill."

Shannon sneaked a look at her watch. She was comfortable with Rosemary, enjoying both her warmth and her honesty, but time was passing. "Let's get back to when you first met Miles," she said. "Where exactly was it?"

Two hours later it was Rosemary's turn to look at the time. "I'm afraid we have to end," she said apologetically. "I have another appointment."

"So do I," Shannon said, remembering suddenly that she was supposed to go shopping with Lynn. She gathered her tape recorder and notebook. "Thank you for sharing so much with me."

"My pleasure," Rosemary said, leading the way to the door. "Call me if you need more."

"I probably will. I feel as if I've just scratched the surface."

"Well," Rosemary said, opening the door. She hesitated and then said, "Be careful in your dealings with Miles."

"What do you mean?"

"He is a destructive man. The people around him often tend to suffer."

Another warning. What a family! Once again, Shannon was not sure how to respond. It seemed so inappropriately personal, coming from someone she had just met. She chose a light reply. "I'm just an innocent bystander," she said.

"Hurricanes do not differentiate between the innocent and the guilty," Rosemary said drily.

"Well, I'll keep that in mind," Shannon said.

She turned when she was halfway up the path and looked back. Rosemary stood in the doorway and lifted a hand to wave. Then she stepped back and the door closed.

Rodeo Drive was just what Shannon had been led to believe it would be—a congregation of immensely expensive shops clustered together on a few small blocks. Glittering stores stood beside small, unprepossessing boutiques, but both shared large price tags regardless of exterior appearances. The shoppers, too, were a contradictory mix. She saw Arab women in veils and Japanese with cameras; expensively dressed and manicured women stood beside those in blue jeans; Rolls-Royces parked beside small, cheap Asian cars.

Lynn seemed quite at home and knew exactly where she was taking Shannon. "Come on," she said, ducking into a small doorway. "This is where we find you a gown."

Inside were soft lights, gleaming mirrors, thick carpets, and an attentive staff who called Lynn "Miss Reid," and asked if they wanted wine or tea.

"A gown?" Shannon said, looking at the obviously exorbitantly priced creation on two mannequins in front of her.

"They'll be dressed to kill at the party tomorrow. You don't want to look like the hired help, do you?"

"I am the hired help," Shannon protested.

"Yes, but that's not something we want to flaunt," Lynn said with a quick smile. "Now, what colors would look good on you?"

Half an hour later they stepped out onto the sidewalk, Shannon carrying a gown with a price tag of $2,840.

"I can't believe we just did this," she said, narrowing her eyes at the sunlight.

"We've only just begun," Lynn said, taking her arm. "Let's go to Giorgio's now. After that we can go to I. Magnin for some more casual outfits."

By the time the sun set, they had spent $11,427.

"Are you sure this is going to be all right?" Shannon asked for the third time as they sat at the bar of the Beverly Wilshire hotel.

"Absolutely," Lynn said, as the waiter placed their drinks on the table. She lifted hers and gulped at it. "Shopping is tiring work, isn't it?"

Away from the house, Lynn looked like a different person, Shannon noted. She smiled more often, seemed more willing to talk, and even appeared to have more color in her face.

"Do you do this often?" Shannon asked.

"What?"

"Go shopping for other people."

"For other women, you mean? Yes, I have bought merchandise for some of my employee's lady friends before."

"And you don't mind?" Shannon asked.

Lynn shrugged. "Mr. Cort can be a very generous man. Believe me, I'm well paid for this. Anyway, I don't mind doing this for you. You're not pretentious like so many other people I've known."

"It seems to be a demanding job. I mean, you're always there. What do you do in your spare time?"

"Spare time?"

"You must have some other life? Friends? Social things?" Shannon asked.

"I suppose I do. A little. But I don't have a lot of time off. I get a vacation every year. I usually travel. Last year I went to Bali and Australia."

"I'd love to travel," Shannon said. "I went to England once to do an interview for a magazine, but I didn't have much time. With Melissa, there hasn't really been much opportunity."

"If that's something you want to do, you'll get your chance," Lynn said positively.

"What did you do before working for him?" Shannon asked.

"Worked as a secretary over at Warners for an executive. Before that I was a script reader. I had some vague idea about a career in film production. I think I've learned more about film working for Miles than working at the studio."

"So, is it still something you want to do?"

Another shrug. "We'll see," Lynn said, and a shadow seemed to fall over her. It was as if she suddenly realized she was discussing a taboo subject: herself.

Lynn took two more sips of her drink in relative silence and then looked at her watch. "We'd better get back. I still have work to do."

"Thank you so much for all of this," Shannon said warmly, trying to bridge the gap that had suddenly opened.

"Don't mention it," Lynn said politely, but she didn't offer to open up again. She drove silently back to the mansion, keeping her thoughts to herself.

Shannon didn't press for further intimacy. Lynn obviously followed her own agenda. Instead, Shannon leaned back in the seat and pictured how she would model the clothes for Melissa when she got back. Melissa wouldn't believe it. Come to think of it, she had trouble believing it herself.

CHAPTER EIGHT

"Of course I was unfaithful to my wives, all of them," Miles said.

"Don't you feel any guilt about that?" Shannon asked.

An eloquent Miles snort. "Of course not. It's part of the package. No one woman could satisfy me for long. I'd die of boredom. They all went into the marriage knowing that."

"What about the vows you made?"

"Look," Miles said, a little perturbed for the first time, "I was a good husband. I provided for my wives and while we were married I loved them. I provided them with money, with security, with sex. No wife ever said she was shortchanged in the bedroom. The fact I was unfaithful had nothing to do with that. It was a separate part of my life. There was the marriage, a complete and satisfying unit, and then there were the other women. Different life, almost a different man."

"That's a remarkable ability you have to compartmentalize your life," Shannon said ironically.

Miles glowered at her. "You wouldn't understand."

"Why not?"

"Because women invented monogamy."

* * *

They rode to the airport in an uncomfortable silence, the memory of the fight they had just had at the apartment still clinging like a bad odor. Every now and then Elizabeth took her eyes off the road and glanced across at the stubborn set of Sissy's mouth. She wanted to reach over and touch her and say she was sorry, but pride kept both her hands on the wheel.

Sissy was in her mid-twenties, three years younger than Elizabeth. A beautiful California blonde, she was five foot six with a figure that made men pant, particularly when she wore a bikini or cut-off shorts, which she often did. With her long legs, honey-browned skin, and perfect features she was the target of more than admiring glances.

The thing was, Sissy wasn't interested in men, a fact Elizabeth discovered soon after meeting her about ten months earlier. After knowing each other a month they had become lovers and Sissy had moved into her apartment.

Elizabeth had had one or two fleeting lesbian adventures in the past, but they had amounted to nothing. She had thought of them merely as diversions from her main and generally futile preoccupation with men. However, meeting Sissy had driven all such thoughts of men from her mind and she felt that she had discovered her true metier. This was her first real love affair, she told herself often, and for the first time in her life she was truly in love with someone, willing to do anything for them, worshipping them. Sissy was her lover.

Sissy worked as a line producer, one of the few vitally necessary people on film projects. Unfortunately her job necessitated frequent travel to film locations. This most recent trip had caused a quarrel between them. For some reason Elizabeth felt more vulnerable now than she had for a long time and she'd accused Sissy of betraying her by taking the job in London. Sissy had accused her in turn of being overly possessive and suffocating, saying that she had a career to think of. Elizabeth had said that she had more than enough money to keep them both living well, but Sissy said Elizabeth didn't understand, this wasn't a matter of money, it was a matter of career. And so the argument had continued, ending with bitter recriminations.

Still Elizabeth had insisted on driving her out to the airport, in spite of the fact it would make her late for her father's party, hoping that they could make up on the way. So far it hadn't worked out too well. She had to do something to fix things. They couldn't leave each other like this. She wouldn't be able to stand it.

They drove down Century Boulevard and into the airport. "Which airline is it?" she asked, her voice sounding thick and artificial in her own ears.

"It's the overseas terminal. They're all there," Sissy said sullenly.

Elizabeth swung into the left lane and into the parking lot, taking the automatic ticket and driving into the structure. She found a spot almost immediately and brought the car to a halt, turning the engine off. Sissy reached over to the doorknob, but Elizabeth put a hand out and touched her shoulder.

"Sissy, you can't leave like this," she said.

Sissy didn't answer and refused to meet her eyes.

"Sissy, I'm sorry," Elizabeth said. "I have no right to make demands on you like this. I'm sorry. It was wrong of me."

"Yes, it was," Sissy said, but this time she looked at her with those wide aquamarine eyes.

"I'm sorry, I really am." She reached her hand up and touched Sissy's cheek.

"All right," Sissy said. "I'm sorry, too." She turned her head slightly and put her mouth on Elizabeth's hand kissing it.

And then they were in each other's arms, both crying with relief.

They entered the terminal with their moods changed

131

drastically. Sissy was excited and Elizabeth excited for her. Sissy had never been to England before and the thought of seeing London was thrilling.

"Now remember you've got to see Carnaby Street," Elizabeth said. She had been to London twice.

"That's where all the hippies were, right?" Sissy said.

"Right. And don't forget, take a boat ride up to Hampton Court. You go up the Thames past Richmond and you'll see it. From the river you can look at the park and see the deer, the marvelous lawns and gardens and the gigantic old trees. Then inside in the palace there are the paintings and the cobbled courtyards. It's wonderful. If you see nothing else in London, see that."

"Well, you also said I should see Kew Gardens."

"Oh, God, yes, you should also see Kew Gardens," Elizabeth said with a smile. "See St. Paul's Cathedral and the Tower of London where all those people were beheaded. And you should go to the British Museum and of course don't forget Piccadilly."

"God," Sissy said. "I'll be lucky if I have a day off. This movie's going to be a real pain in the ass. If I have one day off, I'll be thankful."

"Well, see what you can," Elizabeth said.

As Sissy checked in her luggage, Elizabeth noticed how two young men looked at her. The admiration in their eyes was unmistakable. Another older man, wearing a uniform, gazed at her with open lust. Somehow it didn't upset Elizabeth but only made her feel proud. Sissy was hers and nobody else's. Particularly not any man's.

"Are you going to come to the gate?" Sissy asked, lightly touching Elizabeth's hand.

Elizabeth shook her head. "No, I hate goodbyes. I'm going to go now. You'll be all right, won't you?"

"I'll be fine," Sissy said.

They kissed each other decorously on the cheeks. Elizabeth wished that she could do what any other two lovers would do and take her in her arms and kiss her passionately on the mouth. But it wasn't possible. Not here, not now.

"Goodbye," she said, with tears in her eyes and was immensely touched and gratified to see that Sissy, too, was crying. It filled her with faith and trust.

"Goodbye," she said again quickly and walked back out of the terminal to the garage.

She got back into her car and wound her way out of the structure to the street. Driving through the maze of airport buildings, she remembered the first time with Sissy. They had met at a party and she had invited Sissy back to her place for coffee afterward, seized with an affinity for this beautiful blond woman.

They had sat on the couch, the air stiff between them, sipping coffee laced with Grand Marnier. And then very delicately Sissy had put her cup on the table, reached over, and put her hand on Elizabeth's cheek, simply letting it rest there while she looked into her eyes. Not even knowing what she was doing, Elizabeth, too, put her cup down, and then felt her face being drawn toward Sissy's and then her lips, soft against hers, and a kiss unlike any she had ever experienced with a man. So tender, so gentle, and yet so filled with the promise of passion. A promise that as the following hours unfolded was not betrayed.

She was going to miss Sissy terribly, she admitted to herself. She could already feel an achingly empty feeling as if something had been torn from her body and left a gaping hole.

Anne Cort moved into the corner of the limo, but Allan Prentice was not to be denied.

"You're gorgeous," he said, slobbering over her neck.

"And you've had a little too much to drink, Allan, but thank you," she said as graciously as she could.

Prentice was star of a hot television series. About five years younger than she, with a profile adored by women across the nation and piercing blue eyes that were now shot with red streaks, he was convinced he was in love with her—after two dates. They had slept together once, but since he had picked her up this evening, he had elaborated on his plans to make it a regular occurrence.

She was flattered; it was hard not to be. Prentice was hot, attracting fans and paparazzi wherever he went, but he was also a lush, and this disturbed her. Still, she was realistic enough to know that being seen with him could do little to harm her own career. It wasn't as if eligible men were beating her door down with invitations.

"You're a real woman," he said for the third time, his slurred words sounding like a speech impediment. "A mature woman. These chicks that come on to me all the time, they're kids. You've been around and maintained your dignity. I admire that."

"How much have you had to drink tonight?" she asked, irritation seeping into her voice.

"Hey, I just had a few drinks before picking you up. S'not much." He grinned and picked up the drink sitting on the limo's open bar. "And this one, of course. But it's nothing."

"Listen, you have to promise to behave yourself at the party," she said nervously. "I don't want to be embarrassed in front of my father."

Prentice straightened up, a hurt expression on his face. "Hey, I admire your father. He's one of the—the—icons of Hollywood, babe. I wouldn't do anything to embarrass you. Jeez, I'm just looking forward to meeting him. He's one of my idols."

"Good," Anne said, patting him on the knee.

"Yeah, don't worry 'bout a thing," he said.

"Good," she said again, and picked up his glass. "I think I need a sip of this myself."

She took a gulp and immediately started to cough. It was straight vodka, unadulterated by water or ice.

"Oh, God," she said when she could speak. She was already beginning to dread the evening.

"For chrissakes, hurry up," Orson said to his wife.

Barbara applied the last of her makeup and squinted into the mirror. Not bad, she thought approvingly. She wore a loose-fitting gown, low cut to reveal her best attributes.

"Why are we going anyway?" she said over her shoulder.

Orson appeared in the doorway. He wore a tuxedo and bowtie. "Because Miles invited us," he said.

He raised an eyebrow. When Barbara dressed up, which wasn't that often, she wasn't a bad-looking broad, he thought. He stepped closer and put his hands on her shoulders. "Are you ready?"

"As ready as I'll ever be," she said. "You know how I hate visiting Miles."

"There'll be a couple of hundred other people there tonight," Orson said. "You say hello, you won't have to speak to him again."

"You still hoping for money from him? Is that why you're kissing his ass?" she asked, turning.

"He's my father," Orson said insincerely.

"Ha! You're still hoping for money. Fat chance."

"There may be people there I should meet."

"God, you're hopeless," she said derisively.

Orson glowered at her, then turned on his heels and stalked from the room. "Just hurry up," he said, his back to her.

She stared at the door as he went through it. "Maybe I'll meet my next husband there, schmuck," she said too softly for him to hear.

* * *

Floodlights illuminated the curving driveway all the way from the gates to the mansion where red-coated parking attendants scurried from car to car, scooting any driving machine worth more than thirty thousand dollars around to the parking lot behind the house. Less expensive cars were taken to the street.

The normally somewhat austere mansion was itself transformed by lights pouring like melted butter from every doorway and window, by the hum of conversation, the crescendos of laughter, the music of a band in one of the large rooms, and the sheer glamour of the privileged who attended. Most of the men wore tuxedos and the women gowns running the gamut from the elegant to the outrageous.

Melissa, who was being allowed to attend for an hour, was beside herself with excitement. She and Shannon stood on one side of the grand living room and watched arrivals pay their respects to Miles who was ensconced in his wheelchair in front of the fireplace. They were like subjects paying homage to a king, Shannon thought, realizing with some amusement that Miles had arranged it exactly that way.

"Oh, God, Mom, look!" Melissa hissed between her teeth, her tiny hand almost squeezing the blood from Shannon's. "It's Alex Carr. Oh, God, I can't stand it. Isn't he cute?"

The object of her adoration was a young television actor in his late teens or early twenties. They watched him shake Miles's hand, say a few words, and then move away with his date, a ravishing blonde of the same indeterminate age. He looked like a nice kid, but plain, Shannon thought.

"I suppose so," she said to Melissa, "but he doesn't really turn me on. Not my type."

"Oh, Mom," Melissa groaned. "All the girls think he's cute."

"Well, then I guess he is," Shannon conceded.

She continued to watch Miles. He looked healthy and

robust, in spite of his wheelchair. Clearly, he was eating up the attention. He was also at his charming best, bestowing smiles and even hearty laughs on all who attended him.

"The dress looks beautiful," Lynn said, coming up to them.

"Thank you," Shannon said. "Although, as it was your choice, you really can't say anything else."

It *was* beautiful, though, and she knew it. A glittery ankle-length blue, with thin straps that crossed over her back, a revealing front, and a languid drape from the hips, it was easily the most glamorous thing she had ever worn.

Lynn wore a simple black gown that left her shoulders bare. Around her neck was a single strand of pearls.

"Do you recognize anyone here?" Lynn asked.

"Are you kidding?" Melissa interjected. "I just saw Alex Carr."

"Would you like to meet him?" Lynn asked with a smile.

Melissa suddenly looked frightened. "I don't know what I'd say. I'd probably just stand there like a geek."

"I'm sure you won't," Lynn said kindly. "Come on, I'll introduce you. And you know who else is here? Andrew McCarthy and Fred Savage."

"Fred Savage? Fred Savage is here?"

Shannon wondered if Melissa was going to faint. Probably not. Her face had turned pink, not white. But Fred Savage, the star of television's *The Wonder Years* was the current object of her totally uncompromising infatuation.

"Come on," Lynn said, taking her hand.

"No. I couldn't."

"Come on," Lynn said, giving her a tug.

"Go on," Shannon said with a smile. "If you don't, you'll spend the rest of your life regretting it."

With a final nervous glance over her shoulder, Melissa allowed herself to be led away.

137

It was, Shannon had to admit, an impressive crowd. The actors and actresses were easily recognizable, particularly those from old Hollywood, who predominated. But many of the new, hot Hollywood faces were there as well, probably for the sheer status of attending an event as important as this. Many of the people, however, she didn't recognize, although by the way Miles and others greeted them they were obviously important. Directors, producers, and other less public people, she guessed.

The catering company's staff was very efficient, she noted. They all wore black waiter's uniforms and buzzed through the crowd like bees dispensing their wares. A number of the security staff were also recognizable to her, even though they wore tuxedos as well and mingled with the crowd. Both shifts would be working the party. She saw Peter Corydon, the head of security, move through the room. A tall, dark man with a husky build, his eyes wore never still, constantly scanning the perimeters. She had been introduced to him once, but had not had occasion to speak further with him.

Orson Cort arrived with a pretty redheaded woman Shannon presumed to be his wife. Miles greeted his son without a smile, but mustered one up for the woman.

"Nice party," a man said, sidling up to Shannon.

"Yes," she said. Extremely handsome, he revealed capped teeth in a wide smile. He wore blue-tinted contacts and an attractive dimple sat in the center of his chin.

"I'm Carter Dubrow."

"I recognize you," she replied. She'd seen half a dozen of his films. He'd had a big success in the mid-seventies and had never been able to top it. Lately he'd been getting second billing in second-rate movies.

"And you?" he asked.

"Shannon Ross."

"How do you do," he said, holding out his hand. He shook hers limply and said, "What line are you in?"

"I'm a writer."

"Oh," he said, unable to hide the fact he was not impressed. "I figured you for an actress or a studio executive."

"No such luck," Shannon answered. She already knew how writers were regarded in Hollywood: one step above chauffeurs.

"Well, you're pretty enough to be an actress," he said, mustering up some gallantry. "We don't see too many pretty writers in Hollywood."

"And you're handsome enough to be an actor," she said with a smile.

He chuckled at that, but his eyes were already beginning to search the crowd for more important prey.

"Who are those people talking to Mr. Cort?" Shannon asked, nodding her head at the group of three men who surrounded Miles.

"Three of the most powerful agents in town. The head of ICM, and the other two are from William Morris." His face lighted up at the sight of a woman across the room. "Oh, and there's Rachel. Excuse me, I must say hello. Nice to have met you." He smiled his glorious smile and wandered away.

Shannon decided to get closer to Miles and eavesdrop. It was where the important action was, the "heat," as she'd heard somebody describe it a few minutes earlier. She grabbed a glass of wine from a passing tray and moved through the crowd.

"He's a lightweight," Miles said pedantically.

The three agents listened respectfully. "Why do you say that?" one of them asked. He was from William Morris and had sharp features and small, nervous eyes. "His Q rating is right up there."

"Television, yes," Miles said. "But put him on a big screen and he'll lose it. He's got no charisma, nothing to project. Too weak, too glib."

The two agents from William Morris shot each other

worried looks. "Well, he tested okay," the one who had spoken before said.

Miles let out a scornful bark. "You can't go by tests. They're a few minutes long. You're talking ninety to a hundred twenty minutes. The guy's a pansy. If I were you I'd find someone else. You got better clients."

"Well, I'll certainly think about what you said," the agent said.

"Daddy!"

It was Anne, her lush figure threatening to burst out of her dress. She rushed up to Miles and kissed his cheek.

"What a wonderful party," she said.

"You know these gentlemen?" he said.

"Of course. How nice to see you." She grasped each one by the forearms, enthusiastically kissing the air beside their cheeks.

"Who are you here with?" Miles asked, leaving no doubt in his tone that it would probably be someone he'd disapprove of.

"Allan Prentice. He's a big fan of yours. Where is he? He did so want to meet you." She swung her head around and then waved. "Allan! Over here!"

Prentice made his way toward them. It was obvious to Shannon that the man was under the weather. He looked as if he was having difficulty navigating a path on the deck of a rolling ship.

"Mr. Cort," he said, holding out his hand. "Jesus, I've wanted to meet you for a long time. I really, really admire your work. Really do. Really do."

Miles shook his hand distastefully. "Thank you."

"And your daughter here," Prentice said, putting an arm around Anne and almost losing his balance. "What a girl!" He looked around the room. "And what a party. Man, you sure know how to—how to throw them."

"Thank you," Miles said heavily.

"Come on, let's get a drink," Anne said, avoiding her father's gaze.

"Hey, I want to talk to your old man," Prentice protested.

"Perhaps later," Miles glowered.

There was a nervousness in Anne's eyes now. She took Prentice's hand. "Let me show you around the house."

"Okay, okay," the actor said. He leaned toward Miles and winked. "We'll talk later," he promised.

Miles glared at him without answering.

"Sort of a serious guy, isn't he?" Prentice said as Anne led him away.

Miles lifted a finger and his head of security, Corydon, came up to him. "The man with Anne. If he causes any trouble I want him outta here. Understood?"

"Yes, sir," Corydon said, and disappeared back into the crowd.

"Children," Miles said expressively to the William Morris agent.

"Can't live with 'em, can't live without 'em," the agent said.

Miles grunted and then saw Shannon watching them. "Enjoying yourself, Miss Ross?" his voice boomed at her.

She stepped toward him. "Yes, thank you,"

"A writer from New York. She's doing my biography," Miles said to the two William Morris men. The head of ICM had wandered off.

"Hey," the talkative agent said, "a bio. Who's handling the movie rights?"

"Daddy."

It was Elizabeth Cort. She walked up to her father and kissed him on the cheek. She wore a demure black gown and understated makeup, and looked her usual restrained self.

"Didn't think you were coming," Miles said.

"I always come," she replied.

"Well, get yourself a drink, some food. Mingle," he said.

She nodded politely at Shannon and walked away.

"I think I'll mingle as well," Shannon said. "Excuse me."

"Nice-looking for a writer," she heard one of the men say behind her.

Orson left Barbara talking to a couple they knew and went in search of a young actress he had seen a few minutes earlier. They'd never met, but he'd seen her around. She had given him a speculative look across the room as the woman beside her said something. It was all the encouragement Orson had ever needed.

"Hey, Orson! How's it going?"

It was Cal Fleischman, a director in his thirties. Bearded and long-haired, he managed to look casual and hip, even in a tux.

"Hey, Cal! It's looking good. How about you?"

"Outstanding, my man. Just finished a movie for Paramount. Considering a couple of other projects."

Fleischman was a comer. He'd had a winner a year ago directing a Mel Gibson thriller and had been turning down the work ever since. Before his success, Orson had once talked to him about directing a project of his, but the financing had never come through. Now he'd never be able to afford him.

"Yeah, I've been hearing the buzz about the Paramount movie," Orson said.

"What are you working on?"

"Carrie Pressman," Orson said, naming the actress he was looking for. "Seen her."

" A prime piece of ass," Fleischman said with a wink. "Saw her heading over to the music."

Asshole! Orson thought as he moved on. Arrogant bastard was on a roll. One flop and he'd be standing there with his hat in his hand like all the others. The guy hadn't been around long enough to know that you were only as good as your last movie and that you couldn't have more than three winners in a row. The odds didn't allow it.

He went into the huge drawing room with the dance floor in its center. There was a band at one end: keyboards, bass, guitar, and drums, with a male singer doing a Buster Poindexter takeoff. People sat at tables around the floor, while a few couples danced to some lame Top 40 hit.

There she was, talking to a couple near the bar. He put his drink down on the nearest table and walked to the bar.

"Screwdriver," he said to the bartender.

He got his drink, turned, and seemed to notice the actress for the first time.

"Hey, Carrie Pressman, isn't it?" he asked, stepping up and interrupting them.

She was a brunette, about twenty-three with dark, healthy skin and a strong, athletic body that would one day turn to blubber. For now, it was fine.

She looked at him with ingenious hazel eyes, her companions forgotten, and said, "Yes. And you're Orson Cort."

"Right," he said with a grin. "I've been an admirer of yours for some time. I thought you were wonderful in your last movie. That MOW on ABC, right?"

She grimaced self-deprecatingly. "It wasn't much of a part."

"Yeah, but you played it for all it was worth."

"Well, thanks," she said, almost preening.

"I think you got real talent."

"Oh," she said, remembering the couple she had been talking to. "This is Bob and Michelle. Orson Cort."

"Hey," Orson said, giving them a quick nod. He took Carrie's arm. "I'm working on a project right now. In fact, there's a part in it that might interest you. Calls for a passionate, intelligent brunette."

"Really?" she asked.

"Really." He led her slightly away from the couple. "Maybe you'd like to take a look at the script."

"I'd love to," she said warmly.

He ran his hand up the underside of her arm. "Why don't I give you a call. We can arrange to get together."

She looked up at him, almost slyly. This woman was no virgin in Hollywood. "That'd be great," she said.

Orson grinned at her, squeezed her arm. "Great," he said. "Great."

Shannon saw Elizabeth ordering a drink at one of the bars and went over to her. "Hi," she said.

Elizabeth gave her a cool look. "What do you think of Hollywood?" she asked.

"Interesting." Shannon put her empty glass down and reached for another one filled with wine. She noticed that Elizabeth was drinking Perrier.

"It's right here," Elizabeth said, gesturing at the room. "Most of the power in this town is gathered right here tonight."

"I assumed that. Do you know most of them?"

Elizabeth shrugged. "Growing up in the business, you meet them all sooner or later. They all travel well-worn paths."

"You don't seem overly impressed. I guess familiarity makes you blasé."

"Breeds contempt," Elizabeth corrected with the hint of the smile.

"You don't like the film business?"

Elizabeth looked around the room. "It's a pretend business. Its product isn't reality. Just the opposite. Most of these people here are living that unreality. Pretending."

"What about you?" Shannon asked quietly.

Elizabeth suddenly met her eyes, something like surprise in her own. "Doesn't everyone?"

"To some extent," Shannon agreed. "I guess the key to

reality is to know when you are pretending and know when you aren't. We all create our own realities, one way or the other. It's better to know that you're doing it."

Elizabeth looked at her with interest. "That's true, isn't it?"

Shannon smiled. "It's philosophy. Easy to say, hard to really understand and harder to live by."

"Hmm. What do you think of our family?" Elizabeth asked.

"Everyone asks me that question. I think you're all too complicated for me to judge," Shannon replied carefully.

Elizabeth stared thoughtfully at her. Once again Shannon noticed the amazing depths in her eyes.

"Did you grow up in this house?" Shannon asked.

"Yes." The guarded expression returned to her face.

Shannon looked around the huge room in which the party was centered and through the open doors to the next room. "It must have been exciting. A place like this," she said with a wistful note.

"Would you like to see my room?" Elizabeth asked.

"Yes. Yes, I would. I haven't seen much of the house except for your father's study and these downstairs rooms."

"Come on," Elizabeth said.

The walked through the crowd toward the foyer. There were probably a couple of hundred people here now, Shannon thought as she avoided a burly man who stepped backward without looking. All here to either pay homage or bask in Miles's glory.

"My, how you've grown, Elizabeth," an elderly man said.

Elizabeth smiled and waved casually, not stopping. "To some people you're always a child," she said as they entered the foyer.

They went up the stairs and turned right, walking down a long hallway.

"The children—we all had our rooms in this wing," she

145

said, as the hall turned left. "The adults—Father and his various wives—lived on the other side."

"How old were you when you left home?" Shannon asked.

"Eighteen. I went to college. Here. This was my room." She stopped before a door, hesitated, then opened it and fumbled for the light switch.

"Go on," Elizabeth said, standing aside for Shannon.

It was pink and ruffly, Shannon saw when she stepped in. Very much a little girl's room. A canopy over the bed and layered pink curtains on the window. There were still dolls lined up on a shelf and children's books in a bookcase.

"It's so charming," she said. There was a painting of Mickey Mouse on the wall beside the bed. She stepped closer and saw that it was signed by Walt Disney.

"You must have loved this room," Shannon said.

She turned to see Elizabeth still standing in the doorway, her arms folded across her chest. Her face seemed paler, her eyes distant, lost in memory.

"I hated it," Elizabeth said, an ugly bitterness in her voice. "This room and this house. I hated it."

She turned then and walked back into the hall, not waiting for Shannon.

Quickly Shannon followed, flicking off the light as she passed through the door. She caught up with Elizabeth ten yards down the hall.

"Are you all right?" she asked, coming up beside her.

Elizabeth's arms were still folded as she walked. She shook her head, but said, "Yes. I'm fine."

"What—I mean, it's none of my business, but what upset you?"

Elizabeth gave her a grim sideways look. "It was nothing. Ghosts. We all have ghosts, don't we?"

It was a rhetorical question. Shannon walked in silence beside her. This house, this family, they seemed to have more than their share of ghosts haunting them.

"I'm sorry," Elizabeth said when they reached the bottom of the stairs, "but I'll be taking off now. I've made my required appearance."

"You're all right?" Shannon asked again.

"I'm fine," Elizabeth said, forcing a weak smile.

"Could I call you? I want to talk to you some more. You know, the book?"

Elizabeth seemed to really notice her for the first time since they had been in the bedroom. "Sure. Give me a call. That would be fine."

Shannon frowned as she watched her walk out the front door. No coat, no bag. Probably in her car. What a strange woman.

"My favorite writer."

She turned to see Stephen watching her with a smile. He was very handsome in a tuxedo. His dark hair looked less windblown than when she had seen him before.

"Hi," she said, realizing that she was pleased to see him.

"I've been waiting for a call. My interview," he said, stepping closer.

"Things haven't moved as fast as I'd like," Shannon said.

"Me neither," he said. "Been hanging out with my sister?"

"She took me upstairs to see her bedroom. It seemed to upset her."

"A moody one, our Elizabeth."

"Aren't you all?"

"Not me," he said, holding out his palms. "Stable as the floor beneath your feet. Walked over just as much, too, but I survived."

There was no self-pity in his tone, just humor. Shannon found herself smiling.

"I'd better find Melissa," she said. "I lost her about an hour ago. She went on a mission."

"Ah. Did it involve a male actor? Handsome young man?"

147

"You've seen her?"

"Outside, near the pool. The young crowd is hanging out there." He held out his arm. "You want to check up on her?"

"From a distance," Shannon said, taking his arm. "She's supposed to go to bed soon, but I don't think that's too realistic."

They walked through the hall and out to the back patio. Groups of people clustered around tables. The more causal of the guests had come outside, Shannon guessed.

"There she is," Stephen said, pointing at a group beside the pool.

There were about fifteen young people there, a couple around Melissa's age, but most in their teens. Melissa was listening to a boy of about fourteen, her face serious, then suddenly she laughed.

Shannon leaned back against a brick pillar and said, "It's nice to see her enjoying herself with other kids."

"Is it hard on you?" Stephen asked.

"What?"

"Her kidney problem, the dialysis?"

"Not as hard as it is on her."

"She bears up amazingly well."

"We all adapt, I guess. It was harder at first."

She looked over at Stephen standing beside her, his face still, watching the guests around the pool. He was totally relaxed, she realized. In fact, he always seemed to be at ease, whatever the situation. It was an interesting quality, one that seemed to affect people around him in some way, perhaps as a calming influence.

"I talked to your mother," she said.

"Yes, she told me. She liked you."

"I liked her. She thinks very highly of you, too."

"I'm her son, what do you expect?" he asked with a smile.

"She doesn't feel that way about all her children."

"Rosemary is a realist above all else. It's both a strength and a weakness."

"How so?"

"A strength because it brings clarity of vision, a weakness because it limits her vision. Sometimes you have to see past what appears to be real. As a writer you must know that."

The air was warm outside. Every few seconds an unlucky bug zapped itself against the bug-death light, as Shannon called it, to their right. Someone sitting with a group at a table near them laughed at something and began to cough.

The man standing beside her was one of the most attractive people she had ever met. She wondered what it would be like to be held by him, to be kissed by that sensitive mouth, to be undressed by the elegant hands with the long fingers.

He was staring directly at her, she realized, surfacing suddenly from her thoughts. She felt her face grow warm.

"If you don't call me soon, I'll be calling you, okay?" he said gently.

"Yes," she said, her throat inexplicably dry.

He nodded, his eyes still on her. "Good night."

"You're leaving?"

"Yes. But we'll talk soon?"

"Yes."

A quick, warm smile and then he left.

She leaned her head back against the pillar and folded her arms against her chest. It seemed to take a minute, but she finally began to breathe.

CHAPTER NINE

Miles Cort told Shannon that the unforgivable yet incomprehensibly prevalent sin among people in general was ingratitude. He said that he had done favors for people all his life but that very few had thanked him, let alone attempted to repay him. He said that most of the people he had helped early in his career had later attempted to stab him in the back. When he said this, he held his clenched hand up and brought it down with a vivid grimace and heartfelt grunt. She almost pictured the knife in his hand.

He told her all this during their morning meeting on the patio in the bright sunlight. All traces of the party the night before had vanished, cleared away by hordes of servile minions, while everyone else still slept.

On the table before them were croissants and cheeses, coffee, and orange juice in a tall crystal pitcher.

Miles bit into his croissant and said, "Those agents you met? The one with the nose and the shifty eyes?"

Shannon nodded.

"Nice guy, right?" Miles said, still chewing. "Respects me? Listens to what I say? Sure he is. He'd sell his mother's grave to make a deal. Speaks out of both sides of his mouth at once. You need six lawyers to look over any deal you do with him. They're all like that."

"Surely there are nice people in the business?" Shannon asked.

"Nice, schmice. The nice ones are all dead."

Miles had such an emphatic way of speaking, Shannon almost found herself believing him. But that was ridiculous, she told herself. Every business had its share of creeps and opportunists. Perhaps the film business had more than most. After all, it promised rewards greater than most businesses and the qualifications to enter it were minimal.

But what Miles was saying was impossible, according to the odds. Among the thousands of people working in what was here in L.A. called "the business," there had to be some who weren't venal and corrupt. If that wasn't the case, how could wonderful, entertaining, and sometimes inspiring films be produced, as many were. In the light of rationality, his words sounded like the ravings of a paranoid.

"Have you met all the family?" Miles asked.

"All your children," she said. "A few others."

"So what do you think of them?" Miles finished eating and leaned back in his wheelchair, a cup of coffee clutched in his hand.

"They seem to be a—unique bunch," she said cautiously.

Miles snorted at her evasiveness. "You're going to have to be more outspoken than that if this book's going to be any good."

"I will be when it's time," Shannon said irritably. "I don't like making hasty judgments. Things are seldom all they appear to be."

Miles stared at her with those black eyes and then said, "That's true, very true. Smart."

"Thank you," she said with some irony. He had his area of expertise, but she also had hers. His infringements into her territory were not appreciated.

Miles waved her petulance away with a gesture. "I ask

about the family because I want you to do something for me." He paused, measuring her.

"Yes?"

"I may not have been the best husband and father in the world," he began, for the first time seeming uncomfortable. He shrugged. "My family, they may not exactly love me, right?"

Shannon looked back at him without speaking. It was not her place to agree with the obvious. His discomfort didn't need bolstering from her.

Miles took a piece of cheese and popped it into his mouth. He chewed thoughtfully for a moment. "You're talking to them all. Getting to know them, finding out what they think about me . . ."

"You want to know what they think of you?" Shannon bristled. "I'm not going to report to you like some spy. You can read it when I have it in writing. Everything will be there, I guarantee."

"Shit! I don't want to know what they think of me," Miles growled. "I already know their opinions. I want you to find out something more important than that."

Shannon began to feel exasperated. Why didn't he get to the point? "What is it you want then, Miles?" she asked, using his first name for the first time.

Miles scowled. He looked disgusted: at her question, at having to answer it, at being in this place at this time.

"All right, all right," he said heavily. "I want you to help me find out which member of my family is trying to murder me."

Shannon's immediate reaction was shock and then outrage. Is this what I'm here for? she thought. Is this why he hired me to do this biography? But she fought it down immediately and let her natural journalistic curiosity surface. She began to ask blunt questions.

He told her that a visitor, a girl, had attempted to poison him. Yes, she was paid to visit him for sex.

"A hooker?" she asked.

"An amateur," he said defensively. "A man my age needs sex. You think I want to get married again? Christ, they've taken everything but the skin off my back. I give these girls money, a gift. No complications, no obligations. These girls are actresses mainly. They have a hard time surviving in this town."

"And you're just helping them out," she said sardonically. She couldn't help but disapprove. In her reality, sex was not callous or indifferent, something that could be bought and sold. It was the act that lovers shared.

Miles flared up at that. "Hey, I want a moralist I'll call in a priest or a rabbi. You're a fucking writer. Why don't you act like a fucking writer?"

Right, Shannon thought, mollified. She put her writer's hat back on. "What happened to the girl after you found out she tried to poison you?"

Miles blinked. "We threw her out. She disappeared. Left town I suppose. The point is, my security people investigated her and found no connections to anyone I know. She was an actress, like the others. Worked part-time as a secretary for a shipping company. My people found her in a bar. She knew nobody I know."

"Except the person who gave her the poison."

"Dumb broad, she thought it was knockout drops or something. But I broke my own rule and invited her back more than once. Either she told someone, or someone in the house saw her earlier and then approached her."

"So why do you think it was a member of your family?" Shannon asked, puzzled. "You have enemies. You couldn't have done what you've done and been the kind of man you've been and not made enemies."

"Thank you," Miles said, with a clumsy show of irony. "Well?"

"My enemies could have killed me long ago. I've checked up on the ones who said they would." He shook his head. "Why decide to kill me now, after all these years. Christ, I haven't done anything for years."

"These things fester," Shannon volunteered.

"It's possible. But I don't see a motive," Miles said. "My people did a very thorough check. Corydon is good at this stuff."

There was something wrong here, she realized. The logic had leapt across a chasm. There was something he wasn't telling her.

"So why would your family have a motive?" she asked.

"I ride them all the time," he admitted. "Maybe there was a straw that broke the camel's back."

Shannon shook her head. "I don't buy that. Come on. There must be something else." She looked at him and waited for an answer.

Miles grunted. "Well, there is something, but none of them know about it," he admitted.

"You can't be sure of that," she said. "What is it?"

"Right, you can't be sure." He nodded. "They shouldn't know, but . . ."

"So what is it that they shouldn't know about?"

"I'm making sure they don't get my money."

Shannon tried to grasp the implications. "You're disinheriting your children?"

Miles looked annoyed. "I don't know why I'm telling you this. It's totally confidential, you understand?"

"You want my help, that's why. And yes, I do understand confidentiality," Shannon replied calmly. "So are you disinheriting them all?"

"I am leaving them all a million dollars each," Miles snapped. "The rest is going into various charitable trust funds. Believe me, it's more than they deserve."

Shannon leaned back in her chair, amazed. The man was worth some two hundred million dollars, she guessed. His five children would get a million dollars each. Roughly a hundred ninety-five million would go to charity. Hell, yes, they'd kill him if they found out!

"I'm told a million dollars doesn't go far these days," she said drily.

"Yeah, Orson will lose it on the first movie he makes," Miles said with some satisfaction.

"Then why are you doing it?"

"I worked for my money," Miles said, glaring at her. "My children are just no damn good. They can sink or swim. It's a law of nature and I'm not about to change it. The fittest survive. A million dollars is a damn sight more than most people start with. I think it's overly generous.

"I was going to leave them nothing at all. My lawyer suggested the million. Its payment is conditional upon acceptance of the will. It's iron-clad. They want to waste time fighting it, they get nothing."

"Is this a fait accompli? I mean has it all been done?" Shannon asked.

"I know what a goddamn fait accompli is," Miles said. "No, it's in the works. There's a lot of money involved. It takes time. I don't want any loopholes. I got the best lawyers in the country working on it."

So there it was, Shannon thought. The reason he suspected his family. She might as well voice it. "So," she said casually, "someone could kill you now to stop you from doing this, or think they were stopping you."

"You got it," Miles muttered, sinking into his wheelchair, suddenly looking old and tired.

For the first time since she had known him, Shannon felt pity.

"I'm afraid we no longer have the money available for your project," Blaine Carter said, tapping his cigarette elegantly toward a marble ashtray. He missed his mark and looked with disdain down at the ash on his desk. Carefully, he leaned forward and blew it on the floor. A lock of gray hair fell over his forehead and he flicked it back with a toss of his head.

Fucking faggot, Orson thought, but instead said disgruntedly, "You said it was committed. In the bag."

Carter's blond, blue-eyed partner, Bruce Shaw, ten years his junior, spread his delicate hands in front of him and said, "Orson, you know how fast things change in this business."

The two producers had been jerking him around for months. They had loved the script, adored the stars, been so impressed by Orson's aggressiveness, there would be no problem coming up with the money. It was just a matter of time, of putting all the pieces of the puzzle together. Now, when they were supposed to sign on the dotted line, they were backing out.

"What exactly is the problem?" Orson asked.

"The money people," Carter said. "They seem to have lost confidence in the project."

"You mean that you guys have presented them another one they like more," Orson said.

"The package was weak, admit it," Carter said. "We can't count on video sales to make up our costs these days. You know how the competition is."

"Shit!" Orson said, not suppressing his irritation.

"We haven't given up," Carter said, consoling him. "It's just a matter of waiting. We have other investors, but it could take time." He ground his cigarette out, not looking at Orson, and said, "In the meantime, if you want to show the project to a few other people, we are in no position to stop you."

In other words, kiss off, Orson thought. He realized suddenly that he was close to tears. He had counted on them, wined and dined them, supplied them with coke, given them his time and energy. It had seemed such a sure thing.

He stood up suddenly.

"Are you all right?" Carter asked, all concern now.

"Fine, fine," Orson said. "I have another appointment."

"Keep in touch," Carter said.

"Nice to see you again," Shaw said, sounding like a ventriloquist's dummy.

Orson stormed through the corridors, out the building to where he had parked on the corner of Sunset and Doheny Drive. He opened the door of his Mercedes, got in, and slumped with his head against the steering wheel.

This fucking business, he thought scornfully. Filled with flakes. You never knew until it came time to hand over the check. Shit, no, he corrected himself, you never knew until the check cleared. You'd think he'd have learned that by now.

The past twelve months had been filled with similar disappointments. The pattern was always the same: that initial burst of interest, the ritualistic courtship period, the surges of hope, and always the ultimate disappointment. He was running out of options. You shopped a project around too much and it became tainted. A kind of herd revulsion overcame rationality. Nobody wanted to get near it after a while, no matter how enthusiastic they had all been in the beginning. This one was rapidly approaching that stage.

If only his father would come through with some money—or die. But even death wouldn't provide salvation the way things were going. Apparently he wasn't leaving them any of the money anyway. The thought reminded him that Richard was supposed to call him later with some new information he had been able to squeeze out of the Iceberg. Something had to be done.

He realized the door was still open and closed it. He leaned back in the comfortable seat and sighed. Well, at least something of the day could be salvaged. He was supposed to show the script to the girl he had met at his father's party and had an appointment with in half an hour—in her apartment.

Carrie Pressman was her name. He looked at his notebook. An apartment on Franklin Boulevard in Los Feliz. He drove down a clogged Sunset Boulevard, his frustration tempered by the memory of her athletic body. The girl was probably a dancer before she became an actress, he guessed. Those legs . . ."

Exactly twenty-eight minutes later he pulled up in front of the green two-story apartment building. He parked on the street and walked through the fern-choked entrance, pushing the bell for "Pressman 6."

"Yes," the speaker said.

"Orson Cort."

The buzzer sounded and he opened the metal gate and walked in. There was a pile of old newspapers in the lobby, a dying plant in a pot, and peeling green paint on walls that had once been painted yellow.

The apartment was downstairs near the back of the building. The door opened before he could ring the bell.

"Hi!" Carrie said, a bright smile on her face. She really was attractive, he noted, with strong, jutting cheekbones and thick dark eyebrows above watchful brown eyes.

"Hi! The script," he said unnecessarily, hefting it in his hand.

He followed her in. She wore Reebok hightops and tight blue jeans. He couldn't help watching her legs and the way her ass moved. Very nice.

Carrie Pressman couldn't have been doing too well. The living room was sparsely furnished with stuff she had picked up at garage sales. It was obviously a cheap apartment—one bedroom, a dining nook beside the kitchen—and, like the rest of the building, it needed paint. There were some nice prints on the wall to add color, but it was a sadly heroic attempt.

He sat on the couch and she asked if he wanted coffee. "Or I could probably rustle us up a beer?" she suggested.

"A beer would be great," he said, thinking it was more intimate than coffee.

She came back a moment later with two bottles and glasses, put his on the table in front of him, and sat on the couch, swinging her legs up and tucking her feet in below her.

"How's the movie coming along?"

"Great! Really fantastic. We should be casting soon," he said. "Within a month or two, the way it looks right now."

"And the part you thought of for me?" she asked, looking at the script on the couch between them.

"A woman, tough on the outside, yet soft inside. The character's name is Cassandra. It's not a lead, but a good, meaty part."

"It sounds great," she said.

He tapped the script and looked at her sincerely. "I think you're right for it. I've seen your work and you have those qualities. I've always admired that in you."

He was thinking that maybe she hadn't been a dancer. She wore a loose pink T-shirt and no bra, showing that there was some heft to her breasts. Most dancers he had met were pretty flat.

"Really?" she said. "I'm looking forward to reading it."

"I think you'll like it." He wondered how to make a move on her. She was being friendly, but there wasn't much of anything else going on.

"I enjoyed the party the other night," she said.

"Yeah, Miles throws a good one."

Her eyes lighted with fresh interest. "He's an amazing man. I admired him when I was a kid, and still do. What was it like growing up with a father like that?" She put her arm on the back of the couch and leaned a little closer to him.

God, it works every time, Orson thought with a childlike wonder. The goddamn Miles Cort aphrodisiac. He'd used it since he could get a hard-on and it still worked. The power his father had in this town turned women on. In fact, Miles turned women on. Through some strange contagion, he was the beneficiary.

"I'll tell you all about it," he said with a slow smile. "But first give me your foot."

She looked at him in puzzlement, but slowly untangled one long leg and stretched it toward him. He took her by the ankle and firmly planted her foot in his lap. Then he began to untie her shoelace.

"What are you doing?" she asked with a small chuckle.

"I'm either making us comfortable or I've got a thing for your feet. Which do you like?" he asked, untying the shoe. He pulled it off, followed by the sock.

"They both sound interesting," she said.

He ran his hand over her foot. Her toenails were painted red.

She shifted slightly and moved her other leg over to him. He took the shoe and sock off.

"Are you going to rub my feet?" she asked. She had slipped back from a sliding position so that she rested on one arm. Now she let it collapse and lay back on the length of the couch.

"I'll rub yours if you rub mine," he said, thinking that hell, yes, he was going to rub her feet. It was the greatest turn-on in the world. Then he'd rub the rest of her.

Lazily, her eyes half closed as she watched him, she twisted her right leg and rubbed her toes against his crotch, trying to find the outline of his already hard penis.

He looked down at her, at the hard nipples pressing against the T-shirt, at the tight jeans pressing against the slit of her crotch. She unbuttoned the top of her jeans and unzipped them and he saw the flat brown stomach and silky blue panties.

"Yeah," he said, moving her feet and diving forward. He kissed the warm skin of her stomach and pulled the jeans down over her hips. Then he tore at the panties with his mouth, wetting them, trying to push his tongue through the silk while she pushed her hips up at him and draped one leg over his shoulder.

"Oh, God, yeah," she said. "I suppose—I suppose—I'll read the script later."

And then he tore the panties away and buried his face in the wiry, thick black hair, his mouth searching voraciously for the spot, while she groaned and beat her hands against the cushions of the couch in some rhythm he did not share.

Shannon watched Melissa get her dialysis treatment. Melissa was still excited about the party and was telling the nurse who she had met there, "Everybody was really nice, you know. It wasn't like they were acting like stars or anything. It was really cool," she said.

The nurse was a good choice. She was understanding and communicative, never talking down to Melissa, but treating her as an equal in some ways.

Shannon leaned against the door and half listened, her mind returning to the first time she had seen Melissa get dialysis.

The nurse in New York had been named Linda. Shannon and Dr. Feinstein had watched her take Melissa over to one of the machines and explain what it did.

It had looked like any other machine with dials and knobs and lights, except for the tubes that snaked from it and led into the arm of the small boy on the bed. One tube contained a clear liquid, the other was bright red. Shannon remembered feeling a slight queasiness when she first realized it was blood.

Linda took Melissa's hand and led her across the room. "This is your machine," she said. "And this is your special bed."

During the next half hour, while Shannon watched from a short distance away, Linda explained the dialysis procedure to Melissa. Part of the process involved giving Melissa a doll and some needles and having her inject the unfeeling object with them. It was a wonderful way to

161

familiarize her with the procedure, but Shannon couldn't help but shudder when she saw the dialysis needles. "Horse needles," she thought when she saw how big they were. They were the same size as those used for blood donors, and obviously they would hurt.

When the moment came for the treatment to begin, Linda asked Shannon to hold Melissa's right hand.

She felt the small hand tremble in hers, saw Melissa's eyes grow larger.

"Now, I'm going to give you two small shots of Novocaine to deaden the area so you won't feel the big needles," Linda explained. "They'll just prick a little."

Melissa's hand stiffened while the nurse did her job with cool efficiency.

"Now the other needles." The nurse inserted one, moved it slightly to find the fistula, and then pushed it all the way in. "Very good. You did well," Linda said with a quick grin. "Now we put tape around the needles to hold them there, and that's it. All over."

In a few minutes the pump was doing its job, filling the tube and dialyzer with crimson blood. Melissa's blood! Shannon had realized with horror then that both of them would have to put up with this procedure three times a week until a kidney was found. She had known this before, of course, but at that moment the realization had carried an aura of reality almost crushing with its impact. It had left her with a mixture of anger and desperation and, above all, a sense of helplessness.

She didn't feel much better now, months later, as she watched Melissa's blood move in its well-traveled circle. The procedure still bothered her; she still felt queasy at the sight of her daughter's blood; and she knew how her daughter still hated it.

The telephone rang. She backed out of the doorway and took the call in the office.

"Hi, this is Stephen."

"Stephen?" she said dumbly, her mind still filled with Melissa's ordeal.

"Yes?"

"Oh, Stephen, hi," she said. "I'm sorry, my mind was somewhere else. How are you?"

"I wondered if you'd like to get together tomorrow?" he asked. "I could pick you up, show you where I work. You could hear some of my music."

"Tomorrow?"

"Whenever it suits you."

She suddenly remembered the attraction she had felt for him at the party. It rushed back and flustered her.

"Uh . . ." she said.

"You could interview me for your book," he said.

"Yes, yes, that would be fine. Would the morning be okay for you?"

"As long as it's not too early," he said. "I am a musician, you know. Late to bed, late to rise? How about eleven?"

"Fine," she said.

"I'll pick you up. See you then."

"Yes, see you then."

She hung up the telephone and shook her head as if to clear it. There was so much happening to her, so many changes, so many potentials. There were odd times like this when it all seemed too much. At this moment Stephen seemed too much, an added complication she did not need in an already overly complicated world.

"Damn," she said.

The man stood just inside the doorway of the empty room and looked nervously around. There were gleaming full-length mirrors on two of the walls and another on the ceiling. From its center hung a long chain. In the middle of the room was an eight-foot-long table with a red-and-black X across its center. He stepped forward to look at the leather handcuffs and chains dangling from its sides.

He gave a start as the door opened behind him. A tall woman with blond hair hanging halfway down her back entered.

"Uh, hi," he said.

She stopped two feet away and looked at him coldly with expressionless blue eyes. Her mouth was a tight line. She wore tight spandex pants, high stiletto-heeled shoes and a leather jacket. Her skin was pale, except for her lips which were crimson. She carried a leather riding crop in her right hand.

"I am Mistress Victoria," she said finally. The disdain in her voice told him she didn't care who he was. She tapped the riding crop against the palm of her left hand. "You will not speak unless I ask you a direct question or tell you to. Is that understood?"

"Yes," the man said. He was about fifty, well-groomed but overweight by twenty pounds. His face was flushed, and below the sagging cheeks were the beginnings of a double chin.

"Yes, Mistress," she corrected softly.

"Yes, Mistress."

"You have been a bad boy, I understand."

"Yes, Mistress."

"And you have come to me because you need discipline?"

"Yes, Mistress."

"Remove your clothes."

"Yes, Mistress."

He bent to take off his shoes and socks, then removed his jacket and shirt. Finally, he took off his pants, until he stood there in his underpants. He began to pull them down, but she stopped him with a wave of her suddenly wandlike whip.

"No. Leave those on," she said.

He waited apprehensively. Delicately, she lifted the riding crop and rested the tip on his shoulder. Then she ran it down his chest, circling one of his nipples. His skin rose in goosebumps as the crop continued across his stomach and to his groin, which she again circled.

"You have been very bad," she said. "Get on the table."

He hesitated. "What are you going to do?"

Quickly she lifted the crop and slashed it against his thigh. "You will not ask questions. You will do as you are told," she snapped.

"Yes, Mistress," he said, and went to the table. He clambered on it and looked at her questioningly from an all-fours position.

"On your back," she said.

He did as he was told and quickly she stepped forward and tied one of the leather handcuffs around his left wrist. Then she moved around and did the same on his right side. She lifted her crop and rested it on his chest. She looked down at him, her eyes merciless.

"Now you are mine," she said, her red lips parting into a thin smile. Her eyes judged him. "How should I make you suffer, I wonder?

He looked up at her, not knowing what to say.

"Tell me how bad you've been," Mistress Victoria said harshly. "And then beg me to punish you. Beg me."

Elizabeth Cort turned away from the one-way mirror through which she had been watching the scene. Mistress Victoria, whose real name was Paula Sherman, would take good care of the new customer. She was one of her best girls—one of the few she had personally trained—and had been with her for almost three years now.

Elizabeth walked down the corridor, stopping briefly to peer into another room. The two girls had the man naked on all fours. A tea set sat on his back and the girls chatted politely with each other while serving the drink, allowing just a few drops of the hot liquid to spill onto his back.

This client, a major television executive by day, was being a table. At times, he also enjoyed being sat on as a chair.

She continued into her office in the rear of the building, a renovated warehouse in North Hollywood. She had moved in three years earlier, calling her bondage parlor The Power Exchange, and advertising strictly through word of mouth. From humble beginnings, starting with one girl and herself, she had been built the business up to where she now ran two shifts, each with four girls. The business currently grossed about fifty thousand dollars a month, half of which was profit.

She sat down and turned on the desk lamp. There were books to be balanced, checks to be written, jobs she did herself.

She ran the business like a martinet, carefully screening the girls before hiring them. The game at The Power Exchange was bondage and domination, with absolutely no sex allowed between the girls and customers. In the past, when she had discovered girls working customers on the side with private arrangements, she had fired them immediately. No matter what their stated intentions were, men were there simply to be degraded, and that was the service she provided. A couple of the girls were "switches" who could move from the dominant to submissive role, but that was generally more trouble than it was worth. Dominant male customers were difficult to control, and once one of her girls had been almost killed by a man in a whipping frenzy. Now she provided the service only to trusted older customers.

She seldom serviced clients herself anymore; somehow, the pleasure of it had worn off. Although only a few weeks earlier she had demonstrated for her girls how to do a nipple piercing, a procedure whereby needles were inserted through the victim's nipples. Generally, however, she stayed away from serious sadomasochism. Too many accidents could happen.

Her clients included leading corporate figures, executives in both the film and television industries, at least three judges, and a number of the Los Angeles Police Department's finest. With very few exceptions, they knew her only as Mistress Daphne. If any of them recognized her as Elizabeth Cort, daughter of Miles Cort, they were not in any position to remark upon it.

Elizabeth had discovered the world of bondage and domination shortly after marrying Ellis Brown some four years earlier. Ellis, the heir to a banking dynasty, was immensely wealthy, handsome, and seemingly powerful. All he lacked, she soon learned, was virility. Ellis liked to be spanked before they could have sex. Then he would call her "Mamma" and partake of the act, as long as she made all the moves.

After they had been married three months, she also discovered where he spent the evenings he said he was working. He was, the detective she hired told her, a lifetime member of a Mafia-run bondage parlor ominously called The Chair and the Chain.

There, behind the walls of a gated mansion, high in the Hollywood Hills, serious S&M was practiced, followed by equally serious sex. It was rumored that a number of murders had occurred behind the barred windows and that a snuff movie in which the participants were killed during the act, had been filmed there.

Undaunted, Elizabeth applied for a job there, and after a short training period, she serviced her husband one night. Wearing black leather boots that reached her thighs and a satin mask, she abused her husband mercilessly, hanging him from the ceiling by chains and whipping him with an English riding whip until he bled. Then she removed her mask.

Ellis was first shocked, then abjectly grateful. He now had, he considered, a marriage made in heaven: a wife who was willing to truly punish him. Elizabeth did not agree. She filed for divorce the next day.

When the dust settled a couple of months later and she

discovered that Ellis's money was tied up in trusts, giving her only a nominal alimony settlement, she took stock of her life. She had no desire to suffer the indignity of living off her father's wealth, but neither did she have any marketable skills. The B.A. in English literature from the University of Oregon did not provide her with unlimited employment or income potential. And then she realized, after some introspection, that the night she had beaten her husband had been one of the most sexually exciting experiences she had ever had.

It had been, above all, liberating. She was no longer Elizabeth Cort. She was someone else, someone powerful, dominant, a person who had control. It was strange thought. Afterward she hardly remembered anything of what had actually happened, only the sensation of power.

She went to work part-time for The Chair and The Chain. The same transformation seemed to happen each time. The whole experience was like a distant dream. All that was vivid was the sensation of power. It was a heady freedom.

When she had completely mastered her craft almost a year later, she decided to open her own parlor.

She went to Ellis for financing.

Ellis, who had limited personal finances but did have access to money for "investments," was only too happy to oblige. All he wanted was a lifetime membership. While the marriage might not have been made in heaven, the partnership was—for a time. A year later, she paid him back the fifty thousand he had given her and canceled his lifetime membership. He threatened to tell her father about her business, but the blustering ended as soon as she showed him the collection of photographs she had gathered in the previous months: Ellis chained to the wall; Ellis crawling naked on the floor with a mistress riding his back. Ellis exited her life, muttering to himself about the treachery of women.

Since then, she had made almost a million dollars. Some

intelligent investments in property had given her a net worth to date of almost two million dollars. Just one more year of this, she figured, and she wouldn't have to worry about money for the rest of her life.

The alarm beneath her desk buzzed, disturbing her thoughts. A new client had entered the waiting area. It was her job to screen him, a procedure she entrusted to nobody else. On very rare occasions, just to keep her hand in, she also gave new clients their first initiation.

Perhaps tonight would be such an occasion, she thought with pleasure as she walked down the hall. Watching Victoria had stimulated her.

CHAPTER TEN

"These children of mine are all obsessed by money, they don't understand that money's nothing. You can't even wipe your ass with it. Money is just a symbol for production. It's what you do that counts. None of them have done anything worth a shit," Miles said.

"I've always noticed that it's only immensely rich people who seem to despise money," Shannon said.

"Huh," Miles grunted.

Richard knew there was something he was supposed to remember, but was damned if he could. The blaring rock music didn't help him concentrate, not to mention his friend Darrel's cackle as he danced bare-chested with three shrieking girls in the middle of the living room.

They had partied for about eighteen hours now. Starting the night before with a club-crawl, they had picked up a crowd of twenty and ended up at Darrel's place in Pacific Palisades at about four in the morning. It was now about one in the afternoon and only the dregs were left. He and Darrel and three insatiable girls—only one of whom they had known before the night began.

Who the hell were they? God, he'd been so stoned: booze and coke and pills, and now his nerves were frazzled and he needed some kind of downer to ease him through it. This was the time he hated, when there was nothing that would lift him out of himself anymore. Oh yeah, Annie was the girl they'd known. A frizzy-haired model with a body like a beanstalk. Little bumpy tits and long, thin legs.

He was lying on the couch, trying his best to ignore the commotion around him. It was impossible. The girls were bare-chested, too, wearing only panties. Shit, come to think of it, he was only wearing his underpants.

He peered more intently at the movement in the center of the room. Darrel had his arms around two girls while one danced in front of them. The big blonde with the big tits. Who was she? Vannessa. Worked for a record company. She'd pushed her big brown nipples into his mouth at some stage. Tried to choke him with her tits, he remembered. There was Annie, and then the plump black girl who worked for a PR agency. Had he fucked all three of them? Probably. It didn't matter.

Vannessa saw him watching and bounced over, a big grin on her face. Grasping her breasts with both hands she fell on top of him and rubbed them against his dick.

"Tit-fuck, tit-fuck," she squealed, and laughed.

"Fuck off," Richard said. She must have been about eighteen, maybe a year older. Not just feeling her oats, but sowing, reaping, and harvesting them.

"Oh, baby, don't be a drag now." She sat up and pouted at him. Then, completely unself-consciously, she kneaded his dick with one hand. "Do you want some head? Remember how I give head? Has anyone ever given you better head? Come on, be honest. Have you ever had your cock sucked like that before?"

"Not now," Richard said, halfheartedly pushing her away.

Shit! Orson! That was it! He was supposed to meet Orson and tell him what he'd found out. Where? Had they talked earlier? Oh, yeah, he'd called Orson yesterday and set up a meeting for today. When? Christ, had he missed it? No, it was for four o'clock. He had time to try to get himself half alive and get there.

The music had stopped. Darrel was kissing Annie in the center of the room. He had a raging hard-on that threatened to burst through his underpants. The other girl was behind him, pressing herself against his back, her hand snaking around and finding his cock.

Vannessa had noticed, too. She turned back to him and smiled, cupping her hands below her breasts. "Come on, Richie, say you like them. Be nice. Say hello to my lonely tits."

Richard groaned and turned his head into the cushion. He hated being called Richie, he hated this cunt, he hated being here like this.

There was a noise, a shifting on the couch, and then he felt her hand on his face, her wet fingers on his lips.

"Come on, Richie, suck them, baby. See if this turns you on," she said.

What the hell? Slowly he opened his mouth and she slipped her fingers in. Gently he sucked them and closed his eyes. For a moment the raging in his head died down, leaving a sense of peace. It reminded him of something a long time ago.

By the time Richard arrived at the bar of the Hamburger Hamlet on Hollywood Boulevard, Orson was already on his second bottle of beer. Richard was only twenty minutes late—a miracle considering his condition, he thought.

"Glad you could make it," Orson said.

Richard suppressed a groan and almost fell into the booth.

"Well, you look like shit as usual," Orson said.

"Why don't you order me a drink instead of being an asshole," Richard said.

172

Orson smiled at his brother's obvious misery and signaled the waiter. "What do you want?"

"Double Scotch, rocks. No, wait, make that a triple."

Orson gave the waiter the order and stared at his brother. Richard's bloodshot eyes looked as if they were going to fall out of his face.

"Don't you ever get sick of partying?" Orson asked.

"What else is there to do?"

The waiter brought the drink and Richard's hand trembled as he lifted it. He drank almost half of it in one gulp. He coughed and some color seeped into his face.

"So what did you find out?" Orson asked.

"Like I said, it's charitable foundations. Lynn says, though, that not all of it is going to them. Something like a hundred ninety-five million goes to the foundations. There's five million or something set aside."

"For what?"

"She doesn't know. Hasn't been able to see the paperwork on it."

"Well, Jesus, what use is that?" Orson scowled.

"Hey, if you don't like it, do your own spy work."

Orson gripped his beer bottle angrily. "How can he do this to us? He's giving our money away. Our money!"

"Maybe the five's for us?" Richard suggested optimistically.

"Shit! Why would he do that? He's going to cut us out completely. I know it."

"So what can we do?" Richard asked blearily. He wasn't really interested. The future was too far away for him to worry about. He was too involved in the immediate pain of the present.

"Has this all been done, or is it still in the paperwork stage?"

"She says it's very complicated. Lawyers. It's going to take a few weeks more, maybe longer, for him to set it all up. Could even be a couple of months, I guess."

"Then we have some time," Orson said.

"To do what?" Richard smiled. "You going to go to the old man and tell him we really love him and it's time for him to become a nice guy?"

"I don't know, but I'll think of something," Orson said. "Maybe we should have a family meeting. Let the others know. See what they all come up with. Maybe we could all approach Miles together."

"Oh, yeah, good idea. The others will be a lot of help," Richard said sarcastically. "And Miles would be just thrilled for us all to beg him to change his mind. The last time the fuck changed his mind about anything it snowed in L.A."

"So what the hell do you suggest?" Orson said peevishly.

"Beats me. We could steal some of the paintings. Sell them. Some of them are worth a fortune. There's millions of dollars right there."

Orson looked at his brother incredulously. "Is that the best you can come up with? You know what the security is like. And what the fuck do you know about selling stolen art? Jesus!"

Richard looked uncomfortable. "Well, do better. Let me know when you come up with something."

"Well, obviously five heads are going to be better than one, particularly when the one is yours," Orson said disgruntedly.

Richard ignored the insult. He drank the rest of his Scotch with another long gulp and sighed. "God, I needed that."

Orson looked at his brother with disgust. There was nothing more Richard could do to help. He was mentally impotent, drugged out and besotted. As usual, it would be up to him. He threw some money on the table and stood.

"Let me know if you hear anything else," he said.

"Sure," Richard said. He signaled the waiter for another drink and watched his brother leave. Asshole. He'd always been that way and always would be.

God, he was tired. He wished he could just sleep and sleep and not think about anything. He hadn't slept for days, except for the odd hour here and there. He wasn't able to, no matter how much he tried.

His mind was filled with demons and wouldn't let him. Every time he lay down they raced around the inside of his skull, chattering to each other like stoned monkeys.

He'd give anything to be able to sleep.

Each morning Miles swam the length of the pool ten times. Although his legs were no longer subject to his will, his arms were strong enough to pull him back and forth from one Olympian end to the other. It was probably the only true taste of physical freedom available to him now, those moments in the water when he was able to defy gravity and ignore the refusal of his stubborn lower half to respond.

Melissa swam with him, although she wisely stayed in the shallow end. Shannon watched them both from the shadows of the patio. Miles finished his regime and sat on the steps near Melissa shouting instructions: "Straighten your arms." "Curve your hands more." "There you go."

From the waist up he was a splendid physical specimen for his age, Shannon noted. His barrel chest was covered with thick black hair, and his arms and shoulders were muscular. Below the waist, however, his legs were thin and the muscle toneless.

She had observed his daily habit for a number of mornings and she always noted how he quickly covered his legs once he left the pool. It was if he wanted to hide evidence of his nemesis: those legs. The blood clot that had betrayed him had dissolved, but the legs were still there, proof of his weakness.

"Can you dive?" Miles asked Melissa.

"No, I haven't learned how yet," Melissa said. "But I can swim underwater. Watch."

She scrunched up her face, closed her eyes, and dipped her head underwater and swam two strokes before rising with splutters and gasps.

"That's pretty good," Miles said encouragingly. "Can you jump off the side?"

"Sure," Melissa said, climbing up the steps and standing on the side of the pool. She held her nose with her fingers and then jumped straight down into the shallow water, disappearing beneath the surface. She came up coughing.

"Not bad," Miles said, "but what you have to learn how to do is go in headfirst. That way, you travel underneath the water, and that's what a dive is."

Melissa looked at him and said, "Why would I want to do that?"

"Because it's what everyone does," Miles said. "It's fun."

"Lynn came out of the house and stood beside Shannon. "Is he done yet?"

"I think so," Shannon replied. "He's talking to Melissa." She paused and said, "You do everything for him, don't you? Secretary, nurse, you wear a lot of different hats."

"I do what needs to be done," Lynn said. "Mr. Cort is a very demanding man as you've no doubt noticed."

Lynn walked past Shannon and out to the pool. She stopped halfway down the length of it and said, "Are you ready?"

Miles looked up at her. "In a few minutes. I'm talking to my friend Melissa here."

Lynn waited patiently while Miles continued to coach Melissa in the finer points of swimming, a subject in which she had little interest. Melissa was gracious enough, however, to listen attentively.

Shannon's thoughts went back to the bizarre conversation she had had with him about his prospective murder. "Which one of your children do you think is capable of killing you?" she had asked.

Miles had given his familiar snort and replied, "None of them have the guts."

"But which one might have?" she asked.

"The only one mean enough to consider it is Orson," Miles said. "Richard is too weak, Stephen is too gentle, Elizabeth is too frightened, and Anne is too stupid. If it's one of them, it must be Orson."

"I wouldn't think that Orson would have the courage," Shannon said uncertainly.

"Desperation can sometimes dredge up courage, or at least submerge the fear. I've known desperate men do some extraordinary things," Miles said.

She had told him she wasn't willing to spy for him. "That's not what you hired me to do. You hired me to write a book and that's what I'm here for."

But Miles had brushed her protestations aside. "I'm not asking you to spy, I'm just asking you to listen and let me know if you hear anything that could help me find out who is trying to kill me."

It was amazingly crass of her she knew. Even as she thought it, she was ashamed. But the thought, unbidden, had simply appeared: What a book it would be if she could include the details of the murder plot against Miles Cort by one of his own offspring. Unconscionable, but then so was most journalism. She couldn't help thinking that way. She'd been well trained to place the story above everything else.

"Listen," Miles had said, "my security people are the best in the business and they've found out nothing. They've checked out everyone and come up dry. None of the family trusts them. They all know that these men work for me. They all know who Corydon is. But you're here to write a biography. Everyone likes to tell their story. Probably they will trust you, but even if they don't, hu-

177

man nature being what it is, the arrogance we all have will allow them to tell you things that they would tell nobody else."

"Is that why I'm here?" Shannon asked coldly.

Miles smiled just as coldly back at her. "I want this biography written, I have things I want told and I have scores to settle. But I must admit that the thought did occur to me that there were waters you could stir up that nobody else could."

"I'm not willing to do this for you," Shannon said.

"If you come across information of a criminal nature, all I want is for you to let me know," Miles said patiently.

Shannon shook her head. "A journalist has a responsibility to her sources."

Miles examined her for a moment and then said, "Aren't you curious? Doesn't it pique your curiosity? Wouldn't you like to know which one of my children is trying to kill me? Don't you think it would improve the story you are writing?"

Shannon looked at him angrily. It was almost as if he had been reading her mind. Yes, she was curious. Yes, it would improve her story. Yes, yes, yes. "I'll pay attention and keep my ears open," she said. "That's all I promise. If I learn of something, if I get information that could affect your safety I will do whatever is appropriate with it. That's all I promise."

Miles nodded. "Then that will have to satisfy me."

Standing on the patio, watching Miles ruffle her daughter's hair, Shannon's suspicions rose again. The attempt on Miles's life had occurred sometime before she was hired to do the biography. Was that the real reason she was here? Had Miles simply hired her to stir the pot, to shake the trees and see what would fall out? Was the biography simply a cover? Something he had devised because his own investigations had reached a dead end? She didn't know the answers. She only know that she was being paid well to write a book. She was being treated like a queen and her daughter like a princess. Why should she question his motivations further?

They were disturbing thoughts, not because of Miles's machinations, but because of the selfishness of her own motivations. They would get her nowhere, only leave her swimming in a sea of doubt. She didn't have time for that.

She stepped from the patio and walked toward the trio at the end of the pool. "Melissa," she said as she approached, "you've got to get out now. Mrs. Dalquist is coming to give you your lessons in a few minutes."

"Oh, Mom," Melissa said.

"Hey, we've got a deal," Shannon said. "All play and no work makes a dumb girl."

"Let the kid enjoy herself," Miles said.

Shannon came closer and stopped at the edge of the pool. "Come on, Melissa, it's time to get out now," she said. She looked over at Miles. "My child, Mr. Cort. You take care of yours and I'll take care of mine."

Miles gave his familiar grunt but said nothing more. "You've got to get ready for your lesson," Shannon said as they walked back to the cottage. "I'm going out for a while."

"Where are you going?" Melissa asked.

"Stephen is picking me up and taking me to his studio," Shannon said. "I'm going to interview him."

"Can't I come?" Melissa asked.

"Not today. You've got your lessons."

"But I like him," Melissa said.

"I like him, too, Shannon thought. I like him more than any man I've met for a long, long time. And this is my day with him.

"You'll have another chance to see him," she said.

Stephen lived in a loft in a factory in downtown Los Angeles, on the borders of Little Tokyo. Ten to fifteen years earlier a small artistic and poverty-stricken colony had discovered abandoned warehouses in an economically distraught downtown Los Angeles and rented entire floors for a pittance. Since then, the location and ambience had become fashionable, the downtown area had redeveloped on a vast scale, and what had once rented for two hundred dollars a month now rented for a thousand and up. Considering that the spaces were little more than huge, barren rooms with concrete floors and, in some cases, the simple and inexpensive addition of a bathroom, certain landlords were making a bundle.

"I got in while it was still cheap," Stephen explained. They were traveling up the freight elevator. A bulky, noisy machine, it did not instill confidence that it would reach its destination. "I signed a ten-year lease before the idea became popular. I've been able to put the money I would have paid in rent into improving the place."

It was wonderful, Shannon had to admit. Huge, light-filled windows, a vast high-ceiling space, layered with thick carpet and furnished with a variety of styles that defied categorization. Enormous paintings illuminated whitewashed walls. The kitchen was as modern as anything she had ever seen, with a double sink, garbage disposal, counter space to spare, a double-doored refrigerator, and a sophisticated gas stove. The entire sense of the place was one of aesthetic comfort.

"It's beautiful," she said, standing in the center of what she assumed was the living rom.

"Thank you." Stephen beamed at her approval. He had picked her up at the house and driven her directly here. Dressed casually in blue jeans and tennis shoes and a soft, long-sleeved wool shirt, he looked as charming as anyone she had ever seen.

"You must have sunk a fortune into this place," she said.

Stephen shrugged. "I suppose I have, but I've been here for almost seven years and I've improved it over a period of time. I think it's finally become my home in the last year. I finally was able to make it into what I wanted it to be."

The living room was furnished with blonde rattan chairs and sofas and colorful cushions. A stereo system covered one entire wall with two enormous speakers at each end. Large, framed black-and-white photographs, mainly character studies, hung on one wall, while on the other side of the room was a series of colorful modern prints.

"Come on, let me show you my pride and joy," Stephen said, leading the way down the hall to another large room. He opened the door and ushered her in, flicking the light switch on.

There were no windows in this room. In fact, there was very little space even though it was a large room. Rack after rack of electronic equipment, including tape recorders, equalizers, control boards, microphones, and a lot she didn't recognize filled the room. There was enough space for two people to sit in front of the console, and perhaps another three to stand.

"This is my studio," he said with justifiable pride.

"You record here?"

"Yeah, I compose and record here. I'm doing a lot of work with synthesizers at the moment." He waved his hand at an imposing group of electronic instruments.

He flicked a switch and suddenly the room was filled with sound. "Sit down," he said, pointing at a chair.

She sat while the music, different from anything she had ever heard, swooped and fluttered and dove and shrieked through the air around her. It was a curious fusion of jazz, what she assumed to be ancient tribal rhythms and something far more ethereal. Music of the spheres was the phrase that came to mind, as she listened. It was a music one could imagine being performed in deep space with stars at elbow and foot and fiery comets and exploding suns and beaming moons.

She closed her eyes and felt the music vibrate her body.

When she opened them an indeterminate time later she found Stephen was staring quizzically at her. He flicked a switch again and suddenly silence filled the room.

"What do you think?"

"I think it's beautiful. I think those are beautiful sounds," she said.

He nodded, pleased with her answer. "It's something new. Something I'm working on." He shrugged. "It's so new I can't even judge it anymore.

"It's beautiful," she repeated. She looked around the room again, music still reverberating in her mind.

Stephen leaned against a desk. "If I'm a pauper it's because everything I own is in this room."

"This equipment must be incredibly expensive."

"There is probably a few hundred thousand dollars worth of equipment here," he said. "A lot of it I've bought secondhand, scrimping and saving through the years to create this. It's what I've always wanted to do."

"But you play music as well, don't you?" she asked. "I mean live?"

"Yeah, I play bass guitar and keyboards and a few other instruments and I sit in with groups around town, but this is what I really enjoy, sitting here alone and creating these sounds."

"Do you record?" she asked. "I mean, like for a company?"

"I've just signed a contract with Warners," he said. "That's who this music you've just heard is for."

"Well, maybe you'll make your investment back," she said.

Stephen smiled. "First albums don't make much money, I'm afraid. And I'm not exactly on the commercial cutting edge. But that's okay. I don't do music for money. I do it for adventure."

He tipped his head questioningly. "Do you want a cup of tea?"

"I'd love one," she said, getting up from the chair.

They went back to the kitchen and he put water on the stove asking her what kind of tea she wanted. She chose an herbal tea, and a few minutes later they returned to the living room and she sat on the comfortable rattan couch while he parked on an armchair opposite her. She opened her bag and took out her tape recorder and put it on the table in front of her.

"Ah, yes," he said, eyeing it cautiously. "You are here to work, aren't you?"

"I wanted to talk to you, yes," she said. "I wanted to ask some questions about your childhood."

"Go right ahead."

"What's your earliest memory of Miles?" she asked. She turned on the tape recorder and said, "Do you mind?"

He looked at the recorder and said, "That's fine. I remember as a child, very young, maybe a couple of years old, this looming dark figure, who blew in and out of the house, in and out of our lives. Nothing in particular, really."

"Well, let's look at an incident. What's the first incident you remember with him that sticks in your mind?"

"I remember being about four or five and sitting at the dining-room table. I hated green beans and there was a pile of them on my plate. Miles told me to finish them, but I refused. I remember he put both hands on the table and stood and bellowed down at me, 'You stay there until you finish your beans. I don't care if it takes all night.' I don't know how long I sat there . . . I guess as kids we have a different conception of time. But it seemed to me that it was at least four or five hours. I sat there with the beans in front of me, staring at them, hoping with the intensity of my gaze to make them disappear like some magic trick. But they didn't. They just sat there waiting to be eaten. Every hour or so he'd come back into the dining room and stand in the doorway, his hands on his hips, and look at me without speaking. Then he'd turn on his heels and leave. It seemed to go on forever." He lapsed into silence.

"So what finally happened?"

"My mother came in and stood beside me, also looking down at the beans. I was determined not to cry, I remember that. She asked if I was going to eat them, and I said no. And so with one hand, very quickly she scooped the beans off the plate and left the room carrying them. About half an hour later when my father came back and stood in the doorway, he looked at the empty plate, nodded once and said good night."

"You defied him a lot?" Shannon asked.

"In my own way. Not always in a courageous fashion. It was more a kind of civil disobedience," Stephen said. "Earlier I found that confrontation wasn't a workable system. When he told me to do things I didn't want to do, I'd simply agree and then not do them. Generally he'd forget."

"And when he didn't?"

Stephen's mouth grew hard. "He beat us as children. I think he gave me my last beating when I was about fourteen. He used to take us into his study, hit our bodies with his open palms, both arms swinging. The last time he did it, when I was fourteen, he hit me with his fist, right here." Stephen touched the side of his mouth, as if he could still feel the blow.

"What happened?"

"I fell. He was a strong man, I was just a young boy then. But then I got up and told him that if he ever did that to me again I'd kill him. He must have believed me, because he never hit me again."

"The other kids?"

"As far as I know he continued hitting them."

"So he was a disciplinarian?"

"I wouldn't call him that. Discipline is not a bad thing, I've come to realize. But the term disciplinarian seems to me to imply rational discipline with a purpose in mind.

184

His discipline was always arbitrary, and not always under his control. Sometimes his rages would be quite uncontrollable."

"What kind of things did he discipline you and the others for?"

"Whatever struck his fancy. Generally it was for laziness, for not trying hard enough, for not living up to some image he had of what we should be. Generally it was for something completely unimportant in the larger picture of things. Such as not wiping your feet when you enter the house. I saw him once go into a complete rage at Elizabeth for that terrible sin."

"Was he ever a loving father?"

Stephen shook his head. "Not to his sons. He seemed to care for Elizabeth at times and even showed some tenderness occasionally. But she's the second youngest, you know. I think perhaps he mellowed a little with age. He is far more tolerant of Richard than he ever was with either Orson or me."

"Why do you think that is?"

"Well, maybe it isn't tolerance. Maybe he's simply given up on us all and doesn't see the benefit of continuing to fight. I don't know. Interesting. He spoils Richard in spite of the fact that Richard appears to be the greatest wastrel of us all. The man doesn't try to live up to anything and apparently has no goals. Perhaps that's what Miles wanted from all of us."

"What a strange thing to say."

"Perhaps. Anne and Orson, Elizabeth, myself—we all tried. We really tried. But it seemed that the more we tried, the worst we were in his eyes. Our failures were magnified perhaps. And yet sometimes I look at his motives and I think perhaps it was because we were trying."

"You're saying that he wanted you to fail?"

"I told you that I thought my father was an evil man. It's a matter of motivation. He doesn't have to browbeat

Richard into defeat. Richard is already defeated. He poses no danger to Miles."

"But you did?"

"Perhaps we all did. Perhaps simply because we were trying, because we showed aptitude in certain areas that threatened Miles on some level."

Shannon was shocked and showed it. "That's such a—a—a— "

"Callous view?" Stephen asked with a slight smile.

"Yes, it is, but I suppose it may just be a realistic view."

"You know people by their acts. In his years Miles has destroyed in one way or another many people who have crossed him. I think he attempted to destroy us, his children, just as he did his wives."

"Your mother doesn't seem bitter about it."

"Do I? I don't mean to be."

"No. I guess you're not bitter, you just say it with such emphatic certainty."

"I say what I think is true. I don't have any great emotional turmoil connected with it anymore. At least not since I sorted it out in my own mind once I left home and his influence. But only fools don't recognize things for what they are."

"What about your mother?"

"She's not a fool. But she is a very forgiving woman and perhaps she is a fool where Miles is concerned."

"But to call your father evil? I mean, that's such an uncompromising word!"

"Do you know what invisibility is?" Stephen asked. "Nothing is really invisible. Not atoms, not quarks. The only things that are invisible are those things that are not seen because people don't look at them. Evil is like that. Most people don't recognize it, let alone acknowledge its existence, because they are afraid to look at it, to confront it."

Shannon sipped her tea, then put her cup down on the

table. "Why do you have anything to do with Miles if this is the way you feel about him?" she asked.

Stephen was silent for a few seconds. "That's a good question, one I had to ask myself and find an answer for," he said. "There are ways in which you can deal with someone like him. One way is to have nothing whatsoever to do with the person. Another is to keep things on a superficial level. I chose the second alternative. I visit the house occasionally. I speak civilly to Miles, but in the meantime I conduct my life exactly as I wish. I do that because this family's already been damaged severely enough. I don't see any point being served in disappearing from the scene entirely and leaving some kind of chasm where I once was. So I conduct my affairs with Miles and the rest of the family on this superficial level. That was my choice and I am happy with it."

Shannon didn't know what to ask next. She needed to think about what he had just said, to assimilate it. It was alien to her. She reached over and turned the tape recorder off, then leaned back and pretended to concentrate on her tea. Stephen sat silently, patiently.

Her own relationship with her parents hadn't been without difficulty. It was volatile at times, with angry shouting matches, recriminations, guilt, and all the other garbage that families seem to carry around with them like so much extra baggage. And yet she had never doubted the motivations of her parents. No matter how clumsily they acted, no matter what mistakes they made, she knew that her well-being was of major concern to them.

They didn't really know how to conduct themselves. There was no diploma, no high school course on how to be a parent, or how to be a child for that matter. And while their attempts to help her might not have always been in her best interests, once again she never doubted their motives. How strange to grow up in a family where you felt your father was attempting to destroy you. It was a hard concept to grasp.

And yet, Stephen did not seem permanently scarred from it. If anything, he seemed more rational, calm, and analytical than just about anyone she knew. Perhaps it was simply a pose, she thought. What lies under yon shadows? she found herself ludicrously wondering. He seemed so well balanced, so comfortable with himself. Was he real? After living a life like that, how could he be?

"How can you be so calm?" she blurted out. "How can you not resent it? How can you be so analytical about it?"

Stephen's eyes grew hard, his voice steely. "Because I decided I wouldn't let it destroy me. It was my choice. I could either succumb to this assault on who I was or I could create my own life. I decided not to succumb. There is too much I want to do. There is too much in life that thrills and elevates me to become mired in the past."

"I think you are amazing," Shannon said.

Stephen sipped his tea and then put the cup on the table. He smiled and looked at her with that frank open gaze. "And I think you're beautiful."

She felt like a teenager. There! That flutter in the chest, that rush of blood to her face. Stephen carefully put his cup down on the table. "May I kiss you?"

Nobody had ever asked her before. Usually men just did it, sometimes signaling their intentions with body language, sometimes not. Now, all she could do was nod. He came around the coffee table and sat beside her and then leaned forward and kissed her. His lips were both gentle and demanding. She kissed him back hungrily, feeling a sensation which she could only describe to herself as a melting. And, stranger still, although it was a physical action it felt as if somehow it spiritually joined them.

She couldn't remember ever feeling this way before. Somehow it seemed like a form of complete surrender and, for some reason, that thought scared her. She pulled away, her face flushed.

Damned if Stephen didn't read her mind. "It scares you, doesn't it?" he asked.

She didn't answer, just stared at him.

"It scares me, too, believe me. What are we going to do about it?"

Shannon took a deep breath, and said, "We're going to slow down, that's what."

Stephen smiled indulgently. "There are times when caution is a poor substitute for action."

"Don't smile at me like that," she said, "it's patronizing."

"It's not meant to be," he said. "It's just that there's something amusing about this and it's not you that amuses me, but both of us. It's like we're adults reverting to adolescent feelings."

She knew exactly what he meant, but she wasn't willing to deal with it. Instead she looked at her tape recorder on the table. It seemed suddenly her anchor to reality, her reminder of a more prosaic world where she was a "journalist" and he was her "subject." She leaned forward and picked it up and held it in her lap. "I'm not ready for this," she said.

Stephen shook his head. "Who is? But you're probably right. Let's take it a step at a time."

She was relieved, feeling as if she had just escaped something major. "Let's talk some more about your father," she said, mentally squaring her shoulders.

Stephen leaned back, distancing himself from her a little. "As you wish," he said with a nod of his head.

She had to ask this question. She had to, even though it somehow made her feel soiled. She turned the tape recorder on. "As much as you dislike your father, what about his money? Don't you wish you had it? Wouldn't it make life easier for you?

He shook his head. "No, I don't wish I had it. It's his. He earned it. It's not mine. I don't deserve it, nor do I have any right to it. It's his money to do with as he wishes."

"But surely . . ."

"Oh, sure it would make life easier for me. There are things I could do with a million dollars, five million dollars, ten million dollars. But the things I'd want to do with that kind of money have to do with my music and I'm doing them already. It's just taking a little longer than it might if I had unlimited financing. I don't care, I really don't. His money is a trap. His money is what ties people to him. It's not a pothole that I wish to fall into."

"So you just ignore it," she said.

Stephen stretched his long legs out in front of him. "That's all in the past. What about the future?"

"I don't know," Shannon replied.

"Well, I guess we'll find out," he said.

During the drive home down the Hollywood Freeway Shannon stared out the car window at a striking mural that rose like a fountain from dull rooftops. It was a painting of a gray haired old lady.

It was a portrait of someone for whom the future was now, she thought. And yet, wasn't it true for all of us? Why was she backing off? Why did the thought of involvement with Stephen frighten her so? He evoked feelings in her that were so deep and buried she had forgotten their intensity. He was kind and gentle and wise. If she sat down and wrote a list of the qualities she wanted in a man, she could probably describe him and the list would be complete. Why then the fear, the urge to withdraw? She didn't have an answer readily available.

They took the Santa Monica Boulevard exit and headed west toward Beverly Hills. She looked over at his calm profile as he skillfully engineered his way through the traffic. She knew why. It was because it was too good.

It was too good to believe.

The buzzer sounded on Elizabeth's office telephone. She put the pen she was writing with on the desk and picked it up.

"Hello."

"There are two gentlemen here to see you," her receptionist said. "They say it's a private matter."

"Regarding what?"

"Something to do with business, that's all they'll say."

"I'll be there," Elizabeth said, and hung up. Could they be new clients? she wondered. There had been such a rush of new referrals lately, she was thinking of hiring two more girls on each shift. Business was, as they say, booming. The word of mouth was spreading at a pace she hadn't anticipated.

She walked down the hallway, stopping to look through the peephole into the Interrogation Room. One of the girls was dressed up in a Nazi uniform while her victim was tied to a chair being questioned. She knew for a fact that the customer was a policeman and found herself wondering how he treated his own prisoners.

She opened the door and stepped into the reception area. Two men stood there. One, with short-cropped fair hair and blue eyes, wore a three-piece suit. He was looking at the handcuffs, whips, chains, and other devices in the display case above the desk.

The other man was watching the twenty-six-inch video screen on which a German S&M video was playing. He wore a sports coat and did not look as polished as his companion. Short and heavyset, he chewed gum while his eyes listlessly watched the drama unfold on the screen.

"May I help you?" Elizabeth asked. She was dressed in a dark gray business suit this evening. Her hair was tied back and she wore very little makeup.

The younger, suited man stepped forward and said very politely, "Thank you for seeing us." He looked over at the receptionist, Mandy, who was reading the latest Centurion catalogue, and then back at Elizabeth. "Is there somewhere we can talk in private?"

"What is it you want to talk about?" she asked.

"I have a business proposition for you."

191

"I see," she said. "Why don't you come into my office then?"

She led them back to her office. The younger one seemed quite impressed by what he saw during the walk down the long hall. "It's quite an establishment you have here," he said.

She went into the office, sat behind her desk, and indicated that the two men could sit on the couch.

She wondered what they were selling. The well-dressed one looked like an educated salesman, but the other man puzzled her. With his obvious lack of sophistication, he looked like some ex-cops she had known.

"So what is it you want to talk about?" she asked.

The young man adjusted the crease on his pants. "I'm a lawyer, my name is Brian Parker and I represent a company that is interested in buying you out."

"Oh? And who is that?" she asked.

"Until matters proceed further, they wish anonymity."

"I see," she said. "Well, I'm afraid you are wasting your time. I have no intention of selling this business."

He was undisturbed by her reaction and said smoothly, "Don't you even want to hear the terms?"

"No, it would be a waste of your time and mine. I have no intention of selling."

The other man spoke for the first time, his voice roughened by an East Coast street accent. "I think you had better listen to Mr. Parker's offer." His expressionless eyes fixed on her.

Elizabeth felt the first noticeable warning chill. "I think you should tell me who you represent?" she said to the lawyer.

He smiled at her blandly. "Let's just say a competitor. A competitor who is somewhat concerned about the business you are siphoning off from him. Apparently a number of your clients were once his. He feels it would be more beneficial if the two operations were merged into one."

"Beneficial for whom?" Elizabeth said.

Parker did not answer; he merely smiled.

She knew that some of the bigger bondage parlors in town were run by the Mafia. In fact the place where she had first worked, The Chair and The Chain, had Mob connections. This was beginning to sound like a shakedown to her.

"Well," she said, rising from behind her desk, "you can tell whoever sent you that I'm not interested."

The young lawyer stood as well and shook his head regretfully. "I'm very sorry to hear that. It could cause you certain problems."

"Problems such as what?" she asked icily.

The burly older man waved his hand around the room. "We live in a world that is full of accidents waiting to happen. You could become accident prone."

"Is that a threat?" she asked.

The young man took a card from his pocket and held it out to her. "Perhaps you could call me if you change your mind," he said. "Or perhaps you might just want to hear the terms that are being offered."

She ignored the card and he dropped it on her desk. She walked to the door, opened it, and said, "Goodbye, gentlemen."

The young man went out first. The other one stopped at the door and stared at her for a long moment before leaving the room.

She followed them down the hallway and into the reception area. "Please call me if you change your mind," the young man said at the outer door. She didn't bother answering, just watched them walk out.

When she was sure that Mandy had secured the front door, she turned and went back to her office. She sat at her desk and picked up the business card the lawyer had left. Then she reached for her Rolodex, shuffled through it, and dialed a number.

"Schultz," a voice answered.

It was Lieutenant Charlie Schultz who worked downtown at Parker Center, the L.A. Police Department headquarters. A customer for almost two years, he had helped her a couple of times before when she needed to check people out.

"Charlie, this is Elizabeth at The Power Exchange. Can you talk?"

"Hold on." There was a scuffling sound and then he came back on the phone. "Yeah, what can I do for you?"

She held up the card and said, "I got a visit from a Mr. Brian Parker, Attorney-at-Law. He is representing someone who wants to buy me out—a competitor. I didn't like the sound of it or the man who was with him. There was a kind of a threat. A warning of accidents. Do you know anything about this guy?"

"What was the name again?"

She repeated the name and waited.

"Yeah, I've heard of him," Schultz said. "He's a young hotshot Mob lawyer. There's been a bit of movement in this direction also that I know of. Another bondage place out in the Fairfax area got hit a couple of weeks ago. Apparently some gentleman called with an offer to buy. Two days later the place blew up. It was during the day when luckily there were no customers there."

"It was bombed?"

"Yeah. Professional job. Very skillfully done. Flattened the whole fucking place."

"What can I do?" she asked.

A pause. "Sell," he said.

"Isn't there anything you can do to help me?"

"My hands are tied. You are running a border-line operation as it is. You know we can't give you any kind of protection until after the fact."

"What about the organized crime task force?"

"You want an ongoing investigation? Undercover? All that stuff?" he asked.

"No," she said.

"Hire on a couple of guys to keep an eye on things," he suggested.

"You mean private security guards?"

He snorted. "Hell, no, those guys are useless—college kids or retirees. I can give you some names of real security people, if you like. Ex-cops. They won't be cheap, but they'll be good."

"I'd appreciate that," Elizabeth said. The business was expanding so rapidly she could easily afford the extra overhead.

"I'll call you tomorrow with the names."

"All right, thanks," she said, and hung up.

All right, she had taken precautions, but it still was not good enough she told herself as she felt a knot of fear unwind itself in her stomach.

Shannon's interview with Orson was short. She had tried to pin him down twice before and he finally grudgingly agreed to give her some time today at his office. As soon as his secretary showed her in, he looked at his watch and said, "I don't have a lot of time, I've got to take a meeting."

Shannon sat opposite him and withdrew her tape recorder from the briefcase. "I'll just ask you a few questions in the time that you have then," she said. "Let me know when you want to stop."

Orson leaned back in his swivel chair and looked at her antagonistically. "This is a complete waste of time."

"Why is that?" she asked, turning the tape recorder on and looking more closely at his office.

He sat behind a cheap pressboard desk. On the wall behind him were two framed movie posters. The small bookshelf in the corner had a few books in it and a plant sat dejectedly on top of a gray filing cabinet. That did it for decoration.

"Who wants to read a biography about Miles Cort?

There's a new Hollywood now," Orson said, "that has no place for dinosaurs."

"Your father's name is still very much alive through the films he made," she said. "I think there's a vast audience who's interested in the old Hollywood. Particularly now that it seems to be disappearing."

"It's just another big ego trip for Miles. What's he paying you to do this?"

Shannon looked taken aback. "That's a personal matter."

"Yeah, yeah," Orson said with a nod. "Whatever he's paying you, it's money down the toilet."

"I get the impression that you don't get on with your father," Shannon said, trying to slide into the interview.

Orson laughed a short, abrupt bark at that. "Who does get on with him? Name me one person. Getting on with people isn't one of Miles's goals in life."

"Was your relationship with him always like this?"

"Look," Orson said. "Miles was a drag as a father as long as I can remember. When I was a kid he beat me for every imagined infraction. He still beats me in his way."

"I understand he beat all the children," she said.

"Yeah, he liked that."

"What kind of things did you get into trouble for with him? Can you remember a particular time? A particular incident?"

Orson tapped his fingers on the desk impatiently. "I don't know. It was all kinds of things. I'd get in trouble for being late for dinner, for having dirty fingernails, for sleeping in, for coming home late, for dating the wrong girl, for drinking when I got older, for fighting with the other kids. You name it, I got in trouble for it." He paused and looked gloomily down at his desk. "He was always on my case. He was always harder on me than any of them," he said, self-pity evident.

"Why was that?"

"Who the hell knows. Probably because I was the eldest

196

son, the one who was destined to take over the reins when he passed on or decided to let them go. Whatever, he expected more of me. Hell, he'll probably outlive me."

"But wasn't it exciting?" Shannon asked. "I mean, growing up surrounded by all the famous, glamorous people your father knew?"

"I'll tell you how exciting that was," Orson said, with a glare at her. "I remember a time there was a party at the house, Elizabeth Taylor was there with Eddie Fisher, Eva Gabor was there, so was Marlene Dietrich. There were a lot of the famous and glamorous, as you call them, there. Tony Curtis, Peter Lawford, Ava Gardner, Lana Turner, Joan Crawford—I must have been about fourteen at the time, and I had a terrible crush on Marilyn Monroe and goddamn if she wasn't there. It was probably the most exciting night in my life, until my father got through with me.

"At the beginning of evenings like that he'd line all us kids up like some kind of military squad for inspection and introduce us to his guests. Unfortunately we never knew what he'd say about us. This time it seemed he was in a fairly good mood, because he simply introduced each of us without comment."

Orson stopped talking and stared out the small window.

"And then?" Shannon asked.

"Yeah. When it was time to introduce me, he said, 'This is Orson, Orson's doing his best to fail at school. I think it's because he's discovered sex.' He turned to Marilyn and said, 'And I think it's your fault. He's got pictures of you all over his room. He wakes up in the morning looking at you, falls asleep at night looking at you. I think it's all he can think about.' 'How sweet,' she said graciously.

"I thought that I'd get away with that embarrassment, but Miles didn't leave it at that. I was standing there feeling like the biggest idiot in the world. My face must have been the color of a tomato. I just wanted to disappear. But it got worse because then Miles laughed and said,

'Know what I saw the other day when I was walking by his room, where he has this big photograph of you on the wall? I saw him kissing it. Can you believe that? Kissing a photograph of you.' I couldn't stand it anymore. I remember crying then. Turning and running from the room with the laughter behind me, chasing me."

Orson shook his head, as if to dispel the memory. "I still hear it sometimes, that laughter. It still chases me."

There was silence, and then Shannon said, "Do you hate your father?"

Orson who was sitting half slumped in his chair, looked up at her, his face tired. "I wish the son of a bitch would die."

"What's your relationship with your children like?"

"I hardly ever see them. They're with their mothers. And I stay away from those bitches. They only call me when they want money."

They talked for another ten minutes, and then Orson seemed to exhaust his available supply of frankness. His answers grew terse and his attitude with her became brusque. Finally he looked at his watch. "That's all the time I have."

"I'd like to talk to you again," Shannon said as she rose.

"Yeah, well, I'm real busy," Orson said.

"Well, perhaps I can give you a call and set up another appointment."

"Sure," Orson said, "call my secretary," and ushered her out.

Later that afternoon Shannon met with movie director Gary Farley, who had worked on four of Miles's films, a very successful association, as all four were major worldwide hits. Farley lived high in the Hollywood Hills above Sunset Boulevard. His small two-bedroom hillside house sat on what appeared to Shannon to be distinctly frail stilts.

Farley was in his sixties now, a tall man with silver hair

and gleaming teeth. He was a friendly host and offered her tea and cookies. He struck her as a lonely man. One who had passed his prime, who was no longer called by producers, and who had little to do but dwell on past achievements.

He spoke very highly of Miles. "Say what you like about the man's social graces, he had an instinct for films. He had a commercial sense of what audiences wanted to see that few filmmakers have today. And when he committed to a project he was like a bulldog. He never gave up. He just never gave up."

Farley needed no prompting from Shannon. He was happy to sit and sip tea and reminisce.

Farley smiled. "I remember one film we were doing. We had a young actor, a real up-and-comer. He was getting to be hot. But he was an *artiste*, this young man, and he would agonize over every direction I gave him. I'd tell him, 'Now I want you to walk over to that side of the room and look back with a sad expression on your face.' And he'd go into a long dissertation about exactly how sad he should look, and exactly how he should express that sadness and whether he should be on that side of the room or whether the lights should be highlighting only one side of his face and not the other, and whether he needed to have tears in his eyes and on and on, ad nauseum. It was slowing us down terribly. We were overrunning the budget, because every scene took three times as long to film as it should have.

"Finally, on about the fourth or fifth day, Miles walked onto the set. He went up to our young friend, put his nose up against his, and said, 'Mr. Farley is the director. That means he is the man who directs. You are the actor. The actor is the man who follows directions. Now, you either follow directions or I'm going to beat the shit out of you.'

"The young actor immediately huffed and puffed and said that he had the quality of the film at heart and that he wasn't going to compromise his art for anyone, even someone as important as Mr. Miles Cort. At which point, Miles calmly, deliberately, decked him."

"You mean, he hit him?" Shannon asked.

Farley grinned. "Punched his lights out. The guy was out for about two minutes, flat on his back."

"And then what happened?"

"And then I directed and he acted and the film was finished on time."

"Did you argue much with Miles?"

"Only on the first film, and then I learned to respect his judgment," Farley said. "There were two scenes I wanted to shoot in a particular way, a very arty way. I was a young director and I felt that I needed to make my signature on the films with this arty approach. Miles flat out refused to let me do it that way. And as it turned out he was right. From that point on I respected his judgment not only as a producer but as a filmmaker."

"Do you like Miles Cort?"

"I respect Miles Cort," Farley said, politically avoiding a direct answer to her question. He came to regret his evasiveness because he looked at her apologetically. "Look, let me tell you a story that illustrates what I consider to be the quintessential Miles Cort. A film that Miles and I did together. Jack Random was the cinematographer, and when we were halfway through the movie his wife had a terrible accident. She was in an automobile wreck. Random of course fell to pieces. So what Miles did was personally pick up the tab for her entire hospital bill, plus hire a helicopter each day to take Random from the lot to the hospital. He paid for all of this out of his own pocket."

He asked Shannon if she wanted more tea.

"No, I'm fine. Finish the story," she said.

"Well, I told him afterwards how generous it was and he just laughed. He said it would have been much more expensive to hire another cinematographer. The fact that Jack Random was grateful to him for the rest of his life didn't interest him in the slightest. What interested him was the movie, and he'd do anything to get the movie done on time, on budget with the quality that he had initially set out to achieve. He's a filmmaker. What can I say?" He spread his hands.

"All of us in this business have some sort of obsessive insanity going. And Miles Cort was no exception. He was just more obsessive than most and got more done than most."

"Do you still work as a director?" she asked.

"Not very much. I do some television stuff every now and again. Hollywood's become a young town. We old-timers are considered over the hill," he said with some bitterness.

When she left, he solicitously told her to call him if she had any more questions. "And," he said, standing in the door as she walked down the drive, "don't hesitate to come back if you want to talk more about him. You're welcome anytime. Just give me a call."

She got in her car and drove the serpentine road down the hill. She thought that the town was full of people like Farley, people who gave their lives to film, who had become casualties of the very industry they had supported so strongly. It had ruined them for anything else. Now they were lost.

A complex and contradictory man this Miles Cort, she thought. Respected and reviled and, strangely, the dislike came from those closest to him, the members of his own family. It was a bitter legacy for a man to leave: children and wives who hated him.

And yet, she thought in an attempt to understand his viewpoint, probably that legacy seemed unimportant to him. The real legacy, the one that had meaning for him, was the body of work, the films, the rolls of celluloid.

Shannon shuddered. There was something Napoleonic and inhuman about it. Miles reminded her for some reason of the little French general and his insatiable dreams of conquest, no matter how many bodies were left strewn on battlefields throughout Europe. The dream was all that was important to him. Like many such egomaniacs who achieved seemingly great deeds, Napoleon left behind a wake of destruction that was remembered long after his heroic deeds. Was Miles the same?

If Miles wanted a biography to sanctify his purpose with some kind of human nobility, he was going to be very disappointed. It could as well be titled *Miles Cort, Warts and All*, because that's what she was going to show—the truth as she found it, just as they had initially agreed.

CHAPTER ELEVEN

"You know why I became a success? Persistence. There are a lot of people more talented than I am, some who are luckier than I am, and there are a lot of people more intelligent than I am. But there are very few who can keep their teeth locked around something as long as I can.

"These kids of mine, they want everything to happen now. They want something for nothing. They don't understand. I think everybody in the world's like that these days. It's instant everything. You go in the supermarket: Instant soup, instant pie, instant juice, instant vegetables, instant everything. You turn on the TV you get an instant picture and instant entertainment. Everybody expects things to come easy. It doesn't work that way. It takes time, hard work, dedication, persistence."

"There must be more to it than that," Shannon said. "The film business is so filled with failure. What made you stand above everyone else?"

Miles grinned evilly. "You mean all those dead bodies lying out alongside the trail? How come I made it to the oasis and they didn't?"

"I suppose that's an apt metaphor," Shannon conceded.

Again that grin. "I'm the guy that left those dead bodies there. That's why I'm different," Miles said.

They all met at Agnes Cort's house in Santa Monica: Orson and Stephen, Elizabeth, Anne, and Richard. It was the first family meeting not chaired by Miles, so to speak.

Agnes, although only the mother of Orson and Anne, had demanded Orson hold the meeting there when she heard about it. "I want to be in on this, I want to protect my children's interests," she had told him.

Apart from Orson, of course, only Richard knew what it was about. The others had come in response to Orson's plea that he discovered something about his father that was "extremely serious" and needed to talk to them all about it.

The five children sat in the living room, Stephen and Elizabeth beside each other on the love seat, Richard and Anne and Agnes on the couch, and Orson in an armchair strategically placed in the center of the room.

"So what's it all about, Orson?" Anne asked eagerly. She had tried in numerous ways to find out earlier, but Orson had insisted that they all hear it together.

Elizabeth looked calm but interested, while Stephen looked bored.

"Well, I thought you should all know about this," Orson said. "I thought that if it was out in the open there might be something we could do about it, and it affects us all."

"What?" Anne asked.

"Miles has been in the process of changing his will and it affects us. As far as I know, he's cutting us all out."

"You're kidding," Elizabeth said.

"What do you mean?" Anne asked.

Only Richard and Stephen were silent. Orson tried not to look pleased at the effect he had created.

"How did you find this out?" Stephen asked.

"I can't tell you that," Orson said, shaking his head solemnly. "But the knowledge did come to my attention.

From what I can figure out, Miles is setting up a number of charitable foundations. Of the two hundred million dollars or so that he has, a hundred ninety-five million is going into these foundations. That means we won't see it."

Agnes chimed in, "He's cheating you just like he's cheated everyone else. That money is yours by right."

"What's happening to the other five million?" Elizabeth asked. "Maybe it's being left to us."

"A million dollars each?" Orson asked. "Maybe that's possible. But I think he's out to shaft us completely. Even so, a million dollars is nothing compared to what's there. It's not fair."

"Maybe he's leaving it to all his ex-wives," Richard suggested.

"You've got to be joking," Agnes said. "He loathes us more than his children."

"What do you expect us to do about this, Orson?" Stephen asked calmly.

"Well, we've got to do something," Anne said, her face flushed and her voice flustered.

"I don't know," Orson said. "But I figured that five heads are better than one. And Anne's right, we have to do something to protect our interests. I don't think we should just let him throw that money away and leave us spinning our wheels."

"Maybe this writer has something to do with it," Richard interjected thoughtfully. "Seems like all of this is happening since she started to do this biography. Maybe she's influenced him."

Stephen stood up. "Well, I'll tell you what I'm going to do. I'm going to leave and go back to work. This is really none of my business. Miles can do exactly what he wants to with his money. He earned it. And I'm certainly not going to waste my time coming up with schemes to change his mind."

"That's completely irresponsible," Agnes snapped.

"Still claiming a piece of the higher ground?" Orson sneered.

"Call it what you like," Stephen answered. "But I don't feel we have any right to Miles's money. If he wants to flush it down the toilet, that's his problem. It's certainly not mine."

Orson's face grew red. "That money's ours. We deserve it for putting up with his crap for all these years. We're his children, for chrissakes, and we need it more than some foundation to prevent blood clots or something equally stupid."

"Well, why don't you tell Miles that then, and see what he says," Stephen ventured with a grim smile. "Make a plea to his better nature, tell him how much you want his money."

Anne, ever the conciliator, said, "Well, maybe you're both right. But the fact of the matter is we all could use money and we are Miles's children, and he does owe us something."

"He owes us nothing," Stephen insisted. "He brought us into the world, he fed us, he clothed us, he offered us an education, and now we're adults out on our own. He has his life, we have ours. There is no debt to be paid there, at least not with money."

"Now wait a minute," Orson said. "Don't you need money? Wouldn't you like to have money for your musical career? I sure as hell would. I could use any amount of it right now. And what about Anne here? Forty years old, an actress, divorced? What happens to her? And what about Richard? What the hell's he going to do with his life? All he's good at is being a playboy. And Elizabeth, divorced, struggling—you think she couldn't use a few million bucks?"

"That's not the point," Stephen said. "The point is, the money belongs to Miles. It's his money. He owns it. And he can dispose of it in any manner he chooses. I don't want any further part of this. It was nice to see you all," he concluded with a curt nod and left the room.

"What an asshole," Orson said. "He's always thought himself better than the rest of us with his high morals and great principles. What about the rest of you? I suppose you don't need money either, huh?"

"Well, that's not really true," Anne said uncertainly.

"What are you proposing we do?" Elizabeth asked.

Orson shrugged. "I don't know what to do. That's why we're all here. I thought that perhaps we could go to Miles and approach him on this. I thought that if all five of us showed a united front, it could come to something."

"Well, there are only four of us now," Anne said.

"Is that all the information you have about it?" Elizabeth asked.

Orson nodded.

"Well, I think the first thing we do is see if we can find out any more," Elizabeth said. "Without really knowing exactly what's going on, we're kind of flailing around in the dark."

"What more do we need to know?" Orson snapped. "He's giving away our money."

"I think she's right," Agnes said. "You need to know more."

"Well, it's difficult, but I'll see what I can find out," Orson said without looking at Richard.

"What's your interest in this, Agnes?" Elizabeth asked mildly.

"Orson and Anne are my children," Agnes said self-righteously. "I don't want to see them cheated out of their inheritance. They've had to put up with Miles's bullying all these years, and that's worth some form of payment."

"I see. Well, I think that as soon as we get some more information—some hard facts—we might consider discussing the matter with a lawyer mutually satisfactory to all of us," Elizabeth suggested.

"Not a bad idea," Orson said, looking at her with surprise.

"Well, it seems that there's nothing more to be done right now," Elizabeth said, getting up.

"We can all think about it," Orson said. "If any of us come up with any suggestions I'd be happy to hear them."

"How can he do this to us?" Anne wailed. "How can he treat us this way?"

"What else is new?" Richard asked. "He always has."

"But he's my father and I love him," Anne said in the same tone. "How can he do this to us?"

"Well, you're the only one who does," Orson said. "Maybe he's leaving the whole five mil to you."

"Do you think so?" Anne asked, interest brightening her voice.

"Jesus, give me a break," Orson said.

On that note, the meeting ended.

Just as they were leaving, Richard pulled Orson aside.

"I need to talk to you." They went into a side room and Orson asked what was on his mind.

"I just learned something incredible," Richard said.

"What?"

"Somebody tried to kill Miles."

"What!"

"Yeah, some broad tried to kill Miles. I don't know any more than that, but I've heard a couple of the security guards talking."

"What do you mean? When was this?"

"I don't know," Richard said. "But fairly recently. I heard two of the security guys discussing it. One of them said to the other, 'Anything on the broad who tried to kill the old man?' And the other said, 'Nothing. And believe me, he's pissed off. You know how Cort is.' That's all I heard."

"That's it? You don't know who? You don't know when?"

"No, that's all I know, but it's amazing, isn't it?"

"Yes," Orson said. "Well, okay, keep your ears open. See what else you can find out? Do you think Miss Iceberg knows anything?"

"She would have told me," Richard said.

"She tells you everything, huh?"

"Everything I need to know," Richard said with a smile.

"All right. Well, if you hear anything else, call me right away. Okay?"

"Sure, brother. That's what I'm there for," Richard said, slapping Orson on the shoulder.

Orson kissed his mother goodbye and walked out the driveway. Someone had tried to kill his father. The thought generated the beginnings of an idea.

Stephen called Shannon on Saturday morning. "Would you like to go to the beach? I thought it might be nice for you to get out of the asylum for a while."

"Is this a date?" she asked.

"Only if Melissa can come along and chaperone us. I wouldn't feel safe otherwise," he said.

He picked them up at ten in the morning in a small Honda Accord. Melissa got in the backseat while Shannon sat with him in the front. They drove down Sunset Boulevard and then took the freeway to Santa Monica.

"I'm going to take you to Venice. Have you ever been there?" Stephen asked.

They both said no, and he said, "You should find it interesting."

It was a beautiful day and the freeway was slow, but Shannon didn't mind. In fact, she thought, as she relaxed in the front seat during a period of companionable silence, it was good to get out of the house and away from Miles Cort and his life.

They parked near the beach and walked out onto the Santa Monica Pier. It bustled with vacationers and locals, two easily discernible groups. The locals somehow looked more comfortable.

"I've seen this place in movies," Melissa said.

"Especially the merry-go-round," Stephen said. "They use it a lot on television."

Melissa played a couple of carnival games, winning nothing, and then went for a ride on the bump'em cars. Stephen and Shannon leaned against the rails, watching her from a distance.

The air was fresh and bitten with the tang of salt. A slight breeze whipped whitecaps up beyond the breakers. A surfer caught a wave and rode in beside the pier, looking up to show a flash of white face as he passed.

"You're right, it's good to get away," Shannon said.

"It can get intense around Miles," Stephen said circumspectly.

Melissa ran up. "Can I ride the merry-go-round?"

"You're too old for that," Stephen said. "They only let little kids on."

"Come on, please," she insisted.

"I want to ride it, too," Shannon said.

Stephen watched with amusement as they circled past him.

"Let's walk along the boardwalk toward Venice," Stephen suggested when they dismounted. "I know a nice restaurant where we can have some lunch, and the walk will get our appetite up."

They passed storefronts selling T-shirts, hot dogs, memorabilia, and other tourist junk. They stopped at Muscle Beach and watched a couple of gargantuan men work out. They dodged athletic skateboarders and bicyclists and paused to watch a juggler juggle a chain saw and a magician doing tricks and two long-haired young kids with guitars and a drum machine.

The water itself was a hundred yards across the sand and, when it seemed they had passed the center of entertainment, Melissa tugged at Shannon's arm. "Let's walk along the water." She ran ahead of them skipping through the shallows, oblivious to the fact that the water was still chilly.

At one point, Stephen took Shannon's hand. "Do you mind?" She shook her head, foolishly trying to hide her pleasure. "I like being with you," he said.

"Me, too," she replied.

Melissa ran through a flock of gulls which erupted in a flutter of wings and squawks before settling down again on the sand.

"She's really a nice kid," Stephen said. "I like her, too."

"I never appreciated her as much as I do now," Shannon said, "Since . . ." She let the words trail away.

"Since finding out about her kidney, you mean?" he asked.

Shannon nodded.

"Do you want to talk about it?" he asked. "I'm curious. I don't know a lot about it, but I'd like to. If it's not something you want to talk about, that's fine, too."

"No, it's fine," she said. "I don't mind talking about it. I have to live with it."

"I imagine it was a shock finding out. How was it with other people? How did everybody around you react?"

Shannon gave him a sharp and interested look. "It's interesting you asked that, because that was one of the more fascinating things that happened. Seems as if all my friends changed. They seemed suddenly uncomfortable around me, as if they were walking on eggshells. They were so careful of what they said, and so serious. It's as if they didn't know how to react to our predicament. Although at the time I began to feel as if I were the one with the disease.

"I mean, one of my closest friends, Annette Ball, she's normally this happy-go-lucky redhead, and yet every time I saw her she was so somber. She expressed sympathy and sometimes even interest, but then she'd just close off, and there was always a point where she couldn't look at me anymore. It was almost as if she was feeling guilty."

"It's understandable," Stephen said. "It just makes people uncomfortable. It's hard to face someone else's pain. Particularly if you are not in a position to do something about it yourself. Unable to help in any meaningful way." He paused thoughtfully, and then said, "Of course then there's the matter of selection. Why was Melissa selected to suffer? That thought could make people uncomfortable. If someone as wonderful as Melissa can be smitten by the gods, where does that place them? Are they even more vulnerable or what? I think it makes people very nervous."

"I think you're right," Shannon said. "People don't want to think they live in a universe of chance, of chaos. Tragedy must have a cause! When they see something like this happen they automatically have to create reasons. God, I know, I've been doing it myself. They probably look at us and think 'they must have done something to make this happen, something we don't know about, but something bad.' Thoughts like that maybe make them feel safer or superior."

"Yeah," Stephen agreed, "but deep down they must also know it's bullshit—that they don't really have superiority as a lucky charm. And that makes them uncomfortable."

"So I made everyone aware of their mortality," Shannon said.

"Something like that."

They stopped for a moment and watched a wet-suited surfer come in, riding the wave all the way to the shallows.

"Is she waiting in line for a transplant?" Stephen asked.

"Yes, but it could be a long wait," Shannon said. "There were about ten thousand transplants done last year, there were another ten thousand people with kidney failure on waiting lists for transplants, and there are about eleven thousand new cases each year. The demand for organs exceed the supply. It's also difficult to find a match."

"She can't use one of your kidneys?" he asked.

She shook her head. "I don't match."

"What about her father?"

"I don't know," Shannon answered sadly. "We don't know where he is."

"I see. Well, it'll come. I guess it's just a matter of patience," he said.

"That's an ability I'm learning to develop," Shannon said drily.

Stephen stopped and tugged at her hand, then with his other hand he gently lifted her chin and kissed her softly on the lips.

"What was that for?" Shannon asked.

"Because I like you."

She looked up the beach and saw that Melissa had stopped and was watching them. Stephen put his arm around her shoulders and they walked up to her.

"Are you getting hungry yet?" he asked Melissa.

"I'm starving," she said.

They ate at a small seaside cafe. They were all equally ravenous, and the brunch lasted almost two hours. At the end of that time, Shannon noticed telltale signs of tiredness in Melissa. "We should head back soon," she said to Stephen. "Melissa is beginning to droop."

As they walked back to the car, she explained the cycle to Stephen. "She's due for her next dialysis treatment tomorrow morning. It always goes like this," she said. "She'll be exhausted by this evening. Then she gets her treatment tomorrow and that peps her up for a couple of days. But the toxins build up in the body, and then she gets tired again."

They stopped at one of the storefronts and Stephen bought a Venice, California, T-shirt that Melissa had admired earlier. Then they went back to the car and drove home.

He dropped them off just at the side of the mansion. "It's been a wonderful day," Shannon said.

"Thanks for the T-shirt, Stephen," Melissa chimed in.

"Well, let's do it again soon," he said. "Next time I will allow you to take me out without a chaperone if that's all right."

"Yes, it certainly is," Shannon said.

He kissed her lightly on the mouth and drove away.

She held Melissa's hand as they walked back to the cottage. She could feel the weight of Melissa's every step.

"I think you need a little nap," she said cheerfully.

"Yeah, I think I do," Melissa agreed. As she seldom agreed that sleep was a necessary function, Shannon knew then how exhausted she was.

"Did you have a nice time?" she asked.

"I had a wonderful time, Mom. I really like him. I think you do, too."

Shannon hugged her with one arm. "I think I do, too."

After the pleasant time she had spent with Stephen at the beach, working with Miles on Sunday was a shocking dose of reality to Shannon.

There were no apologies from Miles for meeting her on a Sunday. He was available and apparently he expected her to be available when he was. They met on the back patio overlooking the pool after breakfast. Shannon set her tape recorder up on the table and began to ask him about the first film he had made.

"Never mind that," Miles said with a curt wave of his hand. "I want to tell you about the children."

She thought of protesting but decided against it. In spite of her irritability, she realized that sooner or later they would have to talk about the children and now was as good a time as any.

"You've met them all, and probably formed your impressions. Which one do you think is capable of having me killed?"

"I really have no idea, since I've really only interviewed Orson and Stephen," she said. "You said earlier that it could be Orson and, after talking with him, I'm not even sure that's possible."

"I've changed my mind," Miles said. "I think they're all capable of it if they were desperate enough."

"Why?"

"Because even though they may be failures, they're still my kids, with my genes, and I'd be capable of it," he said, with what she disbelievingly discerned as a note of pride.

He looked at her for a reaction, but she gave nothing away.

"Let me tell you what they're really like," Miles continued, settling back in his wheelchair. "Let's start with Orson. He's the oldest one, and an unprincipled snake. I'll tell you a story to illustrate the point. You will remember, of course, that in 1976 I married Portia. She was, I think, about twenty-five at the time. Pretty woman, like all my wives."

"Yes," Shannon nodded. "I've seen pictures of her, but I haven't met her yet."

"I wouldn't bother," Miles said. "Anyway, Portia's young, pretty, and ambitious like a lot of girls in this town. We'd been married almost four years and it was okay as marriages go, even though her faults soon became evident. But one day, I'm off for a business meeting down in Beverly Hills and almost as I arrive there I get a call on my car phone canceling the meeting. So naturally I turn around and head back home. I come in the front door of the house, everything's quiet, no sign of Portia. She was out by the pool when I left. So I figured I'd get my suit off and I go upstairs, walk into my bedroom, and there in my bed is my son, boffing my wife.

"Yeah," he said with a nod. "Orson is in bed with Portia, fucking her brains out. They both look up at me like I'm a messenger from hell."

"What did you do?" Shannon asked, shocked in spite of herself.

"I beat the hell out of Orson, and dumped Portia. What the hell else could I do? Cost me a bundle, but I got rid of her. She was trash."

Shannon reached over and turned off the tape recorder. "Let me understand you, you want this in the book, about how your son seduced your wife? Or whoever seduced who? You want this printed in your biography?"

"Damn right," Miles snapped. "I want the truth in this book."

"But information like this will reflect badly on everyone," she said. "It's not only destructive, but I don't see that it's necessary."

"I want the truth," Miles reiterated. "Now let me tell you some more about Orson. Keep in mind that he's on his fifth wife now, and still found the time to boff one of mine."

"Well, was he married at the time?" Shannon asked, giving up her protests for the moment.

"Yeah, he was married to what's-her-name—Susan. Got divorced the same time I did. She found out about it. She wasn't too happy about it, either."

"How did she find out about it?" Shannon asked, although she already suspected the answer.

Miles smiled. "I called her and told her to come and pick up her husband after I beat the shit out of him."

Shannon sighed. "Why are you doing this?"

"Doing what?" Miles asked innocently.

"This bitterness. Trying to destroy the reputations of your children."

"Huh!" Miles exclaimed. "I don't have to try and destroy anything. They've already done it. I haven't told you the good stuff yet. I haven't told you how Anne was pregnant at the age of fifteen. And how I had to get an abortion for her—an illegal abortion. I haven't told you about Richard's drug use, and about the time he tried to kill himself with sleeping pills and alcohol and God knows what else. I haven't told you half the story about Orson's proclivity for other men's wives. About the four men who were hired to beat him up by one irate husband. I haven't told you about Elizabeth's marriage to a man who liked to be dressed up like a woman and beaten. Huh! I haven't told you anything yet."

"Why are you telling me all of this?" Shannon asked. "Why do you want me to put it in the book? It's going to damage your reputation, your family's reputation—it's sleaze."

Miles jabbed a finger at her angrily. "It may be sleaze, but I know the public, and I know that this will sell—that so-called sleaze is what sells books. This will be the juiciest Hollywood insider story ever published. If I'm going to do a book, I'm going to do it right, baby."

Shannon shook her head. He was right, of course, it would sell books. It was the type of information the public devoured. One had only to look at the supermarket checkout stand and the paperback rack for proof of that. Yes, it would help the book become a success, but it was distasteful to her. How would she feel with her name on this book? she wondered.

"How about the other side of the coin?" she asked. "How about what the children and other people say about you? Do you want me to write every sordid little detail?"

"Write what you like," Miles said. "I just want the truth in this book. It's your book, you're doing it, you're writing it."

"That means I can also leave out what I like then?"

"I read your other pieces," Miles said with a warning look. "You're a hard-nosed journalist. Those were tough pieces and that's why I chose you. If you're the right person for this job you know that what I'm saying about its salability is true. And you'll put every goddamn word I give you in it. If you're not the right person for the job, I'd fire you now."

"That would be very expensive, Mr. Cort," Shannon said coldly.

"You think I care about money? I've got all the money in the world. I've got more money than I know what to do with. I've got so much money I'm giving it away. You think I care about that?" Again, he jabbed his finger at her. "I care about the book, and I want you to do the best job you can. You write the truth. How people react to that should be of no concern to you."

Shannon began to back down. Getting fired was not a part of her agenda, not now. "I think your real motive for writing this book is revenge. You just want to get back at everybody."

"My motives are no concern of yours," Miles said. "Your concern should be the book, the book, the book." He banged his fist emphatically on the table to punctuate his remarks.

"It is," Shannon said. "But I can't help being concerned about people as well."

"Look," Miles said, his tone suddenly becoming reasonable, "admit it, when you took this job you were worried that I'd interfere in the writing by making you keep unflattering things out. Am I right?"

Shannon nodded. It was true. Usually it was a problem every biographer faced.

"Well, I'm not doing that. Just the opposite. All I want is the truth and, as a writer, that should be all you want. I'm living up to the terms of our agreement, now all I'm asking is that you do the same."

Shannon sighed inwardly. "Very well."

"Good," Miles said. "Now, let me tell you about the first time Anne was arrested for shoplifting. She was only thirteen then."

"The first time?" Shannon asked.

"Hell yes, she's been arrested about—well, at least been

218

apprehended a dozen times. It's cost me a fortune to keep her out of jail."

An hour later, her tape recorder filled with the Cort family dirty linen, Shannon returned to her cottage. She went into her office and tossed the tape recorder disgustedly on the desk. Then she sat heavily in the chair and stared at the computer screen.

She felt ashamed. When Miles had hinted of firing her, her stomach had lurched and she had felt real fear. It had nothing to do with the indignity of losing the job, but was simply a consideration of the material comforts.

She was growing used to this lifestyle: the comfortable house, the television, the stereo, the equipment she was working on, the fully stocked refrigerator, the wine cellar, the seemingly unlimited expense account, the large sums of money she had at her disposal, the type of people she had begun to meet and would continue to meet, this comfortable, almost sybaritic California lifestyle. She was beginning to love it. The thought of losing it to return to a cold and empty New York apartment, worried about where her next check would come from in order to be able to keep Melissa fed for at least another week, was terrible.

She was being bought and she was enjoying it. Where was her integrity? Even when times were hard she had always maintained her integrity as a writer, sometimes even at the risk of losing a magazine assignment. Where was it now?

But she could easily justify what she was doing. Miles was only demanding that she write the truth, and, as he so cleverly pointed out, she had feared exactly the opposite to begin with. How could she argue with that now? And yet, in spite of her eminently logical justifications, the fact that she was compromising her integrity stayed with her. The truth was, on some level she was allowing Miles to dictate the contents of the book. He was making demands and she was acquiescing against her inclinations.

She felt an urge to pick up the telephone and call Stephen. He'd tell her what to do, or at least help her feel better. But she resisted. This was his family, his father, it was them she was writing about. To embroil him in the problems she had with that would not be fair. To ask him for an objective viewpoint of her actions would be asking too much. This was her problem and she'd have to deal with it as best as she could.

She went through the hallway to Melissa's room. She was hooked up to the dialysis machine, her eyes closed, probably napping. The nurse sat in a comfortable chair beside the bed, reading a book. "How's she doing?" Shannon asked.

"She's fine. She was really wiped out this time, but she'll be okay. When we finish she'll probably want to sleep for a while," the nurse answered.

"Great," Shannon said, and left the room. There was the reason she told herself, as she walked back to her office. She'd put up with anything from Miles to create a future for her daughter. The financial independence she'd get from this job would enable them to do just that. And she wouldn't blow it, no matter how much crap she'd have to put up with from Miles.

Orson pulled into a parking spot on Western Avenue and looked at the decrepit bar across the street. The battered neon sign said, "COCK AILS." God knew when the 'T" had fallen off. It looked like it had been missing for years.

He had called Johnny Bell, a stuntman who had once worked on one of his films. Johnny was his in debt, and Orson never forgot people who owed him. An aging jock with a flagrant and obnoxious drug habit, he was seldom hired anymore. Orson had given him the job because he was cheap, not out of the goodness of his heart. But Bell still felt grateful.

"I need somebody to do something illegal," he had told Bell.

"I can," Bell had said immediately.

"No, I need somebody who is a specialist. Somebody who doesn't mind hurting people," Orson had said.

"Hurting people, huh? Yeah, I know a guy."

"Can you put me in touch with him?" Orson had asked.

"Sure," Bell had said. "No problems."

Orson had slipped him a hundred-dollar bill and, as a result of a couple of telephone calls, was now parked on Western Avenue, about to have a meeting with a man he'd never seen. Bell told him not to worry. The man would recognize him.

He turned on the alarm, left the car, and dodged traffic in a dash across the street.

The bar was as depressing inside as it had looked from the outside. One of those places that existed solely to service alcoholics at odd hours. It probably did its greatest business in the morning. It was now afternoon, and there were only three people and a bored-looking bartender.

"What'll it be?" the bartender asked as Orson sat on a stool. He was an overweight bald man with a double chin and disinterested eyes.

"A beer, please." He looked around. Two of the men were in no shape to hurt anyone. They were both in their sixties and had seen better times. The third man at the end of the bar was altogether different. He wore gray slacks and a white open-necked shirt, and with his short crew-cut hair looked as if he'd been in the military.

When the bartender put Orson's beer down in front of him, the man at the end of the bar caught his eye and inclined his head toward a booth. Orson picked up his beer and together they walked to it.

The man didn't introduce himself, but just said, "What do you need done?" He had hard brown eyes and one of those mouths that looked as if it would enjoy biting off the heads of chickens.

"It's a very special job," Orson began.

"I wouldn't be here if it wasn't, I'm sure," the man said.

Orson was nervous. Here he was sitting in a bar talking to a man he didn't know, about to put himself on the line with an extremely illegal request. "How can I trust you?"

The man shrugged. "I come well recommended, don't I? You pay me half the money, I do the job; you pay me the other half, I disappear. That's the way I work."

Orson eyed him for a moment, then dropped his eyes. "Well," he began, "my name is—"

The man held up his hand. "I don't want to know your name," he said. "And you're not going to know mine. Just tell me the story of who you want to hit, and I'll see that it's done."

"Hit?" Orson asked.

"That's what you want, isn't it? That's what people usually want from me. I kill people."

Oh, God, Orson thought, then plunged ahead. "Yes, it is what I want. What do you normally charge?"

"It depends on who the person is."

Orson was silent. Once he told the man the name, he was committed that much more to this course of action. It was insane, he knew, but he did not know what else to do. He made up his mind.

"The man's name is Miles Cort," he said.

There wasn't a glimmer of recognition in the flat eyes staring back at him.

"He's a film producer. Lives in Bel Air," Orson continued.

"How do you want it done?"

"I don't care, I just want it done."

"What about security?"

"There's heavy security at the house," Orson said. "There's twenty-four-hour shifts of guards, plus there are alarms all over the place."

"Do you know where all the alarms are?"

"Yeah, I do," Orson said.

"Can you get me into the house? Into the grounds? I assume this is a mansion."

Orson thought a moment. "Yeah, I can come and go as I please. I suppose you could come in my car."

The man nodded. "That would work if it was late at night. Does he leave the house much?"

"Hardly ever," Orson said. "And I don't know how to predict that."

"So I'll have to go in," the man said, more to himself.

Orson realized his hand was clenched tightly around his beer glass. He looked at it and took a swig.

"Tell me about his habits," the man said. "Where does he work? Where does he sleep? I need to know all that stuff. I also need you to draw me a plan of house and of the alarm system, inside and out." He pulled a notepad from his hip pocket and a pen from his shirt and put them on the table. Orson began to draw. A half hour later, his memory picked clean, Orson leaned back.

"I think it's going to be the pool," the man said. "He takes that swim every day. I don't have to go into the house. I think it's going to be the pool."

"What are you going to do?" Orson asked.

"It's better you don't know. Do you want this to look like an accident or not?"

"I don't care," Orson said. "Somebody else already tried to kill him."

"It's even better."

"So how much do you want?"

"Fifteen grand. Half up front, half when the job's done."

"How do I know you just won't take the half that I give you and split?" Orson asked.

The man gave him a thin smile, the first one. "In my job, word of mouth is more important than in most. What kind of reputation do you think I'd have if I did things like that to my clients?"

"I guess so," Orson said uncertainly. "I don't have that much money on me right now, of course. And," he couldn't help smiling himself, "I don't suppose you'd take a check?"

Unamused, the man scrawled a number on one of the pages of the notepad and tore it out. "You can leave a message for me at this number when you have the money. Just ask for Bill. I'll get back to you within a couple of hours."

Orson took the note, folded it, and put it in his pocket. "All right, I guess you'll be hearing from me," he said. He got up from the booth, nodded at the man, and walked away.

"Hey," the man said after he'd taken three steps. Orson turned. "You're not going to finish your beer?"

Orson didn't answer. He just continued out the door. When he reached the street, he realized that his hands were shaking and his legs were unsteady. He took a deep breath and stepped into the street. A car he hadn't noticed screeched its brakes, stopping just a yard away from him. The driver leaned his head out the window and shouted, "Are you crazy? Want to get yourself killed?"

Orson made it across the street without further incident. Maybe I am crazy, he thought. And yeah, I do want to get someone killed but it ain't me. Jesus, he said to himself, what am I doing?

CHAPTER TWELVE

"People who don't play the game to win die. Some people put it another way and say that people who don't have goals die. Same thing either way," Miles said.

Shannon found Miles an excruciatingly complex character. In spite of her abhorrent feelings about some of his actions, he intrigued her more than any person she had ever interviewed. Contradictions in his character had always been evident to her, but now she found herself almost obsessed with understanding them.

How could this man, who had been what she could only describe as evil toward his children and family, instill such loyalty in a few of the people she had spoken to and be responsible for so many fine, artistic films? It was a contradiction that boggled her mind. Somehow she knew she would have to reconcile it to do this book properly.

She was with Miles in his study and had just heard him recount exactly the same story Orson had told her earlier about Marilyn Monroe. Miles told it without a shade of regret, defiantly, as if to show he had justly punished his wayward son by belittling him in front of the honored group of guests.

"How could you do that to him?" Shannon asked. The

brazenness of his posture demanded some question from her.

"He deserved it," Miles said. "He needed discipline, and that was one way of letting him know who was boss."

"Who had the power, you mean?"

"Yeah, you understand," Miles said with some satisfaction. "It's a matter of power. The father has the power. And power that is not used and demonstrated is lost. That's always been my philosophy."

"But don't you feel it was cruel?" she asked.

He was sitting in his wheelchair near the couch on which she sat. On the table before them was a silver setting of tea and cookies. Miles reached over, picked up one of the cookies, and popped the whole thing in his mouth. Still chewing, he said, "Did I think it was cruel? No, I didn't."

She was too sharp a writer to fall for that evasion and said immediately, "Now! What do you think now? Looking back now, do you think it was cruel?"

Miles studied her for a full five seconds, and then dropped his eyes. In a lower voice he said, "Yes, I do think it was cruel."

"Then why do you continue to treat him the same way?" she asked more gently.

Miles's defiance returned. "Because he's a man and he should be able to take what I dish out. If he can't, what kind of a man is he going to be?"

"But you just said he is a man," she said. "And he is the man whom you've created. How can it help to continue creating that?"

Again, for a brief moment, Miles looked uncomfortable. "I can't change," he said. "I am the way I am, I behave the way I behave. None of them have to stay around if they don't like it."

My God, Shannon thought to herself. The man does have a conscience. Somewhere in that heart of steel is a human heart, pumping with blood and even perhaps with some compassion.

The realization came like a revelation. It was at that moment that she gained her first understanding of Miles. As a writer she was beginning to understand her subject. He was starting to open doors to her that were previously closed and, as always, it was an exciting experience. It was what she loved about interviewing subjects—these moments when the real person somehow, whether accidentally or on purpose, revealed himself.

"Your children then, you don't quite despise them as much as you pretend to, do you?" she asked.

She had gone too far in his estimation. He glared at her. "Why are you asking these questions? What do these things have to do with my biography? What has this got to do with what's happened?"

Shannon smiled patiently at him. "This will have happened by the time the book is published. Everything that you feel now is an important part of your biography. If you were dead, if you had died yesterday, perhaps it would not be an important part of your biography, but you are a living subject, and your insight into your life is going to be a very significant part of this book."

"Huh," Miles said disparagingly. "My insight into my life isn't worth a damn. I don't understand it any more than anyone else does. You tell me who claims to understand their life and I'll show you a liar."

"Everybody tries to understand their life," Shannon said increduously. "Are you trying to tell me that it's a total waste of time?"

"Life is doing, life is about action, life is accomplishment. You know a man by his deeds," Miles said. "You don't know a man by his thoughts and by his wishes. You know him by what he's done. And that's how I want to be known. By what I've done. And I've done a lot in my time, believe me."

"Yes, you have," Shannon conceded. "But even so, I think that like any other man, you wish to understand it."

There was a knock at the door and Lynn entered. Miles

looked slightly relieved at the interruption, Shannon thought, and wondered if she was imagining it.

"You have a doctor's appointment in half an hour," Lynn said. "I just wanted to remind you."

"I don't have to see that damn fool doctor," Miles said. "If he has to wait, he has to wait. I'm busy right now, can't you see?"

"Yes, sir," Lynn said. "When he arrives, where shall I have him wait?"

"Take him to the living room. He can wait there for me."

"Yes, sir," Lynn said, and withdrew from the room.

"Is this just a regular medical checkup?" Shannon asked.

"Yes," Miles said, obviously unwilling to discuss it further.

"Well, let's get back to what we were talking about," Shannon said tenaciously. "I do want you to understand that all of this is pertinent to the book, that I do need to know your feelings now about these things. And, in fact, that I demand to know them. If you want the truth, the truth is not just in the past, it has to include now."

"That's hogwash," Miles said derisively. "People aren't interested in me now. I'm a sick old man, sitting in a wheelchair behind guarded gates. People are interested in what I've done and my accomplishments. What am I accomplishing now? Very little I'm afraid."

"People will want to know if you're truly the bastard you appear to be," Shannon said daringly.

Miles couldn't help smiling at that. "Like I said, a man is known by his deeds."

"Yes, but does he regret them? Does he look back at them with a different perspective? A different philosophy? Surely that must count for something."

"It's just more thinking. Where does that get anyone?" Miles said.

It was hopeless, Shannon thought. Miles had dug in his

heels and wasn't going to budge. There was one last card she could play. "It'll get us a better book, that's what it'll get us," she said. "A more honest book. The book showing a man not only unafraid to reveal his deeds and accomplishments but unafraid to reveal his thoughts, his ruminations, his regrets, and his triumphs."

Miles looked back at her. "What is it you want to know?"

"Your children," she said. "You despise them. You think they've amounted to nothing, right?"

Miles nodded.

"Well," she continued, "how responsible do you feel for that? In other words, what part did you play in creating them so that they are the way they are?"

Miles stared bleakly at a photograph on the wall. "I'm fully responsible," he said.

The silence was palpable after that. Then Miles pressed the controls on his wheelchair and said, "That's all for today, I need to go and get ready for the doctor." A moment later he was gone.

Shannon gathered her materials slowly, her thoughts turbulent. She was poised on the cusp of something, and she was both excited and afraid. Excited because Miles was finally beginning to reveal himself, afraid because he might not go any further or allow her any closer. It was a crucial point in their relationship, and in the evolution of the book.

She picked up her belongings and left the office. In the hallway, she saw the chauffeur approaching. He wore his usual uniform and touched his hat politely as he passed her, saying, "Good afternoon, ma'am."

She walked on three steps and then stopped and turned. "Andy," she called out after him.

He stopped. "Yes, ma'am," he said.

She walked up to him, "Andy, I wonder if I could have some of your time?"

"What is it you need, ma'am?"

"I wanted to talk to you about your relationship with Mr. Cort," she said.

Paxton looked back at her uncertainly, almost confused.

"It's all right," she said. "He has told you, hasn't he, that like everyone else here you should be cooperating with me on this biography?"

"Yes," he said. "What kind of ah . . ."

"Why don't you come along to my cottage for a few minutes and I'll just ask you some questions?" she said easily.

"Well, I do have some time now. All right."

They walked through the garden to the cottage. She took him into the small living room where he sat uncomfortably on a chair. He took his cap off and placed it on his knees.

"Could I get you something? she asked, trying to make him feel at ease. "A cup of coffee, or tea?"

"No, thank you."

He was actually a handsome man, she thought, with his thick black hair, dark eyes, and charmingly masculine broken nose. And yet, she noticed for the first time, there was something vulnerable behind those eyes, something almost childlike and innocent.

"I'm going to tape this if you don't mind," she said, turning the tape recorder on, pushing it across the table toward him.

He looked at it warily.

"Don't worry," she said. "This really has been okayed by Mr. Cort."

"Yes, I know," Paxton said. "I suppose I'm just not used to it."

"Tell me something about yourself," she said. "How did you . . . Well let's start with the beginning. What did you do before you met Mr. Cort, and then how did you meet him?"

"I was in Vietnam for three years, and then I met him soon after I got back," he began.

"Now wait a minute," she said. "What were you doing in Vietnam?"

"What I was supposed to, Miss Ross," he said stiffly. "I killed people."

"Who were you with? Was it some special forces, special operations, or rangers, or what?"

Paxton shook his head. "I'm sorry, I don't talk about Vietnam, not to anyone, I never talk about it," he said, suppressed emotion charging his voice.

"All right. So you came back from Vietnam. What did you do then?"

"I had a buddy in 'Nam, his name was Jeff Allouette, and he was in the movie business and he always told me that I should come to L.A., that he could get me a job as an actor. He said I had the looks for it.

"So I had nothing better to do so I came to L.A. and looked him up. And he got me a couple of small parts in some action adventure movies, nothing to speak of. And then I got a part in *The Volatile Source,* a movie that Mr. Cort was producing. Again, it was just a small part. And I thought I was doing okay, I guess, although I knew deep down I would never get anywhere in this business. I wasn't handsome enough, wasn't polished enough, hadn't studied enough, and I guess I never really cared enough."

He stopped and looked at her, as if for approval. "Keep going," she said encouragingly.

"Anyway, one day Mr. Cort called me over, took me into one of the caravans, sat me down, and said, 'You're never going to make it as an actor, kid, you know that?' Well, I didn't know what to say. What do you say when the boss who's hired you and who's paying you tells you you're no good? Thought I was going to get fired, then and there. Instead he offered me a job.

"He knew everything about my background—what I'd done in 'Nam, where I was before that, what I'd been

231

doing since I'd been here. He has his ways. Said he needed a chauffeur who could double as a bodyguard. And he offered me what was then a very good salary. I've been with him now for fifteen years, his chauffeur and his bodyguard."

"And he pays you well?"

"Very well."

"You've never wanted to leave and do something else? You're happy in this job? Satisfied with it?"

"It's all I've ever wanted," he said. "I got married to an actress when I came back from 'Nam. It lasted about three weeks I think. Twenty-two days, then we got divorced. It was a disaster. I don't have any other family."

"So Mr. Cort is your family?"

Paxton nodded. "As much as I've ever had. I grew up in foster homes up in San Francisco, Catholic homes, run by a bunch of tough old nuns—made Vietnam seem like a picnic. There's never been anything else for me. Mr. Cort gave me the security of a home and more money than I can spend in return for my loyalty."

"As a bodyguard, have you ever had to protect Mr. Cort?" she asked.

"Just a couple of times," he said casually. "Nothing serious. Guys that got out of line, too much to drink, parties, stuff like that."

"Well, what about this attempt on his life? The woman who tried to poison him?" she asked.

For the first time since she had known him, Andy's composure slipped. "He told you about that?"

"Yes, he did," she said. "He also told me that he thinks that it was one of his children who was responsible."

Paxton swallowed. "He told you that?" he repeated.

"What do you think?" she asked. "Do you think one of the kids is responsible?"

"I don't know," he said. "I don't see how they could be. The girls who came here are not connected to anyone in the family. Corydon looked into it thoroughly. The kids

232

would have to know the person, they'd have to be able to get to her. Whoever got to her must have known that this was the third time she was back. He did tell you that, didn't he?"

"Yes, he did," she said. "Are you the one who procures his women for him?"

Paxton now looked embarrassed. "Yes, that is one of my duties," he said sheepishly.

"Well, where do you find them?"

"I still have contacts in the film business. Usually they are actresses. I never get pros for Mr. Cort, he doesn't like them. So I talk to friends, and they know girls who do a little bit on the side to get some extra cash. Or there are a couple of clubs where these girls like to hang out. And I go to those places, talk to them, make the offer. Some of the girls recommend friends of theirs."

"I bet you've had your face slapped a few times."

Paxton smiled. "Yes, you could say that. Although more often they want to negotiate a higher fee."

"So you go back to the same places? The same clubs?"

"Yes, I'm afraid so," he said. "I see now that I shouldn't have. People do talk about these things no matter how discreet you try to be."

"Yes," she said, "I'm sure they do."

"It's all my fault, I should never have allowed him to have the same girl three times. It was his own rule he broke."

"Would he have let you countermand his orders?" she asked.

Paxton shrugged. "Who knows? There have been times when he has. When it seemed to make sense."

"So you have no idea how this could have happened?"

"I don't," he said. "Security's been investigating it, and they've come up with nothing, too."

"And do you think one of the kids is responsible?"

"It's hard to tell with that bunch. Yes, one of them

could be. They certainly have it in them to do something like that."

"You don't like them, do you?" she asked.

"The kids?" he said. "I'm not supposed to like or dislike anybody, I just work here."

"Well, I guess that says it," she said.

"I guess so."

"Do you like Mr. Cort?" she asked.

"Yes, I do," Paxton said emphatically. "He's a fine gentleman. But he's human. Sure he makes mistakes, and sure he flies off the handle. But he's always been straight with me and treated me fairly. When I've screwed up and he's taken me up on it, I deserved it. When I do a good job, he lets me know, too. And he's been very generous to me through the years. He's probably the finest boss anyone could ever ask for."

"I see. Well, I must admit that you're one of the few people I've run across who like him."

"Well, I can see that. He's not an easy man to like. And he's not one to run for a popularity contest. He's a man who believes he has to be a certain way to do what he has to do. And he's done more with his life than most of the people who don't like him. Underneath all of that he's a good man."

"Well, thank you," she said and smiled, adding, "You wouldn't just be saying this about him because you work for him, now would you?"

"No, ma'am. Mr. Cort told me to be completely honest with you. And I have been."

"Well, let me put it another way. Have you ever seen Mr. Cort treat people as nicely as you say he's treated you?" she asked.

"He treats people fair," he said. "If they do the job they are paid to do, he treats them well. Nice isn't a part of Mr. Cort. Nobody would ever call him a nice man. But sometimes that's what it takes to get things done in this world."

"I see."

Paxton shifted his feet and touched his cap. "I got to go now, ma'am. Would that be all right?"

"Oh, sure," Shannon said. "Thanks for talking to me. I may want to talk to you a little more later and get some specifics about—you know, specific incidents during the time you've worked for him, if that's all right."

"Yes, ma'am, that'll be fine," he said.

"Thank you."

She absently watched him leave, her thoughts on Miles. That there was more to Miles than met the eye had always been apparent to her. But exactly what it was had remained a mystery. For a man to instill this type of loyalty he had to have qualities that she hadn't yet discovered. It was, as she had thought earlier, exciting.

She knew from past experience that she was transforming now into a huntress. Miles Cort was her quarry, his life and its secrets the reward of the hunt. If he had mistakenly assumed that she was simply an acquiescent woman, he would soon change his mind. Once she had picked up the scent of a trail she pursued it unflaggingly. While some people got their kicks jumping out of airplanes, and others by getting high on drugs, this is what she loved. This is why she was a writer.

Elizabeth lived in a duplex apartment on a quiet, tree-lined street in Brentwood. It wasn't a particularly prestigious address, but the apartment was a large and airy two-bedroom. She had furnished it elegantly with modern yet comfortable furniture and original paintings she had slowly collected over the years, some of which were now quite valuable. The lucky recipient of a green thumb, she also filled the main room with jungles of thriving plants.

The only jarring note, she now thought, was Anne's presence.

Anne had apparently suddenly discovered a newfound

affinity for her younger half-sister. She had called an hour earlier, saying, "I think us girls should get together and talk about this situation. Can I come over?" Slightly amused by this turn of events, Elizabeth had agreed.

"Well, I think it's just despicable," Anne was saying, drinking a vodka and tonic while Elizabeth cradled a mug of herb tea in her hands. "I mean, how can Daddy do this to us? We are his children and God knows we could use the money."

"I understand that," Elizabeth said, "but why talk to me about it?" Elizabeth wore slacks and a T-shirt, her feet were bare. Anne, as always, wore a low-cut frock and sandals. Elizabeth realized that she had never seen Anne in jeans, at least not since childhood. A certain formality of dress was her distinctive trademark.

"Well, it's all very well for Orson to take charge of this, but I think we girls might have something to contribute, and at least we should talk about it." Anne looked obliquely at her and said, "Besides, I don't trust Orson."

"But he's your brother," Elizabeth said with mock surprise.

"Orson is a little shit and you know it," Anne replied with uncustomary bluntness. "There is only one thing he cares about and that's himself. If he could think of a way to get his hands on all of Miles's money, he'd do it and not give us a second thought."

"Well, I've been thinking about it," Elizabeth said. "And I'm not sure that I really give a damn what Miles does with his money. I think what Stephen said was true, it's his money to do with as he wishes, but more than that I don't think I want anything that belongs to him."

Anne was truly shocked at this unexpected comment. "How can you say that?" she said, waving one hand around the apartment. "You live in a place like this. I mean it's nice of course, I'm not saying it isn't. But it's certainly no mansion in Beverly Hills. And from what I understand, the settlement that Ellis left you after you

236

divorced hardly puts you in a position to make any radical changes."

"I like it here," Elizabeth said calmly.

"Well, I'm sure you do," Anne said. "But I'm sure, like all of us, you wish for better."

Elizabeth shook her head. "I can look after myself. But what about you? Your three husbands have left you in a comfortable financial condition, I imagine?"

Anne waved her hand. "Comfortable, yes, but comfort is not enough. It's all Miles's fault. He brought us up to become accustomed to a certain standard of living, and to expect us suddenly to adjust to not being able to live that way is cruel."

"You'll find another husband, you always do," Elizabeth said.

Anne tossed her hair back. "I don't think I want another husband. Men are so, I don't know—male. I'm really tired of them. It's hard to find an adult male these days. They are all just irresponsible little boys, I think, at heart."

"What happened to Allen Prentice? I saw you with him at Daddy's party," Elizabeth asked.

"Allen Prentice is an over-the-hill lush," Anne said. She suddenly realized she was holding a glass of vodka and put it down on the table. "We broke up after the party. I decided that I didn't want to see him anymore. The man just can't control himself. When he's not all over me, he's unable to perform because he's had too much to drink. The man doesn't have any limits."

"Well, I'm sure there are other fish in the ocean."

"That's not my concern right now. My concern is what Miles is doing with our money."

"I have no idea what to do about that," Elizabeth said. "Miles has always done exactly what he wanted to do, and I don't suppose this time is any different."

Anne narrowed her eyes. "Do you think that writer girl has anything to do with this?"

"Shannon Ross? I don't know," Elizabeth said with a shrug.

"Well, do you think Miles is sleeping with her?"

"It never occurred to me," Elizabeth said. "I suppose he could be. I understand he still leads an active life in that area."

"Maybe she's planning to marry him," Anne suggested. "Maybe he's rewriting his will and leaving all his money to her."

"She's not a foundation. Orson said the money was going to charitable foundations," Elizabeth said.

"Well, you know how complicated things are with money," Anne said vaguely. "Perhaps she is the trustee of the foundations and has access to the money. Or perhaps he's leaving that five million to her. From what I heard, she had nothing when she arrived. It probably seems like a fortune to her."

"It seems like a fortune to me," Elizabeth said grimly.

Anne looked shrewdly around the room again. "How do you live? I mean, what do you do? I thought you weren't left very much money by Ellis?"

"Oh, I get by," Elizabeth said. "I made a few little investments."

The doorbell rang, startling Elizabeth. She wasn't expecting anyone else. "Excuse me."

She opened the front door to find Brian Parker, the young lawyer who had come to her office with the offer to buy. He looked as dapper as ever, wearing a pin-striped, three-piece suit, his hair in place, and the same friendly, insincere smile fixed on his face.

"Miss Cort. May I come in?"

She stood in the doorway blocking it. "No you may not. What is it you want?"

"Oh," he said, sounding hurt. "I just wanted find out if you have thought over our proposal."

"I gave you my answer then and it's still my answer," she said. "I'm not interested in selling."

"Well, I really think you should. As I explained to you, there could be consequences."

She looked past him and saw halfway down the path between the house and the street the burly man who was with him at their previous meeting. He stood, arms folded across his chest, staring at her house. "If you don't leave I'm going to call the police," she said.

"Well, there's no need to be rude. I simply wish to repeat our offer to buy you out. It's a normal business transaction. I don't quite see why there should be any police involvement."

"Because you're harassing me. Now leave. And tell your bosses, whoever they are, that I'm not interested and won't be interested in selling at any time. Goodbye."

She stepped back and closed the door. She leaned against it and took a deep breath, trying to neutralize the surging fear before returning to Anne.

God, she thought, they know where I live. They even know where I live. She'd hired two security men to be at the business at all times, but she hadn't thought of herself. She'd always felt invulnerable in this apartment. It was her world, one which she had created for herself. Now the thought that these men knew where she was and could simply knock on her door suddenly scared her.

It must have still shown on her face, because when she walked back into the living room Anne looked at her with concern. "Are you all right? You look so pale."

"Yes, I'm fine." She sat down again, picked up her mug, and took a sip of tea.

"Who was that?" Anne asked, a puzzled frown on her forehead.

Elizabeth shook her head. "Just a man who's been bothering me. It's nothing. Don't worry about it. I got rid of him."

"Well," Anne said, "do you see what I mean about men? They are such a terrible nuisance. You know what they say, you can't live with them and you can't live without them. Are you dating anyone these days?"

Elizabeth shook her head. "No, I don't seem to be."

"Well, you should," Anne said, blithely contradicting everything she had just said. "You're still young. How old are you now? Twenty-eight, twenty-nine, thirty? You must have men after you all the time."

"Hardly," Elizabeth said drily.

"I'm so glad we had this little talk," Anne said. "We just don't get together often enough. We should see each other more often."

"Yes, we should," Elizabeth said without any enthusiasm. "But I don't see that our meeting has resolved anything."

"I don't know," Anne said, "I think I might just go and talk to Miles about this whole thing, before Orson goes to him and makes him upset."

"I don't think that's a good idea," Elizabeth said. "Miles doesn't like people interfering in his business."

"But don't you see, this is our business, too?" Anne said. "I mean this is our money. We are his children."

"That's what everyone keeps saying," Elizabeth said. "But perhaps Stephen was right: it's not our money, it's Miles's money."

"I don't know how you can talk that way," Anne said petulantly. "Like it or not, we are Corts. And as Corts we are entitled to the family fortune. Surely Miles can see that."

"Look," Elizabeth said irritably, "I don't know what Miles can see and I can't help you on this. I think you're just going to have to go along with Orson if he comes up with a plan."

"Well," Anne sniffed, "I thought you'd be more practical."

When she left, slightly miffed, a few minutes later, Elizabeth took out a spray bottle and watered the large fern

240

in the corner. It was somehow always a soothing activity for her.

She was worried. She didn't really know what to do about those men. They knew where her business was and they knew where she lived. And thanks to her informant in the L.A.P.D. she knew who she was dealing with. God, where is Sissy when I need her, she thought miserably? She had no one else to turn to.

Richard had a bitter fight with his father during dinner that night. Lynn, who had been required to work late, joined them for the meal. None of the other children showed up, even though they had been invited. And Miles's mood was obviously black.

"Don't they care?" he thundered. "Here I am, how often do I see them? Once a week? And they can't even take the trouble to show up?"

"They probably had other things planned," Richard said. "Anyway, I wanted to ask you if I could get some extra allowance this month."

"Jesus Christ, you've spent it already?"

"Yeah, I'm afraid I had some extra expenses."

"What? You ran out of dope? Or you been paying women?"

Richard felt his face flush at that. "Hey, once you give it to me, it's my money," he said. "You always said that. Said it would make me more responsible."

"Yeah," Mils scowled. "And once you ask for more, it's my business. I give you a perfectly substantial allowance. I give you more in a week than most people earn in a month. What the fuck do you do with it?"

"Perhaps Lynn doesn't want to hear this," Richard suggested.

"The hell with that," Miles said. "Miss Reid knows all my affairs. Well, what have you done with your money this month?"

"That's my business," Richard persisted.

"Well then, survive on your business until next week's allowance.

"Look, all I'm asking for is some money. You have more than you could possibly need," Richard said. "I just happen to have some extra expenses. I had to take this woman out somewhere special and it was real expensive, and I owed someone a little bit of money."

"You're a wastrel, a complete wastrel," Miles said bitterly. "Have you ever thought of earning any?"

"Doing what?" Richard asked. "I'm supremely unqualified for anything."

"I've told you this once, and I'll tell you again. I can get you a job anywhere in the industry, all you have to do is ask me."

"I don't want to work in the industry. It's full of flukes."

"You'd fit right in then," Miles said accusingly. "So what's the difference?"

"Look, you agreed to give me an allowance, and that's all I'm asking for."

"You're asking for more than your allowance. Goddamn it! I should cut you off entirely and force you to get out there and work. The only problem is, I know what you say is true. You are unqualified for anything."

"Well, you raised me."

There was a moment's silence as Miles pondered that. Richard continued. "I always have to beg you for money. You know how that makes me feel?"

Miles stabbed a piece of steak with his fork. "You wouldn't have to ask me for money if you lived within your allowance."

"It's not enough," Richard said.

Miles truly erupted then. His voice roared out, "Now it's not enough? Now what I give you, a thousand dollars a week, is not enough? Goddamn, boy, you should see

242

what some people live on. No, no, no! No, you are not getting any extra allowance. You're going to have to wait."

"Goddamn, I need it!" Richard shouted, his face as flushed as his father's.

"The answer is no!" Miles slammed his fist on the table, causing the cutlery to jump. "No! You will not get another penny from me this week."

Richard stood up shaking, pushing his chair back from the table. "Fuck you, you old bastard, fuck you!"

"And fuck you, too," Miles yelled at his retreating back.

Later that evening, when she completed her paperwork, Lynn walked past the pool, out the pathway, past the tennis court to the little bungalow where Richard lived. She knocked on the door and entered at the muffled "Come in."

Richard was lying on the couch staring at the ceiling. She walked over to him and said, "I hate to see him treat you like that, but you really ask for it, don't you?"

"Ah, fuck off," Richard said.

The room was in disarray with dirty glasses on the coffee table and half-filled ashtrays. Newspapers and magazines littered the floor. She started to pick up the glasses when Richard said, "Leave them alone. I don't need you to be my maid."

"I don't mind," she said, taking them into the kitchen.

When she came back he was sitting on couch, a surly expression on his face. "I hate him, you know, I really hate him."

"It's not easy for him, either, you know," she said. "I mean, he really wants to be proud of you, but you haven't given him very much."

"I don't owe him. This is my life. I refuse to live his life for him."

"He's already lived it, he just wants you to live yours. But you don't seem to be doing too much with it."

Richard swung around angrily at her. "What are you? My mother or what? I don't need to listen to this crap."

"Hey, I care for you." Lynn sat on the couch next to him and put her hand on his knee. Angrily he brushed it away.

"Everybody's against me," he said. "Everybody."

"I'm not." She put her hand back again, and gently squeezed his knee.

"Have you found out any more about those foundations?" he asked.

She shook her head. "He's being very secretive about it. It's between him and the lawyers. I don't even get to see the correspondence. In fact, I don't think there is very much correspondence. The lawyer comes, he shows him papers, he signs them, the lawyer takes them away. I haven't typed a single letter to them on his behalf."

"Do you have any idea what's happening to that extra five million dollars?"

She shook her head. "I don't know, I really have no idea."

"Is there any way you can find out?"

Again she shook her head. "It's too dangerous."

Richard leaned back, put his arm around her neck, and pulled her toward him. He placed his most charming smile on his lips, admiring, quizzical, and attractively boyish. It was a very effective smile. "You're a clever woman, Lynn. You could find out if you really tried," he said persuasively.

She rested her head against his chest. "I can try, but I'm not going to take any more risks."

"All I ask is that you try."

"I don't know why I'm doing this for you." She looked up at him, her eyes seeking his.

"Yeah, you know," he said with a smile. "You do this for me 'cause I go down on you better than any guy ever has."

"You don't even care for me," she said angrily, attempting to pull away. But he kept his arm around her.

"I care for you, Lynnie," he said. "I care for you."

"I don't think you care for anyone, not even yourself."

"I just need my freedom," he complained. "I'm like a prisoner here. I'm on the money leash, I need my own money, I need my independence."

"Well, why don't you move out? Live on the allowance he gives you, get a job like he says."

"I don't want a job," he said irritably. "There's nothing I can do. What's an extra couple of grand a month? It's not the type of money I'm talking about. I need big money. I need some of his money. I need some of my money that he's supposed to be leaving to me, instead of cheating me out of it."

"Maybe if you talk to him, maybe if you showed some love toward him."

"Oh, Jesus," Richard said. "Give me a break, will you? He knows how I feel. If I went crawling to him now he'd know exactly why. There's got to be another way."

She ran her hand over his chest and began to unbutton his shirt. "Do we have to talk about this now?"

"Why? You got something else in mind?" he asked cruelly.

"Yes." And even he could tell she hated herself for her subservience.

"Well, come on, baby, let's do it. Let's do exactly what you want."

"Yes," she said again.

Anne sat uncomfortably in the reception area and wondered if everyone there was up for the same part. It was a silly thought, she told herself, as half the people there were men. The women were all so young and pretty though. None of them looked a day over twenty-five. The competition in this business seemed to be getting younger each year, she thought ruefully.

She wondered if she was wasting her time again. The part was for a woman of thirty. The fact that she was forty hadn't deterred her from asking her agent to set up the appointment. She could play thirty if she had to; she wasn't *that* over the hill.

An attractive young man sitting opposite her smiled in a friendly manner. She smiled back. He had long brown hair, brown eyes, looked about six feet tall, with handsome aquiline features, probably in his mid-twenties, maybe thirty, she thought, taking him all in with one professional glance. Too young for me, she thought. Besides, she had told Elizabeth only the day before that she wasn't interested in men.

The secretary sitting at the desk picked up the phone and then replaced it. "Anne Cort?" she said. Anne stood up, feeling a little flustered, knowing that everyone in the room was suddenly measuring her. "You're next."

She went through the double doors into the office. It was furnished like all casting offices were: a couple of movie posters on the wall, movie books on the shelves, a large and imposing desk separating the casting director from the victims.

There were three people waiting for her in the room: the casting director, Milt Thomas, a man she'd met before, graying and distinguished in his fifties; a young lady she assumed to be his assistant; and another man of about forty who could have been the director.

Milt stood up from behind his desk and leaned forward and shook her hand. "It's nice to see you again, Anne. This is Cindy and that's the director, Brian Moss."

"How do you do," Anne responded.

"Please sit down," Thomas said, pointing at the chair sitting in front of the desk.

He shuffled some papers on his desk and cleared his throat. "Anne, I understand you're testing for the part of Cass."

"Yes," Anne said. "I think it's a wonderful opportunity for an actress. The script is excellent."

"Well, Brian and I were talking and you don't seem quite right for that part."

"Well, it's a stretch, but I think I can handle it. If you remember, I don't know if you saw *Michael's Luck*, but the part I played there was very similar in context."

"Yes, I know. Talent-wise I'm sure you can do it. It's just the matter of the look."

My damn age, Anne thought bitterly, that's what he's talking about. I'm too old for the damn part.

Thomas hurried on. "We wondered though if you'd test for the part of Amy. We think you might be right for that."

"Amy?" Amy was a secondary character, a fifty-year-old over-the-hill blowsy blonde. Not exactly the kind of image she was trying to project. "I don't think I'm right for that," she said.

"Well, we think that there's some good potential there," Thomas answered.

"I don't think so. I'm really interested in the part of Cass," Anne said stiffly.

"Well, I'm afraid that won't be possible. However, if you'd like to test for the part of Amy, we'd be happy to give you a few days to read the script over with that in mind and have you in for another audition."

Anne rose slowly to her feet. "Well, I'll think about it and have my agent give you a call, okay?"

"Fine," Thomas said, "fine." He stood up again and extended his hand.

Automatically she shook it and then turned and left the room, trying to slow herself down, trying not to run, which is what she really wanted to do.

She closed the door behind her and stood in the waiting area, engulfed in disappointment. Without looking, she knew that everyone else was watching her. They always did. Everyone looked for little signals: Had the part already gone? Should they just turn around and go home? Was it a tough audition? Were they soft? Was she obviously rejected? And if so, they would try all the harder. Anne squared her shoulders and forced a smile and stepped forward.

"How did it go?" a voice said to her left.

She turned to see the good-looking young man she had seen before.

"Just fine," she said brightly, "just fine."

"May I walk you to the elevator?" he asked, standing. She was taken aback, but only for a moment. Any admiration was better than none at this point. "Certainly."

They walked out of the room into the hall. "My name's Frank Scolaro." The man held his hand out.

"I'm pleased to meet you," Anne said, shaking it.

"I've seen some of your work," he said. "I really admired it."

"Thank you."

"I mean really. I'm not just saying that. I think you have a potential that no director has ever really uncovered."

She looked at him with rising interest. He seemed sincere. "Really?"

He looked a little embarrassed. "I'm sorry if this offends you, but I don't know if you want to hear my opinion."

"Of course," she said, "I'd love to."

"Well, I saw you, oh, about five years ago in something, what was it called? *On the Carpet*, something like that?"

"Yeah, that's right," she said, *"On the Carpet."*

"Well, I saw something there, just in a couple of scenes, that I thought really should have been played up. It was a kind of a vulnerability. Almost a fear in you. Was that something that was in the script? In the director's mind?"

It was interesting, Anne thought. She thought she'd done her finest work in that film. And yes, there had been a vulnerability, and, no, it hadn't been in the director's mind. The film had bombed, however, and the critics hadn't commented on her part.

"No," she said. "It was something I brought out of myself. For some reason the part demanded it, and it was something that I had to give, that I felt should be shown. I felt it was appropriate somehow."

"Right," he said, "that's what I thought. It was just so truthful, it seemed so real, and it seems to me that no one else has brought that out in you, or no part you've done since then has demanded that, and I wish it would, because I think it's a very fine piece of work. I think you've got a lot of fine work in you."

"Well, thank you. What did you say your name was?"

"Frank Scolaro."

"And you're trying out for this movie *Deep Down?*"

"Yeah, I'm trying out for the part of Allan. I don't think it's right for me, but what the hell. You know what I mean? My agent called them and that's the part they thought I should test for."

"Well, you've certainly got the looks," she said.

"Thanks."

He really was a most attractive young man, she thought. With that slim, hard body, not an ounce of waste on the lean face, and those smoldering brown eyes, he looked more leading man material than a fourth billing like the Allan part.

"Miss Cort," he began.

"Yes?"

"I wonder if I could see you again. I'd like to get to know you better."

He was such a child. So much younger. And yet, why not? What did she have to lose? It didn't take her more than a second to make up her mind.

"Yes," she said. She reached into her bag and took out a card. "You can reach me at the number on this card. It's my service, they forward all my calls."

"That would be great. I'd love to talk to you for a while."

"Fine," she said. "I look forward to hearing from you." She pressed the elevator button then.

He looked at her for a moment, and then said, "Well, I'd better get back in there in case I'm called. It was nice to meet you."

"Yes, it was nice to meet you." She watched him turn and saunter away. He had a nice ass.

The elevator came and she stepped in. She was a fool, she told herself. He was young, as young as Richard even. And she was a woman who was too old to get the part of a thirty-year-old character. She was forty, and Frank Scolaro was probably at least ten years younger than she. What on earth did he see in her? Why did he want to see her again? What did he want? Why was she such a fool? The elevator plummeted and with it, the feeling of well-being that she had felt for a moment as she stood before his admiring glance.

I'm an old, blowsy, over-the-hill actress who's destined to play character parts if she wants to continue in her profession, she thought bitterly. Why not face up to it now? Why keep denying the fact? Why not just confront the truth and get on with what needs to be done?

But it was too hard, too painful. By the time the elevator doors opened on the first floor she had fixed that smile back onto her face. And swept through the lobby, fortified by the knowledge she was followed by admiring male glances.

Frank Scolaro called her that evening about 7 P.M.

"Hi, this is Frank Scolaro. We met today at the casting offices."

"Yes, I remember." She was surprised to hear his voice so soon—surprised to hear it at all. "How are you?"

250

"I'm fine," he said. "I was wondering if we could get together for a drink or something?"

"When would you like to do that?" she asked.

"Well, I know that you probably have something planned and that this is ridiculously short notice, but what about this evening? I mean, if you don't have anything else to do."

God forbid she allow anyone to think she had nothing to do, but for some reason this young man disarmed her. What the hell? she thought. "As a matter of fact, I am free this evening," she said a little stiffly.

"That's great. Where would you like to meet? Or shall I pick you up?"

"You could pick me up," she said. "How about an hour?"

"That'd be fine."

She gave him the address of her apartment in Beverly Hills, and hung up the telephone.

It was ridiculous, she kept on telling herself.

She hurried into the shower, rinsed down, not even taking the time to look for telltale wrinkles and sags as she normally did, and then came out to choose an outfit.

He was so young, so much younger than she. What was it he saw in her? Could it be that he had really seen her? That in that film he had spoken so highly of, he had seen the real Anne? The one she had suppressed for so long, and never allowed to escape? The thought both mortified and exalted her.

For once she chose jeans, although she couldn't have explained why. In spite of her full figure, she still looked good in them, she noticed. Could it be that they implied youth? Jeans were young, jeans were happening. The hell with it; her reasons didn't matter. She wore them with a silk, silver blouse and a pink scarf.

Promptly an hour later, she answered her buzzer and heard his voice come up through the speaker, tinny and tentative. "Frank Scolaro."

251

"I'll be right down."

She met him in the lobby. He wore gray slacks, an open-necked cream shirt, and a navy jacket. Somehow he seemed older than when she had seen him earlier in the day, dressed then in blue jeans and a blue shirt.

"Where would you like to go?" he asked as they walked through the door.

He was a struggling actor, just like she was and probably couldn't afford to go anywhere expensive, she thought with unaccustomed sympathy. "There's a little bar down the street. It's nothing much, but it's comfortable and friendly," she said. "I'll show you the way."

"That'll be fine." He led her to a small blue Toyota and opened the door for her. He got into the other side and settled into his seat. "I'm sorry about the car. You're probably used to limos and Rolls-Royces, but this is all I can afford."

"This is fine," Anne said, looking across at him.

He gave her a quick grin and put the car into gear.

It was a small neighborhood bar, with vinyl-covered barstools and vinyl seats on the booths. But it was, as she said, a friendly, safe place. And the drinks they served were honest and inexpensive. When you asked for a gin and tonic you got gin and not some watered-down version.

It was what she ordered. He did the same. "This is kind of amazing for me," he said with almost childlike candor. "I mean, it's overwhelming. I've admired you for so long and seen you in so many movies and to be sitting here with you right now, I'm at a loss for words."

"Well, it's just you and me," Anne said. "Nothing to be afraid of. Why don't we just relax and get to know each other?"

"I feel like I already know you," Frank said. "Just from watching your work. Before that, I was a fan of many of your father's films. He's contributed so much to movies over the years."

"Well, tell me about yourself," Anne said. "You're not from L.A. obviously. When did you come here and why?"

Frank had grown up in New Jersey, the third son of five in a large Italian family. After finishing high school, he had studied drama in New York, attended workshops, waited tables, driven cabs, and followed the normal pursuits of a young actor looking for work. He had played in a number of off-Broadway productions and done a couple of television commercials before deciding to head out to Los Angeles.

"It was always the movies that attracted me," he said. "I grew up with the movies. More than anything I wanted to work in them."

"So how has it been?" Anne asked.

"Well, I haven't exactly taken the city by storm, but I have been working. Mainly small parts. I've been here two years and in that time I've had small character parts in three features and half a dozen TV shows, and I've done two more commercials, one of which was a national spot for an automobile company. That's essentially what I've been living on."

Anne felt a sudden stab of jealousy. The kid had been here only two years and already worked twice as much as she had in that time. Age again, she thought bitterly. The town worshipped youth. Once you lost it, the town ignored and even reviled you. However, instead of showing her thoughts she congratulated him.

"That's not bad for two years," she said. "You may not be taking the town by storm, but at least it's keeping you alive, which is more than can be said for a lot of other actors."

Frank shrugged modestly. "I have talent, I believe that. And I look good on the screen, but so do a thousand other wanna-bes. I'm convinced that it's just going to be a matter of persistence."

"You're right. There are a lot of talented, pretty people in this town. The ones who make it are the ones who keep showing up for work even when it isn't there. Sooner or later it is there. And when it is, so are they."

"They liked me at the audition today, I think I'm going to get a callback on it. How did you do?"

She was going to lie and give the usual cheerful answer, but instead the bitterness seeped through. "I arrived to read for one part and they wanted me to read for another, an older part."

"Oh, you were up for the Cass part. What did they want you to do?"

"Amy, a fifty-year-old has-been actress. I may not be fifty, but I could be considered a has-been, I suppose."

"Don't do that to yourself," Frank said irritably. "You're not a has-been. You may be older than most of those women there, but that's nothing to be ashamed of. Aging is something we all do. The difference is that some of us do it gracefully and some of us don't."

"What do you know about age? How old are you anyway?"

"I'm almost twenty-eight," he said.

"And I'm . . ." She almost said her real age, which was forty, but couldn't bring herself to do it. ". . . in my late thirties. That's very old in Hollywood."

"Not if you're doing the parts you should be doing. Parts that demand a woman of substance."

"You mean character roles?" she asked with a derisive edge.

"Yes, character roles. It's what you're good at. But it's something that you've never really tried to do. Maybe now you'll face up to the fact that that's what you should be doing if you want to work," he said bluntly.

Anne looked at him coolly, her immediate reaction one of irritation. But suddenly there didn't seem any point defending an untenable position; she knew that what he was saying was right. Like it or not, she wasn't the young ingenue anymore. She wasn't the glamorous, svelte young sex symbol. She was a forty-year-old woman who had seen a lot of life and showed it. Hell, maybe he was right. Perhaps if she could get parts that demanded that she utilize and show her experience, she could have an entirely new career, a second chance.

They talked for an hour or more. Frank was attractive, charming, and flattering. A vital young man. She felt seduced by his mere presence. Somehow his youthful enthusiasm enabled her to drop years off her own life. Finally she said, "I should be getting back."

Regretfully he paid the bill and drove her back to her apartment.

"Would you like to come up for a cup of coffee?" she said as he pulled to a stop.

"I'd love to, just let me park the car." He parked down the street, and then went around to open the door for her.

She'd had three drinks in the bar and felt a little tipsy. She almost stumbled as she got out of the car. But he grasped her arm firmly and held her upright. "Oops," she said, and giggled.

Going up in the elevator, Anne felt an unfamiliar nervousness. She was an experienced woman used to the attentions of men, but usually they were men of her own age or older. Somehow, this younger, attractive man made her apprehensive. It was as if his youth served only to emphasize her age.

She opened the apartment door, stepped in, and flicked on the light. "Home sweet home."

"It's very nice," he said from behind her.

It was a small apartment, but everything in it had been chosen with care, from the leather furniture, to the paintings on the walls, to the black lacquer entertainment center and bookshelves, to the small ornaments that filled the spaces where there weren't books.

"Thank you." And then she felt his hands on her shoulders. It was now she would have to decide, she realized, as his hands turned her around to face him.

"Why?" she said, almost in a whisper.

"Because I like you," he said, a softness in the liquid brown eyes.

"But why? I'm old enough to be your mother. You must have your choice of younger women."

"You're not old enough to be my mother," he corrected her, with a flash of that earlier irritation. "You're probably ten years older than I am, and that doesn't mean anything. As for the young girls, I'm tired of young girls who have nothing to say, or think they have a lot to say, based on no experience."

"Oh," she said, and then found herself being pulled toward him.

A moment later, his mouth met hers and all thoughts of judgment or resistance, or anything else for that matter, left. There was only the two of them—a man and a woman about to begin an ageless ritual.

CHAPTER THIRTEEN

"I'm a man, not a saint," Miles said. "Even if I wanted to, sainthood isn't something I could pull off. Not even I could do that."

He was responding to Shannon's question about his famous casting couch. "Was it indeed true that almost every day an actress visited you there?"

"Sure it's true," Miles said. "What am I supposed to do? The most beautiful women in America throw themselves at me, and I'm supposed to say no?" He looked at her doubtful expression and said, "You've got to understand, actresses are harlots. Actresses are different from any other kind of animal. They will all, without exception, do anything to forward their careers."

"Without exception? I find that hard to believe."

"Yeah, well, maybe I'm generalizing. There may be one or two exceptions, but they don't count. They weren't normal. They were angels."

"What are you really doing here?"

Shannon was lying on a lawn chair beside the pool, enjoying a much-needed break from her interviews and other research. She wore only a bikini and the hot sun filled her with a luxurious lethargy. She opened her eyes and struggled to focus on Orson looking down at her.

"Excuse me?" she asked.

Orson pulled over a chair and sat heavily beside her. "What's really going on here? You're not here only writing a biography. That can't be all there is to it."

Shannon sat up, adjusting her bikini top. "I don't know what you're talking about. Is there something I should know?"

"There is something I should know and you're not telling me," Orson said belligerently. He wore a suit and he looked hot even though the jacket was draped over his arm. "None of this makes sense, Miles suddenly deciding he wants a biography written. I figure you've got to be here for some other reason. Are you and the old man getting it on?"

"That's outrageous," Shannon said coldly. "I'm here to write a book and that's all I'm here for. I suggest if you have any further questions you ask your father. Now, leave me alone."

"Yeah," Orson said with a nasty smile, "I might just do that."

He turned and stalked back into the house. Superior bitch, he thought to himself. He entered Lynn Reid's small office without knocking and said, "I'd like to see Miles."

She looked up from the papers she was working on, a slight frown on her forehead. "You don't have an appointment."

"I know I don't have an appointment, but I still want to see him. Buzz him and tell him it won't take long. I just need to consult with him briefly about something."

She reached for the phone on her desk and relayed the message to Miles. He couldn't have been pleased because she said, "He says it won't take long, sir. Yes, sir." She hung up the receiver and said to Orson, "He's in the study, he said for you to go in. He said you have five minutes."

Orson turned without thanking her and walked down

the hall to the study. His father sat behind the desk. He looked up at his son, not wasting time on small talk. "What?"

"I need some help," Orson said. "I'm in a little financial trouble and I have a second due on the house, a balloon payment. I'd like you to lend me some money if you could."

Miles raised his eyebrows. "Lend you some money? Well, that's a pleasant change. Normally you want me to invest in one of your crackpot movies."

"Well, I realize you don't want to do that, so I thought if I could just borrow some money at a regular interest rate, that might be one way of doing it."

"Why don't you earn money like everybody else in the world does?" Miles asked.

"Look, I'm in a little bit of trouble, I'll be out of it soon. I just need your help for me to get through this, that's all I'm asking. I'm not asking for a lecture," Orson said.

"How much do you need?" Miles asked.

"Fifteen thousand dollars," Orson answered.

"Ten percent interest repayable within twelve months."

"That's fine," Orson said.

Miles picked up the telephone. "Miss Reid, come in please." A moment later she entered the study. "Make out a check in the amount of fifteen thousand dollars to my son here. And also write up a promissory note saying that this amount is due with ten percent interest in twelve months. It's a loan."

"Yes, sir," she said.

Orson was shocked at how easy it had been. He'd expected a royal battle, even a refusal. But it had seemed worth a chance. "Well, I guess, thanks."

"You be sure and pay it back," Miles said. "I'll have your ass if you don't."

"Yes, I will," Orson said. "Thanks." He walked back toward Lynn's office.

There was something perfect about it, poetic. He was using his father's own money to hire someone to dispose of him. He couldn't help it, he laughed out loud as he entered Lynn's office. She looked up from her desk with surprise and Orson grinned cheerfully at her. He wouldn't have to pay the money back, there wouldn't be anyone to pay it to.

Stephen took Shannon to dinner in a small Korean restaurant in Korea Town, just south of Olympic Boulevard. The walls were made of bamboo and they sat inside a curtained booth, attended by a discreet Korean waitress wearing a colorful native costume. The food was delicious. From the highly spiced barbequed ribs, to the seafood swimming in some kind of sauce she had never tasted before, to the tasty dumplings, the food came in a never ending stream.

Stephen was relaxed as always and yet Shannon noticed it was like a cat's relaxation. She could imagine him springing into some kind of action at a moment's notice. It was the relaxation of someone who knew that at any moment something could happen, and that he would be prepared for it.

"How's the book coming along?" he asked.

"I find your father more and more fascinating," she said. "I think I'm actually getting to know him."

"Hmm," Stephen said noncommittally.

"You think you know him?"

He looked up from his food, "You know what Miles always says, 'You know a man by his deeds.' It's one of his favorite little aphorisms."

"Would it surprise you to know then, that for the past ten years Miles has been one of the sole supporters of a shelter for battered women in Hollywood?"

For a second Stephen looked surprised, then he said,

260

"Well, he's probably battered a few in his time. Perhaps this is just his conscience speaking."

"Do you believe that people can change?" she asked.

Stephen put down the rib he had been holding and looked at her. "You're really intending to have a serious conversation about this, aren't you?"

"I'm sorry," Shannon said with a smile. "But I'm discovering a side of your father that I didn't know existed before. And I'm just curious to know what you really think, behind that antagonism you show toward him."

"I've told you before what I think," Stephen answered. "Miles contaminates people around him. His thrust for power, his drive toward his own goals sweeps people aside and sometimes injures them."

"You said something about evil."

"I think that is evil."

Shannon leaned forward on the table. "But do you think that people can change?"

There was a momentary hesitation on Stephen's part. He blinked, looked away, and then looked back at her. "Yes, I do think people can change. But for Miles to change at this stage of his life? It's too much to ask for. Besides, I'd rather talk about us."

"Us?" Shannon said, ladling some rice into her plate. "What us?"

"The us that could be," Stephen said. "You can't deny that you're feeling what I'm feeling."

"I'm not being coy," Shannon said deliberately, "but I don't know what you're feeling."

"I feel as if I've known you for a long time." He sipped his wine, looking at her over the top of the glass, his eyes gentle. "I feel that some part of me that's been missing is suddenly here. It's snapped into place. I don't really understand it, but that's the way I feel. A discombobulated man whose pieces are snapping back where they belong. What do you feel?"

Shannon looked at him thoughtfully before answering.

"I think you are the most attractive man I've ever met. But I don't trust that."

"You don't trust your own feelings, you mean?"

"Of course not, not when it comes to an attraction as enveloping as this. I think that based on my experience that this type of, for lack of a better word, infatuation, is either very, very wonderful or very, very disastrous. I'm not sure yet how this would turn out."

"Well, that's the risk we all take, isn't it? Nothing tried, nothing gained."

"That's very glib," she said levelly. "You can do better than that."

He had the grace to look embarrassed. "You're right. It is and I can." He reached across the table and touched her hand with one finger, resting it on one of her knuckles. "I'm just as scared as you are. I haven't felt this way in a long, long time. And all the do's and don'ts keep running through my mind. I feel like an incompetent. I want you, I don't want you. I want to touch you, I don't want to touch you." He withdrew his finger, then put it back again on her hand. "I want to say this, I don't want to say this. And what I really want to do is just crush you in my arms."

It was true, Shannon thought looking into his eyes. He really did feel that way. And he really was scared. For some reason it gave her the strength to acknowledge her own feelings. "I know," she admitted with relief, "I feel the same way."

"So what are we going to do?" Stephen asked.

"We're going to take it one step at a time," she said. "First of all, we're going to enjoy our dinner."

Stephen laughed, delighted by her response. "I agree. While it may be confusing, while it may be intense, there is no need for it to be this serious, is there?"

"No," Shannon said. "There isn't."

"So on that light note, what do you want to do? Talk about my father again?" he asked ironically.

"He is a fascinating man. I wonder why he really wanted this biography written. I thought first that it was simply the egomania of an immensely wealthy man of accomplishment. And then I thought that the motive was revenge." Shannon toyed with a condiment bottle. "Now I don't know. I'm not so sure anymore. I have the glimmerings of something else."

"Of what?"

"I don't know. They are only glimmerings. When I decide I'll let you know."

They ate in silence for a minute and then she said, "How did Miles treat you when you were a child?"

"I suppose you could say, with neutral callousness," Stephen said. "That didn't bother me as much as how he treated my mother."

"And how did he treat her?"

"He was cruel to her. He was unfaithful to her all the time, you know. His little inner sanctum with the casting couch in it was a joke throughout Hollywood. Everyone knew and laughed about it. I even knew about it when I was a kid. Kids used to talk about it in school. My mother couldn't have been ignorant. The indignity of that was terrible."

"But surely she was responsible for enduring that?" Shannon asked.

"I suppose she was. And yet I find it hard to forgive him for subjecting her to it, for placing her in that position. She really is a wonderful woman and deserves better. Always has. Always will."

"I like her, too," Shannon said. "But one thing I've learned is never try and understand the marriage or sexual relationships between people. The agendas are always hidden from the view of outsiders."

"Yes, I know you're right," Stephen said. "But this is my mother, and while I was an outsider to most of what went on in their marriage, I was still a witness."

"She still loves him, you know," Shannon said quietly.

"My mother?"

"Yes. He told me she came to the mansion as soon as he had his stroke and took charge of everything."

"I know she does," Stephen said with puzzlement in his voice. "And that's why I know what you say is true, about not understanding other people's marriages. Because I don't understand it. And yet it's there. It's real. She does love him still after all these years."

"Well, perhaps she saw something in him that you never saw."

Stephen nodded. "Yeah, I came to that same conclusion. It's why no matter what I say about Miles, no matter to what extent I recognize the evil which he's created, I don't hate him. I can't. I only hate those things in him which are hateful. And I suppose everything you were saying tonight is true. But I'm afraid I've just never seen it. So you have to forgive me for not being more charitable."

Shannon reached across the table and put her hand over his. "I forgive you," she said with a mischievous smile.

"Have you had enough to eat? You've been stuffing yourself like a pig."

"Please," she said, "I'm a lady. I've just been doing exactly what you've been doing. You're the one who's been ordering the food."

"Well, have you had enough?"

"I think if I had any more, I'd burst," she said.

"Would you like to go?"

"Where to now?" she asked.

"I thought we'd stop at a club in Santa Monica, some friends of mine are playing there tonight."

"I'd love it."

They drove down Western to the Santa Monica Freeway and then wound through streets she'd never seen before, finally stopping before a small doorway. A club called At My Place.

Everybody there seemed to know Stephen. They either greeted him with a shout or a handshake. And somehow, in spite of the crowd, they were directed to a table a few feet from the stage.

The band was called Last Carousel, four men—a drummer, a guitarist, a bass guitarist, and a singer. And for twenty minutes Shannon sat entranced by their music.

When the set finished, the members came to the table to speak to Stephen and he introduced Shannon to them— Justin, Tony, Marine, and Matt. They were young, at least ten years younger than Stephen, but there was an easy camaraderie between them. Something she had noticed before that musicians, no matter how different, seemed to share. There seemed to be a common refusal to accept the generation gap that had been so promoted by the media in the years past.

"What did you think of them?" Stephen asked.

"I thought they were wonderful. They're young, they must all be under twenty. They seem so much more together than when I was that age."

Stephen laughed. "It seems that way to me, too. I don't know if it's true or not. Maybe we seem together to people who are older than us."

"I doubt it," she said. "I had no idea who I was or what I wanted or where I wanted to go. Did you?"

"Yes, I did," he said. "I think from the age of fourteen, I knew I was going to be a musician of one kind or another."

"How did you start?"

"I started playing clarinet in the junior high school band. Luckily we had a wonderful teacher, Miss McNamara. She was probably a failed musician herself, but she still loved music enough to teach us the basics. And they stood me in good stead. After playing clarinet for a year, I discovered keyboards and started playing them. And then when I got into high school I picked up the bass guitar and knew that that was my instrument."

"So how many instruments do you play now?"

"I play almost everything," he said modestly.

"Almost everything?" she said, kiddingly. "Do you even play drums?"

"Well, yes, as a matter of fact, I do."

"A very versatile man?"

"I'm a musician. I play music."

"But the bass is still your instrument?"

"In a way it is. But in the last three years I discovered synthesized electronic music. It's a marvelous freedom for a musician, because you can synthesize any instrument. And I think since then I've really grown from the status of instrumentalist to one of composer. I'm much more interested in composing music now than in playing it."

The next band to take the stage wasn't very good. After a dozen bars of their music Stephen looked at Shannon and asked if she wanted to leave. She nodded and when they got back into the car, he asked where she wanted to go next.

"I don't want to go home. It's been a wonderful evening," she said.

"Would you like to come to my place?" he asked. "We can have coffee and dessert there."

"Yes," she answered.

When they reached his downtown loft half an hour later, they stood inside his living room and he looked at her with a strange quizzical smile. "Coffee?"

"No."

He stepped up to her then and stopped so close to her that she could feel the warmth of his body even though they weren't touching.

"Shannon?"

"I'm afraid."

He reached his hand out and touched her face with the back of his fingers in a gentle, brushing gesture.

"You have nothing to fear from me."

She looked at him dumbly and then in a shared gesture which she would forever be uncertain who initiated, their

266

mouths met. Their lips opened and their tongues twined and she felt herself sink against him, her arms on his back.

Their bodies clung together as if for warmth, but it was a warmth that generated fire. Soon the passion rose between them and she felt her breasts swell, her nipples grow hard, and felt him grow hard against her. After what seemed like a long, long time, they drew apart.

"Come on." He took her hand. They went to the bedroom and stood beside a queen-size bed. "It's a waterbed," he said unnecessarily.

"I've always been afraid of waterbeds," she said, making the same inane type of conversation. "I always wondered what would happen if they burst while you were in the throes of passion."

"This is a very expensive waterbed," he explained seriously. "There are seven independent lengthwise cushions of water in it. Only one can break at a time, and they never have."

"Do you mean you don't get seasick?"

He reached out and began to unbutton her blouse. "If you move on one side of the bed, I can't even feel it on the other." And then her blouse was unbuttoned and then he pushed it off her shoulders and reached behind her and unsnapped her bra, and the feel of his hands against her skin made her gasp.

She did the same to him, unbuttoning his shirt and then it seemed only seconds later they both stood naked beside the bed. He took her arms and turned her so that the back of her legs rested against the bed, and then slowly pushed her down and knelt on the floor before her, and plunged his face between her thighs. She felt his gentle hands stroke her and the movement of his gentle tongue and lifted her legs over his shoulders, feeling an uncontrollably wild passion and a growing heat like an exploding ball of flame centered from her vagina.

She wanted him close, she wanted to feel him, to touch him and hold him, and, as if he sensed this, he lifted his head and kissed her stomach, her navel, her breasts and then her mouth until they were lying together on the bed, their bodies trying to meld into each other.

She wanted him, all of him, and slid down to encompass him in her mouth, moaning at the taste of leaking nectar.

"No," he begged, "no more. Come here." And again she slid up his body and finally couldn't hold back any longer and thrust herself onto him with a groan. She felt him in her and bounced joyfully on top of him, looking down at his contorted face and feeling the swelling of him, which seemed inside her to be creating another swelling.

And then they both shouted and groaned and came together in a tumultuous climax that left them collapsed against each other dripping with sweat.

"Oh, God. Ecstasy," she murmured.

Two hours later, after they had made love again, Shannon sighed regretfully. "I've got to go home soon."

Stephen, who was leaning on one elbow and looking down at her, asked, "Can't you stay?"

She shook her head. "Melissa would be upset when she woke up in the morning. I didn't tell her I'd be staying out all night."

He ran a finger lazily around one of her nipples, and she couldn't help but feel a stirring again, a reaction that amazed her. He leaned down and kissed her gently on the mouth. "You are wonderful in every way."

She reached her hand over and grasped his penis. "And you're wonderful in the ways that count."

"You're an animal."

"You make me feel like an animal," she said. "I haven't felt this way for a long time."

"Neither have I. I love you and I want to marry you."

She wasn't shocked or surprised for some reason, but she said, "So soon? We hardly know each other."

"I feel as if I've known you forever."

"I feel the same way," she said.

He touched her mouth with his finger. "I've never asked anyone to marry me before."

"I've been asked before, but I've never been tempted to say yes," she said.

"And now?"

"And now, I don't know. This has happened too fast."

He smiled down at her. "But you want to say yes, in spite of your natural caution, don't you?"

"Yes," she whispered in wonder, realizing that what he said was true.

"Well, I won't rush you."

It was four in the morning when he dropped her off at the mansion, but she didn't go inside her cottage. She sat on the porch in the cooling night air and stared at the lights on the grounds and the twinkling lights high in the sky. Body and soul felt replete, satisfied, calm. It was such a wonderful feeling, she didn't want to lose it by going to sleep. Finally, as dawn sent the first brushstrokes of light into the sky, she got up and went inside and climbed into her bed and fell asleep.

Sissy had arrived home from London late the previous night. The reunion made the aching loneliness Elizabeth had felt during her absence seem worthwhile. They had talked and made love with a hunger that only separation can fuel and talked again and finally fallen asleep in the early hours of the morning.

It was now almost noon and they had both staggered out of bed and were sipping their first cup of coffee. Sissy, who managed to look beautiful in spite of the fact she wore no makeup and her hair was in total disarray, was still excited about her trip.

"I love London," she said, "but I really missed you. I think we should take a vacation there together, there's so much we could do. It would be so much more fun with you there."

"We will," Elizabeth promised. "We can do it anytime, as soon as you get a break between movies."

"Oh, God," Sissy said, "I have so much work lined up. I don't know when I'm going to get that break."

"You'll get it anytime you decide to turn a job down," Elizabeth said. "We can just plan for it."

"Yeah, we could. We could go there for two weeks, three weeks, rent a car, drive around the south of England, visit quaint little villages and old abbeys and walk along hedgerows in the countryside. Oh, it would be wonderful."

Elizabeth smiled at her contagious enthusiasm. "I could use a trip myself. L.A.'s getting to be a drag."

Sissy gave her a keen look. "Is anything wrong?"

Elizabeth debated whether to tell her what had been happening, but she didn't want to suppress Sissy's happy mood, and just shook her head. "No, everything's fine. I'm so glad you're back though, I really missed you."

"Oh, God, you know what I missed more than anything, and you know what I want for breakfast more than anything, and I'm going to get dressed right now and go and get it?"

"What's that?" Elizabeth asked, amused.

"A hamburger and fries. Do you know how horrible hamburgers are in London? They call them Wimpy burgers there—something like that. And that's what they are. They are really wimpy. The best hamburger you can get there is like a McDonald's."

She got up and walked toward the bedroom. "I'm going to do it right now. I'm just going to throw on some jeans and run out and get it."

"For breakfast?" Elizabeth shouted after her.

"For breakfast." She came out a moment later, still barefoot but with jeans and a T-shirt on. "Can I take your car?"

"Of course. Maybe you could get me something like an Egg McMuffin or something like that."

"Okay, I won't be long." Sissy blew her a kiss and went out the side door to the garage.

Elizabeth hugged her knees and smiled secretly to herself. She loved Sissy so and had missed her so when she was away. This was what as a young girl she had imagined having a husband would be like. In a way she now had a husband—a lover, someone she loved who loved her as much. It was all she'd ever wanted and all that had ever been denied to her until now.

Faintly through the thick wall she heard the garage door open, and then the car door slam closed. And then she heard the engine kick over and the car back out of the garage into the driveway. It stopped, she heard the door slam again, and Sissy came bursting back into the house, her purse in her hand. "Ah, I'm silly. I don't have any American money, all I have is English money. Do you have a few bucks?"

"Sure, I'll get it for you." Elizabeth got up and went to the bedroom and came back out with a ten-dollar bill. "Here," she said, holding it out.

Sissy took it and then kissed her on the cheek. "I'm so glad to be back."

"And I—"

She never finished what she was about to say because suddenly the sound of the motor was replaced by a peal of terrible thunder which shook the entire house and sent glasses, ornaments, books, and pictures to the floor and had the two of them grabbing each other, staring at each other's confusion with their mouths open.

And then Elizabeth knew suddenly what it was and ran for the side door and into the garage and stood there looking out at the driveway and the tangled, twisted, smoking wreckage of her car as flames licked hungrily into the air and black smoke billowed up through them.

Sissy stood behind her, amazement on her face. "What . . . what happened?"

Elizabeth grabbed her and held her tightly as if she never wanted to let her go. "It could have been you. It could have been you . . ."

The fire department had come and gone and now there was just the police to contend with. The young policeman who stood in the kitchen with them while his partner continued to search through the garage for clues was regarding Elizabeth with sullen suspicion. "Ma'am, why would somone plant a bomb in your car and yet you say you've received no threats of any kind?"

Elizabeth was exhausted. She wanted to scream at him, but instead she said, "I don't know, Officer, I really don't know why anyone would want to do something like this."

I can't say, she told herself, I can't say. Echoing in the back of her mind was that it could have been Sissy instead of her. If Sissy had the correct money with her, if she hadn't stopped the car and run back inside . . .

The explosives expert said the bomb had a timing device set to go off a minute after the car started. They probably wanted it out in the street when it went off, he said.

The young officer repeated his question. "Ma'am, are you sure you can think of no reason anybody would want to do this?"

Elizabeth shook her head.

He sighed and said, "Well, I'm afraid you'll be getting more questions from other officers as the investigation continues."

"I'll be happy to answer them," she said. "I just really can't tell you anything to help you. Maybe it's a case of mistaken identity. Maybe they thought I was somebody else."

"Maybe," the officer said. He went back through the

house to the garage where his partner was. They talked for a few minutes, walked around, and then finally left.

Still shaking, Elizabeth put water on for coffee. Sissy stared at her with a strange, fixed expression on her face. "Yes?" Elizabeth said, irritated by it.

"Do you want to tell me what's going on? I've known you long enough to know you were lying to that policeman, and he knew it, too, by the way."

And so back in the living room, over coffee, Elizabeth told Sissy about the offer to buy her business and about the Mob affiliation. "You mean the Mob, like the Mafia?" Sissy asked.

"Yes, that's what I was told. Jesus Christ, I don't know what to do," Elizabeth said.

"Hell, there's only one thing you do. You call that guy right now and sell him your business."

Elizabeth shook her head stubbornly. "I can't sell. If I sell it I've got nothing. You don't think they are going to give me much money for it, do you? They just want the competition out of the way. They'll probably offer me a buck, just to make it legal."

"Well, can't you go to the police and tell them what happened?"

Elizabeth sighed. "These people are like ants, you kill one and there's a dozen more behind them. There are rows and rows of them. So the police go and question this lawyer, then what? He says he made a legitimate business offer. Besides, it's not like I run a legitimate business."

"It's legal," Sissy protested. "You've always told me that it's legal. That there's no sex, that you are simply acting out the fantasies of your customers. There's nothing illegal about it."

"I go to the police, it gets into the press, my father finds out about it, my family finds out about it, I can't let any of that happen."

"So what choice do you have? You have to sell."

It was all too much for Elizabeth. She couldn't contain

herself any longer. She began to sob, tears running down her face.

Sissy came over to her and took her in her arms and cradled her head against her chest. "It's okay. You're okay, I'm okay. It's okay."

"It's not okay," Elizabeth said between sobs. "It's never okay. I thought I was free, I thought this business gave me the freedom I've always wanted. I've never been free, I never will be free. I'm still trapped."

A half hour passed. There was still no solution in spite of all their talk, but at least Elizabeth was calm now. Finally she got up, saying, "I don't have any choice." She went to the study and took the young lawyer's card from her desk and dialed the number. When he came on the line, she said, "I got your message. I am willing to accept your offer providing it is equitable."

There was only a momentary silence and then Parker said in his cheerful salesman's voice, "I don't know what message you're talking about. I'm afraid my principals have asked me to withdraw the offer," he said.

It was so unexpected she didn't know what to say. And then after a moment she said, "What am I supposed to do now?"

"I would suggest you dissolve your business as of today," the lawyer said. "And I recommend that you do not try to open it at another location. Word gets around very fast in these circles and my principals would not be pleased to hear news like that."

There was a click as he hung up. She stared at the telephone and then put it down. She knew she had no choice but to obey.

Richard thought that sometimes his impulses were completely uncontrollable, like now.

He was at a Beverly Hills party being given by Gary Wylie, a developer worth megabucks. The Wylie name was well exposed in Los Angeles. There were Wylie buildings in Westwood Village and downtown near the Arco Plaza and along Miracle Mile on Wilshire Boulevard. The house where the party was being held, although only two-stories high, was a fairly impressive monument itself. Four wings had been added to the original and already large building, and one of them covered an Olympic-size indoor swimming pool, which is where the main body of the party was taking place.

Richard had been invited by Wylie's daughter, Melodie, who, like her father, was big and blonde, but who, unlike her father, showed little aptitude for anything but enthusiastic sexual adventures. Her favorite activity, Richard had discovered some months earlier, was giving head in the car while her current companion was driving, the more crowded the neighborhood the better.

His impulse now, however—the one that both terrified and excited him—was to make it, not with the buxom daughter, but with Sonya Wylie, Melodie's stepmother. Sonya was probably about forty, dark-haired and full-figured with black penetrating eyes and a wide, thin-lipped mouth that reminded Richard of a hungry predator. She was altogether more beautiful than her stepdaughter.

They were standing to one side of the room watching the milling crowd of a hundred people. When he wasn't talking to her, he felt Sonya measuring him with her gaze. She asked him questions about himself and his family and every now and again a pink tongue darted out to moisten her top lip. She was, he thought, a very sexy lady. "And you've been out with Melodie a few times?" she asked.

"Yes, she's a very nice girl," he said dutifully.

Sonya smiled sarcastically. "I would think she'd be a little too bovine for you," she said. She half closed her eyes and smiled warmly. "You strike me as the kind of man who would at least want his woman to move when he touched the right places."

That did it. It was all he needed. His urges were now

clamoring in an uncontainable chorus. "Do you want to do a couple of lines?" he asked.

"I'd love to," she said. "That's one thing I've never tried. Just follow me. I know a quiet place where we can be alone."

He glanced around the room. Gary Wylie was the center of attention, surrounded by a group of at least twenty people. He was tall, about six foot, with the build of a football player and short-cropped fair hair. He knew from what Melodie had told him that he was as straight as they come. Didn't approve of drugs or much of his daughter's behavior.

Sonya led the way down a long hall until she finally opened a door and stepped into a room. She flicked on the light, and then when he came in, closed the door and leaned back against it.

"Where are we?" he asked.

"It's a guest bedroom. Nobody ever comes here."

"Good." He went over to a glass-topped dresser and spread out four lines of cocaine. Taking a silver straw from his pocket, he handed it to Sonya. She had a curious and expectant expression on her face.

"I just sniff it, right?"

"Right," he said. "One in each nostril."

She leaned forward, showing an ample display of bra-less breasts in the facing mirror. Holding one nostril closed with her right finger, she held the straw in her left hand and took a deep sniff.

"Now the other one," he said.

She did the same again and then stood upright. "I don't feel anything."

Richard grinned, "Just wait a moment." He leaned down and did the two lines quickly. By the time he got up her face was pink.

"Oh," she said, "that feels so good. That feels good, that's almost as good as sex."

Richard felt his blood vessels expand and that familiar rush. "It's better than sex. You know why?"

She shook her head, her eyes fixed on him now.

"Because it makes sex better."

She smiled. "Show me." She sounded like a little girl, daring a risk.

Richard stepped up and kissed her. She pressed against him, her arms creeping around his shoulders, pulling him closer. In less than a minute they were both naked.

Sonya was definitely better looking than her stepdaughter, Richard thought, looking approvingly at her brown-skinned full body. There were no tan lines, either. Her breasts were large, but firm and upturned. Below was a flat stomach and long, muscled legs. She was looking at him with similar approval and then she fell into a crouch and took his penis in her mouth. "Umm. Yum, yum, that's good. That's very good."

For a moment a small voice appeared, a cautionary voice that told him what he was doing was insane, that the risk wasn't worth it. But as he entwined his fingers through her thick black hair, he pushed the voice aside. It was a voice that always tried to spoil his fun, what he had called ever since he could remember, his spoiled-sport voice. He had learned to listen to it less and less of late.

Somehow they made it onto the bed. She lay beneath him and lifted her knees up, opening herself for him, grabbing his penis with her hand and guiding him into her. She was dripping wet and tossed her head from side to side as he began to move, slowly at first but then with increasing frequency, banging hard against her, feeling the whole bed shake beneath them.

And then faintly, through the crimson rush of passion, he heard a sound behind him, but somhow it didn't register. It had no meaning, no significance in what he was doing now.

But then, a moment later, he couldn't ignore the anguished roar that filled the room. He stopped what he was doing, like a car skidding to a halt, and turned his head to see standing three feet away a red-faced and obviously distraught Gary Wylie.

Richard had time only to think, "Oh shit!" before he felt a meaty hand grab his ankle and yank.

"You dirty bastard! Fucking Cort sleaze!" Wylie shouted.

Richard fell to the floor, his hands automatically moving to cover his already limp penis. "You bastard!" Wylie repeated, and his foot whistled through the air, landing on Richard's shoulder.

He fell back with a flash of pain, and then Wylie was pulling him to his feet. Next he felt the fist, this enormous knuckled fist, crash against the side of his head. Before he could fall again, another fist appeared miraculously from the other direction and hit the side of his face. His ears began to ring and his sight grew curiously vague.

"I'm falling," he thought and wondered how he looked naked, spinning through the air, and wondered with some strange detachment if Sonya still had her knees up on the bed and what expression she now wore on her voracious face as she watched all this? The thought occurred to him that she was probably enjoying it.

And then he landed and felt the shoe again, this time in his stomach, and then again in the ribs, and then again on his head, and then the gauzy vision began to turn a bloody red and he wanted above all else to laugh at the stupid scene, at the wife and the young lover and the enraged husband at the party given for the elite of Los Angeles.

Somehow the laughter wouldn't come and the red began to turn, like a fadeout on a movie screen, to a deep, solid black.

"He's tied up on telephone calls probably for another ten minutes," Lynn said apologetically.

Shannon sat in the armchair in the study, her omni-present tape recorder on the table before her and a pad of notes on her lap. "That's fine. It'll give me a chance to go over my notes."

It was hard to concentrate. Her mind was still on Stephen, on the miraculous event that had occurred between them. She found herself missing him—his touch, his smile, the smell of him.

Sighing, she forced herself to pay attention to the task at hand. Miles always expected her to be prepared. Lucky he was late; it would give her a little time to get herself together.

She was used to Miles's erratic apppointments. Whatever other businesses he was involved in (a subject she had not yet broached), they certainly seemed to keep him occupied. Their appointments, originally scheduled for regular morning meetings, had instead taken place at Miles's whim: in the mornings, afternoons, and sometimes even at odd hours in the evening when he had an hour to spare. Essentially, she was on call.

Her notes had covered much of the family history, although to her standards it was far too superficial and would need to be delved into again. They had also covered his early years in the film business and the years before that running the family company. Miles apparently never forgot an anecdote, which was fortunate as it helped make the early years far more entertaining. The canning of foodstuffs was not a glamorous business, but somehow Miles made it appear so, even though he proclaimed that it was the most boring period of his life. He still attacked it with the same gusto that he later became famous for in the film business. "If you can't do it well, don't bother doing it" was one of his favorite sayings.

He was a difficult subject to control, however. Often she found herself beginning a meeting with a specific subject in mind yet ending it on a far different note. At times she attempted to divert him back to her planned passage, but at others the richness of the material was its own reward and she allowed him his divergences.

Her subject notebook was consequently a maze of arrows, crosses, and check marks to indicate what had been covered, what needed to be returned to, and what had been entirely missed.

There was the sound of the door, then the whir of electric machinery and the hiss of wheels. Miles sped over toward her, coming to a stop so that she faced his back and then quickly spinning the chair around a hundred eighty degrees to halt facing her.

"Good afternoon," he said with an uncharacteristically buccaneering smile.

"Good afternoon Mr. Cort," she said, a little taken aback by his show of exuberance.

"There is no need to point out my seniority or my age. For Godsake call me Miles. Everyone else does, including my children."

"Very well, Miles," she acceded.

He rubbed his hands together. "I have been busy on the telephone. I have both bad news and good news for you. First, for the bad. My detectives, so-called, who as you know have been attempting to find your young Melissa's father, have succeeded only in turning up no useful leads whatsoever. It seems he has disappeared from the face of the earth. I'm sorry to have to tell you that."

Shannon was crestfallen. She had been hoping now for weeks that some miracle would occur, that somehow Miles's men would find something she had overlooked and discover the whereabouts of Mark Keller. This news was not encouraging. "I see," she said.

"Their orders are to continue searching until they find him," he said a trifle belligerently, as if their failure reflected upon him.

"I appreciate that."

"But now for the good news." He hesitated, cleared his throat, and began again. "I have grown very fond of Melissa; in fact I must congratulate you upon rearing a child so exceptional under the circumstances in which you had to operate."

"Thank you," she said.

"She is truly an admirable young woman. And I only wish my own children were nearly as acceptable. On the other hand, it does reflect somewhat upon you as a mother and perhaps even me as a father—the differences between our children, I mean."

"I never thought I'd hear you admit to anything less than excellence of anything, even as a father," Shannon said.

Miles frowned at her. "Irony is wasted on me," he said accusatively. "Unlike most people, I know my shortcomings. Whether I admit them publicly or not is my business. However, be that as it may, I have grown fond of your daughter and I wish to help. Do you remember I mentioned the foundations I was forming?"

"Of course."

"Well, I have, or at least will have, a foundation supporting the Miles Cort Kidney Wing at a Los Angeles hospital for children. As you know, I sit as a director on many boards and recently remembered that I was on this hospital's board. I spoke to the president and asked if there was a need for an endowment. Naturally there was, and he encouraged me very strongly to make such an endowment saying it was sorely needed."

"I'm very impressed," Shannon said, as indeed she was. However, although it was sorely needed, it did not make up for the bad news that she had just heard.

Miles seemed to sense her disappointment. "Oh, no," he said, "there's more. I have taken the liberty of adding a stipulation to my generosity, one which the good doctor did not particularly approve of. However, practicality overcame his scruples."

"Oh?" Shannon asked, her curiosity pricked.

"Yes, the stipulation is that the first available kidney

281

with a tissue match for Melissa goes to her. There will be a search made of all available kidneys nationwide."

Shannon was stunned. There was a waiting list of kidney recipients, one which was inviolate. The standards were strict. Those who needed kidneys worst were at the top of the list, but of those who had similar tissue-typing, there were all kinds of priorities. It was, in essence, a waiting line.

"Do you mean that she could get a kidney before somebody who is ahead of her in line?"

Miles nodded. "She will get the first available kidney that matches her," he reiterated.

"How can you do that? How can they do that? I mean, how can they justify it?"

"The endowment is ten million dollars," Miles said drily.

"You mean you are buying her place in line?"

"Essentially that's correct."

"I don't know what to say. The money . . . what you're doing . . ."

Miles misread her confusion. "The money's nothing. I was going to leave it to something else. Now I can put it to a constructive use, the results of which I can personally see. It will affect somebody I know and whom I have developed a fondness for. What more could I ask?"

"It's not just the money," Shannon said. "Although I do appreciate your generosity. I mean, it's unbelievably generous. But there are matters of ethics involved here. I don't know how I feel about it."

"Ethics?" Miles raised an eyebrow. "We're talking of your daughter's life. You've told me how hard dialysis is for both her and you, and of the dangers involved. Each time she gets blood the risk that she contracts AIDS or some other disease mounts. How can you even question this?"

Shannon shook her head in confusion. "I don't know."

"Then don't!" Miles snapped. "Simply accept it for what it is, a stroke of good fortune."

"I don't know," she said again.

"You're not required to know," Miles said, growing angry now. "Think back to your predicament before knowing me. Think back to your financial difficulties and how clouded your future was. And just thank your lucky stars."

"I don't mean to seem ungrateful. I really don't. I'm stunned and overwhelmed by your generosity in this. It's just, it's just a matter of fairness or something." She was at a loss for words to explain her feelings.

Miles refused to acknowledge her qualms. "Some people deserve a little extra luck. Your daughter is one of them. She is a special person and should be treated as such."

"Some people deserve to live more than others, you mean?"

"Of course," he said. "It's only logical. It's only survival. It's how everything on this planet works. The fit and deserving survive. Lower life forms are devoured by higher life forms. People are no different. Those who have the strength, the courage, and determination to succeed do so over the failures of others."

"Such a bleak view of life," Shannon said.

"It is not bleak or any other emotion, it is just simply realistic. And the sooner you recognize it the better."

Shannon's own emotions were flooding her. Yes, there was gratitude, and yes, there was relief, and yes, there was even the strongest hope she had yet felt, but there was also a sense of fear and even horror. Was this the kind of power that money had, that it could buy a life? Something as intimate as a body organ? It was too unsettling. "I have to think about it," she said.

"There's nothing to think about. It's under way. All you have to do is wait," Miles said. "Now shall we get on with the interview?"

* * *

Shannon sat beneath the willow tree in a quiet corner of the grounds. It seemed fitting somehow. Los Angeles had once been arid desert. Now, through influence, money, power, which had brought water from far-off northern sites in California and states even farther north, these unquenchable trees were flourishing.

It was a question of power and money. It often was that way. The criminal who could afford the best lawyers received the lightest sentence. The rich and powerful could achieve the greatest security behind their gated and moated castles, the wealthiest corporations paid the least taxes. General Motors, if she remembered correctly, paid less taxes than she did for the previous year.

Ordinary people who wanted power knew how to play the game. The politicians who sought power first sought money from those who possessed the real power. The affluent East Coast bankers who had squandered the money of their depositors on loans to insolvent countries were supported by the politicians and ultimately the taxpayers. The world was a pyramid of wealth. At the apex, which covered such a small area, were a relative handful of those who controlled the destinies of that wide range below them. It was not fair and never had been fair.

It was, however, the way the game was played. And why should she have compunctions about taking advantage of it now that she was in a position to do so? She wasn't motivated by self-interest. She wasn't doing this for herself, she told herself hollowly. She was doing this for her daughter, the being she loved more than any other in the world.

The thought gave her resolve. It was selfless. How could she refuse? How could she turn it down when Melissa was faced with a solution to her agony? Wouldn't that be more of a criminal act than any other?

A hummingbird fluttered in midair no more than four

284

feet away from her, its brilliant scarlet breast poignantly beautiful. Such a small creature, so alive, moving so quickly, carrying such beauty.

Tears pricked her eyes. Her dilemma was painful. The thought that she had been suppressing surged to the forefront. If Melissa moved up in line to get the kidney she needed so badly, who would she pass? Who would be left behind and wanting?

CHAPTER FOURTEEN

"Everyone's motivated by self-interest. Don't let anyone tell you otherwise. Mother Teresa? She probably wants salvation more than anything else. The thought of hell probably terrifies her. Her good deeds are simply a method of ensuring her attainment of that personal goal. Everyone does what they do because of self-interest. Once you know that fact about people, once you really understand it and apply it, you can manipulate anyone. There is nothing wrong with it either. Self-interest is simply self-survival. Remember that about people. All you have to do is find out what they want most in the world," Miles said.

Orson looked over at the ebony skin of his secretary Wanda. She was snoring slightly, her wide nostrils flaring with each breath. They were in a motel room five blocks from the office at two-thirty in the afternoon.

She was exactly what he had expected. An enthusiastic yet unimaginative lover. Purely physical, she was given to loud grunts and energetic movements, but the giving and receiving of pleasure seemed almost secondary to the gymnastics of the act.

He noted the time and quietly slid out of the queen-size water bed, trying not to disturb her. The room was prepaid and it wouldn't be a shock when she woke to find him gone. He walked across the cheap carpet and clumsily put on his clothes.

He was getting too old for these intense gymnastics, he thought as he tied his shoelaces.

He had introduced Wanda to a producer—a more successful producer than he was—and the man had taken her to dinner and promised her an audition for the film he was currently casting. For all Orson knew, the producer had screwed her. He didn't care. All that mattered was that, in her gratitude, when he had almost absentmindedly patted her on the ass in the office a few hours earlier, she had suddenly rounded on him with an unmistakably sultry look. One thing had led to another, the ultimate end result being the current motel room.

He fumbled in his jacket pocket and pulled out the piece of paper that had arrived unsigned in the mail this morning. The envelope was addressed to him and marked "Confidential," underlined three times.

The note, scrawled on a piece of lined notebook paper, said simply, "Four P.M. at Bristo's Bar," with a hastily scrawled map showing the location of a bar on Lankershim Boulevard in North Hollywood. The note was unsigned, but Orson knew immediately that it had come from his unnamed hired assassin, known to him as Bill. He folded it again and put it back in the jacket.

This whole insane operation filled him with misgivings. Who was this man? And what power would he hold over him after the deed had been committed? What was he getting into? He was dealing with danger, the magnitude of which he had never before experienced. He was actually hiring a man to kill his father.

He looked nervously in the other pocket of his jacket to make sure the envelope containing the money was there. He pulled it out and looked at it again, thumbing through the hundred dollar bills—seventy-five hundred dollars of his father's money.

The thought made him grin again. It was poetic.

He looked once more at the sleeping Wanda and left the room.

He hopped on the freeway at Pass Avenue and then took the Lankershim exit a couple of minutes later.

The bar was much like the other had been, except there was no neon sign, just flaking white paint on a blued background. His unnamed contact obviously had a penchant for dives.

He parked the car on the side street and walked around the corner to the bar. Inside it was as dank and dark as the previous bar had been. A smell of mold permeated everything. The bartender looked like the brother of the one who had served him before at the previous meeting.

Orson squinted his eyes and looked through the gloom. His man wasn't there. He leaned on the bar and ordered a beer. A glass of draft cost fifty five cents, a throwback to preinflation days.

Two minutes later, a shadow filled the doorway. Orson turned and saw his man standing there, his eyes glancing quickly around the bar. Then he stepped in and, without looking at Orson, sat at a nearby booth. Orson picked up his beer and walked over to him.

The man looked at him with those pale, inhumanly expressionless eyes. 'Do you have the money?''

"Yes," Orson said, his throat suddenly dry. This was now reaching a point of no return. He had no idea what the consequences would be, but somehow he sensed that they could be fearful.

"Well?"

"I need to know more," Orson stammered. "What are you planning to do? When are you planning to do it?"

"It's better you know nothing."

"Yes, but . . ."

"Trade secrets," the man said with a thin, humorless smile.

288

"Well, I need to know when in order to get you into the grounds."

"The diagram you gave me with the alarms and sensors, it's up-to-date and accurate?"

"Yes," Orson said.

"Then I'll find my own way."

"You're not going to need me to get you inside in my car?"

The man shook his head. "I've decided that it's better you don't get involved. The more people involved in an operation like this, the more chances for mistakes."

"Well then, when? Are you going—?"

The man held up his hand, cutting off what Orson was about to say. "It's better you know nothing. Just give me the money and go your way, the job will be done. I'll contact you afterwards for the other half."

Orson didn't know what to say, the man was so certain. Obviously a consummate professional in his craft.

"Don't worry," the man said. "It'll be taken care of."

"But when?"

Another grim smile. "You'll hear about it."

"All right," Orson said, beginning to shuffle to his feet. The man's hand shot out and grabbed his wrist. "You're forgetting something."

"Oh, God, yes, of course," Orson said apologetically. He reached into his pocket and took out the envelope of money and handed it to the man.

"Thanks. You'll be hearing from me."

Orson said, "Good." And then not looking at the man again, he rushed from the bar into the sunlight as if he was being pursued.

The talons of the enormous bird raked at his face. The eyes, blood-red and angry, fixed on him, holding him there. The wings beat hot blasts of air into his face. The hiss of breath poisoned him.

289

And as if the attack from the air was not enough, the snakes circled him. Their scales were a myriad of tempting color and their forked tongues darted toward him like pricking swords, knowing that he was helpless, a receptacle simply waiting for the poison sacs behind their fangs to empty into him.

Richard woke with a shudder. He was sweating, every pore of his body awash with water and salt. His head thundered painfully and his mouth was coated with wool.

He wondered where he was, and through narrowed eyes allowed his glance to scan the room. Obviously a woman's room: the vanity, the dozens of bottles of cream and makeup and perfume scattered over it; the pink decor; the crumpled dress on the floor. He looked beside him and saw only the indentation where someone had slept.

It wasn't the horror or the pain that crippled him at this moment. It was self-loathing that filled him. It was something that seemed to grow stronger every day, and no matter what he did he couldn't lessen it. Not with the alcohol, the drugs, or the sex. It simply expanded and expanded and he knew that a time would come when it would encompass him so completely that one day he would no longer be there.

A woman came through the door, a cup of coffee in each hand.

"Oh, God," Richard groaned to himself and closed his eyes. He was still bruised from the beating he had received a couple of days earlier, and, worse, he still hadn't learned his lesson.

It was Elana, an actress at least eight or nine years his senior. She was easily the most beautiful woman he knew and he had avidly pursued her without success on a number of occasions. Apparently last night he had finally succeeded. He felt the bed move as she sat beside him.

"Come on," she said, "have some coffee."

He opened his eyes. She had shoulder-length black hair, the most perfectly shaped mouth of any woman, and green

Irish eyes, now looking down at him with an insufferable kindness. He sat and took the coffee, muttering a "thank-you."

It had been a party, he remembered now. Some film producer, a friend of his. Elana had been there and he, flying high on half a dozen toxic drugs, had approached her with his usual invitation that she leave with him. She had almost shocked him into sobriety with an affirmative answer. The rest of the night had been a haze of motion and warmth and passion.

He sipped at the coffee, enjoying the liquid heat, a relief against his throat.

"How are you feeling?" she asked, her eyes still regarding him seriously.

"Like shit."

"It's not surprising. You were pretty stoned."

"No more than normal," he said, mustering up a weak smile.

"And do you always feel this way?"

"Sometimes worse."

Elana sipped her coffee and then said, "How long have we known each other? Three years? Four years?"

"I suppose. I think I met you at a screening first, four years ago."

"You've been this way ever since I've known you. What are you trying to do to yourself? There are easier ways to commit suicide."

Richard couldn't meet her eyes. Nor suddenly could he speak. Something held his throat and mounted in his chest, something remarkably like grief.

She reached her hand out and brushed some hair from his face. "I think you are the unhappiest man I know."

He drank the remainder of his coffee, still not trusting himself to speak.

"Would you like more?" she asked.

He nodded. She took his mug and left the room.

She had no right to speak to him like that, he thought,

the sadness replaced by anger. Who was she to judge him? How could anyone judge him? God, he didn't even understand himself. He only knew that he had this frenetic impulse toward excess in every direction as if in the hope that somehow he would no longer have to see himself at all.

The urge was like some sort of primordial force, he thought. Something like sap rising in a tree. It had no choice but to follow the path that nature had ordained. And so it was with him. It had always been that way, ever since he could remember. Ever since he had learned to walk and talk he had followed this road which was leading to some obscure and unattainable destination.

She came back with the coffee and once again sat on the bed handing it to him. He took another sip and then said, "If I'm so hopeless, why did you bring me back here last night?"

Again that calm and knowing look. "Because I thought you needed affection."

"Pity?" he asked.

"I prefer to call it compassion," she said.

The anger came again. "I don't need your pity. I'm doing fine by myself," he said bitterly.

"If your wish is to kill yourself, then I suppose you are," she said mildly.

He sat up fully then and put his cup on the table beside the bed. "I don't need a sermon. It's one thing I know I don't need. I've got to get going."

She was undisturbed by his reaction. "I'm sorry, I know you don't need a sermon. Perhaps all you need to do is find out what you do need."

The sadness welled up again, the misery. "Why are you talking to me like this? Why are you doing this to me?"

She smiled. "Because I like you, I've always liked you. You are a charming, intelligent, and, I think, at heart a wonderful person. I just hate to see it all destroyed."

He swung his legs over the other side of the bed and sat

on the edge, his back to her. "It's not going to be destroyed," he said. "I'm going to be fine. Now can I use your shower?"

"Sure, go ahead. Right through the door in front of you."

He got up and, naked, walked into the bathroom. He turned on the hot water, adjusted it, and then stepped into the shower, standing in clouds of rising steam. What did he want? he wondered. All he had ever wanted was some kind of peace. All he had ever wanted was for the misery to stop, and it was something that had never happened.

Why was it this way for him? Other people seemed to go through their lives without this onerous burden. Other people seemed quite happy to live normal lives, to grow up, to go to school, to fall in love, to get married and have children and work and live out their lifespans with some kind of happiness. Why couldn't he? Why was it so different?

He lifted his face directly into the stinging jets of water, allowing them to wash the tears from his cheeks.

"Insane," Sissy said.

She stood with her hands on her hips looking down at Elizabeth, anger stretching every muscle of her body.

"I'm doing what I have to do." Elizabeth sat on the couch in the living room, trying to avoid Sissy's irate gaze.

"Do you know who you are dealing with?" Sissy asked. "These men are killers, this is the Mafia. You can't fuck with them."

"I need the money."

Sissy tossed her head. "You've got money. You've got as much money as you need. You've got more money than you can spend. Surely your life's more valuable than money."

"I don't have enough money to be independent," Elizabeth said stubbornly. "I set myself a goal and it was going to take me almost another year to attain it. I'm not going to give up now. It's such a short time."

"Yeah, well, it was a real short time it took for that bomb to explode. Think about that," Sissy said.

"You're being hysterical," Elizabeth said, finally looking up at her.

"No. That's not hysterical. What was hysterical was a bomb going off in the street in front of your house, in your car. That was hysterical. You must be absolutely nuts."

"I'm going to do what I have to do," Elizabeth said, finally allowing her own anger to surface.

Sissy immediately changed her tactics. "If you need more money, you know you could get it from your father."

"I have never asked him for anything and I never will. You know that," Elizabeth said. "Don't even suggest it, if you value our friendship."

"What can I do to talk you out of this?" Sissy said hopelessly.

"Nothing."

Sissy sat exasperatedly on the couch beside her. "So what exactly are you planning to do?"

"I've already done it. I've rented a small private house in West Hollywood and I'm going to be operating out of there. My equipment has already been moved over."

"How are you going to get clients? As soon as you start, these guys are going to hear that you're back in business. This is a small circle of people we're talking about."

"Word of mouth. I'm simply going to contact my oldest and trusted clients. And let them know that this service is available on an ultra-discreet basis. I'm not going to be able to run the business the size I was doing before. I've come to terms with that. But it won't be necessary. It will be very exclusive and very expensive. The overhead will be less, I'll only have two girls and myself. But the profits shouldn't be that much smaller."

"Trusted clients," Sissy said sarcastically. "How can

you trust people who come to you to be beaten up? Organized crime is everywhere these days. Anyone of those guys could be an informant. The cop you talked to who told you about who these people were could be on their payroll for all you know."

Elizabeth shook her head. "I don't think so. I think I know who I can trust. I'm not going to open the place under the same name. It's going to take a while before any word gets out. I'll just try and stay a step ahead of the game."

"I still think you're crazy," Sissy said.

"Perhaps I am."

"What can I do? You know I'd do anything to help you."

Elizabeth looked at her fondly. All traces of anger had disappeared now. "I'll let you know."

"Oh, baby, I'm just so scared for you," Sissy said miserably.

Elizabeth touched her hand gratefully without speaking. In truth, she was far more scared for herself. But she didn't feel she had much choice. There were things she needed to do. The problem was that it was all happening so fast now. She hoped she could control it all.

On Friday night Stephen invited Shannon to hear him play at a small jazz club in Sherman Oaks. It was a trio—drums, piano, and Stephen on bass guitar. The female pianist sang in a soft, throaty voice.

She discovered Stephen was not only an excellent musician but also a charismatic entertainer. Once again, he seemed to know everyone there. All through the evening musicians dropped in and jammed with the band. The highlight came when Chick Corea arrived and played keyboard on three numbers. Before Shannon left, she invited Stephen to come to the cottage for dinner on Saturday night.

She prepared dinner nervously. For some reason it reminded her of the first time she had ever cooked for someone else—imbuing her with fear of making a cataclysmic mistake. She couldn't pin down why she was feeling nervous except from some childish and superficial need to impress Stephen with her culinary abilities.

It was, however, a difficult dinner to screw up, she thought ruefully, as she peeled the giant prawns. There would be a salad, French bread and brie, a heaping bowl of pasta, sauteed prawns with cayenne pepper and a cheese sauce; all accompanied by three chilling bottles of Chardonnay. Simple yet elegant.

Melissa appeared in the kitchen doorway. "When's Stephen coming?" she asked.

Shannon glanced at the clock on the wall. "Oh my God," she said, "he'll be here in half an hour and I still have to have a shower."

"Take it easy, Mom," Melissa said knowingly. "He won't mind if you're not ready. He's cool."

Shannon washed her hands and dried them on a towel. "Can you finish making the salad while I have a shower?"

"Aw, Mom," Melissa protested.

"Come on, sweetheart, all that's left to do is to slice up some mushrooms and tomatoes. You don't even have to put them in. Just slice them up for me and leave them on the board. Help me out, will you?"

"Okay," Melissa said unenthusiastically.

Shannon went into the bathroom and quickly undressed. She had seen all too little of Stephen in the previous days. They hadn't slept together since that first time in his loft, simply because of conflicting schedules. The gig at the club the previous night had ended with her leaving alone, as he had obviously intended to visit into the wee hours with his musician friends. She didn't resent it, for he had explained the situation before inviting her. But the thought of being alone with him filled her with almost painful anticipation.

She washed quickly, dried herself, and then dressed, slipping on a pair of jeans and a long, loose blouse. Expertly she applied makeup, wondering as she dabbed at her lips what he saw in her.

The question made her smile. She was acting like a child. That thought in turn made her chuckle. It was a nice feeling for a change, this excitement and the accompanying physical tingle in her body.

Stephen arrived fifteen minutes late, thank God. He stood apologetically at the door, a bouquet of flowers in his hand. "I'm sorry I'm late," he said, handing her the flowers. "I had to stop and get these and couldn't find a place that was still open."

"Thank you so much," she said, taking them. "I was running late myself."

"Hi, Stephen," Melissa said, running over to him and giving him a hug.

"Hi, babe." He lifted her up and planted a kiss on her cheek. "Met any stars lately?"

"No, but I was invited to a party. There's going to be a lot of stars there, Vonni Ribisi is going to be there."

"Vonni Ribisi?" he asked.

"Yeah, he's in *My Two Dads*. He's so cute," she said. "I don't know what I'm going to say when I'm there."

"I'm sure you'll think of something. Anyway, he'll think you're cute as well, if he's smart at all."

"Sure," she said cynically.

They sat in the small living room. Shannon offered Stephen wine and poured them each a glass. He sat on one end of the couch while she sat on the armchair beside it. Melissa took a look at them and said, "Mom, can I go and watch television?" When Shannon agreed, she left the room with one sly, backward glance over her shoulder.

"Did you like the show last night?" Stephen asked.

"It was wonderful. You really have a way with the audience. It's as if you are playing for each person, for each individual there."

"Oh, I do," he said. "I always see exactly who's there and make it a point to play for each one of them. That's one of the things I like about music, that you can do that, that there's that immediacy and contact."

"It's something you don't have as a writer," Shannon said regretfully. "Something I think I miss. Sure you have an audience who you communicate to, but you're never able to see their reactions. That privilege seems unique to the performing arts. I'm jealous."

"Well, perhaps it's just a different form of communication. I'm sure there is still a satisfaction."

"Yes, but the satisfaction comes from the craft, not so much from the communication. Of course, when you do get an acknowledgment like a letter from somebody who's enjoyed an article you've written, it's always gratifying."

There was a moment's silence while they sipped their drinks and looked at each other.

"You look beautiful," he said tenderly.

"Thank you." She felt the beginnings of what could only be a blush. She laughed. "My God, I think I'm blushing."

"You are."

Another moment's silence, and then she said, "How late did you stay last night?"

"Oh, till about five in the morning, I guess. The club closed at two, but we jammed for another couple of hours."

"Isn't that like working overtime?"

"No, not at all. When it's just the guys together, nobody cares if mistakes are made or how things are presented to an audience, it's just us having fun. It's one of the best parts of the job. We stop and start and talk in the middle of a song, and make jokes and laugh."

"I'd love to sit in on that some time," Shannon said.

Stephen nodded. "I'm sure you will." He put his glass down and then patted the couch beside him, "Now why don't you come and sit beside me so that I can kiss you.

298

I've been aching to do that ever since I saw you at the front door."

Willingly, Shannon moved around to sit beside him. They kissed for what seemed like a long time. A tender, searching kind of kiss, a question in it.

He drew away from her, his eyes searching her face.

"What?" she asked.

"I love you," he said. "It's like a miracle to me. I always knew this would happen and yet I never really thought it would. It's so miraculous."

She reached up with her hand and traced the strong line of his jaw. "I know. I was thinking about it myself. Out of all the people in the world, out of all the places I could be at this time, how is it that I ended up here on Miles Cort's estate to meet his son?"

"Fate?"

"I don't know what it is. It's like . . . it's so incomprehensible, it's like looking up into the sky filled with billions and billions of stars and imagining two of them colliding in all that immensity of space. How does something like that happen? I suppose fate's as good an explanation as any. Whatever it is, I'm very thankful."

He kissed her again.

"Excuse me."

They drew apart to see Melissa in the doorway. She was grinning widely at their embarrassment. "There's nothing on TV, Mom. I'm going to go outside for a while, okay?"

"Okay," Shannon said, flustered. "But dinner will be in about twenty minutes."

"All right, I'll be back. I'm just going to go hang out around the pool. You behave yourselves, all right?"

"Sure," Stephen said. "Although I really would appreciate it if you were here to chaperone us."

"You're too old for a chaperone," Melissa said, "but I'll be back soon just in case." She left the room.

"I've still got some cooking to do," Shannon said. "You want to come into the kitchen?"

"Sure." He picked up his glass and followed her.

She took a big iron skillet from the wall and put it on the stove while he watched.

"What's for dinner?" he asked.

She recited the menu, and he nodded approvingly.

"Perfect," he said. "I love prawns and I love them spicy."

The dinner was a success, the mood light, informal, and comfortable. Melissa was funny and charming. Stephen was funny and charming, and after they finished the first bottle of wine, in spite of her nervousness, Shannon, too, felt funny and charming.

Afterward, while Melissa prepared herself for bed, Shannon and Stephen sat beside each other on the couch, drinking coffee and liqueur.

"How's the project with Miles going?" he asked.

"Uh, it's coming along okay, I guess," Shannon said. The subject was like a cloud on a bright sunny day, obscuring the sun for a moment and giving her a chill. She wondered why she felt that way, for the book was indeed progressing well. Perhaps it was just the contrast between the seriousness of it and the lightheartedness of these moments.

"Shouldn't I ask you about it?" Stephen said perceptively.

"No, it's all right," Shannon said. "Although I guess you know how it is from writing music. You don't like to talk about something that you're in the middle of. You're afraid it'll disappear if it's brought into view before it's finished."

"Yeah, I know the feeling."

"But it's silly," she admitted. "In fact, the book is going well, and I guess the scariest thing is that I'm beginning to like your father."

"Fatal attraction," Stephen murmured.

She looked at him quickly. "I don't think I have any-

300

thing to fear. I think you are wrong about your father. People can change."

"Even Miles?" he asked ironically.

"Even Miles. I really think he's changed. Even in the short time since I've known him."

"What do you attribute that to?"

She wanted to tell him about Miles's offer to help find a kidney for Melissa, to ask him what his opinion of the ethics of that would be. But, more than that, she didn't want to spoil the evening.

Instead she said, "He's taking stock of his life, and I think he's taking responsibility for it as well. You can't look back over so many years, so many deeds and misdeeds, and not come to some kind of different conclusions about them all. At least I don't think it's possible."

"Maybe you're right. I guess we'll see."

"Sometimes I feel like Miles's confessor," Shannon said. "And sometimes I think that's really what he's trying to do with this book. To confess his sins to the world and to seek its forgiveness."

Stephen smiled. "I'm afraid that analogy is a little farfetched for my imagination to grasp," he said. "I can't imagine Miles seeking forgiveness from anyone."

"Perhaps he's seeking it from himself," she suggested. "I don't know. But don't judge him too harshly. No one is all bad."

"Maybe I have some lessons to learn from you," he said.

"Maybe we could teach each other a few things," she agreed.

Melissa came in to say good night, and kissed them both, announcing that she was putting herself to bed. "I'm going to read for a little bit, okay?"

"Yeah, but not too long," Shannon said. "You have a busy day tomorrow."

"Okay, good night."

"I can't get over what a wonderful child she is," Stephen remarked. "I guess what I really can't get over is how you've helped her stay so sane in spite of the difficulties in your own life."

"It's not easy being a single mother, I'll admit, but rather than a burden, Melissa has been my staff. She's given me strength and encouragement and hope."

"I think you do that for me," Stephen said. "Whenever I'm around you I feel stronger and more hopeful."

She thanked him and then said, "I always felt that you were naturally that way. You don't strike me as a man who lacks either of those qualities."

"Normally I don't, but we all have low points." He grinned to take the seriousness away, and added, "Right now isn't one of them."

They kissed each other again. This time more passionately, as if Melissa's departure had given them new licence.

"Am I going to have to leave soon?"

"Not until I've made you breakfast," Shannon said.

An hour later when Melissa was securely asleep, they went into Shannon's bedroom and made love. It was gentler and more satisfying this time in some ways, although the passion threatened to erupt so forcefully at times it could scald them. Afterward they got up, had dessert, and then went back to bed again. Finally, at about three A.M. they fell asleep in each other's arms. Shannon's last thought was that this was the way it was all supposed to be.

Orson was worried. He was home alone. Barbara was out again, supposedly with a girlfriend. But that wasn't the cause of his concern as he sat in his living room and sipped a vodka martini.

He had come to the conclusion that the whole thing was crazy. To think that he could get away with having someone kill his father. That somehow it wouldn't get screwed up, or somehow it wouldn't be traced back to him. It was, he admitted to himself, insane. For the fourth time he took the piece of paper with the contact telephone number for his man out of his pocket and looked at it.

Shit, he thought, I've got to stop this.

He went to the telephone and dialed the number quickly, knowing that he shouldn't be doing it from his home phone, even as he did so. It was too late to stop now.

As before, a woman's voice answered. Orson said, "I have a message for Bill."

"Yes?" she said.

"Tell him I want to cancel the contract. Tell him to keep the money, but cancel the contract. I don't want the contract fulfilled. Is that understood?"

"Yes," she said, "I'll pass the message on. He probably won't get it until tomorrow though."

"I don't care," Orson said. "As long as he gets it as soon as possible. If you can reach him earlier than that, please do so. This is very important. I don't want the contract fulfilled."

"I have the message," the woman said, and hung up.

Orson went back to the chair, relief pervading him. He'd come up with some other plan. Somehow he'd get the money from Miles. Murder wasn't the solution.

Still nervous, he took his drink and walked to the window. Below him the lights of the San Fernando Valley, grids of human habitation, beamed back at him.

So he'd lost seven or eight grand, it didn't matter. He still had the balance and he'd find other alternatives. There had to be a way to get Miles to part with some of his money or change his mind about his will. It was simply a matter of figuring it all out.

He drained his drink and looked at his watch. Maybe he could call Wanda or someone. He didn't want to be alone and his wife was nowhere to be found. Probably out fucking someone else, he thought. Well, he told himself, two can play at that game. He went back to the telephone and dialed a number.

The man climbed the tree on the sidewalk, took the long branch overhanging the mansion walls like a tightrope walker, and then dropped into the gardens. He wore black clothes with dark polish under his eyes. On his back was a small knapsack.

He peered through the darkness, orienting himself. He had memorized Orson's drawing and quickly spotted the sensors and alarms.

Zigzagging his way through the grounds, he soon found himself at the back of the house. He stopped in the shadows near the pool and took the knapsack from his back. He placed it on the ground before him and opened it, taking out a small box, a long cord, and a handful of tools. Then quickly, expertly, he began to assemble it.

Twenty minutes later he left the way he had come.

Lynn stirred beside Richard in bed. He was lying awake, his eyes open, smoking a cigarette, staring up at the ceiling. He wondered what she saw in him, aside from his obvious good looks. She was a strange bird, he thought. He'd never really understood her. Never bothered to try, now that he thought of it.

He dragged deeply on his cigarette. For once he was relatively sober. Somehow his conversation with Elana had changed something. He wasn't sure yet what. He had left her apartment this morning somewhat humbled. It was the only word he could use to describe what he was feeling, although it was such a strange and unusual emotion that he wasn't sure what it was. He had slept during the day, eaten at the mansion, turned down three invitations to parties, and had only two drinks before dinner and two after.

He had to figure out what to do with his life, he thought, watching the blue smoke coil up in the dim light. That was his real problem. He had nothing to do except follow his impulses. If only he could channel them in some direction. Maybe he should take his father's advice and get a job in the industry. There were probably worse fates than working, although at the moment he couldn't think of any.

He stubbed the cigarette out in the ashtray beside the bed and closed his eyes. But the thoughts wouldn't let him sleep. They buzzed mercilessly around his brain. Thoughts of childhood, of hopes dashed and chances lost, thoughts of women he had known, of friends he had betrayed and, yes, even thoughts of his father.

On some level he loved Miles. The old man was a bastard through and through and yet there was a certain integrity to him that Richard admired. Miles never compromised. You had to give him that. He said what he thought and, more, he acted on his beliefs. He hadn't come across many people who did that.

There was no denying that Miles treated him like shit, but when he really thought about it, he demanded to be treated that way. What had he done to deserve to be treated any other way? Miles had given him everything he'd ever asked for except perhaps affection. But then he had given him nothing in return, nothing that would earn the affection he wanted.

God, he thought, sitting up, that affection I wanted so badly. It was the first time he'd ever acknowledged that need. And once again, it brought unfamiliar emotions swelling to the surface, a sadness that pricked at his eyes.

It was all he had ever wanted from Miles and all that Miles had never given him—affection. A feeling that his father liked him, that there was some pride, some acceptance of who he was. Miles had always denied him that. Instead, the old man had constantly berated him for his failures. It was a bitter pill to swallow and one that had been choking in his throat for as long as he could remember.

There would be no sleep this night. There was too much erupting inside of him.

He got up and walked out to the living room. He opened the curtain and looked outside. A half-moon cast a pale glow on the grounds. There was no movement in the garden or in the back of the mansion that faced him, although lighted windows told him that the security staff were around.

He went into the bathroom, took a towel off the rack, and knotted it around his waist. A swim would be good, clean and refreshing, and somehow symbolic of his mood.

He went outside and walked down the path toward the pool. To his left a night bird broke into a soft song.

Maybe there was something he could do, he thought. Maybe his life wasn't a total waste. It wasn't too late. It could never be too late. People could change. He'd seen people change, so why couldn't he?

He reached the edge of the pool and looked down into its lighted turquoise stillness. He unknotted the towel and let it drop to his feet and poised for a second at the edge of the pool.

The water called him. It was as if his fate was contained there. Tightening the muscles in his legs, he bent his knees and then entered the water in a perfect dive.

There was a blue crackle the second he hit the water.

Ten seconds later he floated on his back, sightless blue eyes staring at the black night's sky.

Richard was dead.

CHAPTER FIFTEEN

"I had hopes for Richard. Out of all the children, he was potentially the brightest, the one who could have accomplished the most. It was wasted, unused potential, but it was there and I always saw it there," Miles said.

In a rare moment of self-criticism he added, "I brought him up all wrong. I was tough on the others and look how they turned out. I thought by giving Richard more leniency he might be different. All I gave him was enough rope to hang himself. And all he did was fritter his life away." Miles shook his head. Were those tears welling in his eyes? "I don't know what to say. All I know is that he was my son. And now he's gone."

Lynn had discovered the body in the early morning hours as the sun was rising. It was immediately obvious to her that Richard was dead. Suppressing a scream and soon realizing her own need for discretion, she went to the two security men on duty. After they came out of the house and looked down at the still body floating on top of the water, one of them woke Corydon, their boss. Corydon went directly to Miles's room and reported what had happened. Within minutes, Miles hurtled out in his wheelchair and started barking orders. "Get him out of the water," he said to Corydon.

The body bobbed aimlessly near the center of the pool. One of the men reached for a pool net to pull it closer. As soon as the metal rod touched the water, a stream of blue sparks erupted. "Jesus," the man said, dropping the pole and thinking how lucky he was that the handle was made of rubber.

"There's an electric current running through the water," Corydon said unnecessarily. Using another net, they managed to pull Richard's body from the water and deposit it on the tiles at the side of the pool. Meanwhile Corydon spotted that one of the pool lights was out and ran over to it. For a few moments he examined it and then came back to Miles.

"What?" Miles said.

"It was set up to electrocute the pool," Corydon said.

"What do you mean, set up?"

"There is a device there, probably to magnify the current from the light outlet. I don't know, I'm not an electrician."

There was a short discussion on what to do next. Corydon thought they should call the police. But Miles seemed doubtful. "They'll poke around, ask questions, find out about the girl."

"No, sir, they don't have to find out. We don't need to mention that," Corydon said.

"They'll want to question everyone here," Miles said. "They'll find out about the girl who tried to poison me. I told Shannon Ross that an attempt was made earlier."

Corydon looked back at him disapprovingly. "I suppose you'll have to speak to her first then, sir."

"Yes," Miles said. He looked at the now still water. "Obviously this was meant for me, for my morning swim."

"Yes, sir."

"Well, either someone here did it, or someone got into the grounds past your security."

308

"Yes, sir."

Miles looked at him blankly. "Well, first find out which and then call the police."

"Yes, sir," Corydon said.

Miles looked at Lynn. "How come you found the body?"

Lynn had a story prepared. "Well, you know I worked late last night, Mr. Cort. So I slept in my room in the house and, ah, woke up early for some reason and came outside for a walk and saw him floating in the pool."

"I see," Miles said.

Her face had lost color and she was trembling slightly. "You'd better have a stiff Scotch for breakfast." He turned his wheelchair and went back into the house.

There were police everywhere. Men and women, in and out of uniform, bustled through the grounds, sifting, searching, and querying.

Miles set up a battle station in his office. The only time he showed surprise was when, after Corydon had woken them, Shannon and Stephen walked in together.

"What are you doing here?" Miles asked after a short silence.

Shannon answered the question. "He was visiting me."

"I see." Miles had a speculative look in his eyes, but he questioned them no further. Instead he got right to the point with Shannon. "The police will be here asking questions. They want to question everybody. When they talk to you I'd appreciate it if you didn't mention anything about the incident I told you about involving the girl."

"Why not?" she asked, while Stephen looked on, puzzled, unaware of what they were talking about.

"Because (a) that should have been reported to the police, and (b) nothing could be proved anyway. It won't contribute anything to their investigation here, now, so I don't want it mentioned. All right?"

"Yes, I suppose so," Shannon said doubtfully.

"What are you talking about?" Stephen interjected.

"It doesn't concern you," Miles said.

"He's your son, he has a right to know," Shannon said.

Miles hammered a hand on the table. "I don't want anything I discuss with you then discussed with him regardless of whatever relationship you presently have with him," Miles said firmly. "Is that completely understood? I have your confidentiality as promised?"

"Yes," Shannon said. "I suppose you do."

"Good," Miles replied. "I'll try and see the police don't talk to the child. She shouldn't be bothered with any of this. In the meantime, I guess we just wait for them to get around to us."

"Yes."

When Shannon and Stephen left the room, Stephen said, "What was all that about?"

Shannon shrugged and said resentfully, "You heard, it's writer/client privileged information. I can't talk about it."

Stephen looked a little put out for a second, but then said, "He's right, I suppose. Whatever it is, it's no business of mine. But who the hell would want to kill him? Because that's what this was, wasn't it?"

"It looks that way," Shannon said.

"But why?"

"You've told me yourself that your father has a lot of enemies," Shannon said.

Stephen looked nonplussed. "Sure he has enemies, but none who would want to kill him. At least none I know of."

Shannon looked at her watch. It was 7:30. "Come on back to the cottage and I'll make you breakfast. Melissa should be waking up around now."

As they walked along the cobbled path underneath an eave of hanging bougainvillea, she looked over at him, remembering the night they had spent together. It had

310

been loving and romantic and very satisfying. He noticed her glance and took her hand with a small smile.

She wished she could tell him about the earlier attempt on Miles's life. But she knew she couldn't. Miles suspected his children, and Stephen was one of them, as ridiculous as the thought might be. Still, he had been here last night. He could have left her bed without waking her. He could have . . . She was dismayed at her thoughts. They were stupid, ridiculous, suspicious, unworthy of her or of him. And yet she couldn't help them. They were there unbidden, as part of the ordeal.

They went into the kitchen and Shannon began to mix some eggs in a bowl. Stephen slumped into the kitchen chair. He hadn't shown any emotion apart from the initial shock when they had been told of Richard's death. Now he grew silent and thoughtful.

"How are you feeling?" Shannon asked.

"I don't know," Stephen said. "I feel shocked, but . . . I don't know."

"Do you feel any grief?" she asked.

Stephen stretched his legs out in front of him and leaned back in the chair. "There were five years between us. I hardly knew Richard. You know how it is when two boys are growing up. When he's eleven, I'm sixteen and there's a big gap between those ages. When he was sixteen and still in high school, I was twenty-one. Perhaps . . ." His voice trailed off.

She ladled the eggs into a frying pan. "Perhaps what?"

"Perhaps if I had taken more time and been a better brother, things might have turned out differently for Richard. I don't know."

"That's one of those things that's impossible to say," she said.

"I know. I'm not beating myself up about it. The truth of the matter is, I never liked Richard that much. He had a smart mouth and a nasty streak. But still he was my brother."

"And blood is thicker than water, huh?"

"I don't know. There is a connection and it can't be denied. It just seems such a waste, but then his life was such a waste. I don't know what he was doing with it, but it wasn't anything productive."

"He was young, though," Shannon said.

"Yeah, he was, but I don't know what he would have done. You can't speculate about those things I guess. It's just that his life seemed so meaningless. It's hard to give a lot of meaning to his death."

After a pause, Stephen said, "The question that's more immediate in my mind is who's trying to kill Miles and why?"

"Would you care?" Shannon asked.

"Yes, I suppose I would," he said. "He is my father. I suppose I would."

Melissa walked into the kitchen rubbing her eyes.

"Hi, sweetheart," Shannon said. She opened the refrigerator, poured a glass of orange juice, and put it on the table.

Melissa sat down, took a sip, and then seemed to notice Stephen for the first time. "Are you still here?" she asked, with all the unself-conscious candor of a child. "Did you spend the night?"

Stephen darted a quick look at Shannon but read nothing there and turned back to Melissa. "Yes, I did spend the night."

"Oh, that's neat," she replied.

Shannon allowed her to drink half her orange juice and then came over to the table. "I want you to know there's been an accident."

"What happened?" Melissa asked.

"There was an accident at the pool, and Richard got killed."

"He's dead?"

"Yes, I'm afraid he got electrocuted. So there are police here now investigating what happened."

312

"The police? Do the police always come when somebody's killed?"

"Yes," Shannon said. "They just need to check into things."

"Wow," Melissa said. "Richard dead?"

"I'm afraid so," Shannon said.

"Wow," Melissa repeated.

"Jesus," Stephen said, sitting upright.

"What?" Shannon asked.

"I wonder if anyone's thought to call Mom. If anyone's going to be upset, it's her."

"Do you want to call?" Shannon asked.

"No, I don't," Stephen said, "but I will right now. Can I use the phone?"

"Take the one in the office."

He got up and left the room. Yes, she thought to herself, there might be nobody around here to grieve for Richard, but a mother would, no matter what she thought of her son, a mother would grieve for his passing.

Corydon entered Lynn's office and pulled up a chair beside her desk. He sat heavily and peered closely at her.

"What is it?" Lynn asked.

Corydon cleared his throat. "You said you left the house, that you couldn't sleep, that you went outside, which was when you found the body."

"Yes."

Corydon shook his head. "You didn't leave the house. Nothing was activated. My men would have known if you'd gone outside. You must have been outside already. Do you want to tell me what's going on?"

Lynn hesitated, but only for a moment. "I've been ah . . . having a relationship with Richard for some time. I was with him that night. Not when he was killed, but in his cottage."

313

"I see. So what were you doing when he left the cottage?"

"Presumably I was sleeping, because I didn't hear him leave. When I woke up I noticed he wasn't . . ." Again a slight pause ". . . in bed. I got up, looked through the house, didn't see him, and went outside wondering where he'd gone. I came to the pool, and you know the rest."

"I see," Corydon said again.

"I don't want Mr. Cort to know this," Lynn said. "You know it would cost me my job."

Corydon regarded her without expression, then nodded his head. "I don't see any reason to tell him. It doesn't add or subtract anything from the equation."

"Thank you."

He rose. "Anything else I should know?"

"No." Lynn shook her head. "That's all I was hiding."

"Thank you for your time," he said, and left the office.

Lieutenant Glenn Collins was in charge of the investigation, a thin, nervous man who seemed to suffer from frequent, momentary distractions. However, Miles did not underestimate the short, watery-brown-eyed policeman. He asked questions in a hurried manner, blurting the next one out before waiting for an answer, but Miles noticed that when there was no answer, Collins always returned to the original question.

They were sitting in Miles's study. Corydon was there and so was Lynn.

"So you have no idea why anyone would want to murder you, or any member of your family?" Collins asked.

"No, I don't," Miles replied. "I particularly don't know what kind of company my son kept. I assume that I was the target because I always go for a swim each morning. Like clockwork. However, there is a possibility that somebody knew Richard would take a midnight swim."

"Well, he took it in the middle of the night or in the early morning hours," Collins said.

"I know," Miles replied, without volunteering further information.

"So do you have any enemies?" Collins asked.

"Of course I have enemies." Miles lifted a piece a paper from his desk. "Here's a list of people through the years who have threatened me." He handed it over to the policeman. His security staff had already checked the people on the list after the first attempt, so he knew it wouldn't give Collins much to work on. However, he wasn't about the tell the policeman that.

Hardly looking at the list, Collins said, "It was a very sophisticated job. And I understand that your security people found the spot where the person came over the wall."

"Yes, sir," Corydon said. "I showed one of your men that whoever it was shimmied over a tree and then dropped down into the grounds. You can see the footprints plain as day."

"Yes, it certainly looks like it was an outside job," Collins said. He looked at Miles again. "And you have no idea who'd want to do this?"

"No, I don't," Miles said. "I've made enemies in my time, and I've received threats, but as far as I know, they weren't made by people who were capable of carrying them out, just heat of the moment stuff."

"No reason to think that anybody would actually do something, huh?"

"No, no reason," Miles said.

The policeman shook his head. "Sure looks like a professional job to me."

"What do you mean, professional?" Miles asked.

"Like I said, very sophisticated. Looks like somebody with a good knowledge of electronics set the device up—somebody who might have been hired to do the job."

"Well," Miles said heavily, "I don't know who and I

don't know why." He looked over at Corydon. "Peter, you help the lieutenant in his investigation. If he needs to speak to any of the staff, make sure they are available to him." He looked at the policeman. "Is there anything else I can help you with then?"

"No, sir. Thank you for your cooperation. We'll continue the investigation and let you know what we've discovered."

"Very good," Miles said.

The lieutenant stood up. "And please accept my condolences on the death of your son."

Miles gave him a curt nod.

The audience was over.

If Miles Cort's interview with the policeman had been relatively painless, his meeting with Rosemary was not.

She arrived half an hour after Stephen called her. Luckily, Stephen had buzzed Lynn and told her of Rosemary's impending arrival after he spoke to her. Lynn, in turn, had informed Miles, whose immediate response had been, "What did the asshole call her for?"

Rosemary arrived wearing jeans, a T-shirt, and a leather jacket, somehow still appearing elegant.

"Where is he?" she asked as soon as she saw Miles, still in his office, sitting behind his desk.

"They took the body away," he said. "I'm sorry. It was an accident."

Rosemary leaned forward on the desk, still standing. "You didn't even call me. Stephen had to call me and tell me about it."

Miles had the grace to look embarrassed. "I'm sorry, there was so much going on here, police and everything else. I didn't think."

"God, what happened?" Rosemary asked, finally sitting down. "Stephen told me Richard was electrocuted.

That's all I know. He said something about, something like it was meant for you."

Miles looked across the desk at his wife. She was still a beautiful woman in spite of her age. The only wife he still had some respect for. She'd always been a lady, every step of the way. And when she'd finally divorced him, he had felt a loss that had only appeared once before, at Isabella's death in childbirth in 1942.

"Yes, it looks like it was for me. Somebody rigged up the pool so that an electric current was flowing through the water. I take a swim every morning, I'm usually the first one in there. But what happened is that last night, Richard must have been restless and decided to take a dip in the pool. Apparently he was killed as soon as he hit the water. There was tremendous voltage going through there."

"My God," Rosemary said. "What are you doing for this to happen, Miles? What's going on?"

"I don't know," Miles said, eyeballing her.

"I know when you are lying, I've always known when you lied," she said. "You know more than you're telling me."

"I don't know what you mean," Miles stonewalled.

"Something's going on here. And if the lives of my children are in danger, I want to know about it."

"The lives of your children are not . . ." Miles began, then stopped. It was useless to say there was no danger— one of them had just died. He took another tack. "You know I've got enemies. You know I've always had enemies. Apparently one of them wanted to hurt me. Unfortunately, Richard took a swim before I did."

"And that's all you know?" Rosemary said disbelievingly.

"That's all I know."

"Jesus, you haven't changed," she said, with an edge of disgust.

"Neither have you." They started angrily at each other for a moment, and then Rosemary's eyes dropped.

"This isn't the time or the place for us to have a fight. Our son has just died," she said, misery in her voice.

Miles was saved from further comment by Stephen's entrance. Rosemary got up and hugged him fiercely.

"I'm sorry, Mom. I tried to tell you more on the phone and I'm sorry I had to break it to you that way. But you were in such a hurry."

"I know, I know." She turned back to Miles. "I want to see the body. Where is it?"

Miles looked confused for a moment. "They took it. You have to talk to the police or to Corydon and find out."

She stared icily at him. "I'll do that."

There was a commotion in the hall, the peal of a high-pitched voice and then Anne burst into the room. She glanced at each one of them and then rushed over to her father. "Daddy, I just heard. I'm so sorry. I heard on the radio that there had been an accident and that Richard had been killed. Are you all right? What happened?" All in one breathless sentence.

"I'm fine," Miles said, trying to disentangle her arms from around his neck. "There was an accident. The pool was electrified and Richard fell in."

"Oh, my God, how dreadful!" Anne wore a short summer frock, low-cut in the front and back, red high-heeled shoes, and her hair and makeup were immaculate. She looked as if she'd just come from a society luncheon.

She appeared to notice Rosemary for the first time, and half trotted over to her, her hands outstretched. "Rosemary, how terrible." She grasped her onetime stepmother's arms and kissed the air beside her cheeks. "This is all too dreadful. I don't know how you can all be so calm."

Rosemary stood stiffly at attention. "Anne," she acknowledged.

Rosemary remounted her attack on Miles, taking a different route. "Do either of you two know what's really going on here?" she asked Anne and Stephen.

Stephen gave a small shrug, and Anne looked nonplussed.

"Wha—what do you mean?" Anne asked.

"I mean why did somebody electrify the pool? Why is somebody trying to murder your father? He insists he knows nothing."

"Rosemary," Miles cautioned.

"Murder?" Anne asked. "What are you talking about? I thought this was some kind of accident."

"Somebody electrified the pool," Rosemary said, her eyes seeking Miles's. "Somebody knew your father's habits. Knew that he took a morning swim each day. Richard was just an unlucky accident. To that extent it was an accident."

"My God," Anne said, turning to Miles. "Is this true, Daddy?"

Miles glowered at Rosemary and then said, "It appears to be true, although why anybody would want to harm me I have no idea."

"Oh, Daddy." Anne rushed back toward him. "Have you told the police? Are you going to get some protection? Are they going to find out who did this?"

Miles shrugged. "Everything's under control. Don't worry about it."

"How can you say that?" Anne shrieked. "My God, somebody's trying to kill you. What are you doing about it?"

"I'm taking every precaution," Miles said. "Now, if you would all excuse me, I have work to do."

"Work?" Anne said. "How can you think of work at a time like this?"

"There is no better time," Miles said. "Stephen, will you take your mother to Corydon? She has some questions to ask him."

"I'm not finished with you," Rosemary said. "I have some questions to ask *you*."

319

"I have no answers, Rosemary," Miles said. "You'd just be wasting our time."

"Very well. But I am going to find out what's happening here. I'm not going to have the lives of my children placed at risk."

"Nothing further will happen," Miles assured her. "I'll see to it."

She wasn't at all mollified. "You think you can fix everything, don't you, Miles? This is a murder we're talking about. And a murderer. This is not just something you can fix like you fix everything else."

For once Miles didn't fight back. "Please," he said, almost entreating. "I can't answer your questions and I want to be alone now."

She gave him a sharp look, opened her mouth to speak, but what she saw on his face must have changed her mind, because she said, "Goodbye, Miles. I'll call you about the funeral arrangements."

"Yes," he said heavily, "call me."

They left him sitting there. He stared down at his desk seeing nothing, a heaviness in his heart. Rosemary was right. This wasn't something he could fix, not yet anyway.

Orson heard about it in his office. He was brooding at his desk wondering what to do about Wanda when the call came.

He heard that one should never sleep with the help and it had always seemed like good advice to him. Unfortunately, it was advice he had never been able to follow, much like his father. Ever since he had slept with Wanda, twice—no, make that three times—he had lost the employer/employee edge.

It started with an inappropriate familiarity in the office and was soon followed by requests for extra time off, a raise, and introductions to people who could further her career. He had talked to her about it at one point, saying essentially that simply because he slept with her and found her attractive didn't change anything in their professional relationship. However, as the professional relationship as such had hardly existed, the words did not seem to affect Wanda much.

He was thinking a trifle regretfully that soon he would have to fire her, when the call came. He picked up the phone and Wanda announced that the call was from Lynn Reid. As any call from Lynn was usually tantamount to a summons by his father, Orson said, "Put her through."

The shock he felt when she told him what had happened did not have to be prevaricated. When he hung up his whole body was shaking.

My God, he thought, the wrong person, the wrong person. He tried to clear his mind and think rationally about it, but the words kept running through his mind: the wrong person, the wrong person.

He knew immediately what had happened. His man, the one he had hired to kill Miles, had set the trap. He himself had told him about Miles's habits, including the one of swimming every morning. For some unknown reason Richard had decided to test the pool out first. And Richard was the one who had died.

Orson buried his face in his hands and groaned. "Oh, God," he said aloud, "what am I going to do now?"

It didn't help when ten minutes later Wanda announced a call from someone named Bill.

Orson grabbed at the phone and shouted into it, "What the fuck happened? Do you know what you did?"

Bill's measured, emotionless tones came through the line. "I heard it on the radio. Apparently someone else tried to take a swim first."

"You fucking idiot!" Orson yelled. "Why did you do something that wasn't targeted exclusively to Miles? He's the one I wanted to—"

"We can't talk on the phone," the man interrupted him

sharply. "Meet me at the same place as last time. And bring the balance."

"The balance? You've got to be kidding. You totally screwed—"

But there was a click and he realized that Bill had hung up.

The man was a maniac. He had arranged a murder which could have claimed any victim and had, in fact, claimed the wrong one—and now he expected to be paid. Christ, talk about looney tunes!

Orson grabbed his jacket and his car keys off the desk. However, after hesitating for a moment, he also took an envelope from his file cabinet containing the balance of the money and placed it in his briefcase. The man had sounded emphatic about his request. He remembered the killer's cold eyes. He'd argue the point, but somehow he suspected he wouldn't win the discussion.

He drove to the bar on Lankershim where they had last met, parked carelessly, and scurried around the corner and into the darkened room. Once again Bill wasn't there. He went to a table and sat, his thoughts black.

"Can I help you?" the barman said.

Orson realized he hadn't ordered anything and got up. "I'll have a beer," he said, walking to the bar. "No, make that a Scotch on the rocks." He needed something stronger than beer. He took a gulp of the Scotch as soon as the man handed it to him, then walked back to sit at the table.

A moment later, "Bill" entered and sat opposite him.

"Jesus Christ," Orson said, "you really screwed up."

"I simply followed a plan according to the data you gave me," the man said, staring at him without remorse or regret.

"You killed my brother," Orson hissed.

A slight shrug from the man. "It's not my fault. You didn't tell me he'd be taking a midnight swim."

"Oh, Jesus," Orson groaned, rubbing his forehead. "I

322

know I didn't tell you, but surely you could have come up with something smarter than that."

"It worked, didn't it?"

God, the stupid fuck. Was that pride in his voice? "It worked on the wrong person," Orson snarled.

Another shrug. "It wasn't my fault. I'd like the other half of my fee, please."

"You expect me to pay you after this? Not only do you not kill the person I hire you to kill, but you kill my brother. I should be asking you for my money back."

"Nobody gets their money back. And I'll have the rest of my fee." His eyes looked even colder than normal and Orson felt the chill.

"Look," he said, "let's just call it quits. You screwed up, but you're going to walk out of here with seventy-five hundred dollars, half the fee. It's more than you started out with."

"Uh uh." The man shook his head slowly. "I did the job based on the data you gave me. The fact that you didn't tell me anybody else swam in the pool is your fault, not mine."

"No way," Orson said. "You are supposed to be the professional. You are supposed to be the one who knows what he's doing. That's what you were getting paid for. You didn't finish the job. Miles Cort is still alive."

"You want me to finish the job?" the man said quietly.

"No, I want you to get the fuck out of my life. Take the seventy-five hundred I already gave you and forget we ever met."

"I can't do that."

"Then what?" Orson asked.

"Give me the balance and I'll walk out of your life and we'll forget any of this ever happened."

"But you didn't do the job."

"I did the job," the man said. "My job is killing people. And based on the information you gave me, I would have killed Miles Cort. The fact that somebody else walked into the situation isn't my fault."

"Forget it!"

"Listen," the man said to him quietly. "I have a policy I never violate. As soon as I do a job, I leave town. Right now I can't afford to leave town. You owe me seventy-five hundred dollars."

"So take a bus," Orson said.

The man reached across the table and grabbed Orson's arm by the wrist. "You're forgetting one thing, mister," he said in that same quiet tone.

Orson tried to pull his wrist away, but the grip was powerful and he felt it more dignified just to leave his arm there.

"You're forgetting what I do for a living."

At that moment Orson knew what the outcome would be. He could feel it in his gut, in the surge of adrenaline that pumped through his body. "What do you mean?"

"You know exactly what I mean," the man said. "I don't only do it for business. Sometimes I do it for pleasure. Now give me my money."

Orson scanned his alternatives. What choice did he have? He couldn't go to the police and tell them that he'd hired the man to kill his father, who instead had killed his brother and was now going to kill him. In fact there was nothing he could do except hand the man his money.

Orson stared back at him for a moment but what he saw in those eyes did not console him. "All right. You can have your money and then get the fuck out of my life. I don't ever want to see or hear from you again."

"The feeling is mutual," the man said.

Orson reached into his jacket pocket, took out the envelope, and dropped it on the table.

The man released his arm, picked up the envelope, and stood, all in one motion. He gave Orson one last look, then turned and left the room as quietly as he had entered it.

Orson stared at the open doorway, then picked up his Scotch.

It could have been a large funeral. According to what Lynn told Shannon, more than four hundred messages of condolence had reached Miles in one form or another in the past two days. However, both Miles and Rosemary chose to restrict it to immediate members of the family and their guests, and a few of Richard's old friends.

The other compromise came in the form of the ceremony. While Miles wanted what he called "no religious nonsense," Rosemary, who was raised as and was still a practicing Episcopalian, did want some religious words said. They compromised on this by avoiding a church and having her minister say a few words at the gravesite.

"Do you want me to come?" Shannon had asked Miles uncertainly.

"You are my chronicler and this is part of family history. You should be there," he said tersely.

So she stood with the others at the site of the grave, on the green rolling hills of Forest Lawn Cemetery.

Stephen was there, wearing a sports coat and tie. Orson was with his wife. Anne was with a young man Shannon had never seen before, a man who looked at least ten years her junior. Elizabeth was there alone, dressed in black with a veil across her face, as were Rosemary and Lynn. Miles was there in his ubiquitous wheelchair, glowering down at the grave and the coffin resting inside it.

Two young men in their twenties and a pretty dark-haired girl stood a little to the side. They were, Shannon presumed, Richard's friends.

The minister said his words, calling Richard an "up-standing young man, cut down in the prime of his all-too-short life, a young man with dreams and ambitions unfulfilled, a young man who has gone to join his maker, perhaps for a more compelling reason than the one that kept him on earth."

The others looked on with stony, blank stares during this paean of hypocrisy.

And then after the casket was lowered into the grave, and it all seemed to be over, Miles said from his wheelchair, "I have something to say."

He launched into what Shannon considered to be an extraordinary monologue.

"Richard was my son, and as such I hold some responsibility for the man he became. You all know who he was and what he became. Richard was lazy, irresponsible, dishonest, weak. Not the type of son a father could be proud of. And yet, in my way, I loved him, because he was of me and a part of me, as you all are. Whatever he became, Richard did not deserve to die this way and at this time."

Miles paused and glared at each of his children in turn. "If you don't already know, I must tell you now that Richard died in my place. His death was the result of an attempt to murder me. And not the first attempt, I might add."

They just stared back at him, too shocked to speak. Shannon noticed that Anne's hand went up to her mouth in a gesture of surprise. They were shocked not at the content of what he said, Shannon guessed, but at the fact he chose to say it now. It could hardly have been news that Miles was the intended victim of the trap.

"There is probably more you should know. You should know that in my mind, among those who would wish me dead, you are included. Why? Well, if you don't know already, I am reorganizing my fortune. The vast majority of it will be left to various charities and foundations. I've set aside five million dollars, one million for each of you. Now it'll be one and a quarter million for each of you. And if you keep killing each other off, it'll still be five million for those of you who are alive. I don't know if you know of this, have found out about it in some manner,

326

but I have assumed that someone discovered what I have been planning, and I assume that greed, a basic motivation, is perhaps motivation enough to murder me before the reorganization is complete."

They stood there as if not believing what they were hearing. It was Rosemary who was the first to react. "Miles, this is neither the time nor the place for this," she snapped. "Show some respect for Richard, for the first time in your life. Even though it's too late."

"It is too late," Miles said. "And I mean no disrespect. But we are gathered here and it seems as good a time as any to put all the cards out on the table, for everyone to see."

"How can you even think that one of us would consider something like that?" Anne said, a sob in her voice.

"I think you are all capable of anything, as I am as well," Miles said. "I have one last thing to say. My business affairs might not yet be complete, but at this stage they are irrevocable, unless I choose to revoke them. There is five million dollars to be divided among the surviving children. The rest, as I said, will be going to charities and foundations that are in the process of being set up. I want you to know that, so that if there is indeed a murderer among you, he murders me for the right purpose, not to change my course of action, but simply for revenge."

With that Miles gave a tight small smile and spun his chair around, not waiting to hear the hum of conversation that rose behind him.

Stephen, standing beside Shannon, murmured, "I don't believe it," and shook his head.

Anne raised her voice at Orson and said, "How can he think that of us? How can he?"

Rosemary stood silently, her hands folded in front of her. Through the veil Shannon could see the glistening light of tears on her face.

Stephen noticed as well. He moved closer to his mother

and put his arm around her shoulders, not speaking, simply consoling her with his presence.

Shannon felt very much like an intruder so she turned and slowly followed the path Miles had taken down the hill.

According to Miles, the only secure method of defense was to attack. When Shannon questioned him the next day about his surprise announcement at Richard's funeral, he brushed away her intimations of impropriety. "They were all together. I said what needed to be said."

"I don't think it was the right place," Shannon ventured.

"Yes, it was," he countered. "I wanted my cards out on the table. I wanted everyone to know what I know. And I want no more subterfuge. If it truly is one of my children who is trying to have me killed, it will soon become plain."

"Why?" Shannon asked. "Now that they know you know, surely whoever it is will simply burrow underground and forget the whole thing. Besides, by saying that your plans are irrevocable, you've taken away the motive."

Miles smiled. "I have, haven't I?"

"Except, as you pointed out, the one of revenge," she said, reacting to his smugness.

They were sitting at the pool. Miles seemed to have completely recovered from the ordeal of Richard's death and the subsequent funeral.

It was another perfect southern California day, the temperature in the mid-seventies, the air somehow miraculously devoid of smog, the green of the vegetation around them piercing against the blueness of the sky.

"One more thing," Miles said. "I want to make sure you understand this. Anything I say to you doesn't go any further."

"Of course."

He didn't seem mollified. "I mean Stephen," he said. "I don't care what you two have going, it's none of my business, but whatever it is, the two things can't overlap. That is understood?"

"Yes," Shannon said, "that is understood."

"Good," Miles said, and wheeled his way back into the house.

Ten minutes later Miles zoomed out of the house at full speed, and skidded to a halt beside Shannon's chair where she was still working. She'd never seen him like this. His black eyes were dancing and his cheeks were flushed and there was a broad smile on his face.

"I have some good news. I just got a call from the hospital I told you about. They think they have a kidney."

Shannon felt her heart miss at least one beat. She grasped the sides of her patio chair, an involuntary grip that probably could have broken the metal. "Are you sure?"

Still grinning, Miles shook his head. "No, it's not positive, but they think it's a close match. They're going to need Melissa for tests. The kidney became available last night."

"Oh, my God," Shannon said.

"Yeah, the director just called. He said there's another kid in front of her for the kidney, but in view of the circumstances, meaning the generous gift I'm giving them, he feels that they can make this one available to her."

Shannon's feeling of elation stopped dead in its tracks. "What do you mean?"

Miles brushed it away. "It's nothing. They had another child there who needed a kidney, who was waiting for one, and he happens to be a very similar tissue type to Melissa, but this one's come up, and because of everything that I'm doing for them, they are willing to give it to her."

"Wait a minute," Shannon said. "You mean that this kid's been waiting, and now Melissa is going to have a . . . Wait a minute, there's something I don't understand."

Miles cut her off. "There's nothing to understand. All you have to do is get Melissa down there and see if it's the right one. If it is, it can be done."

"I need to think about this," Shannon said.

"Think, think, you always want to think," Miles said impatiently. "This is your daughter, it's time to do."

Shannon got up from her chair and glared down at him. "I need to think about it, Miles," she said emphatically. "I don't care whether you understand that or not, but I need to think about it."

She walked away, leaving him staring after her, a bemused expression on his face.

CHAPTER SIXTEEN

"Studios today, they're filled with pussycats. Run by accountants and other suit people in corporations. They also own soft drink plants, publishing companies, ten-minute automobile tune-up centers, and fast food franchises. What do these people know about movies? They hire executives who are supposed to know about movies, but these guys are so worried about their jobs that they don't take a chance.

"Last time I took a meeting with studio executives, I almost threw up. We were thinking of doing a joint venture on a movie. The stars were there, two young men, one of them with a drug habit, the other one with limp wrists. Light in the loafers, you know.

"But the stars were hot at the time. The stars made a joke, the executives laughed. Didn't matter that it was a bad joke.

"Every time the stars asked a question, the executives fell over each other trying to answer it. Every time I asked the stars a question, the executives all looked worried.

"One of the stars makes a real dumb suggestion: Let's think about making the lead character a plastic surgeon instead of a used car salesmen, he says, with all the wisdom of his years. The executives all nod at each other—good idea they say, brilliant idea—stroke of genius.

"Pussycats. They expected me to put my money into a project like that? Hollywood isn't what it used to be. I don't want any part of what it is today," Miles concluded.

The hospital in West Los Angeles was an imposing structure of steel and glass containing nurses in starched white uniforms and huge potted plants, with elevator music piped through every internal orifice.

The administrator, Dr. Paul Dailey, was what Shannon could only describe as a politician, a term she used for people for whom public relations was more important than substance. He was a man in his late forties, with wavy brown hair, a charming smile, and candid brown eyes. He was cheerful when he met her, a pose he no doubt maintained at all times in front of others.

She had insisted to an irate Miles that before she made her decision she needed to at least speak to the hospital personnel to gather data. She had called and made an appointment.

Dr. Dailey greeted her in his office, an antiseptically modern room furnished with smoked glass and chrome. A room in which dust was anathema.

"I'm so pleased to meet you," he said, shaking her hand enthusiastically and crinkling his eyes warmly at her. He indicated a chair opposite his desk and sat down. He placed his elbows on the Plexiglas and formed his hands into a steeple. "I understand you wanted to talk to me before we continued with the procedure."

"Yes, I did. I wanted to ask you a few questions."

"Of course, of course. You must have hundreds of questions. This is a very important step you're taking—for all of us."

"Yes, so I understand," Shannon said drily.

"Mr. Cort has offered us a wonderful opportunity," Dailey said. "I don't know what your relationship is with him, and of course it's none of my business, but we are

332

all very grateful for his support, and of course we're willing to do anything we can to assist you."

"I understand that there's another child to whom this organ could be given," Shannon said.

An uncomfortable expression flitted across Dailey's face, gone almost before it could be noticed. "There is another child who has a similar tissue match to your daughter. However, we feel that this will be of great benefit to her and that a kidney will soon be forthcoming for the young boy."

"I see," Shannon said dubiously. "How long has he been waiting?"

"Oh, I'm afraid I don't have that information right now, but that shouldn't be any concern of yours. I just want to assure you that your daughter will receive the finest treatment available anywhere in the world here for her transplant. And I'm sure that it will be one hundred percent successful."

"Well, I have no doubt of that, but I would like to know a little bit more about the circumstances," she said.

"The circumstances?"

"Dr. Dailey, don't you understand that if my daughter is stepping ahead of someone else in line that I might feel a little uncomfortable about it?"

Dailey looked almost shocked. "It's not a question of stepping ahead in line," he said, in a pained voice. "It's a question of whether the kidney is right for her, and we feel that it is an excellent match, and therefore she's entitled to it."

He was stonewalling her, and she knew it. She had interviewed enough politicians in various aspects of government to know when it was happening. Questions were never answered directly. God knew where people like this learned the technique, but the man was a consummate artist at it. Which is probably why he ran this hospital at such a young age.

"I wonder if I could talk to the chief surgeon in charge

of organ transplants, or at least kidney transplants," Shannon said. "I do have a few questions."

"Well, I'd be happy to answer any questions you have," Dailey said. "I don't really see the necessity of talking to the staff."

"I'd like to talk to the man who'd be in charge of the procedure. I need to assure myself of certain conditions on that," Shannon said. "I'm sure you can understand that."

"Well, yes, I suppose so, uh . . ." Dailey said uncertainly. "However . . . well, I'm sure that Dr. Roxford could answer your questions. Why don't we go and find him?"

They left the office and walked down a long corridor. "He should be in his office," Dailey said. He pointed as they passed a room, "As you can see, we have the most modern equipment here. We really are an excellent establishment. Of course the funds that Mr. Cort is promising us will enable us to upgrade even further. We will no doubt become a leader in the field of kidney transplantation in the country. It's very generous of him, very generous."

"Yes, it is," she agreed.

They came to a door and Dailey said, "This is Dr. Roxford's office, let's see if he's in here." He knocked, then opened the door without waiting for a reply.

Shannon peered across his shoulder, and saw a slight, sandy-haired man in his late thirties poring over folders at a desk.

"Peter," Dailey said, the good cheer returning to his voice. "This is Miss Ross. Her daughter Melissa is in line for a kidney transplant. If you remember, we discussed the case this morning."

Peter Roxford looked up from the folders he was studying. A frown knitted his forehead. He had wintry gray eyes and the haggard face of a workaholic. "Yes," he said, "I remember."

"Well, she'd like to ask you a few questions about the procedure. Do you have a moment to spare?"

Roxford glanced quickly at his watch. "Yes, I suppose I do." He didn't seem too pleased with the intrusion.

"Well, I'll leave you two to it, then," Dailey said, taking a step backward. "Why don't you come back to my office when you're done, Miss Ross, and I can answer any other questions you might have."

"Thank you," she said, and stepped into the room. She waited until he closed the door behind him before speaking. "I hope you don't mind the intrusion."

"Well, now that you mention it, I do," Roxford said in an unfriendly tone.

Without being invited, she sat in a chair in front of his desk. "I want to ask you some questions. I want to find out what's going on here."

"Oh?" His eyes came alive with interest. "What do you mean?"

"I understand that there was someone ahead of my daughter waiting for this kidney that just arrived."

Roxford closed the folder on his desk with a snap, and leaned back in his chair. "Yes, there was," he said. "A young Saudi Arabian boy, eleven years old. He's been waiting three years for a kidney. The good news is that the kidney arrived, the bad news is that his tissue type closely matches your daughter's."

"You don't approve of this, do you?" she said unnecessarily.

"I don't approve of favoritism when it's a matter of life and death. Not even when vast sums of money are involved."

"I want you to know that this wasn't my doing," she said. "I never asked for it."

"I don't care whose doing it was. The fact of the matter as explained to me is that a very large donation upon which this hospital is dependent has enabled you to place your daughter at the front of the line. It's not only illegal, it's unethical."

"So why are you agreeing to do it?"

"I'm a doctor," he said. "I'm not a politician, I'm not an administrator. I'm a doctor. I know how to do a job, just like a mechanic knows how to do a job on a car. It's what I've been trained to do. Not only that, but I'm dependent upon this job for my livelihood. When I'm ordered to do something, I become a good soldier and do it. It's easy to justify. I can sit here and say how much we need that money. How many lives that money could end up saving. Compared to that, what's the life of one boy?" His voice was bitter and his eyes hard as he spoke.

"You talk of a life," she said. "What is the situation with the boy?"

"As I said, he's from Saudi Arabia. He's been waiting for three years at his government's expense. They are giving him one more month and then they're taking him home. They are going to give up the waiting. It's costing too much."

"And?"

"He's not going to get a kidney. He's going to spend his life on dialysis, such as it is. With the care they have there, who knows how long his life will be?"

"Oh," Shannon said hollowly.

"Yes," he said, "that's the situation."

"I didn't know."

He rose from his chair, "Well, now you do, Ms. Ross. Do you have any more questions? If not, I need to get on with my job."

"Can I see the boy?"

He raised an eyebrow. "The boy who's been waiting for the kidney?" he asked, surprise in his tone.

"Yes."

"Certainly, come with me." He walked around his desk to the door and opened it.

She got up and followed him into the corridor. They walked five paces and then she stopped. "Dr. Roxford."

He came to a halt and turned.

"I've changed my mind, I don't want to see him. Thank you for your time."

He smiled grimly, "It's much easier that way, isn't it?" He turned and stalked away.

Shannon stood in the hallway, watching his back. She wanted to scream at him. He was being unfair. What did he know of the choice she faced? This was her daughter, not his. She wanted to scream, but instead she turned and walked back the way she had come.

Shannon drove home distractedly. Twice, impatient drivers honked at her, as she delayed when traffic signals turned green. She didn't care about that. She cared only for her daughter.

Whatever the ordeal she was going through, she knew it was nothing compared to what Melissa was suffering virtually on a daily basis. It was a state of affairs that she would be subjected to for the rest of her life if something wasn't done. Here was a chance. Her daughter, the child she loved more than anyone in the world, had the chance to end her suffering and to lead the normal life that other children were lucky enough to have. All she had to do was say yes.

And yet somewhere in that hospital, behind the glass windows, was a small and frightened little boy, from a country far away. He, too, had been suffering and he, too, had been waiting—longer than Melissa.

But Miles was promising a virtual fortune to the hospital. A sum that would, as the charismatic Dr. Dailey had said, allow them to upgrade their equipment so that they could be on a par if not better than any hospital in the country. It was money that would in the long run save the lives of children like Melissa and this unnamed boy from Saudi Arabia. It was a force for the good, of great benefit, not only directly to the hospital but to society.

It was easy to justify, just as Dr. Peter Roxford had said. All you had to do was look at the numbers. How many people would it benefit compared to the discomfort and disappointment of one? How could you look at something like that and not decide that such a gift and the conditions attached to it was the greatest good for the greatest number?

But she couldn't think that way. The greatest good for the greatest number was an abstract. She knew that the only way to maintain a viewpoint like that under these circumstances was not to see the boy, not to see the human face waiting there. It was why she had changed her mind about seeing him, just as the contemptuous doctor had guessed.

When things were taken out of the abstract, away from the philosophical, and brought down to a point of individuality, of human feelings, of a single individual's hopes and fears and dreams and pain, then how could she justify any kind of philosophical argument?

She didn't know the answer to that. It was a question that man had wrestled with probably since the dawn of time. And the answers were as varied as the paths of men had been since then.

She arrived back at the mansion, entered the gates, and parked in the garages on the side. She sat in the car, her mind still alive with speculation and uncertainty. This was her daughter, this was not an abstraction. This was *her* daughter, she told herself fiercely. If she had to choose between the life of her daughter and an unknown boy, could she be blamed for choosing her daughter? She doubted that anyone in the world would blame her, except perhaps the young boy's parents, and except perhaps for Dr. Peter Roxford.

She got out of the car and walked back toward the cottage.

"Hey, Mom," she heard Melissa shout, and saw her run down the pathway toward her.

"Hi. How are you?"

"I'm just fine," Melissa said. "I've finished my school work and I'm going to go to the pool for a while, okay?"

"That's fine," Shannon said.

She turned and watched Melissa jog down the path toward the back of the mansion. How wonderful normality would be for her, no longer a prisoner of that life-giving machine.

She turned again and walked toward her cottage. Twenty yards away she stopped, and went back to the mansion.

She walked through the side entrance down the hall into the main hall. She passed Lynn's office, walked to Miles's study, and opened the door without knocking.

He looked up from his desk, surprise on his face. People never walked in without an appointment, let alone without knocking.

Shannon marched up to his desk, and before he could speak said, "No, I can't do it. The answer is no."

Miles argued, threatened, flew into a rage. He called her ungrateful, he called her stupid, he called her short-sighted. He told her she didn't care enough for her daughter.

"It's not right," Shannon said stubbornly, her anger matching his. "I don't give a shit what you say, it's not right and I'm not going to do it."

"What if you put it to Melissa?" he asked. "What if you told her that this was a chance for her to have a new kidney and that you were going to turn it down? What do you think she would say? What if you let her make the decision? What decision do you think she would make?"

"She'd make the right decision," Shannon said. "She's my daughter. But I would never consider placing that onus on her, never. And if you ever discuss it with her, or even mention it to her, I'll walk right out this door and you will never see me again."

"I wouldn't do that," Miles said. "It was just a hypothetical question."

"Well then, forget it. Hypothetical questions don't apply to real life and you know it," she snapped.

"You're sure about this? Absolutely certain? You don't even have a single doubt?"

"I have a thousand doubts," she said. "What do you think I am? A machine? I'm a mother and this is my daughter we're talking about. I'm filled with doubts, but I've made up my mind and nothing you say will change it."

"Very well," Miles said. "So be it."

The sadness in his voice mentally snapped her to attention. It was genuine, there was no doubt about it.

"I'm sorry," she said, "I really am. And I really appreciate your intentions, and I really appreciate what you're willing to do, and I really appreciate your generosity. But I just can't do it. I couldn't live with myself. And I couldn't allow Melissa to live with my decision. Please understand that."

Miles nodded. "I understand. I don't agree, but I understand. And I respect your decision."

Orson was in a black mood. On the way home from work he stopped at a bar on Olive Street and sat at a small table by himself, hardly noticing the three cute secretaries at a table a few yards away or the short-skirted waitresses he normally joked with. Instead, he stared into his glass. When it was empty, he ordered another.

He had screwed up terribly. He was out fifteen grand, he had a dead brother and a father who was not only very much alive, but now knew beyond any doubt that someone was trying to kill him. The only bright side was that

Miles didn't know there were two people trying to kill him.

Orson had an optimistic thought: Perhaps whoever had made the first attempt would try again and succeed this time. If only. As for him, he had no intention of doing anything like that again. It had been a stupid, stupid move, born of desperation. Probably the dumbest thing he had ever done in his life.

He was running out of money and hope. Nothing seemed possible to him anymore, he thought morosely.

Vaguely he remembered when he was younger. He had dreams then, dreams of becoming a great producer of fine films, dreams of beautiful actresses hanging on to his arms, and, above all, dreams of respect from his father. None of it had happened. Oh sure, there were women, but somehow it was empty, except while it was happening. Afterward he felt hollow and unfulfilled.

"God," he said aloud, and drained his third drink.

"You want another one?" said the waitress who appeared at his shoulder.

Orson nodded. It was all he could do, drink to drown his feelings, to hide from himself.

Poor Richard. Poor miserable son of a bitch. Maybe it had been for the best. He would have died one way or another before a year was out, Orson would have bet money on it. But Jesus, to go like that, electrocuted in a swimming pool—victim of a mistake. How pathetic.

It wouldn't be traced to him, he was almost sure of that. Bill, or whatever his name was, was a real pro. He wouldn't have left any clues. God knew how many people he'd killed. But he hadn't been caught before and wouldn't be caught now. Besides there was nothing that could lead him to Orson. There was no way to trace the cash back to him. He'd been careful about that.

What if the man blackmailed him though? What if he came back a year later and asked for more money? Silly, paranoid thought. How could he do that? He'd committed the murder. There was no way he could incriminate Orson without incriminating himself. No, that was the least of his problems.

The waitress brought his drink and set it down on the table in front of him. "Three-fifty, please," she said.

Orson took a five, put it on the table. She made the change and then moved away. He should go home. He should go sit in the hot tub and stare up at the cool black sky and icy stars and pray for inspiration. That's what he should do. He gulped at his drink and looked around. He recognized some people from NBC a few tables away. He didn't walk over to them as he normally would have. He didn't want to talk to anyone. Another gulp and then another. When the drink was finished, he got to his feet and left the bar.

Traffic was barely moving on the Ventura Freeway. Orson twiddled his radio dial, found a talk station, listened for a moment, switched it to an oldies station, then turned the radio off.

He found his thoughts circling back to the past, seeking the crossroads. There was a time, he knew, when things had seemed okay, when dreams and goals had seemed attainable. When exactly had it started to change? What had happened? He wished he knew.

It had something to do with the job at Charisma, he thought. That had been the pinnacle of his career, a pinnacle that came when he was very young, in his late twenties. Back then Miles still ran the studio. It was already past its prime by then, of course, but it was nevertheless a working studio, still producing a dozen films each year. Sometimes more. He'd started out there in the mailroom. Then worked in development and then in production. Miles was training him to take over the helm, he was told.

The peak came when he was appointed executive in charge of production. It was a horrendous job, dealing with budgets, unions, cranky crews, volatile actors, insecure directors, and grasping producers. But it was power.

The kind of power he'd never personally experienced before, but only seen secondhand in his father. He was feted, wined and dined. He was courted by the famous and the not so famous.

It was a heady period. Women were his for the taking, dope arrived unasked for, mounds of it, and money was available in every direction he turned. Much of it under-the-table payoffs.

He thought he was doing okay at the time. Sure, a number of films ran over budget, and a few of them could even have been called disasters. But he was more shocked than anyone when after eleven months, Miles hauled him into his office and told him he was fired. Not just demoted, mind you, but fired. Off the lot before you wreck it, Miles had said.

He'd taken it in his stride, he thought, and moved into independent production. Hell, with all the contacts he'd built up through Charisma, he thought he could succeed. But he wasn't at Charisma Films anymore and the contacts somehow dried up. He was just another struggling independent, trying to make a go of it.

People he considered his friends no longer returned his telephone calls. And business associates spoke only of the bottom line, and the magnitude of the talent he could sign, and the marketing potential. He'd known how fickle people were in this town—indeed, he'd lived by the same code himself, but this was ridiculous. Since then business had been very difficult.

That was the turning point and it was all Miles's fault, he thought bitterly. He threw his own son out to the wolves. And even when the wolves started to nibble at his heels, and even when the wolves tore his limbs from his body, the unforgiving old man simply watched. Oh yeah, he'd invested money in a couple of Orson's films. But as soon as it became obvious that the films would become financial embarrassments, the funds dried up.

Miles's problem was that he couldn't take a joke. He took money too seriously, Orson thought grimly.

There was still time to show him, to show them all. That was the one thing about Hollywood, you were never counted out until you were really out. It was a town of miracles, of replenished dreams. Anything could happen and usually did. Fortunes could suddenly be reversed. Luck, that whore who wandered to other beds, could suddenly return.

He had seen too many people reverse declines not to believe that. He had seen actors make splashy comebacks, writers who went to live in the desert return in gleaming black limousines, directors whose last three films had prevented them from getting anything except the most degrading work, suddenly become hot again. It had happened to them, and it could happen to him. All he needed was a project, one project, and everything could change. But of course, to get that he needed money.

He had his eye on a script. It was the work of a first-time writer, and somehow the script had escaped the scrutiny of studios and other production companies and landed on his desk. That wasn't surprising, considering the quantity of product everyone looked at.

If there was the slightest risk, it was usually a pass. If it was at all like something else, it was a pass—even if it was simply a similar title or setting. If the reader had a hangover that morning, it was a pass. Great scripts had done the rounds for years in many cases before some insightful or lucky executive had grabbed them.

This was the story of an eternal triangle, set in the arena of law enforcement. It wasn't a totally original concept, but the writing was bright and vigorous and the characters were not hackneyed. It was a quality piece of work, something he rarely had the opportunity to acquire.

His problem in the past was that he had needed to make a film—any film—just for the sake of making one. Admittedly, the quality hadn't been the highest. The scripts

344

hadn't been great, the talent had been minor, and the subjects weren't particularly commercial in the big sense of the word. He had to change that. He needed to go for quality now, something that would lend credibility to his name. This story could give him that chance.

What he needed to do was option the script. Once you had something hot, then interested some major talent in it, the doors usually began to open. He needed to tie the script up. God, if he'd kept that fifteen grand instead of . . .

His hands clutched the steering wheel tightly and then released it. No point in regrets now. He had to look ahead. The past was a morass, an inescapable swamp of failed intentions. He needed to see a future, something that could guide him forward.

He drove up the winding hill and into his driveway. Barbara's Volvo was parked in front of the house, the trunk open. He got out of his car and walked past, noticing a suitcase in the back. He wondered if she was going on a trip. He couldn't remember her saying anything about it.

He walked through the garage and into the kitchen. Stopping at the fridge he took out a beer and unscrewed the cap. He took a long swallow, and then with the beer still in his hand, walked down the hall. The living room was empty, as was the dining room. He headed for the bedroom.

Barbara was packing another suitcase. It was open on the bed.

"Hey," he said, "what's going on?"

Barbara turned to look at him over her shoulder. "I'm packing."

"Yeah, I can see that. Where are you going?"

She returned to her packing, her voice muffled. "I'm leaving you, Orson."

For a moment he didn't understand what she was saying. "A trip?"

"No. Leaving."

"What?" He moved quickly and grabbed her shoulder.

She straightened up. "I'm leaving you. I've had enough of this sham, of this excuse for a life. Of worrying where the next dollar is coming from and what the future holds. That's it for our marriage, it's over. Now let me get on with my packing."

Orson felt as if the breath had been knocked from his stomach. He stood there, not knowing what to say. And then the anger came. "You're leaving me?" he said stupidly.

"It's over. Done. Fini. Kaput. I'm out of here," Barbara said without a trace of regret in her voice. She snapped the lid of the suitcase closed and locked it.

"Where are you going that's so wonderful?"

"I met a guy, I'm moving in with him. You'll hear from my lawyer." She hefted the suitcase off the bed and put it on the floor. "I've still got some stuff here. I'll be back to get it some other time."

"You're just going to walk out of here like that? This is the end of our marriage? You're going to walk out? Some other guy? Who is this guy?"

"He's a director. He works. He earns money. It's not a lot of money, but it's enough. And he cares for me," she said defiantly.

"Who? What's his name?"

"John Bellows. I met him through friends. He's a nice man."

"John Bellows? Ha!" Orson snorted. "I know Bellows, he started off in porno, for chrissake. This is the guy you're leaving me for?"

"I know how he started off, but that was then and this is now. Yeah, he might have started in porno, but he's made something of himself. He's now a respected director. He works in television. He works in features. He has work all the time. It's not like you, Orson. You started off with a golden chance and made nothing of it."

This was too close to his own self-recriminations. He didn't need to hear it form anyone else. "You bitch!"

"Yeah, well, I'm going to be a happier bitch, that's for sure."

"Fuck you, you're not walking out of here like this."

She looked at him dangerously. "Don't try and stop me, Orson. It's not going to work. There's nothing you can do to stop me."

He glared back at her. "I could break your neck."

"You don't have the guts."

Orson's anger dissipated. He *didn't* have the guts and, besides, it wasn't leading anywhere. "Listen, can't we talk about this? I mean, we have been married. We are husband and wife. Maybe we could work things out. Things are changing for me, you know. I got a new deal, a real exciting new script. And I think this is going to be the one."

Barbara shook her head, her eyes stony and her mouth set. "I've heard it all before, Orson. There's no point. It's always the next one. It's always something that's going to happen, but it never does. I've had it. Let's just call it quits."

Orson sat heavily on the bed. He was still holding the beer bottle, he realized. He took a sip. Fuck her. There was no point arguing. There was just no purpose to it. Let her go. He'd be better off without her. She was a cunt anyway, always had been. Shouldn't have married her in the first place. Just a bad habit of his.

Barbara hefted the suitcase up and marched toward the door, stopping to say, "I'm going to be filing for divorce, Orson. You'll be hearing from my lawyer."

"Don't expect anything from me. You want support, you're out of luck."

"I gave up expecting anything from you a long time ago," she said and continued out the door.

Orson stared down at the narrow opening of the beer bottle. He swirled it in his hands, watching the foam lap up the sides. Well, he could make a fresh start, he thought. A fresh start with everything.

And then to his own consternation, he mysteriously found himself beginning to sob.

Peter Corydon walked into Miles's office and stood before him at the desk while Miles finished signing a letter. Corydon stood patiently, easily. He was used to Miles and his idiosyncrasies, and didn't mind them. He'd been with him five years now and liked the job. It sure beat the Beverly Hills Police Department. You always knew where you stood with Miles, which was more than you could say for working in a bureaucracy.

Miles pushed the paper aside and looked up at Corydon. "The guy Anne was with at the funeral . . . Frank . . . some wop name. Scolaro?"

Corydon nodded.

"I want him checked out. I want you to find out everything there is to know about him. Okay?"

"Yes, sir," Corydon said. "Is there anything else?"

"I assume you've maintained contact with the police? And I assume they have discovered absolutely nothing about the setup at the pool?"

"That's correct, sir. They can't trace the equipment, nor did they find any fingerprints, or any clues at all. They maintain it was done by a professional."

"And you? What do you think?"

"It looked like a professional job to me."

"So, he was hired by someone?"

"Yes, sir."

"I gave Orson fifteen thousand dollars because of money he had due on a second trust deed loan. Check through the title office and see if that money was due, will you?"

Corydon's eyes grew interested. "Yes, sir, I'll check on that right away."

"Good. Let me know on both of those things as soon as possible."

"Yes, sir," Corydon turned and walked out of the room.

"And Peter?" Miles said.

Corydon turned. "Yes, sir."

"I assume that security precautions have been studied and corrected so that no intruder can get into the grounds again?"

"We've installed new ground sensors and video cameras to take up the blind spots. It won't happen again."

"Good," Miles said.

The wiley old bastard, Peter thought. He didn't miss a trick. He'd check up on Orson all right. And he'd bet just like Miles was probably betting that there wasn't any such loan. It didn't prove anything, of course, but it was one more piece of the puzzle.

Anne said, "When I was a child I used to watch a lot of cowboy movies, and Daddy always reminded me of the tough rancher, the one who was the villain or the town boss."

"Why was that?" Shannon asked. She was sitting in Anne's apartment in the second hour of her interview. Anne wore jeans and a loose T-shirt, as did Shannon. It looked to Shannon as if Anne had lost weight recently. She also seemed more cheerful. Surprisingly, she was also more intelligent than Shannon had thought.

"Well, in those movies the town boss or the bad rancher was always giving orders to bunches of tough men, who'd go out and beat up some poor innocents. The thing was, the bosses were always tougher than the men they gave orders to. They never backed down, and they were the ones who always ended up being shot by the good guys. Daddy was like that, I think. I always saw him surrounded by tough men, or important men. He always seemed bigger than all of them. He was the one who gave out the orders."

"How did he treat you when you were a kid?"

"He was gruff and I didn't see all that much of him. But he was very protective. Probably too protective. I know he scared off a few of my first boyfriends."

"Can you tell me about that?"

"Well, I remember a time when I was about seventeen, a guy from high school came to pick me up to take me to a party. He came into the house and was shown into Miles's study before I was called. When I came downstairs he was just coming out of the door and his face was as white as a sheet.

"We went outside and I asked him if he'd met my father, and he said, 'Christ, yes.' I asked him what Daddy had said to him and the guy replied, 'He said, "When I was a young man I remember exactly what I wanted from young girls. If you are thinking along those lines you won't even live to regret it.'" The poor guy was terrified. He didn't touch me the whole night. I was the one who had to kiss him good night. He never asked me out on a date again."

"Did this happen often?" Shannon asked.

"A few times. He always checked out my husbands before I married them. He's probably checking out Frank right now."

"Frank, who was at the funeral?"

"Yes. And, knowing Miles, he'll probably find some deep dark secret in Frank's past, but it doesn't bother me. Everyone has done something. I don't care. Frank is good for me and that's all that counts."

"So, over all, what do you think your father thought of you when you were growing up?"

Anne twisted her fingers together. "He was disappointed. He was disappointed in all of us. He wanted me to go to college. I wanted to be an actress."

"What did he say? Did he try to dissuade you?"

"He said if I wanted to be a bimbo—nothing but a bimbo for the rest of my life—I was welcome to go try acting. He said I had no talent. Just because I was pretty wasn't enough. He said Hollywood was full of pretty girls. He may have been right."

"Do you really believe that?"

Anne hesitated. "For a long time I did. But now I don't think so. I mean, I'm not a major star or anything, but I like acting. And I think it's something I could be good at. I still have a lot to learn, even now. I just took a lot of wrong steps in the wrong directions. But it's not too late to turn around and move along another path. Believe it or not I'm actually attending an acting workshop right now. It's quite amazing. You think you know how to do something and then find out you've been doing it wrong all these years."

"That must be fun," Shannon said.

"It is, but it's also hard work. You know, I think that was the thing I never realized—how much hard work it would take to become a good actress. I never really worked at it. It was just something I did, something I thought came naturally to me. It didn't really."

"Well, that must be very exciting," Shannon added.

The doorbell rang and Anne's face suddenly came alive. "That's Frank. Do you have enough? I did tell you our time was limited, right?"

"Yeah, that'll be fine," Shannon said. "But maybe I can talk to you again."

"Sure," Anne said as she hurried to the door.

She opened it and Shannon looked curiously on as Anne and the young man kissed each other. They walked back into the room, their arms around each other.

"Frank, you remember Shannon Ross? She's writing my father's book," Anne said.

Frank walked up to her and smiled, his hand outstretched. "Of course, I met you at the funeral. It's nice to see you again, under happier circumstances."

Shannon stood up and shook his hand. He had open eyes and an easy smile, and she found herself liking him. He had to be ten years younger than Anne, she thought. Yet Anne seemed radiant in his presence.

"Well, I guess I'd better be going. Thanks for the interview, Anne."

"Anytime." Anne took Frank's hand in hers. "Just give me a buzz and we'll set up another appointment if you need more."

"I'll always have more questions," Shannon said, walking toward the door, "but usually they don't come till later. I'll let you know."

When she left, her last sight was of Anne nuzzling her boyfriend's neck.

Shannon was spending the night with Stephen. Both Melissa and the baby-sitter were prepared, and, in fact, Melissa was quite excited at the idea of spending a night at home without her mother.

They went out to dinner at a small Russian restaurant downtown. Shannon found herself telling him about what she had just been going through regarding the availability of a kidney for Melissa.

Stephen was slightly incredulous. "You mean he was willing to donate all that money, just so Melissa could get a kidney?"

"Absolutely. At least the people at the hospital were convinced that was so."

"Amazing," Stephen muttered. "Really amazing. The old bastard can still surprise me. Maybe there is a spark of warmth in that cold heart."

"It's more than a spark, Stephen," she said. "It was an incredibly generous gesture. Actually it was a lot more than a gesture, he was really putting his money where his mouth was. And all because of Melissa." She fiddled with her glass of wine, twirling it on the table. "I'm still wondering if I did the right thing. It was a hard decision."

"I love you because of it," Stephen said.

She looked up, caught off guard. "What?"

"It was the right decision. And you couldn't do anything but make it, being who you are, and that's why I love you," he said. "I know how hard it must have been. I don't know what I would have done under the circumstances. But you did the right thing."

Shannon couldn't help it. She began to cry. "God," she said between sobs, "it was so difficult to decide. It means so much to Melissa and to me. But I knew that I would have hated myself afterwards. I just couldn't do it. I guess unlike Miles, I just don't have what it takes to really go for something without any qualms or second thoughts. It was so hard."

Stephen reached across the table and took her hand in his. He rubbed it gently. "But you know what? It's going to work out. You did the right thing, and the right thing's going to happen. Somehow another kidney will turn up. And it'll work out without feeling rotten for the rest of your life, hiding the fact from Melissa that some other child had to suffer because of her happiness. I just know it'll work out."

"Oh, God, I hope so," she sniffled. "I hope so."

They finished their meal and walked out of the restaurant. It was only two blocks from Stephen's loft, and they had chosen to walk in spite of the derelicts and homeless crowding the street with their hands outstretched.

"They know me," Stephen had explained. "I'm not known as a soft touch. There are a couple of people I give money to every now and then, but that's it. If I started giving to everyone, I'd never be able to get a block from my house."

They were halfway home when Shannon suddenly grabbed Stephen's hand and stopped. "You said you love me," she said, as if suddenly realizing the importance of the words.

"I did." He smiled.

"Did you really mean it?" Her eyes searched his. "Was that really what you meant to say or were you just trying to console me?"

"I meant every one of those three words. I love you, Shannon Ross. You're the best thing that's happened in my life."

She was filled with such strong desire for him that it almost made her fall. She clutched his hand and started to move down the sidewalk, almost pulling him behind her.

"What?" he said with a foolish smile. "What's gotten into you?"

"I want you. I want you now. Come on, let's hurry." And she broke into a run, the laughing Stephen half a pace behind her.

CHAPTER SEVENTEEN

According to Miles, regret was for wimps. "Sure we've all made mistakes. Even I have. But you can't regret them. You can't carry that millstone around your neck for the rest of your life. You've got to move on and look forward. Regret is something like quicksand. It keeps a part of you stuck there forever. People who regret are weak. They use it as an excuse not to act. I can't do that, never have, never will."

The family dinner was well attended. Shannon was there and so were all the children: Stephen, Elizabeth, Anne, and Orson. Anne had Frank with her, and somehow his presence seemed to fill the void that Richard's absence left. Frank looked slightly nervous but was still able to be charming and talkative.

Miles was uncustomarily pleasant. When he heard from Orson that his wife had left him, he simply said, "You're better off without her," and didn't mount the withering attack he could have under the circumstances.

When they had finished their food and sat sipping coffee and liquor, Miles spoke directly to Frank, who he had been virtually ignoring throughout the meal. "I understand you were married before."

"Yes," Frank said.

"Did you know that, Anne?" Miles asked with mild curiosity.

"Yes, of course. Frank was only married for six weeks. It was a mistake."

"Did he tell you that he tried to sue his wife for alimony?" Miles asked.

Anne's eyes grew wide. She recognized the impending storm. "Yes, he told me. But it's not your business or anybody's else's here."

"How can a man sue a woman for alimony?" Miles asked.

Frank dove in. "Anne's right. It's none of your business," he said bravely. "But since you bring it up, she was an actress, too. In those six weeks, she spent the ten thousand dollars that I'd saved and she was working and I wasn't. All I wanted was the money back when I found out what a mistake it was. I don't like getting ripped off. Do you, Mr. Cort?"

"I see," Miles said. "Simply a repayment of a debt."

"I'm not going to justify it any further than that," Frank said stiffly. "I don't owe you any explanations."

"I understand you also got arrested for drunk driving about a year ago," Miles said, still in that same calm, dispassionate voice.

Frank glared at him.

"And when you were twenty-one you were arrested for selling cocaine to an undercover police officer. Got off with probation, though."

"I don't do drugs anymore," Frank said hotly. "I was young then. I made mistakes. I'm sure even you have."

"How dare you bring this up in front of everyone now. How dare you even bring it up!" Anne shrieked. "What right have you got to interfere in my life? What right do you have to poke around in Frank's private life?"

Miles was unfazed by the attack. "Simply protecting your interests as always. Here you have a young man, young enough to be your goddamn son, sniffing around you. You don't think I'm going to check into it?"

"He's not young enough to be my son," Anne said, enraged. "And it's not your damn business anyway."

"Regardless of what you think, Mr. Cort," Frank said, "I love Anne. The fact that she's older than me has nothing to do with it. The fact that I've made mistakes in the past has nothing to do with it. I love her and that's all that matters to both of us."

"That true, Anne?" Miles asked.

"Frank is the nicest man I've ever met. I don't care what he's done in the past, he's told me everything anyway. And I don't give a shit what you think about it. Why don't you just stay out of our lives?"

"Very well," Miles said, and sipped his cognac. Then he held it up. "To the young lovers."

The others had watched this scenario with varying degrees of interest. When Miles made his toast, they all did nothing except Stephen, who raised his glass and said without a trace of irony, and genuine warmth, "To Anne and Frank, may you be happy together."

Miles gave him a sharp look but said nothing. He had apparently been mustering his energies during the meal, because now he turned his attention on Orson. "By the way, Orson, that fifteen thousand dollars you borrowed from me . . ."

Orson, who had been solemnly regarding his glass, suddenly came to attention. "Yes?"

"You said it was for a payment due on a second trust deed."

"Yes."

"I did a little checking. You don't have any payment due on a second trust deed. You cashed the check I gave you and took it all out in cash. What was it for?" Miles asked with disarming interest.

Orson's hands clutched at his glass and he avoided his father's look. He waited for three full seconds before answering. "It was for a gambling debt. A gambling debt that was due. I didn't want to tell you about that."

"I see," Miles said. "This is a new vice you've taken up then? Gambling's never been one of your many vices."

"Yes," Orson said dully, "a new vice."

"I see," Miles said thoughtfully and dropped the subject.

After finishing coffee, they moved to the living room. Orson took his briefcase from the floor, put it on his lap. He took a bound script out of it, put the briefcase down and held the script, looking at it dubiously as if uncertain what to do next.

"What's that?" Miles asked.

Orson hesitated, then walked a few steps to his father and handed him the script. "I'd like you to read this."

"What is it?"

"It's a very exciting script," Orson said. "Something I want to acquire."

"Are you going to hit me up for money again?" Miles asked.

"I just want you to read it," Orson said irritably.

"Why?"

"I'd like your opinion. I'm very excited by it, but I'd really like your opinion."

Miles looked surprised. "You're asking me for my opinion now? You mean it has some value? All those other things I advised you against, my advice which you so wisely ignored? Now you want my opinion?"

"I do," Orson said uncomfortably.

"Good. Then I'll read it."

"I saw Rosemary today," Stephen said. "She asked how you were."

It had been a week since the funeral and, although still sad, Rosemary had apparently recovered her equilibrium. Stephen had talked to her for a long time.

"How is she? How is she about Richard?" Miles asked.

It was the first time his name had been mentioned this

358

evening, and somehow it seemed to send a jolt through the room. Elizabeth looked up from the magazine she was studying, her eyes wary. Anne looked down at the floor.

"She's doing pretty well," Stephen answered. "I think she's come to terms with it."

Miles nodded. "She's a tough woman, your mother. Tougher than she looks. She'll get over it."

"And you?" Stephen asked. "How are you feeling about it?"

"I'm tougher than your mother," Miles said.

Later, as they sat in Shannon's cottage, Stephen said, "Elizabeth's the one I'm worried about. She's so quiet and withdrawn. I tried to talk to her about Richard but she's just ignoring the whole thing as if it never happened. You know there was one time they were pretty close."

"Really?" Shannon asked.

"There's only two years between them," he said. "They grew up together. Closer to each other than they were to me, because of the age difference. I think during the high school years in particular they were pretty good friends."

"And then later?"

"They went their different ways. Elizabeth is, I suppose, the ultimate loner. And Richard seemed intent on his own path."

"She hasn't expressed any feelings about it?" Shannon asked.

"Nothing."

"That's not a good sign. You're right," she said.

"I'm going to see if I can talk to her more," he said.

"Do you want some more coffee?" Shannon asked.

"I'll never get to sleep."

"I'm not planning to let you get any sleep tonight," she replied with a smile. "You are staying the night, aren't you?"

"Couldn't make me leave."

After a few moments Shannon said, "That was quite a performance your father put on tonight."

"It wasn't up to his usual standards," Stephen said. "I'm beginning to think you may be right. He's changing. He could have gone for the jugular quite a few times and he chose not to. It's not like him."

"Well, maybe he's mellowing. Maybe Richard's death has something to do with it," Shannon guessed.

"Whatever it is, it's an improvement. I'm not going to question it. Now let's talk about something more pleasant than Miles."

"Like what?"

"Like whether Melissa is sound asleep yet and whether we can go into your bedroom and make delicious and noisy love."

"Now that's worth talking about," Shannon said.

Dorothy Kite lived in a small ramshackle bungalow below Santa Monica Boulevard. Miles had given Shannon her name, saying, "Here's a woman who really hates me. She'll tell you some great stories."

Mrs. Kite was small and bent but her eyes were bright and alert, and although she had a tremor in both hands, she seemed to be physically robust. She sat opposite Shannon in a small, dowdy living room with old flower-print furniture and said, "What do you want to know about that animal?"

"Why do you call him that?" Shannon asked, unobtrusively pushing the on button of her recorder.

"Because he killed my daughter. He murdered her."

"You mean he actually killed her?"

"As good as," Mrs. Kite said, her mouth pursing and her tone growing sullen.

Shannon decided to backtrack. This was going too fast. "What was your daughter's name, Mrs. Kite?"

"Sandy Kite. She was a wonderful actress. She could

have been one of the great ones. She could have been up there with Marilyn Monroe and Elizabeth Taylor until he ruined it."

"Tell me what happened."

"Do you want some tea?" Mrs. Kite asked, half rising.

"No, thank you. I'm fine."

Mrs. Kite sat again and looked down at her trembling hands without speaking.

"What happened, Mrs. Kite?" Shannon prompted gently.

"My daughter got pregnant. It was a shameful thing, but not shameful enough to bring about her death. She was just an innocent, the poor girl."

"When was this?"

"It was 1953, the summer. I'll never forget that year. Stalin died in the spring and then Julius and Ethel Rosenberg were electrocuted for being spies, and my little girl got pregnant. It was the wrong time for her to get pregnant and the right time for her in everything else. She made her first film and was on the way to being a star. The public adored her. She was doing her second film for Mr. Miles Cort. They'd already started shooting when she found out she was pregnant. Mr. Cort of course, browbeat the information out of her."

Her voice trailed away and the tremor in her hands increased noticeably. She clasped them together as if to stop the involuntary movement.

"And then what happened?" Shannon asked.

"He threatened her. She wanted to have the child even though she was not married. He threatened to ruin her career. First, he said that he would sue her for breach of contract and then he said that he would see that she never worked in this town again unless . . ."

"Unless what?"

"Unless she had an abortion." Mrs. Kite, who had been staring down at her hands, looked up at Shannon. "Abortions were illegal in those days. Mr. Cort arranged the

361

whole thing. Some filthy shed somewhere in East Los Angeles. My little girl went there. She had no choice and she died there. Although her body was found later some miles away sitting at a bus stop. She had bled to death."

"My God, that's terrible," Shannon said. "What did you do?"

"There was nothing I could do. I couldn't prove that Miles Cort had arranged the abortion. I couldn't prove that he had threatened her. It was kept between them and I only heard it secondhand from her. There was nothing I could do except mourn my little girl."

"And now you hate Miles Cort?" Shannon said, more to herself than to the woman.

"He took two lives. He will always be a murderer in my eyes."

"Two . . . oh, you mean the child?"

"My daughter and my grandchild," Mrs. Kite said solomnly.

"What about the father? What did he have to say about all this? Surely he must have been enraged at Mr. Cort."

"No," Mrs. Kite said.

"Oh?"

Mrs. Kite hesitated, a sly look on her face. "Mr. Cort was the father," she announced. "He was the man who got my little girl pregnant. May God rot his soul."

Later, driving back to the Cort mansion, a bewildered Shannon wondered why Miles had sent her on that interview. There was such a thing as candor, but why on earth would he want an ugly story like this known? It was beyond her understanding.

It was one A.M. when Elizabeth arrived home. To her surprise the lights were still on and loud rock music was blaring. She closed the front door behind her, locked it securely, and walked down the hall to the living room where the noise was coming from.

Sissy was curled up on the floor in a fetal position, her long blond hair a tangled heap. A dozen compact discs were spread out in disarray around her, and beside her was an empty glass and a quarter-filled bottle of Scotch.

Elizabeth stood there in shock. Sissy rarely drank more than a glass of wine at any one time and never touched hard liquor. "Sissy," she queried, stepping closer, "are you all right?"

Sissy struggled into a sitting position. Her eyes were bleary and her face tear-streaked and she stared at Elizabeth as if she were a stranger. "I'm fine, just fine." Her words slurred.

Elizabeth dropped her purse on the couch and went over to Sissy. She dropped to one knee beside her. "You are really bombed."

Sissy seemed to have trouble focusing on her face. "I'm celebrating."

Elizabeth eyed her cautiously. "Oh? What are you celebrating?"

A crafty look entered Sissy's eyes. She shook her head and said, "Have a drink. This is good Scotch."

"I don't want a drink," Elizabeth said tartly. "I want to know what's going on with you."

A crooked grin from Sissy. "Nothing's wrong with me, I'm celebrating the fact that I'm a free woman. Here's to freedom," she said, reaching for the glass. She slopped some Scotch into it and then took a gulp. She grimaced at the taste but managed to swallow it with only a small splutter.

Elizabeth looked at her with concern. This was a new and different Sissy, one she had never seen before. Of course she'd never seen her this drunk before. But why the drinking? "Why don't you tell me what's been happening?" she said in a more reasonable tone.

"Nothing's happening. I'm drunk," Sissy said unnecessarily.

"Oh, I can see that."

"Everyone has the right to get drunk now and again. It's good for you. It's good for the soul."

Elizabeth got up off the floor and took off her jacket. She walked over to the couch and threw it down on the end. Then she sat and watched Sissy sitting six feet away.

"How's business?" Sissy asked. "Still beating up men?"

"Business is fine," Elizabeth replied. Now wasn't the time to discuss it. In truth, business wasn't wonderful but it was okay. Limiting herself to only a few trustworthy clients, she found it more and more necessary to service them herself. There were only two of the girls she could trust to keep the entire operation a closely guarded secret. However, on the other side of the coin, when she was required to service clients herself, she charged them more than double the going rate, almost two hundred fifty dollars an hour. Tonight she had made seven fifty in three hours, basically through rendering a man into a whimpering mess.

What she also didn't tell Sissy, however, was that her friend from the L.A.P.D., Charlie Shultz, had come in this evening. She trusted him implicitly and included him on her new list of acceptable clients.

Shultz had given her a warning. "You can only get away with this for so long," he said, shaking his head at her. "This is a small town when it comes to this kind of activity and word's going to get around." She had told him she didn't need much time, but he wasn't mollified. "You're taking a big risk. If these people find out you are still in operation, the consequences could be severe. They don't mess around. And there's nothing I can do to help you. You know that."

"I know the risk I'm taking," she had said. "I need to take it for just a little longer."

Now she wondered if it was worth it. She did have a lot of money. The target amount she had set to attain by a certain time was totally arbitrary. Was it worth risking her life to reach it? She had thought it was. Now however, she wasn't so sure.

Sissy had also apparently been thinking in a philosophical vein, because now the question on her mind came bursting out. "Do you think men deserve it?"

"Deserve what?" Elizabeth said.

"Deserve to be treated that way. The way you treat them," Sissy said. "Do you think men are such bastards that they deserve to be treated that way?"

"They like it. They pay money for it. I don't drag them in there."

"Yeah, but do they know what they're doing?" Sissy thought about her own question for a moment, then shrugged it off. "I don't care, I'm celebrating my freedom. Have a drink."

"I don't want a drink," Elizabeth said. "What is this freedom you're celebrating? What are you talking about?"

Sissy stared back at her, then blinked, looked away, and then looked back at her again. "I can't tell you," she said, a tremor entering her voice.

"Can't tell me what?"

"I'm too ashamed," Sissy said. "I can't talk about it. Let me drink, that's all I want to do."

"Tell me what?" Elizabeth persisted.

"I gave up a burden today. I'm free of it."

"Gave up what? Come on, Sis, you know you can tell me anything."

Sissy drained the rest of her drink and then said, "I had an abortion today."

For a moment Elizabeth was speechless and then the words burst out. "An abortion? You were pregnant?"

"Well, you have to be pregnant to have an abortion, don't you?"

"I don't understand. How did you get pregnant?"

"Well, it wasn't from you, was it?"

"Who? How? What happened?"

Sissy began to sob, her shoulders shaking. "On the last

movie I had a fling with one of the actors. I didn't take any precautions and neither did he. So I got pregnant. That's what happens, isn't it? Today I had the abortion."

"With one of the actors? Who the hell was it?" Elizabeth demanded.

Sissy's sobs became sniffles. "What does it matter? It happened. It's over. I've taken care of it."

"What does it matter? How could you do that to me? How could you betray me like that?" Tears pricked her own eyes now. "I thought we loved each other. I thought we had something special. How could you do that to me?"

"I didn't do anything to you. I'm the one who's had the abortion."

"But how could you do that? With a man?" Elizabeth said, endowing the noun with distaste.

"I was lonely and he was available and he was very flattering, and it just happened."

Elizabeth slumped on the couch. She felt as if she'd been struck. Sissy had betrayed her. Worse, she had betrayed her with a man. It made nothing of everything they had together.

"Well, don't sit there like that," Sissy said sharply. She had apparently regained herself. "I'm the one who had her insides ripped out."

"How does it feel?" Elizabeth said dully.

"It feels like I had my insides ripped out," Sissy said. "I feel empty. I feel as if I've lost something precious. I feel as if I've committed a murder. I feel as if I'm nothing. I feel like shit."

Elizabeth just shook her head. She was beyond sympathy. If there was any sympathy, she was feeling it for herself. She was the one who had been hurt.

Even through her own anguish, Sissy seemed to sense her pain. She got up off the floor with difficulty, came over to the couch, and sat beside Elizabeth. "I'm sorry."

"How could you do it? How could you cheat on me?"

"It didn't mean anything. It's just something that happened. It doesn't affect our relationship," Sissy said.

Elizabeth's grief turned into anger. "Yes, it does. How can I ever trust you again?"

"Because I chose you, because I came back to you," Sissy said plaintively. "When I told him I was pregnant he wanted to marry me. He says he's in love with me. He said he'd look after me and the baby. I said no. Because I wanted to come back to you. And I got rid of the baby because of that. That's how you can trust me. I had a choice and I chose you."

"You betrayed me," Elizabeth insisted.

"I'm sorry," Sissy said, "I really am. I'll never do that again, I promise. I'll make it up to you. You know I love you, you know I'd do anything for you. You know I want you to be happy."

"How can I believe that now?" Elizabeth asked, her doubt showing on her face.

"I'll prove it to you. Any way you want, I'll prove it to you."

Elizabeth gathered herself and sat up straighter. "How? How can you prove something like that?"

"Any way you like," Sissy said. "But I'll prove it to you. You wait and see."

"Yes," Elizabeth said, scanning the possibilities. "I suppose you could."

Anne felt the tiny needles vibrate as the slight electric current coursed through them. She was lying on her back, on her acupuncturist's table. Needles dotted her face. This monthly treatment was something she swore kept the skin on her face tight and smooth and far away from the scalpel of the plastic surgeon.

Anne felt like smiling, but it was impossible. Her face was supposed to remain expressionless throughout the course of the treatment. But she felt good, better than she had for a long time.

It was all because of Frank, of course. Ever since meeting him she had discovered a level of fulfillment that she hadn't known before. Frank was a wonderful, kind, attentive, and loving man. And he made her feel not just like a woman, but like a special person, someone unique, someone gifted and lovable.

Anne was no neophyte in the area of relationships with men. She'd been married three times and had had dozens of boyfriends. But somehow this was different. The marriages had been disasters. Two had lasted five years each, and the last one, in 1987, to Martin Lawson, a film director, had lasted six months. As for the boyfriends, some had been fulfilling and some hadn't. But the level of fulfillment in this was different.

She wondered if it was because of the age difference. She had never been with a man ten years younger than she. And she knew that she was feeling her age. She was at that treacherous cusp of forty when all she could see before her was a long stretch of middle age. And all she could see behind her was lost youth.

Frank made her feel younger, that was true. But was that the only reason she felt so happy in his company? She felt girlish and fresh. She also felt that she was able to give him what he needed, although exactly what that was she wasn't sure.

She wasn't used to such introspective thoughts. They'd been coming more frequently of late, since she had met Frank.

She had been thinking about her career, of revitalizing it. She'd been thinking of it in terms of a craft to be learned, as opposed to a way of being. She'd always been first Miles Cort's daughter, and then an actress. It was a persona, something that she projected, like a name, an identity. But that wasn't really who she was, as Frank had pointed out to her one night. She was herself. A unique individual, and acting was just something she did. As for the fact of being Miles Cort's daughter, that was simply an accident of fate. It wasn't her identity.

Sometimes they talked late into the night, about matters like that. It was a new experience for her.

The acupuncturist's nurse, a slim young Chinese girl who barely spoke English, came into the room, turned off the current, and began to remove the needles from her face.

Anne paid her bill and then hurried into the parking lot. She was supposed to meet Frank at his apartment, and then they were planning to go to the beach somewhere in Venice for dinner.

She climbed into her baby Mercedes convertible and backed out of the lot, taking Santa Monica Boulevard to Hollywood, where Frank lived in a small, unkempt apartment building of four units.

That was another thing she liked about him, she thought as she passed a bus belching blue smoke. He was totally unpretentious. It's not that he wasn't proud, but he didn't care about things he didn't consider important, such as the kind of car he drove or where he lived or where he was seen.

Once, soon after first meeting him, she had tried to explain how important appearances were in Hollywood. He had shrugged her reasons away. "I'm an actor," he said. "That's something I do, it's a job. I have to do it on my own terms, otherwise when I succeed it's going to mean nothing to me. I'll have tarnished its value." Soon she found herself agreeing with him. He was also a persuasive advocate of what he believed.

She parked outside the brown stucco building on Gower Street. After activating her car alarm she went up the steps with a spring in her walk and rang his doorbell.

"Come in."

She opened the unlocked door and stepped in. It was small but a warm, comfortable apartment, with eclecticism the reigning impression. Somehow there was no unity in either the furnishings or the paintings on the walls, or the throw rugs on the floor. And yet, they all fit together, simply because Frank liked each one, each piece.

He was speaking on the telephone. She stopped in the middle of the living room and watched him.

"Yes, thank you very much," he said. "Yes, thank you, thank you. I'll talk to you soon." He hung up, stared down at the phone for a second, and then turned to face her. He looked shattered, as if something totally unexpected had just happened.

"What's the matter?" she asked, concern in her voice, moving toward him.

He just shook his head and stared at her.

"What?" she asked when she reached him, putting her hands on his arms.

"That was my agent."

"Yes?"

"He said I got the part."

"The part you tested for? The part in that movie where we met?" she asked, a smile beginning on her face.

He shook his head. "No. Not that part."

"Then what?"

"The lead. I didn't get the part I tested for. I got the lead," he said. "They liked the test so much that they offered me the lead. I tested for Allan and they offered me the lead."

Anne let out a whoop of pleasure and hugged him. She understood his shock. These things didn't happen often to actors. When they did, they were almost unbelievable, beyond comprehension.

"That's wonderful," she said. "I'm so happy for you. That is really great." She meant it, too, she realized with surprise.

Before, she'd always been jealous of the success of other actors. The competition in the business was so fierce that often somebody else got apart because you didn't get it, because someone thought you weren't good enough. Or because you didn't hear about it and were not able to test for it. Or because you were not called in, or because they slept with the casting director and you didn't, or . . .

She'd always greeted the success of others with hypocritical good wishes, all the while listening to a voice inside her saying, "Why didn't I get it? Why didn't it happen to me? What did he or she do to deserve such luck?" But now she was genuinely happy for him. It was wonderful.

"My God," he said, "I can't believe it. I've got to sit down."

She took his hand and pulled him toward the couch and plunked herself next to him. "It's incredible," she said. "It's fabulous and you deserve it."

"I don't know," he said.

"Of course you do. You know how talented you are. They saw that, too."

"Wow," he said. And then he suddenly seemed to realize what had happened and leaped to his feet and shouted "Wow!" at the top of his voice, and stamped the floor with his feet and shouted "Wow!" again.

Anne leaned back on the couch and laughed at him. He really did deserve it. He was a tremendously gifted actor and he'd worked long and hard at his craft. If there was any justice in this world, he deserved to succeed.

She remembered something that Miles once told her: "There are a thousand talented actors in this town, but talent isn't enough. It takes talent plus a little bit of luck, but, above all, persistence and hard work."

He was fond of saying that about many fields of endeavor. It was one of Miles's universal laws of life.

But Frank had shown persistence. He turned out for every interview he'd been called on. He'd prepared for them. He'd worked hard. He deserved a little luck.

It took him twenty minutes to calm down. And then the jitters set in. "Can I do it? Can I pull it off? It's a hell of a challenging part."

"Of course you can do it," Anne said, patting his hand. "You're good. You've told me that yourself."

"Yeah, of course I have. You have to keep telling yourself that, otherwise you don't keep going in this town. But am I really good enough?" he muttered, staring off into the distance.

Anne put her hands on his shoulders and turned him toward her. "Listen to me," she said seriously. "You're as good as any other actor I've seen. And you're going to do this well. You're going to succeed at this, this is your break, and there is no way after all the work you've put into this that you are going to blow it. You know that and I know it and the people who've chosen you for this part know it, too."

Frank just looked back at her without speaking. And then he reached a hand out and touched her cheek gently. "You are a wonderful woman, Anne. I really love you, you know."

"I know."

"I want you to marry me," he said.

And now it was her turn to be shocked and amazed, and flabbergasted and speechless.

"What?" she said finally.

He nodded. "I think we should get married. I think it's the best thing for both of us. I love you and you've said you love me. Why the hell don't we get married? That's what two people in love do."

Anne's mind, for some reason, scanned every failed relationship she'd been in. They'd all started with words of love and proclamations of eternal fidelity, and they'd all ended in recrimination and disappointment. Here was a man she felt she truly loved, maybe the first time she had ever loved any man, and he was asking her to marry him. But once again there were declarations of love and implied intimations of eternity. It scared her.

It would be too terrible to lose him. It would be something she wouldn't be able to bear.

"Maybe we should give it some thought," she said hesitantly.

"I have thought about it. I'm not just blurting this out on a wave of euphoria. I've thought about it a lot. But I wanted to ask you when it seemed as if there was some future for me. At a time when I had something to offer you, some kind of security in a financial sense."

"You have so much to offer me," she said with an involuntary laugh. "Money doesn't even enter into it. You've given me so much already."

"I want to give you more," he said fiercely. "I want us to share everything, to be together always."

Anne grew practical. "I'm ten years older than you. When you're forty, I'm going to be fifty. When you're fifty, I'm going to be sixty. When you're sixty, I'm going to be seventy."

"So what?" He shrugged. "I'll probably still die before you. Women live longer than men. Look, that's not important. Age isn't the issue."

"Women lose their looks before men," she said. "Age does enter into it."

"It's not a matter of looks. It's a matter of who you are and what I love. It's not your looks I love, it's you."

Anne felt trapped. His arguments were so logical and yet so glib. "Look, you're just about to embark on a successful career. You're going to be tempted by all kinds of beautiful women, young, beautiful women. How can I compete with them? If we got married, how could we sustain our relationship in the face of that? You've no idea what it's like. Believe me, I've seen it. I've seen it with both men and women. The temptations are incredible."

"Oh? Then we should break up now, right?"

"What do you mean?"

"Well, if the temptation is so horrendous and you're so old and I'm so young, and all these young women are there waiting for me, we should break up now because whether we get married or not, our relationship doesn't stand a chance of succeeding, according to what you're saying."

"That's not what I'm saying," Anne protested.

"Then what are you saying?"

"I guess I'm saying I'm scared to make a commitment like that. I've been married before, it hasn't worked out."

"I'm not interested in young women," Frank said, touching her face again. "I've had young women. The problem with young women is they are young. It's you I love. It's because you've done what you've done and lived as long as you've lived and been where you've been and all that stuff. I want to marry you, Anne. Yes or no?"

"My God," she said.

She sat in silence. He was really leaving her no alternative. She had to decide. He was completely certain, totally assured. He loved her and he didn't have a single doubt about it, at least not that he showed.

And what about Miles? What would he think about it? He's laugh himself blue in the face. He'd tell her she was chicken stealing. He'd mock her as an old woman chasing young men. The hell with him. That wasn't important. That shouldn't even enter into her calculations. Miles was who he was, but she was an adult and she had her own life to live without worrying about his reactions.

"My God," she said again.

"Do you want to think about it for a while?" he asked quietly.

Anne shook her head. She could think about it from here to eternity. and the same fears and doubts and longings would crowd her mind. What was the point of thinking about it?

"Well?" he asked.

"Yes," she said. "Yes, I'll marry you."

Anne's telephone call to Miles was almost comical in its brevity—in view of her misgivings.

374

"I'm getting married, Daddy."

There was a momentary pause on the other end of the line and then Miles said, "To who? The young guy?"

Anne braced herself for the attack, the onslaught of withering sarcasm. She took a deep breath. "Yes. To Frank Scolaro."

"Good. Don't fuck it up this time. This is the best man you've had yet."

Anne was so surprised she didn't know what to say except, "Yes, Daddy."

Melissa had a viral infection of the liver, a form of hepatitis. It had probably been transmitted through the blood during one of her transfusions. Luckily it was spotted quickly and she was placed on medication almost immediately.

After distraughtly asking the doctor how this could possibly happen and listening to his apologetic "no blood screening is one hundred percent effective," Shannon began to blame herself. It was strange that this had happened right after she'd turned down the chance for Melissa to get a new kidney. But it was a short-lived period of regret because ultimately Shannon saw that there was no logic to it. She had made the decision she needed to make and the illness now was simply coincidental.

Melissa was exhausted and demanding and her nerves were obviously on edge. Shannon did all she could to help, tending to Melissa's needs as often as possible while still trying to work on the book.

Right now she was sitting in her office scrolling through her computer and studying some of the transcripts of her earlier interviews, making notations, underlining important sections, and generally evaluating what was usable and what wasn't.

When the telephone rang she answered it absentmindedly.

"This is Dr. Peter Roxford," the voice at the other end said. Shannon's immediate reaction was, "Oh, shit, the doctor who thinks I'm a schmuck. The doctor who despises me for wanting to jump ahead in line."

"Yes," she said defensively.

"Miss Ross, I just wanted to thank you for the decision you made. I want to let you know that I understand how much courage it took for you to make the right choice."

"Thank you," Shannon said tiredly. "There really was no other choice."

"I understand," he said. "I thought you'd be interested to know that the young boy received his transplant this morning and it seems to have gone very successfully."

"Oh, I'm glad," she said more warmly.

"Yes, I thought you would be. He'll be going home as planned, but in this case it'll be with a functional kidney. It'll make all the difference in the world for the rest of his life. I also want you to know that I don't hold any rancor at all. I don't quite understand what happened here, but when your daughter gets her kidney, as she will, I hope she comes here because she'll get the best possible care."

"I never doubted that," Shannon said.

Roxford cleared his throat. "The gift from Mr. Cort was very generous. I was of the understanding from Dr. Dailey that the gift was dependent upon a kidney for your daughter. However, I was very happy to find out that wasn't the case."

"The gift?" Shannon asked. "Do you mean Mr. Cort's still making his donation?"

"Yes, I thought you knew that. Yes, he is and it's very generous and very needed."

"Well, that's great," Shannon said. "I'm happy to hear it."

"Well, I just wanted to let you know about the boy."

"Thank you, thank you very much for calling," Shannon said, and hung up.

It was amazing. Miles had used the gift to blackmail

them into shoving Melissa ahead in line. When she had refused to play along with that she was sure Miles would retract the gift. Apparently he hadn't. She shook her head. Miles was still giving them the money. Why? She wasn't much closer to understanding him now than she had been when she first arrived.

CHAPTER EIGHTEEN

Miles admitted that he often said things he didn't believe. The secret to winning, he said, was never to let anyone know that you'd lost. You did not publicly admit your mistakes. You just kept forging ahead. There was nothing worse than a wishy-washy man, he said. You stated your position and then you stuck to it, right or wrong.

"But I've heard other people say that it takes a big man to admit he's wrong?" Shannon asked with some amusement.

"Bullshit. Admitting you're wrong is easy. Most people do it all the time. It's knowing you're wrong that's hard. A big man knows when he's wrong and he acts accordingly. He doesn't have to admit it to anyone."

"So now are you saying what you mean?" Shannon asked.

"Probably not," Miles said.

Lynn informed Shannon that her late-afternoon appointment would be held in his bedroom instead of the study. "He's a little under the weather," Lynn said. She added a warning. "Don't bring it up though. He doesn't like to talk about his physical condition."

"Is he okay?" Shannon asked.

"He says he's fine. He says he's just not feeling a hundred percent."

Lynn led her upstairs, knocked on the bedroom door, then entered. The head of the bed was raised so that Miles sat in an upright position. A tray containing papers sat over his lap. He wore striped pajamas below a burgundy robe and looked somehow like a decadent king receiving his loyal subjects.

He waved his hand at a chair and a small table set up beside the bed. "Sit down."

"Is there anything else, Mr. Cort?"

"No, Lynn. Thanks."

Shannon sat and looked over at Miles. There seemed to be a grayish tinge to his skin and he looked tired. In spite of Lynn's warning she said, "Do you want to do this interview today? If you don't feel up to it, we could do it tomorrow instead."

"I'm fine," Miles said in a mild growl. "Let's get started."

Shannon took out her tape recorder and placed it on the table, then she leafed through her notes.

"Did you see the Kite woman?" Miles asked.

"Yes," she said. "I'm puzzled."

"By what?"

"Why did you want me to see her? Why did you want such a damaging story told? Is it true?"

"Yes, it's true," he said.

"You're the one who got the girl pregnant?"

"Yes."

"And you're the one who arranged the abortion?"

"Yes."

"But you denied it at the time?"

"What do you think I am, stupid? I didn't want to go to jail. I did what I had to do for the sake of the picture. I thought it was the best thing for her at the time."

"But it wasn't, was it?"

"No."

She went back to the question he had avoided. "So why do you want that story told? Why are you casting such a bad light on yourself?"

"Because it's the truth."

Shannon shook her head at what she considered a simplistic evasion. "I don't understand you, Miles."

"What's to understand? I want the truth to be told. There are enough lies in the world without me continuing to add to them." Pugnaciously he jutted his chin out at her.

Shannon sighed. "Miles, in the last week, in addition to Mrs. Kite, you've given me six other names of people who hate you, who have nothing nice to say about you whatsoever, who only have damaging stories. I find it curious."

Miles smiled. "Yeah, I came up with a list when I was trying to think of who was trying to kill me. These are all the people who have reason to hate me. I figured they'd have something to contribute."

"They certainly do," Shannon said. "Not only a mother who says you are responsible for her daughter's death. But a cameraman who says you seduced his wife and ruined his marriage. A banker who says you single-handedly brought about his financial ruin because of some vendetta. And on and on."

"It's all true," Miles said. "I did all those things."

"Yes," Shannon said carefully, "and I've been wondering why you want them known. It's been really bothering me. And then I realized what you were doing."

"What?" His eyes suddenly grew more alert.

"A strange thing for an irreligious man," Shannon said. "You are seeking redemption. This book is your confession, isn't it?"

Miles stared at her silently. She could see a vein throbbing in his left temple. His eyes were fixed on hers. He lifted his right hand then, and pointed across the room.

"There's a bar over there. Get me a drink and get yourself one, too. Scotch on the rocks for me."

She put the pad she was holding on the table and stood. "Should you be drinking?"

"Hell, yes! It's one of the last pleasures left."

She walked over to the well-stocked bar, mixed him a Scotch on the rocks, and poured herself a gin and tonic.

Miles took the drink she handed him and watched her sit again. He sipped at it, then put it on the bedside table.

"You are a very smart woman, very perceptive," he said thoughtfully.

"Thank you."

"Do you believe in redemption, Shannon?"

"Like you, I'm not a religious person," she said. "I don't believe that there's some omnipotent god up in the sky who will forgive us for what we've done."

"But do you believe in redemption?"

Shannon nodded. "Yes, I believe that we can forgive ourselves once we accept responsibility for what we've done. And I believe that's the only true redemption there is."

"I knew you'd understand," Miles said with a satisfied smile. "I read an article that you did about three years ago. You talked about redemption in it. It was the story of an execution, do you remember it?"

Yes, she did, vividly. It was the execution of a man named Ted Warwick, a man who had killed three women. She had written the story for a magazine.

It was one of the most unforgettable experiences of her life. She had watched the execution, stood with the other reporters and sightseers outside the gas chamber. And she had written a story afterward about a man who seemed completely at peace, a man who had accepted responsibility for his acts and was willing, even eager, to pay the penalty.

"Yes, I remember it."

"When I read that story I knew that you were the right

person for this job," Miles said. "You see, I, too, believe in redemption. But I believe you must not only admit responsibility for your acts but you must atone for them and make amends for them in some way. I am announcing my acts to the world and, in the time I have left, in some small way I will atone for them further."

"And it was because of your stroke that you decided to do this now?"

Miles narrowed his eyes at her. "I trust you, you know. I'm going to tell you something that can never go beyond this room, but for the sake of the book you should know."

"Yes?"

Miles said that in nine months he would be dead.

"It's not the stroke," he said. "The stroke's nothing. I've beaten the stroke. But this one I can't beat. I have cancer. And I have nine months left."

Shannon sat there, her mind frozen, her tongue still, "Oh, my God" chanting in her head. "Oh, my God," she said finally.

Miles held up his hand. "It's all right. I've known this now for fifteen months, I've come to terms with it. But there are things I want to do before I leave, and this book is one of them."

"There's no chance that it's a misdiagnosis? Or that it will go into remission? Or that the predicted time is wrong?"

"I thought I could beat it when it was diagnosed," Miles said with a scowl. "I've beaten everything else. I thought this was just one more ordeal for me. But it's eating away, according to its timetable, right on target. There's nothing I can do, and there's nothing that medical science can do. I am going to die in about nine months, give or take a few weeks. I finally realized that—came to terms with it—only recently."

Shannon reached for her forgotten gin and tonic and almost drank it all down in one long gulp. She put the glass back down on the table. "I'm sorry. I'm very, very sorry."

Miles bobbed his head. "Appreciate it," he said gruffly, "but it doesn't help. Let's just get on with the job at hand."

"So this is why you want redemption?" she said. "It wasn't the stroke, it's that . . . it's that you see the end coming?"

"Yes, I see my death. I've always heard that men who know they are about to die cast their vision back on their lives and examine them. Look at the failures and successes, their regrets, and try perhaps to seek atonement. I never believed it, I thought it was for pussycats. But it's true. You have no future to look at. Only the present with its fears and the past with its victories and defeats exist, at least in your mind."

Shannon felt tears well up in her eyes. She couldn't help it. She knew that they would make Miles angry, but it struck her as so sad. This man, who had accomplished so much in his life and who now was so lonely.

She was right about his reaction.

"Don't pity me," Miles snapped at her. "I don't need that. It's not going to help."

"It's not pity," she said. "It's just sadness."

"Well, let's get on with the book."

"I can't," she said, "not now. Can we do it tomorrow instead?"

"You're a professional, aren't you?" Miles yelled at her. "This is what you do for a living, isn't it? Well then, do it. I don't want you sniveling on my time."

Shannon's tears disappeared and she stiffened her back. "You are such a bastard, Miles."

Miles grinned. "Right, and don't you forget it."

"You said I'm to tell no one, that it can't go beyond the walls of this room. What about your family? Have you told them?"

"It's none of their business. This is my life, I don't owe it to them."

"But they could help you," Shannon said. "They could share this with you if you shared it with them."

Miles laughed out loud. "What, Orson help? Anne help? Elizabeth? Stephen? You've got to be kidding. They will fall to pieces. They'll make my last nine months a misery. Anne will be bringing me daily news of quack cancer cures. Orson will try to borrow as much money from me as he can. I'll have them whining around me all the time."

"You underestimate them, Miles, I think you always have," Shannon said. "Stephen for one deserves to know this, and he deserves the chance to be able to help you."

"No. I don't need any help," Miles said stubbornly. "And I forbid you to mention this to anyone, is that understood?"

"Of course," Shannon said.

"All right, let's get to work."

Shannon sat alone in her living room. It was late at night. She had cooked dinner and put Melissa to bed. Stephen had called, but she had not called him back. She didn't feel like talking to anyone, not even him. She had poured herself a strong gin and tonic and now that it was finished, she poured another.

Poor Miles, she thought, sitting back in the armchair. So sick, so scared, and so alone. A man who had spent his life surrounded by people, now with nobody to lean on. How was he really feeling? Had he truly come to terms with it?

Death had a way of making nothing of man's endeavors, she thought morbidly. At least that was how it seemed. There had to be a lie there somewhere. Such a depressing and nihilistic viewpoint couldn't possibly be true. It made nothing of everyone. And that wasn't right.

She knew firsthand that death was a subject most people tried to avoid. She, on the other hand, had been forced to think of it when Melissa's kidney failure first happened. For most of her life, she had done her best not to. Fortunately, due to medical technology, her child's illness did not automatically mean death as it had in the past. Miles, however, had no such respite. He was being forced to confront his death.

She shuddered at the thought. What do I have to show when I die? she said to herself. What will I have to look back on? Will I be proud? Will I think that the world was a better place for my being there? Will I think that I have at least affected some lives in a positive manner? Or will I look back and wonder what the point of it all had been?

Miles was being forced to take stock now. He was doing it with a brutal honesty that she could only admire. Perhaps the brutality was abhorrent to her, but it was what he felt was necessary and who was she to argue with it? She wasn't walking down this path in his shoes—no matter how deeply she tried to understand it on an intellectual level. This was his path and she was a pawn in his game. She was being paid to be a pawn, and somehow at this moment, she did not resent that. What she resented above all else was the unfairness of it all. Death was indiscriminate when it chose its victims. There didn't seem to be any justice involved.

And yet justice was simply a concept concocted by men. It was something men used to bring some order to the elementary chaos in which they lived. Earthquakes, hurricanes, disease, and disaster didn't subscribe to that view. Nor did death.

Shannon lifted her drink and said aloud, "To life," because that was all men had to cling to. She drank and then put her glass unsteadily down on the table.

She would regret it tomorrow, she knew, but she was planning to get very drunk tonight.

* * *

Orson lay on the big water bed, staring up at the ceiling, wondering what was going to happen next. He was wearing blue silk pajamas. There was a sound in the hall and then the door opened. He turned his head and watched the nurse approach.

It wasn't a regulation uniform. It was cut three inches above the knees and the three top buttons were undone to expose a deep cleavage. Curly blond hair poked from beneath the white cap and baby blue eyes stared curiously at him.

"Are you Mr. Cort?" the nurse asked.

"Yes," he said nervously.

"Don't worry. Just do everything I tell you to do and it'll all work out."

"Yes, nurse," he said.

She came up to him, and he smelled the scent of Opium perfume. "Now first let me check you out." She leaned forward and unbuttoned his pajama top, then ran her hand over his chest, pinching his nipples as she did so.

"Ow!" Orson yelped.

"Now, now, just relax," she ordered. "Let me do my job." Her hand crept down across his belly toward his crotch. It circled the area then came back and grabbed him.

"What are you doing?"

"You don't want a shot now, do you?" she asked sweetly.

"No," he said, "not a shot."

"Well then just behave and let me do my job."

The skillful hand began to knead his penis. In seconds Orson was hard. "This part of your job?"

"Oh, yes, this is what my job's all about." She dropped her head then and took him in her mouth.

After a half a minute, just as his hips thrust up into the air, she quickly withdrew.

"Aren't you going to finish?" Orson gasped.

"Do you want me to call the doctor?" she threatened.

"No, no doctor."

"All right then, just relax," she said, still fondling him with her hand. "Now I want you to just lie there, while I take care of you." And with that she pulled the tight skirt up over her hips.

She was wearing nothing underneath—no stockings, no panties. With a deft movement she put one knee on the bed and then swung over so that she was kneeling above him, one leg on either side of his thighs.

"Now, do what Nursie says." Then she lowered herself down onto him.

Slowly, he entered the moist warmth and felt the sides of her vagina clutch at him.

"Now, isn't that the best medicine?" she murmured.

"Oh, God," he groaned. "The best."

Just a suddenly she withdrew, leaving his penis sticking up in the air.

"What are you doing?" he complained.

She smiled down at him. "Medicine has to be taken in small doses, otherwise it's not good for you."

She unbuttoned her blouse, exposing her breasts. He reached up and fondled them. At the same time, she grasped his slick penis with one hand and pumped it. Then she guided it into position and lowered herself again.

Orson thrust up at the same time, but she held him down with her weight, controlling him, not moving and not allowing him to move, leaving him throbbing inside her.

She narrowed her eyes down at his frustration. "Oh, the poor patient. Maybe I should give him some more medicine. He looks as though he might die without it."

"Yes," Orson said. "Give it all to me. I don't care if it kills me."

Slowly, she moved her hips, feeling the swollen tip of his penis slide across the top of her vagina. She closed her eyes and parted her lips and threw her head back and groaned.

She was the one out of control now. Her tempo increased until her hips bucked wildly against him, faster and faster.

Five minutes later, an exhausted Orson looked over at Pat. "Everything's fucked."

"What?" she asked lazily.

"My life. The only good thing is fucking you. Nothing's happening the way it should."

"Has it ever?" she asked.

It was a good question. There had been moments when things seemed to be right, but they were so vague, in such a distant place, they had very little meaning under the present circumstances. "I don't know."

"Well then, why worry about it?"

"Because I want things to be better," he said.

Pat didn't answer.

They lay in silence for a few minutes. Orson thought that Pat was one of the only stable facts of his life. Whenever he called her, he knew he would always be ensured some kind of sexual extravaganza. She had a virtually unlimited imagination when it came to sex. She loved to play games and so did he. He wondered why he had divorced her in the first place. No, he remembered, that wasn't it. She'd divorced him. He had no money, and she wanted money. That was it.

"You know what?" he said.

"What?"

"I think we should get married again. I think you're the best wife I ever had."

There was a chuckle from Pat. She rolled away from him to lie on her back. "You've got to be kidding."

"No, think about it," Orson argued. "We get on well. Ever since our divorce we've become friends, our sex is great. There's never a dull moment."

"I wouldn't marry you if you were the last man on

388

earth," Pat said. "As a sometime lover you're great, but as a husband you are a real dud."

Orson wasn't at all hurt. The idea was growing on him and his enthusiasm for it was mounting. "Come on, who else can give you this? Why do you keep on seeing me if that's the way you feel?"

Pat seemed to look at the ceiling for an answer. There was a long silence. Then she said, "Orson, let's get one thing straight. There's only one reason I keep on seeing you. And that's because a good fuck is hard to find."

Peter Corydon entered Miles's bedroom at the barked command. The old man was sitting up in bed glaring at him.

"I hope this is important," Miles said.

Corydon felt like smiling. He had his pride and he felt badly about letting the intruder into the grounds and the accident at the swimming pool. He'd hoped to make up for it in some way and now he had.

He suppressed his pleasure and said blandly, "Yes, sir, it is."

"Well?"

"The girl," Corydon began, "the one who tried to poison you?"

"Yes, what about her?"

"Well," Corydon said, "we came up with dead ends. Couldn't find any connections. Couldn't find out much about her other than the fact that she was an out-of-work actress. There seemed to be nothing that would lead her to your door."

"I know all that," Miles interrupted impatiently. "So what did you find out now?"

"Well, there was a woman who lived in the apartment next to her who just moved out a few weeks before the incident. We tried to find her so that we could question her and ask her about the girl. But she'd gone to Europe to shoot some movies. Nobody knew exactly where."

"And now you've found her?" Miles said, looking at him with a glimmering of admiration in his eyes. "You never give up, do you, Corydon?"

"No, sir, I don't. And yes, we did find her. She came back a week ago. One of my men interviewed her, and then I did. She wasn't exactly friends with the girl next door. But they knew each other and they talked and had drinks occasionally."

"So what did you find out?"

"Well, she'd seen some of the guys who were dating this girl. And she even knew some of their names," Corydon said. "We found out that one of them was a Cort."

"A Cort?"

"Yes, sir," Corydon said with some satisfaction. "The girl who tried to poison you had been dating one of your sons."

"Which one?"

Corydon told him.

Shannon noticed a curtain of smog in the overhanging sky as she hurried to the house. Miles had summoned her unexpectedly. Their appointment was not until the afternoon, but at nine A.M. promptly Lynn had called and said, "Mr. Cort would like to see you now."

She entered the house and went directly to Lynn's office.

"One moment," Lynn said when she saw her. She lifted up the phone, dialed an extension, and said, "Miss Ross is here to see you." She hung up the phone. "He's in the study, just go right in."

Shannon found Miles sitting at his desk. Clutching her tape recorder in her left hand she sat.

"You won't need that," Miles said, noticing the recorder. "I have the name of someone I thought you should see here." He slid an envelope across the table. "That's Dr. Gerald Deakins, a psychologist. You need to interview him."

"What's his relationship to you?" she asked.

"I saw him briefly," Miles said. "That letter to him gives him permission to disclose everything I discussed with him."

"You mean you were a patient?" she asked incredulously.

"Briefly," Miles said, not meeting her eyes. "The man's a charlatan. He couldn't help a mouse find cheese. But I did see him for a short time and he does have records. That authorizes you to have access to those records."

"What's it about?"

"Talk to him. He'll tell you."

"You could save me a lot of time by telling me now," she stated.

Miles opened his mouth to speak, then hesitated. She noticed some color had returned to his cheeks. He looked better than the previous day in the bedroom, less haggard and drawn.

"Why don't you just tell me about it?" she prompted.

Miles shook his head. "I can't. Just go and see him."

Shannon was going to argue the point further, but decided against it. A curious emotional stress seemed to envelop Miles, one she hadn't seen before. "All right," she agreed.

"His phone number and address are on the envelope. Call and make an appointment."

"Okay."

He shuffled some papers on his desk, looking down. She realized she was being dismissed. "Miles?"

He raised his head. "Yes?"

"I've been thinking. I wish you could find it in yourself to tell Stephen about your illness. He's really a special person, and I think it would be helpful to you both if you did that."

Miles looked at her with a curious expression. "Tell Stephen?"

"Out of all of them, he's the one you should talk to, who you would be able to confide in."

Miles chuckled, an ugly sound. "That's funny," he said with no amusement. "Stephen."

She looked at him, puzzled by his reaction. "Why not?"

His face contorted into a nasty scowl and the words seemed to have difficulty leaving his mouth. "Because Stephen is the one who tried to have me murdered."

"That's not possible," Shannon whispered.

"No? You know the girl who tried to poison me?"

Shannon nodded.

"Well, Corydon just found out Stephen used to date her. What does that tell you?"

CHAPTER NINETEEN

"I've always wanted to be remembered as the man who made great films, and I've worked hard all my life to earn that reputation. I don't know if all that work was worth it. Today, I look around Hollywood at the type of product that's coming out, at the people who are involved in producing it, at the literacy level of the audience, and I wonder if that's still how I want to be remembered.

"But that was the path I chose and there's no turning back now. It's too late. I'm not going to be remembered as a loving father, or a faithful husband, or a warm friend, or a great humanitarian. I closed those doors behind me a long time ago. I am what I am and like all men I will be remembered for what I am," Miles said.

Shannon had tried to call Stephen immediately after her meeting with Miles yesterday. She really had no idea what she would say to him, but knew only that she had to talk to him. However, when his answering machine came on, she remembered that he had gone to Santa Barbara for a gig that evening and wouldn't be back until the next day. She was forced to keep her tumultuous thoughts to herself.

She found it impossible to believe that Stephen was the one responsible for the attempts on Miles's life. He wasn't that kind of man. If there was something unpleasant to be done, he would do it himself. He would never hire other people to do his dirty work for him. It just wasn't in his nature. Nor, she believed most importantly, was it in his nature to cause his father any kind of harm.

She had said all this to Miles as well, but he had brushed aside her protestations, saying that the facts spoke for themselves. She had asked him what he was going to do about it, and his certainty was shed like a coat. "I don't know yet," he had replied, the confusion showing on his face.

Now, the next morning, she dialed Stephen's number again, still not knowing what she was going to say to him but still feeling the necessity to talk to him.

The recorded message on his answering machine came on. Frustrated, she left a message asking him to call her immediately and hung up.

She looked at her watch. She had another appointment with Miles and she was already two minutes late. Quickly she gathered her materials and after briefly looking in on Melissa, who was doing much better, she hurried out of the cottage.

The sky was hazy with fog that had rolled in from the ocean. The gardener saw her and tipped his hat to her, as he always did. In the far distance she saw one of the security men walking through the grounds.

Miles was waiting for her in his office. When she entered he looked at his watch without comment.

"I'm sorry I'm late. But I had something to take care of."

Miles didn't acknowledge her apology but said, "Did you see the quack?"

"The psychologist? I have an appointment for later today."

"Good. What do you want to cover today?"

She sat in the chair opposite his desk and looked at her notes. "I want to go way back and pick up some stuff from the forties."

Miles looked irritated. "I thought we covered all the early years."

"There's an area we haven't talked about much, and I wanted some information. It's about your first marriage to Isabella," she said.

"That's not important. I was only married to her for a year and a half, I was just a kid then."

Again Shannon looked at her notes. "Yeah, you married her in 1940, you were twenty years old then, she died a year and a half later in the middle of 1942 in childbirth. She was only nineteen when you married her."

"So?" Miles said, uncooperatively.

"Tell me about her. How did you meet? What was your marriage like? And what happened to her?"

"Is this necessary?" He began to shuffle some papers on his desk.

"Yes," she said, and then added, "Why don't you want to talk about her?"

Miles's head shot up and he gave her an ugly look. "What do you mean? It's not that I don't want to talk about her, it just doesn't seem important."

"Well, I'm the writer here, so let me decide what's important," Shannon said sweetly.

Miles grunted.

"So where did you meet her?"

He gave her a baleful look but then relented. "All right, you want me to talk about Isabella, I'll talk about Isabella. She worked for my father's company as an executive secretary. I'd known her slightly in high school, as a matter of fact. We dated a couple of times, but nothing came of it. And then at the office I started to take her out. We fell in love, we got married. She got pregnant, and there were difficulties. There was a son, stillborn, and Isabella also died."

It was a shorthand, truncated version, a bone thrown out to pacify her. Shannon wasn't about to become an obedient puppy and gnaw on it.

"What was she like?" she asked, probing further.

Miles rolled his eyes and grimaced. "She was a beautiful woman, very young, of course, and immature, but a sweet woman. And very intelligent."

"What kind of a relationship did you have? I mean, was it romantic? Did you talk a lot? How did you two get on together?"

Miles seemed to grow more comfortable, leaning back to stare up at the ceiling. "We were friends. Above all, we were friends. I could talk to Isabella about anything. Even then I was thinking about movies, and in the evenings we would sit and I would tell her my plans. She was tremendously supportive of me. She told me I could do anything I decided to do, and said she'd do everything that she could to help. She was also interested in films, from a business viewpoint. She thought that the whole business was going to change over the next ten years because of television. She was remarkably visionary in many ways."

"So there was a lot of communication. Was it a romantic relationship?"

"No other woman satisfied me as Isabella did," Miles replied. "Yes, it was romantic. We were both young, and we both believed in romance back then. Plus it was the forties, a very romantic time, I suppose. We'd hold hands like kids. I suppose we were kids then, come to think of it. Kiss each other in public, all very lovey-dovey."

"And the pregnancy? Was it planned?"

"Yes, we both wanted children," Miles said. "Actually I wanted children more than she did. She wanted us to accomplish great things together. She felt children would get in the way in some manner. But I was the one who persuaded her that a family was just as important."

His voice sank on those last words, then he swung his chin up and looked defiantly at her.

"And you blame yourself for the fact that she died?" Shannon asked gently.

Miles hesitated, then nodded his large head. "Yes, I was the one who made it happen, I was the one who persuaded her, I was the father. We couldn't have anticipated the difficulties of course, but nevertheless they happened."

"And how did you feel after her death?" Shannon asked, her voice still quiet.

There was a long silence and then Miles said, "I felt nothing. I probably have felt nothing ever since. She was the only woman I truly loved, if you must know. The only one."

"What happened afterwards? How long before you started seeing other women?"

Miles lifted his hand and rubbed his forehead, then ran it down his face and across his mouth. "I didn't see anybody for a year after she died. And then slowly I started to meet other women."

"So in 1945 you married Agnes? That was three years later," Shannon said.

"Yes, that was the first of my numerous mistakes," Miles replied, with a strained attempt at humor.

"Did you still want to have a family? Did you still want to have children?"

Miles shook his head negatively. "Agnes was the one who wanted to have children. She had Orson and Anne, of course. After that came Rosemary, I married her in '57 I think. She also wanted to have kids. I aim to please."

"So your hopes of a family died with Isabella? And the families that you did have after that weren't of your own choosing?"

"I suppose you could say that," Miles said disapprovingly. "Although it sounds like you are trying to make some kind of psychological gobbledygook out of it."

Shannon ignored the comment and said, "I don't have any pictures of Isabella. Could I have one and see what she looks like?"

Miles waved over at the shelf. "There's an album over there. There are some pictures of her in it."

She got up and walked over to the shelf, thinking that indeed she was making gobbledygook of it. Here was a man who had lost his dreams of love and family when the women he loved had died. Since then, he had had three wives and five children, none of whom he had wanted. No wonder he resented them all so much. They must have done nothing but remind him of his early loss.

"Over there," Miles pointed.

She took a heavy, brown-covered album from the shelf and brought it back to her chair.

"Here," Miles said, "give it to me."

She handed the album over and he opened it, leafed through a few pages, and then said, "There she is." There was a look of fondness in his eyes, and sadness.

He turned the album over and she stood and looked down at the beautiful dark-haired woman.

"She looks so familiar," Shannon said.

"She was a beautiful woman," Miles said.

And then Shannon realized who she looked like. "It's amazing. She looks so much like Elizabeth."

"Yes," Miles said. "It's quite a coincidence. Rosemary was Elizabeth's mother, of course, there was no possible way that she could look like Isabella, but there is a strong likeness. I noticed it, too."

It was amazing. The woman had the same eyes and mouth as Elizabeth, although she looked far more vibrant and beautiful than Miles's demure daughter. She looked

398

like a woman who would grab life with both hands and shake it until it gave her what she wanted.

They talked for another hour, at the end of which time Shannon had a thorough understanding of the relationship Miles had with his first wife. They had been both lovers and friends. For him it had been that idealistic first love that so many people cling to. Isabella had been everything he had wanted in a woman, and when she died she had left a vast emptiness that he'd never been able to fill. Her death had, in effect, changed his life.

From that point on Miles had become a driven man. Driven to attain the goals that both he and Isabella had shared, in some attempt to memorialize her memory. Isabella was, in Miles's own words, the finest thing that had ever happened to him. Nothing else had come close in his life. Nobody else had a chance beside this idealized memory.

When she got back to the cottage the nurse told her that Stephen had called. She went into her office, took the tape out of her recorder, put it in an envelope for the transcriber, and then called Stephen.

"I need to see you," she said, as soon as he answered.

He seemed a little taken aback by her lack of social niceties. "Sure. What's happening? Is this a sudden onslaught of lust?"

"I just need to talk to you. Can we get together?"

"Sure. When?"

"How about now?"

"You want to come down here?"

"That would be fine," she said. "I have another appointment, but I'll stop in at your place on the way." She was sounding too serious, she knew. And she didn't want to cause him any concern. "How was the gig in Santa Barbara last night?" she asked in a more casual tone.

"Oh, it was great," he said. "It went really well."

"Good. Well, you can tell me about it when I see you."

"Okay."

She hung up and stood indecisively in front of her desk. She still had no idea what she was going to say to him. She didn't even know what to think.

Miles had spoken to her in confidence, but . . .

She sighed and walked over to the window. The gardener was cutting roses, placing them reverently in a big straw basket. The only thing that she really knew was that she loved Stephen. She couldn't conceive of him doing something like this. But if he had, for some reason she couldn't understand, what then should the correct course of action be for her to take?

She didn't know the answer.

Stephen greeted Shannon with a passionate kiss. She kissed him back hard, enjoying the smell and feel of him.

"I missed you," he said with a warm smile. "Just a day and a half from you and I already miss you. What does that tell you?"

He looked tired, she thought with concern. But then that was only understandable. If he'd had a gig in Santa Barbara last night, that probably meant that he hadn't gotten to bed till two or three in the morning, maybe later. Slept a few hours there and then driven back home.

"We have to talk," she said. "It's very important."

Stephen took her hand and led her to the couch. He sat beside her and looked at her with concern. "Has something happened?"

Shannon took a deep breath. She knew now what she had to do. She loved this man. "Stephen, I'm going to tell you some things that I shouldn't tell you, but I have to. Miles thinks that you were responsible for the attempts on his life."

Stephen's mouth dropped open. "What? Me?"

"Yes. He thinks you're the one."

"That's crazy. Why on earth would he think that?"

"You went with a woman named Dana for a while, didn't you?"

Stephen looked puzzled. "Dana?" he said queryingly. "I don't think I . . . Oh yeah, right, there was a woman, Dana Coleman, I think her name was. An actress. I took her out twice, I think. It didn't work out very well. A nice person, I guess, but there was just nothing between us. Why? What's she have to do with this?"

"Apparently she is the woman who tried to administer poison to Miles in the first attempt on his life," Shannon said.

"You're kidding."

Shannon shook her head. "No. She's the one, and Miles has found out that you used to see her. He's put one and one together and come up with three."

"That's totally ridiculous," Stephen said. "I hardly knew the woman, for chrissake. In fact, now that I think of it, I seem to remember hearing something about her dying a few months ago. Something about an accidental drug overdose."

"Really?"

"Yeah, I either read it or somebody told me about it."

"All right," Shannon said. "Let's take a look at this now. Let's assume for the moment that she is the person who tried to poison your father, and that this is the woman you knew. How did you meet her?"

Stephen rubbed his head. "I can't remember. I was going through some dating phase at that time, and I took quite a few women out. I guess I met her at some party somewhere, thought she was a pretty woman and asked her out. But we discovered that we had nothing in common."

"Can you think of exactly where you met her?"

"I don't know. I can't remember. It was months ago. She was one of, I think, four women whom I took out in a month." He smiled at her. "I was feeling lonely."

Shannon noticed the time and said, "I've got to go. You

need to try and remember. If there is anything else you can remember about her, we need to talk about it. It may help."

"Yeah, I will," he said. He gave her a stern look. "You didn't think I had anything to do with this, did you?"

Shannon was a trained observer of people. She knew when they were lying and she knew that Stephen's surprise had been genuine. She was ashamed at the relief she felt. But it was only natural. "No," she said, "I never thought for moment that you'd do anything like that. I told Miles that."

"But you came to warn me just in case," Stephen said cautiously.

"If there was any truth to it, it would have served as a warning," she said cautiously. "But I'm really telling you this because it's got to be cleared up. You can't have your father thinking you tried to kill him."

"I'll go and talk to him."

"This places me in a very difficult position," Shannon said. "I was sworn to secrecy and confidentiality."

"So what do you want me to do?"

Shannon thought for a second and then said, "In for a penny, in for a pound. There is something else you should know." She hesitated. There was no easy way to say it. "Miles is dying. He has cancer. He has something like nine months to live."

Stephen's face grew pale; he was truly shocked now.

"I'm sorry to have to tell you like this." Shannon reached for his hand. "Miles has been keeping it a secret, nobody in the family knows. But I really feel that you have a right to know."

"Miles? Dying?"

"It's incurable. It was diagnosed fifteen months ago," she told him. "He figures he has about nine months left, and it doesn't look like there's any chance of remission. I told him he should talk to his family about it. That you could help each other. But he laughed. Then I told him that you, above all the others, should be told. That you would understand and be a strength to him. And then he told me about Dana, and that he thought you were responsible."

"I've got to talk to him," Stephen said.

"I know."

"What about you? This places you in a difficult position."

Shannon shrugged. "All I have to lose is my job. Go and talk to him, I don't care. It needs to be done." She stood up. "Now I've got to go."

"Will I see you tonight?"

"Yeah, I'll be home about four. You can give me a buzz."

"Shannon," he said, putting his hands on her shoulders. "I can't believe how much I love you. I just seem to fall more and more in love with you each day."

She reached up a hand and touched his cheek affectionately. "I love you, too." They kissed and then she left.

Dr. Gerald Deakins was a short-wizened man in his late seventies, Shannon guessed. He peered at her though thick eyeglasses, a worried expression on his face, and rubbed the top of his head with a liver-spotted hand. Thick, unkempt bushes of gray hair sprouted from the sides of his head; the top was completely bare. He looked like one of the Marx brothers gone to seed, if such a thing were possible.

When she'd called to set the appointment, he had said that this was most irregular, but agreed to see her. Now, as she followed him to the living room of his Benedict Canyon home, he muttered the same thing again. "This is very irregular."

She handed him the letter that Miles had written and sat on the couch while he read it. He stood in the middle of the room and opened the envelope, his fingers trembling, from both nervousness and age. Peering through his glasses he read the letter, muttering to himself.

"This is most irregular," he said. "There is such a thing as patient/doctor confidentiality." He looked at her over the top of his glasses, the whites of his eyes abnormally large.

"But this is, in effect, a release from the patient," she said.

He nodded quickly. "Yes, yes, I know. But . . ."

"Do you have the records?"

"Yes. I pulled them out." He walked over to a table on the side of the room and came back carrying a yellowing manila folder that had once been brown. He sat down in an armchair and opened the folder on his lap.

"He only came to me three times," he said. "I told him that I could help him but that it would be a long treatment, that he would have to see me for at least a year. But he only came three times. He called me a quack. I remember now. A terrible man."

"Why did he come to see you?" She took the tape recorder out from her purse, flicked it on, and put it on the table between them.

Dr. Deakins almost jumped in alarm. "No, no, no tape recorder," he said, waving his right hand wildly at her.

Shannon reached over and turned it off and put it back in her bag.

"It cannot be known that I have given you this information. I don't care that the patient authorized it," he said. "I can't let anybody know. I have my reputation to consider."

"I understand," Shannon said. "I'll respect your anonymity."

He nodded, "Very well, very well."

"So why did he come to see you?"

He consulted the folder in his lap again, shuffling pages.

"Yes, yes, it was a terrible thing. I remember it all. It was terrible."

"What was terrible?" Shannon asked patiently. "What did he want your help with?"

"The man had a serious problem. He was referred to me by another patient. He wanted me to help him overcome a certain, shall we say, pattern of compulsive behavior."

"And what was that?"

The frightened doctor closed the folder and looked at her. "This is most irregular," he repeated.

"I understand that it's irregular," Shannon consoled him. "And I understand your reticence to discuss it, and I respect that. But Mr. Cort himself wants me to know. You do understand that, don't you?"

"How do I know that this letter was written by him?" he challenged her.

"Would you like his telephone number? You may call him yourself."

The temporary reprieve seemed to energize the doctor. He jumped to his feet and said, "Yes, yes. I will call him. I must make sure that this is indeed from him."

Shannon gave him the number. He excused himself and hurried from the room.

She looked around, noting that Deakin had obviously seen better days. The heavy oak furniture had probably once been expensive, but now the wood was scarred and the upholstery frayed. A bookshelf against the nearest wall contained mainly old hardbacks. There was dust everywhere.

He came back about three minutes later, shaking his head, and sat down again in the armchair. He picked up the folder and turned it in his hands a number of times. "I don't understand," he said. "Why does he want this known?"

"That shouldn't concern you," Shannon said. "I assume you reached him."

"Yes, yes, he told me to speak to you."

"So tell me," Shannon repeated. "Why did he come to see you back then?"

The doctor squared his shoulders and finally looked at her. "He had a problem that he wanted me to help him with. The man was molesting his daughter. He was unable to help himself, he said."

"My God, he was molesting Anne? What do you mean, molesting?"

"He was having sexual relations with his daughter. He was forcing her to have sex with him. He was very ashamed and realized he was sick and came to me for help. I offered him help, of course, but then he decided that I could not help him. He called me a quack."

Shannon was stunned. The implications, the very act. Miles molesting his daughter! It was unbelievable.

"How long had this been going on?" she asked.

"Almost two years, he told me. He said it had happened by accident, and then it was something that he had done again and again, at least four times."

"But how could she have stood for it? I mean, she must have been in her mid-twenties by then. If he was unable to help himself, she must have—."

"No, no," the doctor said, interrupting her. "No, she was much younger." He opened the folder and looked through his notes. "She was fourteen at the time."

"Fourteen?" Shannon said, as comprehension came. "What was her name?"

"Elizabeth," the doctor said. "His daughter's name was Elizabeth."

Shannon walked slowly along the wet sand near the water on Santa Monica Beach. The sky had clouded over, yet there were still hundreds of people there, enjoying the open space, the smell of salt, the freedom that somehow the ocean always carried with it.

She had been first confused and then disgusted. The thought of driving home, at least back to her cottage in the Beverly Hills mansion, had seemed repugnant to her. She had come to the beach instead.

Now, all she felt was a deep and terrible sadness.

Poor Elizabeth, and yes, poor Miles, she thought to herself. For both had carried this burden for almost fifteen years. It must have been a crushing weight.

And yet in some insane way it made sense. Miles, the patriarch, the patron, the father, the king. Miles, still grief-stricken after more than three decades, by the loss of his love, Isabella. And his daughter Elizabeth who looked so much like her. A lonely man, and a scared young girl.

Shannon looked out at the tumbling breakers. There were a handful of surfers out there, all waiting for the last waves of the day.

How had a horror like that happened? How could something like this have been kept a secret in a family so large? But not a close family, she reminded herself. Each was encased in his or her own world. Each had their own dragons to slay. The fact that one of them, a powerless young girl, had been unable to face the fiercest dragon of all could easily have escaped the rest of them.

And what of Miles? Miles, so strong and intractable and convinced of his own rightness in everything he did. For this one time, he must have known without doubt that he was involved in evil. She knew it was why he had finally gone to see Dr. Deakins. How this must have preyed on him, tore at him.

Indeed, it must have caused the very cancer from which he now suffered, the stroke which had incapacitated him for so long, the misery which he carried around with him like a shield. She felt only pity for him now, and pity for Elizabeth, and pity for the whole miserable family. The Corts, the kings of Hollywood, trapped on a stage without control, actors in a play, in which they were like puppets, acting out a script which none of them had written.

A young boy and a young girl ran past her, laughing, running through the shallows and splashing each other. The girl was about fourteen, the boy, fifteen. God, she thought, how terrified Elizabeth must have been. How alone. She had nobody to turn to. Nobody to confide in.

She'd read of incest. She knew that the incestuous father always thought of himself as a proud owner of possessions. That the children were merely other possessions to do with as he wished. No matter what private agonies he had gone through, Miles had felt that he owned Elizabeth, that she was his to do with as he wanted.

How had this affected Elizabeth? She knew that incest left terrible scars. The victim was usually left without real love, forced to partake of this substitute. What longings and conflicts it would leave! Usually incest survivors felt betrayed by both parents: the father for what he had done, the mother for obviously failing to satisfy him and for not protecting the child.

She shook her head again. So ugly, so pathetic, so sad, so horrible. She wanted to leave. Leave Los Angeles, leave the Cort family, leave the man she loved, leave the book that she had grown to love. Take her daughter and go far away from here.

Her daughter. She thought of Miles and Melissa in the pool. The young Melissa, with her tiny breasts budding out like flowers, and Miles so possessive, telling her how to dive.

Oh, God, she thought. She had to get back. And then she chided herself. There was a difference between a child molester and an incestuous father. A vast difference. There was no need to get paranoid or hysterical. Nevertheless, she had to get back.

She cast a last, longing look at the ocean, this wide expanse of water and oxygen, of creamy foam and blue depths, and at the carefree people, running and laughing and swimming and surfing and fishing off the pier as if nothing in the world was wrong. As if nature was simply taking its intended and preordained course. It was illusion, all illusion. Nothing was as simple as it appeared to be.

She turned her back on the ocean and trudged back across the sand to her car.

CHAPTER TWENTY

"Everyone says that what they want more than anything in their lives is peace. I've never wanted peace in *my* life. It's a ridiculous desire. We thrive on conflict. Peace is too much like death. Peace is when things are quiet and still, when nothing's happening. Peace means you are not accomplishing anything of any importance. Peace is for grazing cows, not for people who want to get things done. And yet, when I look back at my conflict and the conflicts I have created, there are some things I wish had never happened," Miles said.

Anne arrived unannounced at Elizabeth's home in the middle of the day.

"I'm sorry, I should have called, but I was driving by and thought I'd stop in," she said when Elizabeth opened the door.

"What for?" Elizabeth asked, not inviting her in. She wore jeans and a T-shirt and was barefoot. She wore no makeup.

Anne seemed a little taken aback by the cold tone and unfriendly face. "I wanted to talk to you about this thing with Daddy. The fact he thinks someone is trying to kill

410

him. It's so upsetting. I thought two heads might be better than one."

"Oh," Elizabeth said.

"Can I come in?" Anne asked.

"I suppose so." Elizabeth stepped back and let her enter. Then she led the way to the living room.

A beautiful blond woman was sitting on the couch, dressed as casually as Elizabeth. In skirt, blouse, and full makeup, Anne felt overdressed.

"This is my friend, Sissy," Elizabeth said offhandedly. "This is Anne, my half-sister."

"How do you do?" Anne said, offering her hand.

The woman shook her hand and smiled pleasantly at her. "So, you're the other Cort female?"

"Yes," Anne said, not knowing what else to say.

"Sit down." Elizabeth pointed to an armchair.

Anne sat and said, "I wanted to talk to you, but I didn't realize you had company. Perhaps another time would be better."

Elizabeth looked at Sissy. "Would you make us some tea?" she suggested.

Sissy got up without comment and went through a door into the kitchen.

"So?" Elizabeth said.

"Well, I wondered if you had any ideas. I can't believe that Miles suspects one of us."

"Why not? As he said, we're all capable of it."

"You can't believe that!" Anne protested.

"Why talk to me about it? I might be the one."

"You're not that interested in his money," Anne said definitively.

"But it may not be about money."

"Then it's not one of us. It's some enemy who wants revenge," Anne said. She hesitated and added, "The only one of us who is that interested in Miles's money is Orson."

411

Elizabeth shrugged. "Well, he's your brother, not mine. Do you think he's the one?"

"I don't know," Anne said exasperatedly. "Sometimes I think he announced this just to set us off against each other. I wouldn't put it past him."

"Well, I can't help you, Anne. I have no idea who could have been behind it, and I'm not about to start guessing," Elizabeth said.

"Surely you must have wondered about it," Anne suggested.

"Actually, I really don't want to discuss my musings," Elizabeth said tartly. "I don't think it would be productive. Nor do I see why you have to pick on me to have these discussions with."

Anne was hurt. "I thought . . . I don't know what I thought. I didn't intend to upset you."

Elizabeth didn't soften. "Look, Anne, we've never been friends and it's too late to start now. Why not just keep things the way they are?"

"Because we should be better friends," Anne said, her own irritation rising. "It's not right that sisters should be such strangers."

Elizabeth sighed and said in a tired voice, "Anne, you know nothing about me, or my life. I like it that way. I want it to stay that way."

"I'd like to know more about you," Anne said softly, giving it one more try.

"All right," Elizabeth said cruelly. "The woman you just met . . . Well, Sissy is my lover. Does that make you feel better, to know that?"

Anne stared at her for a blank second. "You mean?"

"Right. I don't like men. I'm what's commonly called a dyke," Elizabeth said defiantly.

"Oh, dear," Anne said mildly.

Sissy came back into the room. "Do you want a cup of tea, Anne?" she asked sweetly.

"I think Anne is just leaving," Elizabeth said.

Sissy's eyes darted from one to the other. "Oh."

"I don't care about your personal life like that," Anne said stiffly. "That isn't what I meant."

"Well, whatever, that's the way it is," Elizabeth said carelessly.

Anne got up and so did Elizabeth.

"I'm sorry, this is obviously a bad time," Anne said. "I guess I'll be going."

Elizabeth stood close to Sissy and made no move to show her out, so Anne walked herself to the front door.

As she left the living room, she turned in the doorway to speak. The last thing she saw was Elizabeth with one arm around the blond woman, her hostile eyes on her sister.

Anne swallowed her words and showed herself out.

"I understand that you think I tried to murder you," Stephen said. He stood with his hands in his pockets before his father's desk.

Miles looked shocked for a second and then his face grew stony. "Shannon told you."

"Yes, of course she told me," Stephen said.

"She's about to lose her job!" Miles snapped angrily.

Stephen shrugged. "I love Shannon and she loves me. I'm going to marry her. How can you expect her not to tell me of such a terrible thing? What effect do you think it had on her?"

Miles considered this for a moment and then said, "Well, did you?"

"No."

Their eyes locked, as if each were trying to read some truth behind them.

"Why should I believe you?" Miles asked.

"Why on earth would I want to have you killed?"

"The money."

"Miles, I don't give a damn for your money. I never

have and you know that. I've never asked you for any and I never will. I lead my own life. I'm not dependent on your money."

Miles looked uncertain. "The girl? What about the girl? She was a girlfriend of yours."

"I dated her twice. It didn't work out. I never even slept with her," Michael said. "That's hardly a girlfriend. I certainly didn't know her well enough to ask her to do something like kill you. Give me a break."

"Then who?" Miles asked.

"Now, that I don't know," Stephen said. "Shannon also told me about your illness."

"Goddamn it!" Miles roared. "She had no right to do that." He slammed his fist on the desk.

Stephen was unaffected by the display. "I'm not going to tell anyone. I just wanted you to know that I'm sorry. Nobody deserves that."

"Not even me?"

"Not even you."

Miles grunted. "I've always said people get exactly what they deserve in life. I don't see how I'm any different."

"If there's anything I can do for you—" Stephen said, leaving the question in the air.

"Find a cure," Miles said ironically.

Stephen shrugged. There was no answer to that. His father looked old, he suddenly realized. There was a pallor to his skin and his eyes seemed to have lost their habitual brightness. He felt a stirring of pity.

Miles cocked his head to one side and looked back at his son. "Do you hate me, boy?" he asked unexpectedly.

Stephen shook his head. "No, I don't hate you."

"I haven't given you an easy life," Miles replied.

"Nobody said it was going to be easy," Stephen replied. "Besides, you've never given anyone an easy life, including yourself."

"Do you resent me for it?"

"Sometimes, yes, I do."

Miles pushed himself away from the desk a little. "I had hopes for you. I had hopes for all of you. I wanted you to carry on my dreams, I suppose. I didn't care too much about yours. I wanted the Cort name to continue in filmmaking. What do I get? A daughter who is a has-been actress? Another one who does nothing? A son who's a has-been B-movie producer? And you a musician?"

"It's what I love to do," Stephen said.

Miles nodded. "I understand that. I love to make films. I just couldn't understand why you didn't as well."

"We follow our talents."

"I know that," Miles said irritably, and then softened. "Are you any good?"

"Yes, I'm very good," Stephen said. A simple statement of fact.

"Maybe I can hear some of your music sometime," Miles said.

"Sure." It was the first time his father had ever asked to hear his music. It was a little thing. And yet it was enormous. "Sure," he said again. "I'll drop off a tape sometime."

"Good."

"Well, I've got to go," Stephen replied. He stood there for a second, then turned and walked away. After five or six paces he stopped and looked back at his father. "Do you believe me?"

Miles took a long time to answer, then he said, "Yes. I do."

"Good." Stephen continued on his way.

He walked out of the house into the garden. Something had just happened between them, he thought. But he wasn't sure what. The beginnings of a bridge, of something connecting them? It had been a long time coming. Funny how it came when it was almost too late. He shook his head and walked down the pathway to Shannon's cottage. He walked up the patio and rang the doorbell.

Shannon opened the door. "Hi," he said, kissing her.

"Come in." She put her arm through his. "Do you want some coffee?"

"Yeah, I could use some. How's Melissa doing?"

"Much better," Shannon replied. "Go say hello to her. She'll be pleased to see you."

Stephen knocked on Melissa's door and then walked into the room. "Hi, babe. I hear you're doing pretty well."

"Hi, Stephen," she said, her face lighting up. "Yeah, I'm doing fine. I'm feeling a lot better."

"That's great." He gave her a hug. "What are you up to?"

"Just reading and watching TV. How about you?"

"Courting your mother, the usual stuff, you know—mushy stuff."

Melissa grimaced. "Are you two going to get married?"

Stephen was surprised for a second, but then he said, "Yes, although your mother doesn't know it yet."

"And I'll have you for a father?" Melissa said.

"I guess so. Beggars can't be choosers."

"Hey, you'd be pretty neat for a father," Melissa conceded.

"Well, we'll see. Talk to you later."

He went into the kitchen where Shannon was pouring coffee. "I've just been talking to Miles," he said. "He wants to fire you."

"Really?" Shannon asked, for some reason feeling no concern.

"I doubt it. He'll calm down. I think it'll be fine."

Shannon wore blue jeans and a thin cotton T-shirt. She was wearing no bra. He reached a hand up and casually cupped her right breast in it.

Shannon playfully pushed his hand away. "Animal!"

"Around you I can't help it."

He took the coffee she handed him and sat at the kitchen table. Stephen suddenly clicked his fingers. "Oh, right! That was it!"

"What?" Shannon asked.

"I've just remembered how I met that woman," he said.

"How?"

"It was at a party. Elizabeth introduced me. It was a party at Elizabeth's house, as a matter of fact. She was a friend of hers, or maybe they'd worked together. Something like that."

"Elizabeth," Shannon said.

Shannon sat at the table as well. She hadn't seen Miles since her visit to the psychologist the day before. For some reason she dreaded seeing him. She was still horrified at what she had discovered. It was so ugly, this final sin that Miles wanted to confess. And when she saw him during their appointment, set for tomorrow, she knew they would have to talk about it.

"Are you going to tell Miles that?" she asked.

Stephen shook his head. "No. He'll just jump to more conclusions. I think I'll talk to Elizabeth first."

"Good."

"What is it?" Stephen asked, watching her carefully.

"Ah, nothing," she said. "Just let me think."

Miles sat in bed, waiting for the sound of the limousine to come down the driveway. He looked at his watch; it was nine o'clock. Outside he could hear a wind shifting the trees and tapping branches against the windows of the house.

He wasn't as excited as he should have been. Perhaps he was getting too old for this, he thought. And yet Andy had told him that this one was a real knockout. She'd been recommended by another of the girls he'd had earlier, and he'd checked her out carefully. She worked in the business and earned a fair amount of money when she was working, but she wasn't averse to earning a little more during her down-time.

Elizabeth was in the house sleeping in the room she had slept in when she was a little girl. She'd called just before dinner and said workmen were in the process of destroying her apartment and asked if she could spend the night there. He had agreed.

Immediately after dinner she had said she was tired and that she was going to bed, which suited him just fine.

He thought again of the girl who would be coming. Like all of them, she would be beautiful and young and eager to please, and yet tonight for some reason the thought didn't even cause a stirring in his loins. He'd known so many women in his life and used so many of them. He'd lost count of the number of women he'd fucked, maybe twenty years earlier. Once he used to keep score, writing the names down in a book. But the book became a crowded and ultimately futile testament.

He wondered what Shannon thought of him now. What everyone would think of him. A man who had sex with his own daughter. That had been a terrible thing and he still did not know why he had done it—simply because it was available, it seemed at the time. The psychologist had tried to talk to him to find out stuff about his childhood and what had happened to him. But he didn't subscribe to nonsense like that. He simply decided to stop doing it, and so he had.

But the shame of it had clung to him like an odor, through all the years of triumph. If there was anything in his life that he wished he could relive and take back it was that.

He thought of Elizabeth alone in her room now, just like then. How then he had gone to that room and touched her and—

Perhaps it was these thoughts that had taken the thrill away from his pleasures this night.

There, the limousine, he heard it. He heard the engine come closer and then die, and then the sound of the door.

He waited, his interest mounting. So, he wasn't dead after all, he thought. A new and pretty one always prom-

418

ised something different.Thank God he still had that to look forward to. There was a knock at the door.

"Come in."

The door opened and the girl walked in.

Andy had not lied. The girl was startlingly beautiful. Tall, long blond hair and blue eyes. She had a full, almost insolent mouth, and she wore high-heeled shoes, tight black leather pants that hugged her long legs and curving hips like a second skin and a white silk blouse that accentuated her deep, full breasts.

"Hi," she said, walking up to the bed and smiling down at him.

She was, he thought, the epitome of the perfect California girl.

"Good evening," he said.

She carried a small garment bag which she put on the floor beside the bed.

"Would you pour me a drink?" He waved at the bar. "And fix yourself one, if you want."

He watched her walk, a lilting sway to her hips. The girl had it all. A great body that she know how to use, he thought admiringly.

"What would you like?" she asked over her shoulder, tossing her blond hair pertly to one side.

"Scotch on the rocks, please."

"I'll have the same." She poured the drinks deftly and then turned, a glass in each hand, and walked back to him.

Her good looks were so innocent and unself-conscious that it almost pained him.

"What's your name, my dear?"

"Sissy." She smiled and handed him his drink.

Elizabeth sat stiffly on the edge of her bed, unable to relax, waiting. She hated this room, she thought, with its pink ruffles and little-girl decor. She had known fear in this room.

She remembered the nights he'd come in, the soft sound of the door opening and then closing. The movement of the large body as it approached, and then the shifting bed as he sat on it. And then the hands groping and insistent while she tried to make herself disappear.

"No, Daddy," she would whisper.

"Shh," he would say, and his hand would stroke her hair.

And then later she would lie there in the dark, sobbing dry sobs, her body wracked with misery.

They had a secret, something only the two of them shared. And yet she had despised everyone else in the family for not knowing it, particularly her mother. She had feared him and hated him and loved him. A vortex of emotions too complex for a little girl to understand.

Now all that remained was the hate.

She looked at her watch. Another five minutes. She only had to wait five minutes.

The girl sat demurely on the edge of the bed, and then her eyes fixed slowly on Miles and she slowly unbuttoned her blouse. She was not wearing a bra, and perfectly formed firm breasts with cherry-colored nipples came into view.

Miles felt almost like saying a prayer at the sight of them. He reached out with his left hand and ran a finger around one of the nipples.

"Do you like them?" she asked, coquettishly.

"Mmm," he said, his throat suddenly so dry he was unable to speak.

"That's just the beginning," she said. "I'm going to make you feel like a king."

Miles felt his erection swell beneath the blankets. This

420

was the best one in a long time. This one was something special.

"I know how to please men," she said, her pink tongue lightly moistening her lips. "That's one thing I learned how to do really well. I've never yet had a man and left him unsatisfied. I know how to do things that have never been done before to you."

It was unlikely, Miles thought jadedly, but he was willing to let her try.

"What do you like?" But she didn't wait for an answer and said, "I bet I know." She reached a long-fingered white hand over and put it right on top of his penis. It was hard, and she felt its outline through the blankets. "Can I see?"

Miles pushed the covers down below his hips and she reached into his pajamas and, without hesitation, released his short, thick penis. She fell forward in a cascade of blond hair and took it deep in her mouth, flicking at it with her tongue and sucking.

Then, just as quickly, she raised her head, her hands still on his penis. "Do you want me to be your little girl? Is that what you'd like? Perhaps not," she chattered on. "Perhaps you'd like me to sit on it."

Miles didn't speak, he didn't need to. His cock felt enormous, as if it was going to burst.

She looked at his face and smiled. "Do you like to be teased? Do you know that I could tease you so sexily that I could make you come without even touching your cock?"

"That would be a good trick," Miles said, finally speaking.

She leaned forward, and as her face approached his, she whispered, "Let me play with you," and then she kissed him.

Miles kissed her back hungrily. When they broke apart he said, "What do you want to do?"

She pressed her breasts against his chest and with her face still close, so close he could smell her skin and feel her soft warm breath, she said, "I want to tease you, I want to make you so excited you go mad. I want you to want me so badly that when I finally give myself to you, you explode."

She sat up suddenly, leaned down to her garment bag, and took something from it. It looked like some kind of a belt, Miles noticed, although he was more intent on watching the sway of her breasts as she moved.

"What's that?" he asked.

"Don't worry, you'll like it," she said. "Now you have to do something. You have to close your eyes so I can surprise you."

Obediently, Miles closed his eyes, wondering what she was going to do. He felt something close around his wrists and then a sudden sharp movement as his arms were pulled back over his head.

He opened his eyes and saw his hands were tied to the headboard, encased in some sort of handcuff.

"What the hell are you doing?"

"Trust me," she said, "you're going to enjoy this."

She reached into the bag again and brought out another item that also looked something like a belt, although it was made of cloth. Then, in one swift movement, she pushed it down over his head and across his mouth.

"Jesus Christ," Miles thought wildly. It was a gag.

He tried to speak he couldn't. Only gurgling sounds came from his throat.

"There," she said sweetly. "now you're ready for the real fun."

She stood up then and began to button her blouse.

What the hell was the bitch doing? he wondered. What the hell was he doing? What was going on here?

He looked over on the side of the bed, wishing he could reach the alarm, but there was no way, his arms were tied and his legs are unable to move.

And then came the totally inexplicable. The door opened, and Elizabeth walked into the room.

Miles's eyes almost bugged out of his head. She was wearing high heels like Sissy and a gleaming leather body suit. In her hands she carried a small black briefcase.

"I see it went as we planned," Elizabeth said, coming to the bed and looking down at him with a curiously disdainful expression in her eyes.

"It was just fine," Sissy said.

"You did wonderfully," Elizabeth said, and then she kissed the girl full on the mouth. Not a friendly kiss but a passionate one. The type a man gives a woman.

Jesus, Miles thought.

He began to feel real fear.

"This is my lover, Daddy," Elizabeth said, one arm still on Sissy's shoulder. "Isn't she beautiful?" She kissed Sissy lightly on the cheek and said, "You must go now. Paxton will be in the kitchen. Just go down there and tell him that Mr. Cort told him to take you home."

Sissy looked at Miles on the bed, and then at Elizabeth. "What are you going to do to him?"

"Don't worry," Elizabeth said. "I'll take care of him."

"Okay." Sissy kissed Elizabeth and said, "Be careful." And then, picking up her bag and zipping it closed, she hurried from the room.

Elizabeth put the briefcase on the bed and opened it. It was filled with shining steel instruments and looked like a doctor's case. There were needles and knives and rods, all with sharp points.

"You're wondering what I'm going to do to you, aren't you, Daddy?" Elizabeth gave him a quick, sidelong glance.

Her cheeks were flushed and her eyes feverish, he noticed. God, he thought, what can I do? She's insane. What can I do?

"I want you to see what I've become, what you've made me," Elizabeth said. "Yes, Sissy is my lover, but that's only a small part of my life. Do you know that I am one of the most famous dominatrixes in town? That I specialize in giving men pain? And fulfilling their desires for punishment and degradation. I'm very good at it, Daddy. I should be. I've known enough pain myself." She reached into the suitcase and pulled out a thin steel needle about four inches long. She held it up and squinted at it. "That should do for a start."

Miles had a funny feeling he knew what she was about to do. He wished he didn't.

"Andy is so stupid," Elizabeth said. "At least two of the women you've had have worked for me, including the one who was supposed to poison you. It was so easy to plant them."

Right, he thought, friends recommending friends. It was so easy and he had been so stupid.

"I'm going to make you suffer pain, like you've never suffered before." She turned to face him, her eyes glaring down at him. "Yes, I sent a woman to poison you. I thought killing you would be enough. But I think killing you is too kind. I've thought about it, and no, I'm not going to kill you. I'm going to treat you to a couple of hours of the most intense agony you've ever experienced. It's nothing, of course, to the agony you've caused me. But it'll make me feel a little better.

"You won't be able to scream, Daddy, but you'll feel it, I promise you. You're going to look like a pin cushion by the time I've finished with you, and you're never going to be a man again, either. I'm going to make sure of that with a piercing right where it counts. No more hard-ons for you, Daddy."

She smiled craftily at him. "And then, I'm going to unpluck everything from you and untie you and leave you here. And you know what? You won't be able to do a thing about it. You'll never mention it to anybody, because you know that I'll tell everyone if you do."

But I have already told, he wanted to say. I was so sorry and ashamed that I told myself. But, of course, he could only stare at her.

424

She hissed the next words out. "I'll tell everyone what happened in the little girl's room down the hall."

A smile that turned into a painful grimace. "I love you, Daddy, but I hate you more. And now you're going to find out just how much."

Shannon closed the folder of notes and yawned. She should go to bed, it was late and she was tired. But there was some kind of demonic energy in her and she felt restless. Maybe a walk would help, she thought.

She stood, turned off the small desk lamp, and walked out the front door to the patio. The wind had died down and now there was only a soft breeze. It brought the smell of the ocean with it.

She loved it here, she was thinking—California, Los Angeles, this house, these grounds. If it weren't for the project she was working on and the ugliness surrounding it, it would be an idyllic existence. Perhaps when it's over, it will be different, she thought.

Faintly, from the front of the house, she heard the sound of a car move along the driveway.

She walked along the well-lighted path knowing she wouldn't trip any alarms if she stayed on the prescribed circuit. Her arms were folded across her chest as she walked, wondering what Stephen had discovered. When he left this afternoon he said he would try to talk to Elizabeth this evening.

"I'm sure there is some simple explanation, that they were nothing more than acquaintances. I'm sure Elizabeth didn't have anything to do with any attempt to kill Miles," he had said.

The words had sounded hollow to her. She didn't tell him about what she'd discovered about Elizabeth. She didn't have the heart to bring it out from her thoughts into the harsh light of the real world. It was so damaging, so unbelievable and abhorrent that she just couldn't bring herself to say anything about it.

But she thought to herself, yes, Elizabeth could kill Miles. A little girl molested by her father? Growing up so quiet and demure with the knowledge eating away inside her and the hatred building and building. Yes, Elizabeth could easily have arranged it. And probably did. Sooner or later it would all come out.

She came toward the pool, and a man suddenly stepped out of the shadows.

"Oh, it's you, Miss Ross," the guard said. "I thought it was Miss Cort."

"I'm just taking a walk to the pool," Shannon replied.

"That's fine, ma'am, have a nice evening."

Shannon took step and then stopped. "Fred?"

"Yes, ma'am."

"Why did you think I was Miss Cort?"

"Oh, she's staying here this evening, ma'am. You just looked like her for a moment."

"What do you mean, staying here for the evening?"

"Oh, she's sleeping at the house tonight, in her old room."

"Oh," Shannon said. "And where's Mr. Cort?"

"He probably has gone to bed."

"Oh." She stood there and felt an ugly feeling crawl over her skin. Something terrible was happening. She knew it.

"Fred?" she said. "I think you'd better check on Mr. Cort and I think I need to speak to him."

"Well, he can't be interrupted, ma'am. I'm afraid that's impossible."

"It's urgent," Shannon insisted, "very urgent."

Fred stepped closer to her, an uncertain expression on his face. "I can't do that, Miss Ross. He's just had a visitor and is probably sleeping now."

"Is Corydon here?"

"He's probably in his room."

426

"Get him," Shannon demanded, and headed fast for the back patio doors.

The guard caught up with her just as she reached to patio. "Ma'am, you can't do that. You can't just burst into the house like that."

"Take me into the house to see Corydon, *now!*" Shannon ordered.

"What's happening here?" Fred asked.

"I don't have time to explain to you, take me to Corydon. You'll hear my explanation then. Now move!"

The man finally believed that something was wrong and hurried ahead of her, opening the back door and walking into the house.

"Wait here, I'll get Mr. Corydon," he said when they were in the kitchen.

She folded her arms across her chest again, clutching it tightly. Events were intersecting at their destined point, she knew it beyond a doubt.

She couldn't wait. She moved toward the door. She had to get to Miles's room.

Corydon came in wearing a bathrobe. "What is it, Miss Ross?"

He was still awake, thank God, and looked alert enough. "I think we need to go up to Mr. Cort's room right away. I have a feeling he's in danger."

"In danger?" Corydon asked raising an eyebrow.

"Let's just get there. I don't have time to explain now."

"I'm afraid that's not possible," Corydon said. "We can't disturb him."

Shannon wanted to stomp her feet on the floor, but there was no time for that. "If you don't want to see Mr. Cort dead, I suggest you get up to his room right away. If he's safe I need to tell him something."

Corydon looked dubiously at her, but the word "dead" seemed to impinge. "Tell me what's going on," he said, taking her arm and leading her down the hall at a fast trot.

"I think Elizabeth is the one responsible for the attempt on his life," Shannon said, "and she's here tonight. I have a feeling that something terrible's going to happen."

Corydon broke into a trot and took the stairs three at a time with Shannon close behind him. Upstairs, they ran down the hall.

Corydon didn't even bother to knock at Miles's door but swung it open and stepped in.

"Jesus," he said, coming to a halt so sudden that Shannon almost collided into his back.

Miles was lying on the bed, his hands cuffed to the posts with some latex device, his mouth gagged.

Elizabeth stood over him like an apparition from hell. Six pins of varying lengths were sticking out of his chest.

"Jesus Christ," Corydon muttered, then rushed to Elizabeth, pulling her away.

Shannon stepped closer, hardly aware of what she was doing. She felt like a puppet, disembodied.

"But I was just beginning," Elizabeth complained in a little-girl voice.

Shannon looked over at Miles, at the blood running down his chest, down his stomach, at the devices of torture, and at his bulging eyes.

Shannon wanted to be sick. She was going to be sick. Her stomach lurched. She was sick.

CHAPTER TWENTY-ONE

According to Miles the concept of forgiveness was dreamed up by losers, weaklings, and cowards. "You've just had your ass kicked, you've just been beaten up by somebody bigger, smarter, and stronger than you are. What are you going to do to make yourself feel a little better about the ignominy of it? You forgive them. There's this guy on the cross, right? What's he going to yell out? 'Fuck you?' They're just going to laugh. They're not hanging there with nails through their palms. Instead he says, 'Forgive them.' It makes them scratch their heads, makes him feel a little more righteous. I've never forgiven anyone in my life. I'm proud of my grudges."

Miles was apparently back to normal within two days. The wounds had been superficial, needing little more than cleaning and bandaging. Elizabeth had indeed not proceeded too far with her task of torturing him.

As for Elizabeth, she had retreated from responsibility into the past, and continued to talk only in that little girl voice. Miles, ever the maverick, had refused all suggestions to have her institutionalized. "What do I want to do that for?" he said. "Those people are quacks. They shoot her full of dope, give her a little electric shock therapy, talk to her for five years, and she comes out of there a vegetable. That's not what I want. She deserves real help." Instead he had placed her in the care of private practitioners, people who spoke of cures based upon communication and understanding.

"My daughter's going to be fully functioning, and she's going to recover from what I did to her and what she did to me."

Miles announced this during a dinner the entire family had been ordered to attend.

And yet, in spite of his posturing, Shannon noticed a subtle change in Miles. Oh, he was still the same cantankerous old man, but he seemed more deliberate and thoughtful in his actions and words. It had to do with responsibility, she thought. Perhaps he had finally realized that every action had a consequence, that no matter how much a man tried to isolate himself he still affected those around him, in sometimes incomprehensible ways.

If he hadn't learned that lesson she certainly had, Shannon thought. It had been an astounding journey for her. From hardship in New York to luxury in Beverly Hills, from a life containing its own tragedies for her to what ultimately turned out to be a far more tragic arena, involving many more people. In the process her own life had changed in ways she realized she had yet to discover.

She remembered her conversation with Miles earlier that day. They were walking through the gardens, Miles in his motorized wheelchair and her beside him.

"What do you want me to say about you and Elizabeth in the book?" Shannon had asked with great difficulty. It was still a subject she found hard to deal with.

"Say what you wish."

"You can't really want me to include that," she said. "There is no point. It hurts too many people. You don't really want that, do you?"

Miles had stopped his wheelchair and looked up at her,

pain in his eyes, despair in the heavy lines of his face. "I must."

Shannon sensed what he was going through. It was not altogether rational but it was understandable. "Miles, I know you need to atone for what you have done, but by admitting it to your family, surely you've done that. There's no need to publicly dismember yourself. It won't serve any purpose."

Miles moved his wheelchair on without comment.

Now, looking around the dinner table, Shannon saw what courage it had taken for Miles to come this far. They all knew: Anne, who refused to meet her father's eyes; Orson, who seemed unchanged, the same as he always was, surly and short-tempered; and Stephen who was more on edge than usual.

It was at this point that Miles pushed his plate aside and said, "I must say something to you all."

Four heads lifted and stared at him.

"You know me well enough to know that I'm no good at apologizing," Miles said brusquely. "So I'm not going to do that. I've done much to hurt each one of you throughout your lives. I've done much to hurt Richard, who's no longer with us. And as you know, I hurt Elizabeth terribly. And I'm sure that it has shocked you all beyond understanding.

"I don't ask that you forgive me, I don't ask that you love me, nor do I expect you to respect me. But I must say what I have to say. What happened with Elizabeth happened. Perhaps I was a sick man at the time. I don't want to say that, because somehow that seems like an excuse, as if I'm absolving myself of responsibility for what I did. And I did it. But there did come a point where I stopped, when I realized that what I was doing was dreadfully wrong. And I want you to take that into account. I want you also to understand that is has weighed heavily on me for many years and perhaps affected me in ways I don't understand. Be that as it may, I have chosen to make my transgressions public. It was a matter of free choice, of responsibility. Maybe it was my impending death that gave me the courage to do that. If so, what kind of courage is that? I don't know. But I have done it. I have taken all the responsibility I can take for my actions. I don't know what else to do. I shall also attempt to create a new and different life in the time that I have left. That's all I have to say."

There was a silence, the clearing of a throat, the movement of a silver knife against china, the lifting of a glass, and then Anne said, "How could you do that, Daddy? How could you?" Her voice was trembling with emotion.

Miles looked away and then forced himself to look at her. "I don't know. I don't understand it any more than you do. I can't answer that question."

"Perhaps you should see someone," Anne said, her voice still trembling. "Perhaps you should get some help."

There was a grim smile from Miles at that. "It's too late for me, my dear. I'm going to die. And I'm going to die not knowing the answer to that question. But that's all right. I've done what I can. First I stopped doing what I was doing, and now I seek redemption only from myself, in my own way."

"And have you found it?" Stephen asked.

Miles seemed to sag in his chair. "I don't know. I really don't know. I think perhaps I still have a way to travel along this path."

After dinner Miles beckoned to Orson. "Come into my office." The two of them went into Miles's office.

"Sit down," Miles said, beckoning toward the couch. Orson sat uncomfortably on the edge, his elbows on his knees, while his father brought the wheelchair close to him.

Miles looked down at his son, his face hard. "You tried to have me killed."

Orson sat upright, his heart thumping, his face a shade paler. He stared back at his father, unable to speak.

"That fifteen thousand dollars I gave you, that's what you used it for, isn't it? You had no mortgage due on your house, and you're no gambler, Orson. I know you well enough to know that. You paid somebody to come and fix the pool, knowing that I would be swimming in the morning. You were trying to have me killed. Unfortunately, Richard was the casualty."

Orson swallowed, then said, "You can't prove that."

Miles grimaced. "I don't have to and I don't want to. It's enough that I know what I have done."

Orson stared at him perplexedly. "What *you* have done?"

Miles nodded. "Yes," he said, his voice tired. "You are another creation of mine, Orson. What you have become and what you are today is largely because of the way I've treated you, the way I've brought you up, the values I've failed to instill in you and the values I tried to enforce upon you. I'm sorry."

Orson stared at him incredulously. "You're sorry? You say I tried to have you killed and you say you're sorry? What is this?"

"You don't understand, do you? It wouldn't be in your nature. Doesn't matter. Just know that I know, and know that it doesn't matter."

Orson didn't know how to think, nor how to react. He sat in silence, while his father's gaze lingered on him. "Well," Orson said finally, "was there anything else?"

Miles shook his head.

"Well, all right," Orson said, starting to rise.

"Oh, there is one other thing," Miles said. "That script you gave me to read."

"Yes?" Orson said, sitting again. "Did you read it?"

"I did."

"And what did you think?"

"I'm surprised. I'm surprised that in view of your lack

of ability in this area in the past you now seem to have the ability to recognize a good script."

"You liked it?" Orson asked, brightening.

"It's a wonderful script," Miles said. "The writer is very talented and has a great future ahead of him. It stands head and shoulders above anything that I've read or seen lately."

"Oh," Orson said. He had no idea what to do next. Originally he'd intended to ask Miles for the financing to option the script. Under the circumstances, that seemed a farfetched idea.

"I bought the script."

"You what?" Orson exclaimed a yelp of surprise.

"I bought it outright. I now own it."

"You stole it from me. You had no right to do that," Orson protested angrily.

"I didn't steal if from you," Miles said. "I've bought it and I'm going to provide the funds to produce it. You will produce it under my supervision. That way I'll ensure that you don't screw it up."

"You'll finance the film?" Orson said weakly.

"Yes, I will. And you'll produce it. But you'll do it under my supervision. You understand that?"

Orson nodded. "Yes, of course. Yes, I do. That's wonderful. I can't believe it. Why are you doing this?"

Miles paused and then said, "Because I think I owe it to you. But that's not the main reason."

Orson opened the palms of his hands in bewilderment. "Then why?"

"Because it's a fucking good script, that's why," Miles said. "I haven't been excited about a story like this for a long, long time. I just think it could give me a new lease on life. Do we have a deal?"

Orson looked at his father, puzzlement still apparent in his eyes. Then he stuck out his hand. "We have a deal."

* * *

"How do you feel?" Shannon asked.

She and Stephen sat in her kitchen, each clutching a cup of coffee. Stephen was quiet, withdrawn.

He shook his head. "Sad."

"Do you hate your father?"

Again he shook his head. He looked up at her without speaking, his eyes filled with volumes of emotion and unspoken words.

"What?" she asked. "What do you feel?"

"I think I'm closer now to Miles than I've ever been," he said. "I don't hate him. How could I hate him? I've seen that the god has feet of clay. It's not that I revel in his weakness. By no means. But I see that Miles has been a tortured man and that my anger and resentment have been misdirected. I can only feel compassion for him now."

Shannon reached across the table, put her hand over his. "Maybe one day there will be a way for all men to be as great as they set out to be," Stephen said.

"Maybe," Shannon said.

He turned her hand over in his and ran a finger across her palm. He looked at her intensely. "Will you marry me, Shannon?"

She examined his kind, strong, understanding face and felt a warmth envelop her. If, out of all this, only that could come, it would be worth it.

"Yes. As soon as the book is done, I'll marry you."

Stephen nodded. "Good, good. That's good."

When the telephone rang the next morning Shannon was surprised to hear Miles's voice, not Lynn's. "Could you come to my office now, please?"

"Yes, I'll be right there," she said, and hung up the telephone.

Melissa was having a dialysis treatment. Shannon poked

her head through her daughter's door and said, "I have to go to the house, I'll be back soon."

Melissa ignored her, but the nurse nodded.

She hurried down the pathway, wondering at this change of operation, why Miles had called her. She shrugged the thought aside. By now she shouldn't be surprised at anything that happened in this house.

She went directly to Miles's study and knocked on the door. Not hearing anything she opened it and peered in.

Miles was sitting at his desk. "Come in."

She walked over to him.

He regarded her with a curiously somber expression, and then lifted a sheet of paper and handed it to her. She looked at him questioningly and then took it. On it was a name and two telephone numbers.

Shannon felt suddenly faint. And then she felt so many emotions she couldn't differentiate between them.

"I just got the information. One number is the home phone, the other is business. They are both in San Francisco. The rest is up to you."

"God," Shannon whispered.

"It's up to you," Miles repeated. "Nobody's contacted him."

"God," Shannon repeated, then turned and left the room in a daze.

She went directly to the office and dialed the business number. "Mark Keller, please," she said to the secretary.

"May I say who's calling?"

"Shannon Ross."

She waited for what seemed an interminable length of time for Melissa's father to answer the telephone.

Finally a male voice came on. "Shannon, I'm sorry it took me a little while to figure out who you were. It's been a long, long time. How are you?"

"I'm fine, Mark," she said. "It's good to hear your voice. You've no idea how good."

"Oh?" he said, puzzled.

"I don't know how to begin, I don't know how to say this," she said.

"Shannon, before you go any further you'd better know that I'm married now. I have a wife and a young child, and the past is the past and I have a life here now."

Shannon made a sound, she didn't know whether it was a sob or a laugh. And then she said, "That doesn't matter, Mark. That doesn't matter. I have to talk to you, that's all. I need your help and I have to talk to you."

The flight to San Francisco had been torture. She had told Mark that they had a daughter, not intending to shock him, but he had been shocked. She had then told him that she needed to talk to him about her, assuring him that he had no paternal responsibility and that she was not in any way trying to make trouble for him. She said only that her daughter was ill and he could help, adding that she didn't want to discuss it over the telephone and asking if she could get the next flight to San Francisco and meet him there.

The puzzled father, Mark Keller agreed.

If the flight seemed agonizingly slow, the cab ride into the city from the airport was worse. Finally Shannon reached her destination in downtown San Francisco on Market Street, paid off the cabbie, and went into the office building where he had told her to meet him. She took the elevator up to the eleventh floor and entered the stock-brokerage office. Walking up to the receptionist, she asked for Mark Keller.

"May I say who you are?" the woman asked.

"Shannon Ross."

"Please sit down and make yourself comfortable," the woman said.

Shannon couldn't sit. She paced the floor.

A moment later, a door opened and Mark came in. It was a very different Mark from the scraggly bohemian she had once known in the Village. This was an older, clean-shaven, pleasant-looking man, with short hair and a three-piece suit. He greeted her warmly and asked her to come into his office.

"A stockbroker," she babbled on as they walked into his office. "I never expected to see you this way. It's not how I remember you."

He closed the door behind them. "We all change. You still look wonderful, though, I must admit."

"Well, thank you," she said, sitting as he moved behind his desk.

He sat and shook his head. "I had no idea you were pregnant when I took off. I really want you to know that."

"Oh, of course. I know. That's fine, you had no way of knowing. I found out after you'd gone and came to your room, but they'd said you left and nobody knew where you were. It doesn't matter. I had the child. It was a daughter, I named her Melissa. She's a wonderful girl."

Shannon reached into her bag. "Here, I want to show you some pictures." She took half a dozen photographs out of the bag and put them on the desk in front of him.

"There," she said, pointing. "That's Melissa when she was two. That one was taken, I think, when she was about six, and so was that one in Central Park. That one was when she was seven at a birthday party. Those are her friends from school. And these were taken very recently in Los Angeles. She's twelve now."

Mark clucked his tongue as he looked at the pictures. "She's a beautiful girl, she really is. Melissa is her name?"

"Yeah." Shannon shrugged. "It's just a name I liked."

"She's lovely," Mark said. "I have a two-year-old son. But a daughter? Wow. This is completely mind-blowing, you know that, don't you?"

Shannon nodded. "I know and I'm sorry to spring it on you like this, but there is some urgency."

Mark leaned forward, his elbows on the desk. "You said she was ill. What's the matter?"

438

"Do you know anything about kidney failure?" Shannon asked.

"No. No, I don't know much about it at all," he said.

Shannon launched into a thorough explanation, starting with when she first discovered Melissa's kidney failure and the sequence of events after that, explaining the dialysis treatments she was having now that were keeping her alive.

After about ten minutes of this she said, "She needs a kidney transplant. She's in line waiting for a kidney. But it could be years before a matching kidney turns up. And this is where you come in."

"I don't understand," he said.

"I was willing to donate one of mine to her," Shannon said. "Everybody can live on one kidney. It wouldn't have been any detriment to me. It's a simple operation and I would have been able to function perfectly with only one kidney. But there was no tissue match."

"That's too bad," he said. "But I don't understand where I come in."

"Kidneys match according to a certain sequence. The closest match is a sibling. The next closest is a parent. My tissues don't match, but yours might."

Michael moved his elbow off the desk and leaned back as comprehension entered his eyes. "You mean that one of my kidneys might be good for her?"

"Yes," Shannon said. "It's not guaranteed, but there's a good chance of it, and it's worth a try."

Now came the predictable confusion. Mark looked at her and then away and then back at her. "You mean that they could operate on me and take one of my kidneys and transplant it to her?"

"Yes," Shannon said. "If you are willing to do that, they could. If the tissue match is close enough."

"There are tests that I'd have to undergo?"

"Yes," she said.

"I don't know," he said doubtfully. "I mean, I have a

wife, a family, a life—to undergo an operation like that, I just don't know."

"Mark, this is our daughter, your daughter we're talking about. This is not something dangerous for you. It's done all the time. It's something you could do that could change her life."

"I know, but . . ."

"You've done nothing for her all your life. I'm not blaming you," she added hurriedly. "You never knew that she even existed until now. I know that this is a shock for you, but she is your daughter. There is a connection there. You are tied together. This is your chance to do something for her so tremendous, so wonderful, something that she would be forever grateful for." She paused, seeing his thoughts turn inward.

He pondered what she was saying, examining it. Questioning it. "My wife is a wonderful person. I know she'd understand," he muttered.

"We could just take it one step at a time," Shannon said, suppressing her excitement. "All you'd have to do first is take the tests, find out if the tissue does indeed match. Then the next step, if it does match, would be to decide whether or not you are going to do the transplant."

He looked down at the pictures on his desk. "She's a beautiful girl. She looks so happy in spite of this."

"She's a wonderful girl. She's intelligent, precocious, loving, exceptional. She's the most wonderful girl in the world. She's our child," Shannon said.

He looked down at the pictures again, shuffled them on his desk, and then looked up at Shannon and nodded. "All right, I'll take the tests. Do I need to come to Los Angeles?"

"It would be better. There's a hospital there. It's all set up to take care of stuff like this."

He nodded again, his mind made up now. "I'll do it. I'll have to talk to the doctors first, of course. Get all the medical facts, but I'll do it for our daughter. It's the least I can do."

"Yeah!" Shannon exclaimed, unable to contain herself. She jumped up and ran around the desk and hugged him. "Yeah!" she said again. "Yeah! Let's see. Even if there is only a chance, let's see."

The flight back was less tumultuous. Shannon leaned back in the seat listening to the drone of the aircraft's engines. There were some things you just knew in spite of logic, in spite of anything. These glimpses of knowledge came from some deep reservoir inside oneself. She knew that there would be a suitable tissue match. She knew that soon Melissa would be free of this terrible curse under which she had lived for so many months.

She closed her eyes and pressed the button on the seat, letting it fall back even further. Melissa was waiting for her, Stephen was waiting. Soon she would be home. Soon they would all have a new beginning.

EPILOGUE

"I don't want a bunch of people pretending to grieve when I die. I never did like that. Hell, I'll be off wherever I'll be, doing whatever I'm doing. Grief is selfish. Most people are crying for themselves, for their loss. Let them do it on their own goddamned time, not at my funeral. Instead, throw the mansion open and have a big party. Make sure the booze is good and there's plenty of it. Have a ball," Miles said.

More than four hundred people attended Miles Cort's funeral. Most of them were or had been involved in the film business, but there was also a large representation of other community leaders and celebrities.

The eulogy was given by Mrs. Shannon Cort, at the request of the immediate family.

The tall slim brunette surveyed the throng with calm green eyes and began to speak without notes:

"As many of you personally know, Miles Cort was an unusual man among men, a complex man and, above all, an honest man. I will therefore not speak of him with words of hollow praise and flattery. It was not his way and not the way he would have wanted it.

"When Miles told me of his cancer, he had nine months

442

to live, according to the most expert medical advice available. But Miles was not one to take advice, nor was he one to follow the well-trodden path and go gentle into that good night. As always, he set his own agenda. Miles lived fifteen months longer than the directors said he would.

"Many of you know Miles as the last great Hollywood legend, a dedicated filmmaker who made history and set standards in this industry for generations of filmmakers to follow. This was, indeed, his passion. He was known as a man who would do anything to get a film made and, in that process, he made his share of both admirers and enemies. Many of you will remember him as a cantankerous, bellicose tyrant, a man whose own vision took precedence over all else.

"That, it is true, is the Miles Cort I first met. He was a tough, cynical son of a bitch who cared little for the feelings of his own family, let alone those of his associates and friends.

"But, as I said, Miles was a complex man, and this is not the Miles I learned to know, or the Miles he finally became.

"In the last two and a half years of his life, Miles took stock of where he had been, what he had done, and what legacy he would leave this world. In that time, he reentered the film business and financed a movie produced by his son, Orson. He lived to see the film released to great critical acclaim. In that time, he also worked with me on his biography, *Miles Cort: The Last Hollywood Legend*. And he lived to see the book published last month to popular acclaim, as witnessed by its immediate rise on the best-seller lists.

"More important than either of these achievements, however, was another Herculean task Miles undertook, one which would have daunted any lesser man. Miles attempted to right his wrongs. He looked back down his life for those deeds where he truly felt he had wronged another and then set about trying to right that wrong.

"You see, Miles believed that he was fully responsible for his own redemption and, I think he attained it.

"The legacy of his recent efforts includes a number of significantly endowed foundations to benefit his country, his city, and the business he loved so much. It also includes a family immutably forged through fire, one that has rediscovered the profound meaning of that unique set of relationships.

"As new members of that family, my daughter Melissa and I are proud to share the Cort name.

"Miles once said of love that it was something people didn't understand. He said, 'It's not making calf-eyes at each other and walking off into the sunset. It's not like the movies, for chrissakes. Love is some kind of confusion that a man and a woman feel for each other for a short time. It's not that big a deal.'

"Miles often spoke to shock and often he did not mean what he said. During these past two years, Miles rediscovered the meaning of the word love. His last comment on the subject was, 'Do you know what love really is? Not that heart-thumping crap. Love is caring for the survival of others.'

"Miles learned to care. And he has demonstrated his lessons well.

"A few weeks ago, I asked him how he wanted to be remembered. He replied, 'Miles Cort, a great filmmaker who cared.' And that is how I ask you to remember him today."

Shannon stepped back and looked over the heads of the crowd. She saw Orson and his new wife Michelle, who had worked as his secretary prior to the marriage, Anne and her husband Frank, Rosemary with her daughter Elizabeth. Far in the back was Shannon's husband, Stephen. He had lifted Melissa onto his shoulders so that she could see her mother speak.

Melissa lifted a hand and waved, a proud smile on her face. Shannon waved back.

ESPIONAGE FICTION BY WARREN MURPHY AND MOLLY COCHRAN

GRANDMASTER   (17-101, $4.50)
There are only two true powers in the world. One is goodness. One is evil. And one man knows them both. He
knows the uses of pleasure, the secrets of pain. He under-
stands the deadly forces that grip the world in treachery.
He moves like a shadow, a promise of danger, from Mos-
cow to Washington — from Havana to Tibet. In a game that
may never be over, he is the grandmaster.

THE HAND OF LAZARUS   (17-100, $4.50)
A grim spectre of death looms over the tiny County Kerry
village of Ardath. The savage plague of urban violence has
begun to weave its insidious way into the peaceful fabric of
Irish country life. The IRA's most mysterious, elusive, and
bloodthirsty murderer has chosen Ardath as his hunting
ground, the site that will rock the world and plunge the be-
leaguered island nation into irreversible chaos: the brutal
assassination of the Pope.

*Available wherever paperbacks are sold, or order direct from the
Publisher. Send cover price plus 50¢ per copy for mailing and
handling to Pinnacle Books, Dept.17-212, 475 Park Avenue
South, New York, N.Y. 10016. Residents of New York, New Jer-
sey and Pennsylvania must include sales tax. DO NOT SEND
CASH.*

NON-FICTION FROM PINNACLE BOOKS